HER FACE WAS INCHES FROM HIS

Brianda could taste his breath, see the satisfaction in his eyes, the gleam of the conqueror.

"Don't look at me, John," she whispered.

"Why not? I love you like this. You are fully mine, and you always will be. No other man will ever know these pleasures. . . . Brianda, you are mine. All mine."

"Stop saying those things!" she entreated.

"Why?"

John was driving her mad with desire. Soon she would be powerless to stop its path.

Her head fell backward, every muscle taut with pleasure. She heard herself call his name.

Harper
Monogram

To Love
and
To Cherish

 ANNE HODGSON

HarperPaperbacks
A Division of HarperCollinsPublishers

This is a work of fiction. The characters, incidents, and dialogues are products of the author's imagination and are not to be construed as real. Any resemblance to actual events or persons, living or dead, is entirely coincidental.

HarperPaperbacks   *A Division of* HarperCollins*Publishers*
10 East 53rd Street, New York, N.Y. 10022

Cover illustration by Jacqueline Goldstein

First printing: December 1993

Printed in the United States of America

HarperPaperbacks, HarperMonogram, and colophon are trademarks of HarperCollins*Publishers*

❖ 10 9 8 7 6 5 4 3 2 1

1

Her eyes opened slowly, her chest rising and falling in shallow breaths. She was afraid to move, for moving her body would surely bring pain, pain with which she was too familiar.

She was lying on her side, and she could feel the stickiness of blood drying on her upper thighs and her back. She pushed herself up on one arm, wincing as fingers of agony reached across her spine. Slowly she sat upright, taking several deep breaths to suppress a wave of nausea. She looked down at the floor and saw blood where she had lain. How long had she lain thus? she wondered. Hours? Days? And what had brought on Edward's latest brutal beating?

Taking another slow, deep breath, she pulled herself upright and waited until the dizziness passed. Unable to stand erect, she shuffled toward the door. And as her mind began to clear, she remembered what had set Edward off. Dakota!

*   *   *

Brianda recalled walking quietly along the upper hallway and down the first flight of stairs. She had heard the men's voices. The night of gambling had just ended, and Edward's guests were leaving. A deep, resonant voice demanded possession of the horse at once. Edward, his voice high-pitched, almost whining, was trying to persuade the stranger to let him deliver the animal in the morning.

Who could this man be, to whom Edward was cowering? Unless . . . unless it was the mysterious Lord Fauxley, Earl of Manseth, rumored to have recently returned to his land and holdings.

"I will take the stallion now, sir," the stranger said.

His back was to Brianda, and all she could tell was that he was exceedingly tall and broad-shouldered under the heavy winter cape he wore.

No matter who he was, how dare he? Dakota was hers! The stallion was all she had left. Since her father died three years ago, Edward had gambled away everything. Now he was using her horse to pay a debt!

She quickly descended the decrepit wooden stairway, then suddenly remembered that she was clad only in her night chemise. Helplessly, she watched the stranger leave through the front door, Edward trailing behind him. She ran back up the stairs and down the empty hallway to the window facing the stable. With tears streaming down her face, she watched as Dakota was led from his stall and out into a night as black as he.

Fury filled her. She wanted to kill Edward with her bare hands. She ran back down the stairs quickly and was there waiting for him when he walked into the house. "What have you done, Edward?" she railed.

"I will not hear any of your mouth tonight, Brianda," he growled through clenched teeth.

"You have no right to use my horse as payment for a gambling debt!" She stood her ground as Edward took a menacing step toward her. "Dakota was a gift to me from Father! You have managed to lose almost everything we own. Damn your gambling!" she shouted at him, heedless of his reaction.

"Brianda, say one more word, and I swear to you that you will regret it," he responded softly, a gleam of barely controlled rage in his eyes.

She had seen the look before, had heard the hushed threat many times. She knew that if she failed to cease her tirade, he would vent his wrath on her, but she was too grief stricken to heed her own instincts.

"Get him back! I want him back. He is all I have!" she cried.

Edward's hands flew to her neck and grabbed the chemise. He pulled her savagely to him, her face within inches of his. "I warned you, you worthless bitch," he snarled. "If you *were* worth anything, I'd sell *you!*" He started toward the stairs, ruthlessly tugging her behind him.

She struggled to get free of his grasp, hoping he had drunk too much brandy to persist, but her efforts were rewarded with a blow that made her see stars. And in her stunned state, he dragged her to the third-floor attic room.

As she opened the door now to call for Nellie, one of the three servants who remained on the estate Edward had gutted, she realized that the loyal family retainer would doubtless put her to bed and make her stay there for days. That could not be. She had to get Dakota back.

Slowly, painfully, she made her way down the steep, winding stairs and crept along the hallway to her room. There, she pulled on her boots and opened the closet to find her long black cape. She knew she could not bear the weight or texture of normal clothing on her damaged body and would have to make do with only the night chemise under her cloak. Draping it carefully over her shoulders, she pulled the hood over her head and tucked in the long strands of her spun-gold hair.

It was easy enough to slip down the main staircase and outside without being seen, as the house was nearly deserted. The three remaining servants kept to themselves as much as possible, none of them wanting to incur the wrath of young master Edward.

Brianda hurried along the path leading to the sea. The wind was high, the afternoon shadows lengthening; a storm would be making landfall soon. She stayed as close as she could to the cliff wall, seeking shelter from the blustery gusts.

Each step she took caused pain to ricochet up her spine, but she took a deep breath and soldiered on. She had a long trek ahead of her; it was at least three miles to the property line of the Earl of Manseth.

Brianda had overheard some women talking at the market stalls last week about Lord Fauxley's impending arrival. They were hopeful that upon his return he would take the affairs of the village in hand and provide the aid and direction that was so sorely needed. Brianda hoped so, too, for she knew Edward was the only other landowner in the county and the parish, and her mean-spirited brother did not give a damn for the villagers or their problems. For years Brianda had pilfered food-stuffs from the stores of Cliffshead Manor whenever she could and distributed them to the most needy, making sure each family had something special to eat through the long winters.

Since childhood she had been drawn to the village folk. The village folk and Old Megan. There were some who thought the young lady of the manor shouldn't spend so much time with the Medicine Woman. Many villagers thought the gruff old woman a witch who might harm Lord Breedon's neglected little daughter in some way. Witch or not, Old Megan's healing powers were well known, and since doctors were strictly for the gentry, the poor folks relied on Old Megan and her knowledge of ancient healing arts.

Over the years Brianda had learned many of the old woman's herbal remedies, and as she grew into adolescence, she often accompanied Old Megan on her visits to the ill and to birthing mothers. She wished the wise old woman was there now, with a shoulder to cry on and a remedy for her young apprentice's injuries. But Brianda was alone, and she had to keep walking.

By the time she reached the edge of Lord Fauxley's property, she was near exhaustion. The pain from the whip marks on her back was unrelenting. She gathered her inner strength and forced herself to concentrate on her goal of getting Dakota back. Picturing herself once more riding bareback across the windswept moors, she continued up the path toward Manseth Manor.

Though she had lived nearby all her life, she had never seen the great house up close. It was set well within the extensive property and was surrounded by huge old oak trees. She had, however, heard stories of its legendary proportions and beauty. The grounds were immaculately kept by a full staff of gardeners. The present earl's late mother had had a love for roses, and accordingly there were hundreds of bushes planted in myriad formal gardens, each a showcase of a particular genus of rose. They were said to be a glorious sight in the spring, and in the summer the scent of the various buds wafted through the manor on the light afternoon breezes.

Manseth Manor was one of the oldest estates in the country. Built solidly of local stone, it easily withstood harsh winter winds and snows. The Earl, having ordered the south and west wings closed upon the death of his father, mother, and younger brother in a boating accident, was rumored to occupy only the north wing, which itself could accommodate at least fifteen guests. Although the Earl was rarely at Manseth Manor, evidently disdaining entertaining in the country in favor of his London residence, the house was kept completely staffed and in immaculate order.

The rain had begun to fall as she walked silently through the thick forest and now was a veritable downpour.

When she neared the enormous manor house, she glanced to the right and left of the building to find the stable. There it was, not far at all! For a moment she thought perhaps she would just go and get Dakota, and explanations be damned. But doubtless there were grooms within, and, although Lord Fauxley might be dishonorable enough to gamble and take a girl's horse, *she* would do the right thing. She would go to the manor house and have it out with his Lordship.

John Fauxley, the Earl of Manseth, stretched his long legs out before him and gazed into the fire in his study. It had been a tiring day, filled with meetings with his property managers, and his head was overflowing with countless details. He was glad his staff was so diligent and competent. All seemed to be running smoothly.

One bit of information, however, disturbed him greatly. He heard from more than one retainer that the villagers were suffering at the hands of the other lord in the county. It seemed the young Lord Breedon, with whom John had spent much of the previous evening, cared little for the welfare of the people depending on the landowners for their livelihoods. Evidently John's prolonged absences from the region had not helped their situation.

John ran his long fingers through his coal-black hair and wondered how any member of the gentry could be so cold and uncaring. On the other hand, was he himself completely exempt from his own criticism? It was becoming more obvious to him that, in his own way, he had sorely neglected his duties as Earl of Manseth and that he had to spend more time here to see how he could better the lives of those who worked his lands.

John's two best friends sat nearby, also enjoying the warmth of the hearth. Angus MacKenzie, his most trusted employee and bodyguard stood, his six-foot eight-inch frame casting a mammoth shadow as he went to stoke the fire. John's professional colleague, Paul Martin, sipped his brandy and listened to the wind toss raindrops against the windowpanes. The men had come with him to Manseth Manor for a well-deserved holiday three days earlier, and he was glad of their company. Following the death of his family, he had been reluctant to remain in a now sorrow-filled Manseth Manor, and, having ensured that the country holdings were being overseen with care, he had hastened to return to his life in London.

John's father, a good master, fair and just, had lived in the manor from the time of his marriage and had raised his two sons in the country, hoping that in adulthood, when they inherited the estate, they would care for the land and its people as had the Fauxley ancestors for hundreds of years. Obviously, he had hoped the most of his elder son, John. But the hopes of the Earl were not to be realized.

To the horror of his whole family, after completing his studies at the university, John had decided to remain in London to attend medical school. It was unheard of, said his mother, that a titled gentleman would consider such an occupation! Working professions were for those less blessed. But, as usual, John did not give a damn what anyone thought. He wanted to study medicine, and he did, finishing first in his class.

His mother could not imagine what on Earth he would do after he completed his training. Surely he would not consider practicing in London, coming into contact with the lower classes? The thought was simply too much to bear, sending Lady Fauxley to bed with migraine headaches. John's father had rubbed his chin and worried in silence.

But practice in London is exactly what John did. He and Paul opened a surgery clinic and began treating London's less fortunate. On the staff of the city's biggest hospital, they became, in several years, the most highly respected surgeons in town. As word of their skills spread, they began seeing a new breed of patients, members of the upper classes, dressed in cloaks and hats to hide their identities. John and Paul would smile at the folly, but, rich or poor, all patients were treated equally.

Now, back home in the country after a five-year absence, John found it felt surprisingly good to sit in the quiet study, watching the flames jump and play in the fireplace and listening to the storm that seemed to have greater intensity than it would in the city. Nature was somehow closer in the country.

Life had been exceedingly hectic the past few years. His practice had grown with his reputation, and there were many days when he worked sixteen hours straight, only to sleep for a couple of hours and be back at the surgery table again. He and Paul had decided they would take a fortnight holiday in the country, where John could attend to estate matters at the same time. Now he found it hard to believe that it was only a few days ago that a belligerent drunk, cut up from a brawl, was swinging his burly arms at them, calling them names the gentry seldom heard. Yes, two weeks of peace and quiet would be just what the doctor ordered, he thought with a wry smile.

Angus, too, had welcomed the change for his exhausted master, even going so far as to suggest that a quick love affair would not hurt. Although the Earl of Manseth could have all the women he wanted whenever he wanted them, of late he had wearied of courting the opposite sex and had cut all ties, even with the beautiful Susana Smythe. Women were just too much trouble. All any of them wanted was to marry him and get their dainty little hands on his fortune. But John had no intention of marrying anyone. He was quite content as he was, single, free, and happy to be both.

He called out to Stevens, the butler, to bring more brandy into the warm, cheerful study. It was then that he heard a pronounced thud. "Was that thunder, or did either of you hear a noise?" he asked, sitting up straight.

"I am not sure what I heard," replied Paul.

Another louder thud came from the direction of the main door. Angus made to leave the study to investigate, but John held up a hand to stop him. A third bang resounded through the mansion.

"What the bloody hell!" yelled John. "Stevens, for the love of God, answer that door!"

"Yes, my Lord, right away."

Stevens hurried to the door, unable to imagine who could be out on a night like this. He unbolted the door and looked out into the pouring rain. He saw nothing.

"I am here!" Brianda called over the howling wind.

Stevens tilted his head downward, and he was so surprised that he couldn't say a word. He simply stared at the tiny person hiding in the sodden cape.

"Are you going to leave me standing in the rain all night?" she demanded. "I have business with his Lordship, and I must speak to him right now."

Undaunted, Stevens addressed the dubious visitor in his most distinguished tone. "I am sorry . . . miss, but his Lordship does not see anyone without an appointment, and certainly not at this late hour." He began to close the massive oak door.

"Are you mad?" Brianda countered, sticking her foot in the path of the door. "An appointment? In the rain, at night? Obviously this is an emergency! I bid you call Lord Fauxley at once!" she demanded.

"What in hell is going on out there, Stevens?" boomed John's voice from the study.

"You wait right here, young lady, and do not dare to put one foot inside this door until I return." Stevens hurried to the study.

"For God's sake, what is the matter, Stevens?" John asked, irritation in his voice.

"A young woman is demanding entrance, sir. I have not the faintest idea who she is, sir. She says it is an emergency."

"Demanding, is she?" he mused. "Well, show her in, Stevens."

"Yes, sir. But, sir, she is soaking wet, and the floors are just cleaned. Maybe I should have her go to the kitchen door. Maybe she is just a beggar with a bent mind."

"Show her into the study, Stevens," John said firmly.

"Yes, sir."

When Stevens opened the front door, she was still there, standing in the pouring rain, waiting.

"Come this way, miss. His Lordship will see you now," Stevens stated, his voice tight with unveiled disgust.

"Thank you," she said through clenched teeth, taking in the beautiful tapestries and paintings along the hallway as she followed the irritating butler.

As Stevens held the study door open for her, a wave

of warmth—and nausea—washed over her. She knew she had to fight off feeling ill until she got Dakota back. Taking several deep breaths, she struggled to hold on a little longer.

"The young woman, my Lord," Stevens announced.

Three men turned to face the visitor, and Brianda, disoriented, had no idea which one was the famous Earl of Manseth. She addressed the man with the kindest face. "Sir, I have come to retrieve my horse," she spat out quickly, so nervous that her knees were knocking.

"I am Lord Fauxley, young woman, and I do not have any idea what you are talking about. What horse?" John rose from his chair and placed his hands on his slim hips. He was so tall and broad shouldered that the mere sight of him made her pause. Gamely, she continued, "Why, the horse you took from Cliffshead Manor last night. You had no right to him. He is mine."

Stepping closer to see into the folds of the cape, John said, "I have no idea who you are, young woman, but the horse I won in a gaming encounter last night is now my property, and I have the ownership papers to prove it. Now, if you will excuse me . . ."

She was being dismissed! She had not come all this way simply to be thrown out! "I will gladly leave, sir, but only when I have my animal." The dripping wet cape was like a shroud of ice, and, feeling the nausea return, she grasped the back of a nearby wing chair for support.

"Are you well, miss?" Paul asked.

"I am fine, thank you, sir." Turning back to the haughty Earl, she stated, "The person who is mistaken is you, sir. Any papers you may have are false. I have the only legal papers on the horse. I will take this matter up with the local authorities. You will not get away with this!" she said with a great deal more bravado than she felt. Her breathing began to quicken, and her stomach began to roll. Brianda knew that she had to control herself, so as not to become ill in front of these gentlemen.

"Angus, please get the papers from the top drawer of the desk and show them to the lady," said John, his temper beginning to flare.

Angus retrieved the documents, approached the young woman, and held them out for her to see. Her hands shook as she reached for them. Standing as close as he was, Angus could hear her labored breathing. He was no physician, but he knew the raspy sound was not normal. He motioned to John with his head that something was amiss.

Paul, noticing the silent communication, rose from his chair and approached Brianda. "You are very wet, miss. May I take your cloak, while you sit down to look at the papers?"

"No!" she almost shouted. "I . . . I will keep my cloak, thank you, sir. But I will sit down for a moment, as I am a little tired. Thank you for your kindness. It is obvious that you, sir, are a gentleman." She glared in the Earl's direction and gratefully sank into the large wing chair, careful not to lean back.

Brianda turned her attention to the papers and could not believe her eyes. These were, indeed, the legal documents of ownership for Dakota! How had Edward found them? She had taken such care to hide them, along with the few pounds she had been able to save. She supposed they were gone now, too. Tears filled her eyes, but she fought them back.

"Would you like a small sip of brandy to ward off the winter's chill?" Paul asked gently, now close enough to hear her breathing and not liking what he heard. She did not respond but continued staring at the papers. Paul looked at John over the top of her head and motioned for him to draw nearer.

As the earl started toward her, Brianda was once

again struck by the sheer size of him. Everything about this stranger frightened her. She pushed herself up and stood on wobbly legs. "These papers are correct," she said in a small, defeated voice. "It seems my brother has truly given you the title to Dakota." She turned toward the door, her sodden cape dragging. Barely audibly, she said, "I don't know what to do." She tipped her head back and looked up at John. "Would you consider contacting my brother and making other arrangements for his debt? Edward had no right to use my horse as payment without my permission."

It was then that John saw the huge violet eyes staring at him from the cave of wet wool. So struck was he by their beauty that for a moment he could not respond to her question.

Taking his silence as a refusal, and knowing that at any moment she might vomit right there in the earl's elegant study, she said, "Forgive me, but I am feeling tired, and I have a long way home." She held the documents out to him. She was shaking so badly that the papers rattled in her hands. John took them from her, and just as he was about to speak, she whispered, "I am sorry for any trouble I may have caused. Please excuse me now." Brianda turned and started for the door.

"Just a moment, if you please," John commanded.

Brianda continued toward the door as if she had heard nothing. The pain was beginning to wrap its fingers around her, and she knew that she had to get out of this house. She would go to the stable and steal the horse, and she would deal with the repercussions the next day. The nausea returned with a vengeance, causing small beads of sweat to appear on her upper lip and forehead, and she hurried her steps.

"Just a moment, I said, young woman," John repeated icily as she hurried out of the study toward the main door.

"Let me talk to her, John," Paul said. "You are too gruff with the poor thing." Addressing Brianda's back, he called out, "Young lady, please, you must wait a moment. We will make sure your carriage is ready before you venture out into this most nasty evening."

"Do not trouble yourself further, sir. I will be fine," she said, and she slipped out the door.

"We can't just let her go out into the storm," Paul announced flatly.

"Let it be, Paul. It may be that this woman is not quite right in her mind. Tomorrow morning I will ride to Cliffshead Manor to see about the matter. Now I suggest we all retire." John signaled to Angus to accompany Paul up the grand staircase.

"Good night, then," Paul said dubiously as he mounted the stairs.

When he was out of sight, John opened the front door and looked out into the night, but all he could see were the trees blowing in the wind and a heavy curtain of rain.

2

Brianda made her way slowly toward the stable. The rain was coming down so hard that the drops were painful against her back. Drawing strength from her resolve to find Dakota, she reached the stable's huge door and slid it open just enough to slip through.

It was so dark that she could not make out the stalls. "Dakota, where are you, boy?" she called softly.

The huge black stallion whinnied in response.

"I hear you, boy. Quiet now, I am coming for you," she whispered into the inky darkness. She started forward, her hands out in front of her, to avoid bumping into anything in the dark.

At last she found Dakota's stall. She reached to unlatch the sliding bolt, but the movement made the fire in her back flare again. She grimaced and waited for it to subside. The green heat of nausea swept up her throat. Once again, she breathed deeply to ward off the horrible sensation. Finally she was able to grab the leather halter, and the horse followed her out of the stall.

"In England they hang you for horse stealing," came a familiar voice out of the dark.

Brianda froze. "I am only taking what is rightfully mine, my Lord. I am sure no court in this land would find me guilty for retrieving my own horse," she said with as much confidence as she could muster.

"I would not be so sure of that, Miss Breedon, seeing that I am in possession of the deed to the animal. I thought that I had made myself quite clear on this subject a short while ago. Now I suggest that you let go of the horse's halter and I will return him to the stall."

She raised her chin, gathering her courage. "I am not going to leave here without Dakota." She began walking the horse toward the door.

"If you move one foot farther, I swear you will regret it."

"Sir, I warn you that Dakota will protect me if he senses danger. We have been together since he was born, and he answers to no man. He is mine."

Ignoring her warning, the imposing Lord Fauxley moved toward the small woman and her massive horse. Brianda expected Dakota to become agitated, but the stallion merely stood placidly, as if waiting for Lord Fauxley.

She felt a wave of exhaustion wash over her. Would this ordeal never end? Her knees went weak, and she held tighter to the halter, letting the horse's strong head and shoulders hold her up. She closed her eyes against a sudden rush of dizziness and slumped against Dakota. Dakota shifted uneasily.

John noticed the young woman sway and quickly took her arm. "What troubles you, miss? Are you ill?"

Brianda heard the words but could not reply. She tried to look up at him, but her head would not cooperate, and her eyes were unable to focus.

"You are cold from the rain," John said, his voice

softening as he realized that she was indeed ill. "We will go inside and talk when you feel better."

"Oh, no, I cannot! I must get home," she said weakly, her voice rising with concern.

"You are wet to the skin, Miss Breedon, and will surely become ill if you do not get a dry cloak, at the least. And where is your conveyance?" He could not believe that a member of the gentry would have condoned her walking to a neighboring manor, especially in a rainstorm.

"My conveyance is no concern of yours, sir, and I must leave at once. Please let us go now," she intoned weakly. She took an unsteady step forward.

John quickly put his arm around her back to support her.

Brianda screamed. The pain, instantaneous and unforgiving, was too much for her, and she felt herself slipping into darkness. Her fingers slid from the halter.

John was able to catch her just before she hit the dirt floor. "Bloody hell! Thomas! Thomas, come quickly!" John yelled for his head groom.

Thomas, resting in the warmth of his cottage near the stable, jumped from his chair at the sound of his master's voice.

"Mollie, get my coat! I hear the master calling from the stable!" he cried to his wife.

He grabbed his coat and, in a flash, was out the door and in the stable. "Yes, my Lord," he said, trying to keep his voice calm despite the sight of the girl in his Lordship's arms and the black stallion prancing about, obviously unnerved.

"Get the animal back into his stall, Thomas. Settle him down, and then return to your house. You will say nothing of this to anyone. Is that clear?"

"Yes, my Lord."

John carried his small burden easily to the door and then ran with her in his arms through the pouring rain. He marveled at how light she was.

"Paul! Where are you?" he called as he entered the house and headed up the curving staircase.

Paul hurried from his room, and seeing John carrying the young woman, exclaimed, "Here, John, in the room adjoining yours."

"Is the bed ready?" he asked as he carried Brianda into the bed chamber.

"What has happened, John? Have you harmed the poor young woman?" Paul asked with concern.

"Of course not, Paul. Don't be an ass! I found her in the stable trying to take the horse. She became faint. When I reached out to steady her, she screamed and then lost consciousness. This whole thing is quite strange. I think we had better examine her."

John laid Brianda on the bed, then rang for the housekeeper, Mrs. Brady. Both physicians began removing Brianda's cloak, and both were astonished that beneath it was only a night chemise, wet and molded to the frail body.

John's eyes swept over her. She was so small!

Paul looked at his friend. "I'll lift her, and you pull the chemise off." As Paul's hands passed under her back, Brianda moaned deep in her throat. John quickly pulled the chemise over her head, and they gently turned her over onto her stomach.

Each man drew in a deep breath at the horrible sight. Ugly welts covered her back, buttocks and upper thighs. Blood and purulent fluids oozed from the wounds. In some places, the tissues were torn down to the underlying bone.

"Oh, my God," said Paul in a hushed voice. "Oh, good God, the poor thing."

For a moment, John was unable to speak. Then, gathering his professional composure and suppressing his disgust at whoever could have done this to her, he said, "Come, Paul, we must clean these wounds quickly before she dies from infection." He glanced out the door.

"Mrs. Brady!" he yelled, "come quickly!"

"Yes, my Lord?" huffed the housekeeper as she hurried into the chamber.

Elvira Brady, somewhere near fifty years old, was a most efficient household manager, calm, kindly, and discreet.

"Boil water in two separate pots," John instructed her. "Boil pieces of cloth in one, and cool the other. Do these things as soon as possible, Mrs. Brady," he ordered.

"Yes, sir. Right away."

Brianda moaned, and Elvira Brady caught her first glimpse of the young woman. She could not suppress a horrified gasp at the sight of the young woman's ravaged back. "Good God, my Lord, what evil has been brought upon the lass? What kind of animal could do a thing like that?"

"We don't have any idea who did this, but right now we need to treat these wounds, so that she may have a chance of surviving. Please go for what I need now, Mrs. Brady," John said gently.

"Yes, sir." Mrs. Brady hurried off to do as she had been told.

The doctors spent considerable time cleaning and dressing the wounds. Brianda did not respond in any way during the entire procedure. But for her shallow breathing, Paul might have thought she had died. The fever started near midnight. They had just finished the last dressing, when Paul noticed the heat beneath his fingers. "The fever has begun, John.

Now we will see how much fight she has left in her."

"She will have to be a strong fighter, I'm afraid, Paul. I have seen men die from less grievous injuries." John smiled ruefully. "But from what we saw earlier, she may yet have the will. She seemed aggressive enough for ten men. Let's see if we can get her to swallow a little water. She will need it to fight off the fever."

They carefully lifted and turned her, and John tried to get a few drops of water into her mouth, but she was unresponsive. "It is too dangerous now. I'll drown her if I keep trying. We will have to try later. We can only leave her on her back for a short while, as these wounds need to get air."

The exhausted men found chairs on opposite sides of the bed and let themselves down heavily into them.

Paul closed his eyes and instantly fell asleep. John sat and looked at the girl, seeing her as if for the first time. Earlier she had been heavily cloaked. Later he had been busy trying to save her life. Now he found himself surprised at how pretty she was. Mrs. Brady had brushed her long blond hair back from her face and fashioned it into a braid. It was the color of delicate corn silk but was thick and luxurious. Her face was small and oval. Long dark lashes curled over her closed eyes. Her cheeks, with the unnatural blush of fever, almost looked painted, like those of the whores on Barley Street in London. But there was something altogether innocent about her.

The sheet was pulled up almost to her chin, covering her small breasts and angular frame, the bones protruding from her too-thin body.

John rose and gently turned her onto her side, propping her with soft pillows, allowing the awful wounds to air.

There was a quiet knock on the door. "Come in," John called out softly.

Mrs. Brady entered with a tray of tea and biscuits. "I thought you two could do with some tea, my Lord."

"Thank you, Mrs. Brady. I could surely do with tea. We missed our supper, but I think Dr. Martin needs sleep more."

"Very well, sir. Shall I pour your cup?"

"Please." Rubbing his eyes, he tried to ease his fatigue and clear his mind. His hands were as steady as ever, though, as Mrs. Brady handed him the cup.

"Is there anything else, sir?" the housekeeper asked.

"No. Go and sleep now. Thank you for all you've done this evening, Mrs. Brady."

"It was done with a willing heart, sir."

It was early the next morning when John awoke. For a moment he didn't know where he was or why he was sleeping in a chair. Suddenly he remembered and looked to the bed.

The girl lay just as she had the night before. Paul, too, was still asleep.

John rose slowly, letting his cramped muscles unwind. He placed a hand on the girl's forehead. She was afire!

He shook his friend awake. "Paul, the fever is raging. If we don't get fluids into her, she will die."

"Aye, John." Paul stretched and rose. "Let me help you."

"We must go very slowly with the water, Paul. We don't want her to breathe any fluid into those boisterous lungs of hers."

"Aye," answered Paul.

John cradled Brianda in his arms. Even this ill, she smelled sweet, and her skin was petal soft. He gently opened her mouth with his fingers, and Paul let a few drops of water slip through her teeth. They waited while the water slowly trickled into the back of her throat. She swallowed! The physicians smiled at each other.

"Let's try some more," John suggested. Once again she swallowed.

Mrs. Brady entered the room with breakfast for the two doctors. "How is the young thing this morning, my Lord?" she asked.

"She remains febrile, but if she continues to take small sips of fluid, she might have a chance. She is far from being out of danger yet, but at least now she may be able to give it a good fight."

Elvira Brady smiled at the fierce determination in his voice and set the tray on the table between the two chairs.

Edward Breedon slept fitfully in the massive wooden bed in the master suite of Cliffshead Manor. His mother, Blanche Reed Breedon, had taken much pleasure in decorating the suite when she moved into it with her new husband, but in twenty years, not one thing had been changed. The once grand draperies and bed covers were now faded and tattered, the carpet worn nearly to the floor beneath. Nellie tried her best to keep up the manor house, but Edward's room, where he sat and drank cheap ale until he became ill, was difficult to keep presentable.

Edward awoke in the late afternoon to the full force of an English storm. He groaned with a hangover as he slowly rose. Then he remembered Brianda. He couldn't recall much of what had happened the night before, but he knew that she had misbehaved, and he had beaten her again. He languidly made his way to his secret attic room.

She was not there. Where could she be? He searched all over the house, but she was nowhere to be found.

Not even in her special hiding places. Odd, she had never disappeared in the past. He didn't want to ask that old fool, Nellie, for she would just start a ruckus if she knew Brianda was missing.

What if he'd killed her? he thought to himself. But, no, if the bitch were dead, he would have found her body. Maybe she had wandered down to the ocean. His face lit up with a perverse thought. Maybe she had drowned! That would be wonderful. If she were in the water for a long time, no one would be able to detect the marks from the beating he'd given her.

He grabbed his coat and ran down the old staircase to the kitchen door, which led to the path to the cliffs. He hurried down the muddy path, and, though impeded by the darkness of approaching night, he scanned the waves crashing at the base of the path for a body.

Nothing!

He was furious. He made his way farther down the slippery path as carefully as he could, checking the water line. No sign of a body. Looking toward the base of the cliffs, he searched farther up the beach, where the tide might have washed her.

Still nothing. He pounded his fist on a huge rock and swore. He slowly climbed the hill to the top of the cliff, his chest heaving with the exertion. He had never been one for exercise or sporting. He even hated riding, preferring to go about by coach. He was not like his little sister, who would, at any opportunity, jump on the back of her precious horse and gallop off onto the moors.

He felt a jolt of glee at the thought of using the horse to pay that debt last night. But where could Brianda be? He decided to check the barn. She was always hanging around the stable, talking to the servants as if they were equals. Imagine thinking that servants would have anything of interest to say! They were all worthless slobs who only wanted to live off his money and eat his food.

Yes, maybe the stable. She was always with that blasted horse of hers. It had been a gift from their father just before he died. She loved that horse more than anything in the world. It had given him perverse pleasure to dispense with her most precious possession.

He stopped cold. Fear spread through his veins. What if Brianda had gone to Manseth Manor to try to get the horse back? He trembled at the thought. If a man as powerful as the earl discovered his penchant for brutality, he would be ruined.

Impossible. No female would venture that far alone. He went to the barn and asked the stable boy if he had seen Lady Breedon that morning. The terrified boy shook his head.

Well, thought Edward, *I will wait this out a little while longer. If she does not show up on her own, I will go and pay a call on the Earl of Manseth; maybe ask his Lordship's aid in finding her.* He would play the distraught brother, desperate to find his little sister. That would look good in the earl's eyes. Yes, that was what he would do.

Before he did anything, though, he had to post a letter to his hired thug and inform him that Manseth Manor was now occupied, and that they might have to change some of their plans for the forthcoming business deal. He would have to word the letter carefully, as Biff Blanders was not very bright, and the woman who owned the boarding house would have to read the message to him. Yes, he would have to be careful, indeed, both with Biff and with John Fauxley. But he would succeed. He just needed to take his time and plan everything well.

On the evening of the second day of his vigil, John was awakened from a fitful sleep by a knocking on the door. He forced himself to rise, running his fingers over his eyelids and then through his hair. He shook his head slightly to clear his tired mind. He looked over to the bed where his patient lay, still unconscious. The fever continued to rage, rising and falling slightly but never stopping its assault. He had done all he knew to help her through this crisis, but so far he had seen no change in her condition.

Once again, someone knocked on the door. He crossed the room quietly and opened the door to find Mrs. Brady.

"Sir, there is an old woman at the door who states she is a friend of the young woman and demands to see her. When I refused, knowing her condition, she insisted that she be granted an interview with you."

"Show her into the library, Mrs. Brady. I will be there directly," John said, thinking that these country people certainly did a lot of demanding.

3

Megan Sloan was born to the medicine woman on the outskirts of the village under the rule of the Earl of Manseth. During her fifty-eight years of life, she had learned all that her mother and her mother's mother knew about the medicinal powers of herbs, and at her mother's death, Megan herself assumed the mantle of Medicine Woman. Though she was known to all the village families and had shared in many of their joys and grief, attending their birthings and deaths, she lived apart from them all in a cottage at the edge of the property owned by the Earl of Manseth. It lay deep in the forest that provided the plants to be mixed according to ancient lore into restorative powders and salves. Having never sought company, she had never found a man to father a child for her, destining her to be the last Medicine Woman.

Until she had met Brianda.

She had first seen the child when Brianda was nine years old, crying alone in the woods near the old pond. Old Megan was on her way home from a birthing, laden with her valises, when she heard the soft sobs. Moving as quietly as a field mouse, she found a child sitting beside a large boulder, resting her head against the cold stone. Tears streaked her dirty cheeks, her clothes were old and torn, and she had no shoes.

Old Megan could not imagine where she belonged. She knew all the villagers, and this child was new to her. Could she be an orphan from a neighboring village who had wandered into the forest?

Old Megan had plenty to worry about in her own village. Everything had gone badly since the recent tragic death of the Earl of Manseth. Lord Fauxley had been a just and fair master, and under his guidance, life had been decent for the villagers. Now, with the loss of his leadership, the poor were suffering. For the only other local landowner, Lord Jacob Breedon, cared not a whit what happened to village folk.

Old Megan wanted to ignore the child and start on her way again, but the girl looked up and stared straight at her, her swollen eyes wide with curiosity.

"What are you looking at, child?" Old Megan asked.

"I was frightened by a noise, and I thought it might be a wild animal. My brother told me there were plenty of them hereabouts that liked to eat little children." She looked dismayed, then hurried on. "Who are you, if I may ask, ma'am?"

"I go by Old Megan to most that live around here. I know just about every person hereabouts, lass, but I have not seen your face before. Where do you come from?"

Brianda did not answer, appearing frightened by the question.

"Come, I'll not tell anyone. You can trust me."

"I am Brianda, daughter of Lord Breedon. I am not allowed to leave my father's property, but I got into trouble this afternoon, and I came here to be by myself."

Old Megan could not believe her ears. This raggedy child was the daughter of Lord Breedon? Lady Breedon had been in poor health when she carried her second babe and had died after childbirth. Megan had assumed the infant had soon followed her mother to the grave, for in all these past eight years she had never heard a word about the child. She was a pretty little thing, with her gold hair and large violet eyes, but she was a little thin.

"Could I interest you in a cup of tea, Miss Breedon? My cottage is not far from here," the old woman offered kindly. She smiled at the little girl and extended her hand.

Brianda did not take long to consider. She was on her feet in a flash and at the woman's side. "No one has ever asked me to tea before, Old Megan. I am honored by your invitation. But I will need to be back home before too long," she said, as she slipped her fingers trustingly into the woman's large, rough hand.

And thus a friendship was born.

"I am very happy that we met today, Brianda. I have lived here all my life, child, yet I have never seen you before. I know that you have an older brother, Edward, but why is it that I have heard naught of you?"

"I am not allowed to leave the immediate area of the house," Brianda explained. "My father is very strict. My brother, Edward, has been sent to school—Father feels that a gentleman needs to be educated, but he says all I will do is marry, and I do not need an education for that. Nellie, my nanny, tries to teach me things. She made this dress, too." Brianda twirled to show Old Megan the handmade shift. "She makes all my clothes from old fabrics. My father will not spend good money on new fabric for me. He says I don't need new dresses. Who is going to see me anyway, other than the servants at our house?" Brianda chattered on, thrilled to have someone to talk to.

Old Megan smiled and squeezed Brianda's hand, and they walked on together through the forest.

When they reached the cottage, Brianda's eyes widened at the sight within. There were bottles of every shape and size and color on nearly every surface. "What are all the bottles for, Old Megan?"

"They contain herbal preparations I use to help people when they are sick."

"There are so many! Do you use them all?"

"Every one of them, child. Maybe I could teach you how to use them, too," she said, a small smile on her kind face.

"Do you mean it?" Brianda asked excitedly.

"Do you think that you would be interested in learning?"

Brianda clapped her hands together with joy. "Oh, yes, I would love to learn to help people!"

"It will take a lot of time, and you will have to study very hard."

Brianda nodded eagerly. "I will, I promise!"

Old Megan smiled at her. "We will have to go deep into the woods to find our herbs and plants. It will take patience and hard work to find and gather them, then dry them and prepare the poultices and elixirs. Then you will have to learn dosages and applications. None of this will be easy. Are you still sure you are interested?"

"Oh, yes, Old Megan! I would love to learn. I will work hard, I promise. I will come to you every day. Though I am forbidden to leave the manor, the truth is, no one really notices where I am. The only time my father talks to me is when I have done something to anger him. He lectures me and has Edward give me my punishment."

"Your brother?" Megan was surprised. Edward Breedon was only about three years older than his sister. This all seemed very strange indeed.

Brianda nodded. "My father loses his temper and yells at me—sometimes he gets the strangest look on his face—and then he tells Edward what punishment I deserve. Usually I get the switch. Today I was late for breakfast, because I was helping birth a calf. My father was furious. He told me that girls have no place in a barn. I didn't get any breakfast, and I got ten licks with the switch for my punishment. My father never would have found out if Edward hadn't told him," Brianda said softly, her eyes on the wood plank floor.

"Will you show me where your brother switched you, child?"

Brianda trusted the woman, so she turned around and lifted her shift.

Disgust rose in Old Megan's throat. Edward had taken the switch to her bare back! "Come, child, I will prepare a salve that will make those welts feel better." Using the contents of three different jars, the Medicine Woman quickly prepared a salve and applied it to the child's back. Her skilled hands felt the girl relax almost immediately as the pain lessened. She put the remainder of the salve into a small jar and gave it to Brianda to take home.

"Thank you," the girl said, tears forming in her eyes. No person, other than Nellie, had ever shown her such kindness.

"There, that's all right." Noting the tears, Old Megan felt her heart ache. She hugged the frail little girl to her ample chest. "Here, sit down, and we will have some tea and muffins. I made wild blueberry muffins this morning." Old Megan walked across the one-room cottage and put the kettle on.

Brianda shyly offered to help. She was given mugs for the tea and plates to put on the small wooden table. Her eyes were glued to the plate of muffins, but she waited politely until her hostess offered them. Then she ate with relish, having had no breakfast that day.

"We need to make some plans, child. Tomorrow you will come as soon as you can slip away. But if ever you arrive and I am not here, I will leave a sign for you that I have been called away to aid someone. I will tack this wooden star to the trunk of the tree right next to my front door. If you see the star there, you will go home and come the following day. If ever you are not here by the time the sun has reached the second branch on the tree, I will go about my business, knowing that you are unable to come that day. Do you understand all that?"

Brianda nodded gravely. "I will come every day that I possibly can. Now that I will have something wonderful to do, I am sure I will not get into trouble as much. It is boring for me at home."

"There is one more thing, Brianda. If you are ever in need, lassie, ask Richard's boy to come for me. I know your stableman and his family. Richard was loyal and true to your poor mother. You can trust him. Do you understand?"

"Yes, I understand." Brianda looked at the floor for a moment, then up into Megan's eyes. "Will you tell me about my mother one day, Old Megan? It is forbidden to talk about her at my home, but I would like to hear about her."

"Yes, lass, I will tell you all that I know. But for now you must run along home. It grows dark, and I don't want you to be in trouble again." Old Megan leaned over and kissed the child's forehead.

Brianda felt blessed. "Thank you for being my friend. I will always remember this day," she solemnly told the old woman.

In the years that followed, Brianda spent countless hours learning about herbs and plants under the tutelage of the wise old Medicine Woman. Old Megan also taught Brianda to read and write. She herself had been taught as a child, so that she could learn and record recipes for medicinal herbal concoctions. Brianda was bright and learned quickly.

At thirteen, she was ready for new subjects. To the best of her ability, Megan Sloan instructed the girl in etiquette, attire, and social amenities. Brianda found the entire idea of class structure perplexing and absurd. She considered everyone her equal. Old Megan explained that, nonetheless, Brianda must conform to the rules of society, under which servants and villagers were never the equals of the gentry. Brianda remained dubious, and, since she never went anywhere, paid little heed to social graces.

Midway through her thirteenth year, Brianda awakened with an aching abdomen and her thighs smeared with bright red blood. Frightened, she made her way to Old Megan's cottage, where she pounded on the door, tears streaming down her face and terror in her heart.

Old Megan thought that surely the girl had been beaten again. She pulled Brianda into the house. "What has happened? Tell me, child!"

Trembling, Brianda explained her alarming symptoms. "Am I going to die?" she concluded in a quavering voice.

Old Megan just sat back in her chair and smiled. "Yes, my little one, but not for many years. What has happened is normal, Brianda. It happens to all young women." Old Megan pulled Brianda into her arms and held her close. "I thought I had a little more time before I would have to tell you about these things. You are always surprising me." And she gently expanded the girl's education to include the wonders of a woman's body. Before sending her home, Old Megan prepared a warm herbal drink to lessen the cramps.

And once again Brianda felt blessed by the friendship of wise Old Megan.

Brianda began mixing and preparing herbs, learning

the various concoctions each contained in the curious looking bottles. Gradually, under Old Megan's supervision, Brianda learned how to dispense remedies. At word of a birth, Brianda would grab all the bottles that they might need, both for the mother and for the baby. She knew to administer the bitter-tasting liquid after the child and the afterbirth had been born, so that the mother's womb would cease bleeding. Gradually, the villagers became accustomed to the sight of Brianda's presence at their bedsides.

The subjects of the Earl of Manseth, being fiercely loyal to their lord, went way beyond the boundaries of convention when they took the now beautiful young woman into their homes and hearts. She was a member of the ruling class, and there were some who secretly feared that her friendship would someday bring trouble from the absentee lord. Yet no one could turn away from her smile.

Brianda was seventeen and more beautiful than she could have imagined. She was short, only an inch or two over five feet. She was slender, and her body was well toned from walking miles every day. She rode her stallion every day at dawn, galloping bareback with the wind blowing her long blond hair behind her like a veil. Her natural beauty was only enhanced by her unselfconscious nature.

Her father had been dead for three years now, and Edward hardly ever came to Cliffshead Manor anymore. He was too busy gambling and womanizing to care about his only living relative.

Brianda returned to the manor every nightfall, and Nellie made sure that there was dinner prepared for her. No one at the manor asked where she had been. They really didn't want to know. That way, if Edward came home for a short visit and asked about her, they could truthfully tell him that they did not know and thereby avoid his rage.

Brianda would go up to the master suite during Edward's long absences and gaze out over the moors. As the moonlight danced across the land, she would dream about her mother's first ball, when, according to Old Megan, her father had swept her beautiful mother up into his arms. Brianda imagined that other young women were going to dances and parties, and she longed to go to just one! And she swore she would have the most extraordinary gown of all!

4

Jacob Breedon was an angry man. Indeed, he had been an angry child. He did nothing but work hard and paid close attention to all matters relating to the management of his father's lands. By the time he was thirteen, he was able to manage the estate better than his father could. So when his father died and left his title and the entire estate to Jacob, he set himself down and wrote out a set of plans.

He was twenty years old and decided it best that he marry and father some sons to help him with his work and to carry on the family lineage. He wasted not a moment on thoughts of love. He needed a wife, nothing more.

Still, finding a wife was a new endeavor for a man who thought only of rents and crops. In keeping with his plans, he set about finding a wife as another man might purchase a brood mare. He really didn't care much how she looked, or what her family's social standing was. What he wanted was good breeding stock. London was reported to offer the largest selection, and with his foreman in charge and one bag on his shoulder, young Breedon departed for London.

Given his ignorance in matters of love and romance, no one could have been more surprised than Jacob at the sight of the lovely Blanche Reed. At the first gala ball of the season, Jacob was standing along the wall, when she entered on the arm of her father. Jacob took one look and was instantly and completely in love.

Blanche had been told by her physician to stay in bed. She had defied his orders and wept until her father agreed to take her to the ball. Sickly all her life, she was tired of being left out of all the fun! This was her first ball, and she was going to enjoy herself!

Jacob had no idea how to arrange a meeting with her. Nor did he know how to dance. But seeing that several other men had noticed the beautiful, delicate young woman, he knew he had to make his move. Boldly, he walked right up to her and asked her to dance, thinking only that he had to have this woman in his arms.

Blanche looked up into the stranger's face. He was so handsome and tall, with such broad shoulders! His brooding face had smoldering green eyes that seemed to penetrate her very soul.

She placed her delicate, small hand on his arm, and allowed him to lead her to the dance floor. As he put his arm around her, they began moving to the music. She felt his body move against hers, and suddenly found it difficult to breathe properly. He was much bigger than she, and his size gave her comfort. She liked everything about this strange, quiet young man.

They were married in a fortnight, much to the distress of her parents and friends. No one could believe that she would want to go to the English countryside to live year round! Why, the young lord claimed he had no need of the social season in London. Blanche's father and mother could not bear to think that she would be lost to a life like that, alone with the stranger who had come out of nowhere to steal their daughter.

Blanche stood firm, insisting she loved Jacob and wanted to go to his family home. It did not matter that it was far from friends and parents.

For Jacob, the lovely Blanche had seemingly cast a spell upon him. He smiled at people and even made pleasant conversation! A miracle had happened. He swore he would treasure his lovely wife, as the king would one of his crown jewels. He barely heard Blanche's parents warn him of her delicate state of health. They were together, and that was all that mattered. He would take care of his wife.

To their joy, Blanche became pregnant as soon as they were married. But soon after, Blanche began experiencing difficulties with her pregnancy. The Breedons did not have a full-time physician on staff, and the Fauxleys did. Jacob swallowed his pride and went to Manseth Manor to ask for aid. The warm and generous Earl of Manseth sent his personal physician, Dr. Holmes, immediately to Cliffshead Manor to see to the needs of the neighboring lord's young wife. The doctor put Blanche to bed and told her anxious husband that she must stay there for the entire pregnancy.

Jacob worried about her every moment of every day. But Blanche would have no part of sadness or worry. She was so thrilled to be giving Jacob his first child that it didn't matter to her that she had to stay in bed. She maintained her cheerful attitude and scolded him for his grumpy one. Near the end of the pregnancy, she secretly sent for the Medicine Woman. Megan arrived and took an immediate liking to the brave young woman. Megan brought her herbal teas and counseled her, and they became friends.

When Blanche finally went into labor, Jacob summoned Dr. Holmes, and Nellie summoned Megan. The three of them stayed with Blanche throughout the twenty-four hours of agonizing labor. She gave birth to a son at long last. She wanted him named Edward after her husband's dead father.

Jacob was thrilled with his infant son. The baby thrived, but Blanche did not. The long months of pregnancy had taken their toll. Blanche cried and pleaded with him that she could care for her child, but Jacob stood firm. He found a wet nurse for the baby boy.

Dr. Holmes strongly advised against Blanche's ever becoming pregnant again. He told Jacob that she could not survive another pregnancy.

Jacob was frightened. He stopped working to care for her, spoon-feeding her and kissing her forehead. Gradually her health improved. She gained a little weight and shared the care of her son with the nurse. Blanche was unutterably happy.

After some months, she brought up the subject of having another baby. Jacob refused to discuss it with her, but she kept after him, and finally he divulged the doctor's dire prediction.

Blanche swore to him that she was able to bear more children, that the doctor was a fool. She could not bear the thought of not giving Jacob all the sons he wanted.

Jacob took her in his arms against her feeble protests and told her that his mind was made up. No more babies.

Blanche did not bring up the subject again with Jacob. His resolve was strong, but she knew hers was stronger. She took good care of herself and gradually became stronger and stronger.

Megan came to visit her whenever Jacob was absent, and together they worked out a plan of nourishment and herbal therapy to strengthen her frail constitution.

Blanche avoided telling Megan about her desire for more sons; she was sure that she would once again meet with opposition. Instead she told the woman that she wanted to regain her health, so that she would be better able to care for her son.

It was months before she could lure her husband back to her bed. He was afraid to touch her, so fearful of another pregnancy that he was willing to give up their sexual relationship.

She pleaded with him and flirted with him. She explained that he could withdraw at the last moment, shifting her eyes from his when she lied like that, but her goal was more important than telling Jacob the complete truth. She whispered into his ear how she needed his touch, his body within hers. Her touches became more seductive. She knew all of his sensitive areas, the places where he most enjoyed her attentions, and she used this knowledge to lure him into a tender longing for her.

Jacob resisted her soft advances as best he could, but finally he could do so no longer and fell into her arms in tortured bliss. He made love to her with a tenderness that not even she knew he was capable of. They soared together into the realm of ecstasy.

The first few times, he withdrew before his seed could spill into her. In the silence of her secret world, she knew that she would have to do something to make him stay within her. So she began moving her hips differently than she had ever done before. She dreamed of how she could make herself more physically desirable to her husband; whatever it took, she would do.

Jacob responded immediately to her wild passion. The two lovers were caught simultaneously in an explosive, tumultuous climax. Later Blanche smiled contentedly as Jacob lay sleeping, his arms around her. She prayed that on this night she had conceived the forbidden child.

When a couple of months later she knew she was pregnant, she cried with joy. It was, however, a joy that she could share with no one. If Jacob knew, he would immediately summon Megan and the doctor, and he would insist they do whatever had to be done to rid her of her child.

She lived with her precious secret, taking the most special care of herself. She was obsessive about her health, eating fresh vegetables and fruits and taking long walks to strengthen her muscles. When she completed her sixth month, no one noticed any bulge in her abdomen. She feigned exhaustion and headaches to keep Jacob from her bed. He complied with her requests without objection, so great was his love for her.

She spent as much time with little Edward as she could. Now three years old, he was a difficult child and not easy to love, but Blanche tried to hold him and to show him how she loved him. But he pushed her away. He seemed to have eyes only for his father.

Jacob spoiled him in every way, thinking Edward would be his only offspring. He ignored the many warning signs of the small child's obvious character faults. At three years old, he seemed to enjoy hurting things, abusing the cats and dogs, and destroying his playthings. He convinced himself that the worrisome behavior would pass as Edward continued to grow.

Blanche felt as if she were losing her small son. The more she tried to hold and love him, the more he stared at her with a strange look in his eyes. As the pregnancy progressed, she felt herself withdraw from her peculiar little boy. He was a stranger in her world. She began concentrating all of her love on the unborn child.

＊   ＊   ＊

Late one night in mid-May Blanche pulled the cord in her room to summon one of the servants. The frightened woman ran to fetch her master. Blanche's contractions had begun and she was worried; if her calculations were correct, she was several weeks early.

Jacob entered the room on the run and paled when he saw her lying on her bed in obvious discomfort. "What is wrong, my darling?" he asked, his voice unsteady.

"Jacob, my love, listen to me now," she pleaded with him. "Don't do anything until you have heard me out. Do you promise?" she asked, her eyes begging him.

"I promise. But what is wrong, my darling, what is causing you to look so distressed?"

"I will tell you everything in a moment, my love, but first I want you to sit here with me and hold my hand and look into my eyes and then tell me that you love me."

Jacob sat carefully on the bed and took a cool, clammy hand into his. He lifted her hand to his lips and held it there. "I love you more than anything else on this earth, and I want to be with you always."

"Thank you, darling. Will you give me something, Jacob?"

Surprised, Jacob smiled at her. She never asked for anything. "I will give you whatever it is you wish for or want, my Lady. What is it?"

"A most precious gift from God. I want it more than anything I could ever possibly dream of."

"Come, tell me. What is it?"

"Our baby."

"You already have him, Blanche. Edward is yours and will always be."

"I am not speaking of Edward, Jacob. I am now in labor with our second child."

Jacob's face hardened. "What in the hell are you talking

about, Blanche? Are you so ill that you are imagining things?" he asked, his voice rising, his hand tightening on hers.

"I asked you not to raise your voice, Jacob. I have accomplished this pregnancy without your knowledge and against your will. I admit this freely. No one else on this Earth knows of it, I swear to you. If you are angry, I am sorry, but I will not apologize for the child. The child is innocent, and I want it more than anything else. Please help me now by going for Megan and the physician. I need them to help me, as the pains are getting stronger. Please hurry, my love."

Jacob stood over her and watched as her abdomen contracted. His heart felt as if it were made of ice. His limbs did not want to respond. Finally, he forced himself to move, and then found himself screaming orders at the servants. He went to fetch the doctor and sent a stable hand for Megan.

The strenuous twelve hours of labor took their toll on the young mother, but she never once cried out or complained. Dr. Holmes watched as his patient worsened, afraid to mention anything to Lord Breedon. The young man was clearly overwrought.

At last the baby was born. It was a girl, and she cried lustily. Barely conscious, Blanche reached out for her. Dr. Holmes placed the crying bundle into the loving arms of her mother.

With some effort, Blanche put the babe to her breast and smiled as its tiny mouth firmly grabbed onto the nipple and suckled. After a moment, she glanced up at Jacob and was frightened by the look on his face. He was looking at the baby as if he wanted to be rid of it! Blanche gathered her strength and said to her husband, "I am so happy here with you, Jacob, here with you and our new baby girl. There is nothing you could have given me that would have made me happier. I love you and her and, of course, little Edward. If you truly love me, then you must also love our children. You do, don't you, Jacob?"

"Yes, my darling. Of course I love the children. Nevertheless, I cherish you more than my own life. This has been such a surprise for me, that's all. We will all be fine very soon. But one thing I will tell you, my Blanche, there will be no more children. I will not discuss this further with you. If it takes my absenting myself from your bed for the rest of our days, I will do so to keep you alive and with me. Understood?"

"Yes, my darling." Blanche wiped the tears of gratitude from her eyes. She raised her arms, offering the infant to its father. "Here, take your daughter. Feel how small she is, and look how beautiful she is." She laid her tiny daughter in her husband's strong arms. "You look wonderful together, Jacob. She is as much yours as she is mine. Promise me that you will love her as much as you do Edward. Promise me!" she implored.

"I promise," Jacob swore as he stepped back. "Even so, my darling, you are tired and pale that you ought to sleep for a while. I'm going to summon a wet nurse."

"Oh, please don't take her just yet . . ." she pleaded, her arms outstretched toward the child.

The doctor stepped between them. "You must rest now, Lady Breedon. You have lost a good amount of blood, and I must complete my examination. Then I want you to sleep. You have the rest of your life to care for your baby."

Jacob called to Nellie to come and take the child. When Nellie left the room with her small charge, Blanche called out to her, "Nellie, promise me with all the love that you have for me, that you will swear by your life to love and protect my baby."

"I swear it, my Lady," replied Nellie, as she held the small bundle close to her heart.

"Take the child out now, Nellie!" said Jacob, his voice rising with concern for his wife.

"Her name is Brianda, Jacob. Brianda is the name I have chosen for our daughter, as it has always been my favorite name, and she will be my only daughter. Do you approve, Jacob?"

"Whatever you choose, my love. Now lie back and let the doctor finish his work," he answered, as he held her hand and gently pushed her back onto the bed.

Blanche Breedon never saw her precious daughter again. She hemorrhaged a few hours after the birth, and there was nothing that the doctor could do to save her. The following day, Lady Breedon was laid to rest.

After the funeral, Jacob made arrangements for the children to be cared for, then took to his room. He spent two months in his room, drunk, wishing that God would take him, too. When he realized that he was not going to die, he took up his life as best he could.

He indulged Edward's every whim, giving him anything he wanted. Anything but love, for there was no more love in Jacob to share.

Brianda hardly existed. He never asked for reports on her progress, never wanted to see her. Each day she looked more and more like Blanche, and the sight of her made him so sad that he couldn't bear it. The child had robbed him of his greatest love.

When a servant reported to Jacob that Brianda had been disobedient, he allowed ten year old Edward to punish her. At first, Nellie tried to tell Jacob that Brianda was receiving unjust punishment from Edward, but Jacob refused to listen. It did not matter to him that the punishment was unwarranted. He refused to see that his son had become a cruel, mean little boy. The servants stood by helplessly and kept silent. They knew the master was indifferent to his daughter, and none of them could afford to lose his position, as they needed to feed their own families. After Edward had beaten Brianda several times, Nellie went to Jacob and told him of the cruelty. Jacob screamed at her never to question the actions of the future lord again. His son had his full permission to treat Brianda in any way he saw fit. Nellie left the master's room quietly. All she could do now was to try to protect Brianda from the permanent wrath of her older brother.

Every few months, Brianda would eat with her father and brother in the now shabby formal dining room. Jacob and Edward shared every meal together when Edward was home from school and occasionally, Jacob would suffer one of his rare bouts of guilt and would include Brianda for dinner. But it would always end with Edward teasing her unmercifully, and Jacob could not stand the stress of the situation. Brianda looked so much like Blanche when she was sad, and when she looked up at him with her big violet eyes, he would feel a stab of real pain in his chest.

Brianda was a very lonely little girl. She spent her days in the stable, tagging along after Richard, the head groomsman, or his son. When they were too busy, they would gently shoo her off, and she began talking to the animals, giving them the hugs and kisses that others did not seem to want. Then, when Brianda was nine years of age, Old Megan entered her life, and she at long last found a haven for her heart.

The day Brianda turned fourteen years old, her father called her into his study for the first time.

Afraid, she entered the room. "Yes, Father?" she asked, timidly, standing just inside the door, hands clasped behind her back to hide their trembling. She saw him flinch when he heard her say "Father."

"Come here and sit down, child," he said, unable to

look at her. It was painful. She was just like Blanche. He
would watch her through a window and see his wife,
beautiful and young, with a life in front of her. The
vision ate at him.

"Yes, sir." Brianda walked to the chair near his desk
and sat, back straight, hands in her lap.

"Brianda, I have just been told by Nellie that you
have reached your fourteenth birthday. I haven't been
one to give much thought to birthdays, but seeing as
how this is your fourteenth birthday, I have bought you
a present."

Brianda was too shocked to respond.

He seemed not to notice. "I have been told that you
spend a great deal of time with Robert and the animals."

"Yes, Father."

"Which of the animals do you like the most?"

"The horses, Father. Although I like all of the animals
so much . . ."

"Fine, thank you," he said, interrupting her. He could
not bear hearing her soft voice. "I had the opportunity to
buy a young stallion from an American trader who told
me the horse was once owned by a tribe of Dakota Indians.
I am giving this animal to you. He is young and wild. He
will need a great deal of work. You have plenty of time,
so I think this will be a good present for you. I have
informed Robert, and he will make sure that you have
all that you need to care for the animal. I am going to
give you the papers that state that the animal is legally
yours. Put them in a safe place." Jacob Breedon turned
to the papers on his desk. The look of joy on his daughter's
face was too much for him.

"Thank you, Father!" Brianda was hardly able to
contain her excitement! A horse of her own!

"I assume that you will marry one day soon. You have,
after all, reached age fourteen. Have any young men
come here to see you?" he asked, genuinely interested.

"Why no, Father. Other than the servants and the lad from the village, I do not know any young men."

"What lad from the village?" he asked, his eyes rising to meet hers for the first time.

The look in his eyes scared her. She lowered her gaze to the carpet. "Over the years, I have gone into the village and I have met some of the people who live there, Father," she said, as calmly as her rapidly beating heart would allow.

"Are you telling me, young lady, that you have gone into the village when you were strictly forbidden to do so? You were not accompanied by Nellie or someone else from the house staff?" he fairly bellowed at her, suddenly concerned how it would look for the master's daughter to be wandering around the village.

"I have always been accompanied, Father," she answered in a small voice, praying that he would not ask who she had been with. She was sure he would not like the idea that she had been spending so much time with Old Megan; it was no secret that Jacob Breedon still blamed Old Megan for the death of her mother.

"You are not to go into the village again unless I give my permission. Is that clear?"

"Yes, Father."

"Edward will be home for a holiday from school soon and I'm going to make him aware of my order."

Brianda flinched, and Jacob felt a sudden guilt stab his gut.

He found himself falling into the pools of her eyes. They were so beautiful. He shook himself to stop the thoughts that haunted him. He didn't think often of his broken promises. So many years had passed since Blanche had died, he could scarcely remember what he had said to her. If he thought hard enough, he would remember every word, as if they had been burned into his skin. But he didn't want to recall any of it. All he wanted to do was to get through each day until he could die and be with Blanche again. He looked away. "Leave now and go to see your horse. Remember my words, child."

"Yes, Father, and thank you for the most lovely present of my life. I will take good care of him, and I hope someday you will be proud of me," she said, as she quickly crossed the room and slipped out the door, closing it quietly behind her.

Jacob laid his head on his crossed arms and felt the tears burn his eyes. Try as hard as he could, he could not stop them as they rolled down his cheeks, leaving hot tracks across his face. They gave him no comfort or solace.

Brianda spent every free moment with the black stallion. Theirs was a case of love at first sight. She offered him so much love, he gave his in return; the young animal, too, sensed her need.

She named him Dakota after the American Indian tribe. He had a powerful name because he was her protector, and she felt safe when he was near. She would take him to the ocean, and together they would gallop through the breaking waves. She rode bareback without a bridle. They seemed to have formed their own language since their first encounter, and she needed no leather straps to get the huge horse to do as she bade.

Dakota loved Old Megan's house. The grass was sweet there, and Old Megan always had a treat for him. Dakota became a permanent companion to Brianda and Old Megan.

Brianda continued to visit Old Megan, just as she had done before her father's proclamation that she could no longer visit the village. From experience, she knew that he had forgotten all about his threats.

*   *   *

One cold January morning, Nellie came to Brianda's bed chamber and told her that she had best come quickly to the master's suite.

Brianda threw on her robe and followed Nellie to her father's room. Suddenly, the fourteen-year-old girl was afraid to cross the threshold; she had never been allowed to enter this room. She had seen Edward enter often enough, and had even heard some of the arguments the two men had late at night, usually about Edward's gambling and wasting his father's money.

Nellie pushed her slightly from behind. Brianda stumbled through the door and saw Dr. Holmes standing near Father's bed. "What is wrong, Dr. Holmes?" she asked in a very small voice.

Dr. Holmes turned his kind old face toward her and motioned for her to draw nearer.

It was then that she saw Edward. He, too, was standing near the bed, and the look he gave her made her shiver.

"Come here, my child," the doctor said gently. "My how you have grown. I haven't seen you since the day you were born, and you were a beautiful little thing then, too." He shifted from one foot to the other. Looking into her grave little face, he said, "My dear, I have some bad news for you." He took her small hand into his large one. "Are you a brave girl? I think that you must be. Now listen carefully. I am sorry to inform you that your father has had an attack that affected his heart. He is dead."

Brianda simply looked at him, not moving at all.

"Are you all right, Lady Breedon?" he asked gently.

"Why shouldn't she be all right?" sneered Edward. "My father could never stand her anyway. She doesn't need to be here. Why did you bring her here?" he asked angrily.

"I beg your pardon, Lord Breedon, but she is the rightful daughter to his Lordship, just as you are the rightful son," said Dr. Holmes sternly, keeping a firm grip on Brianda's hand. She slipped behind him, trying to put a barrier between herself and her brother.

"I am sure you are right there, doctor, as you were the physician attending my mother when she gave birth to this girl, were you not?"

"You know very well that I was here, Edward."

"You know, then," Edward continued, looking straight at Brianda, "that my mother died because of her. She bled to death while her precious little baby lived."

"That is enough, Edward! I also brought you into the world. I will not have you saying things like that to Brianda. She is not at fault for your mother's death!" he proclaimed, his voice raised in anger.

Brianda stood behind Dr. Holmes, her small hand entwined in the fabric of his coat. She was unable to speak. How she had longed to hear news of her mother all these years, but no one had ever dared speak of Blanche for fear that Jacob would overhear. Her name had never been spoken aloud at Cliffshead Manor until a few minutes ago when Edward had just accused her of being the cause of her mother's death. Could it be true? And with her father now dead, would Edward blame her for his death, too?

Brianda felt very cold and strangely alone. She glanced briefly toward the corpse and felt no grief, for truthfully she had never been loved by the man lying dead in the bed nearby.

Nellie shuddered to think of what would happen to the young mistress, now that Jacob was dead. Edward would now have full rule of Cliffshead Manor—and his sister. Her life would be in danger. Nellie was sure that seventeen-year-old Edward would never return to

school, now that Lord Breedon was dead. He always
hated school and only went because his father had
forced him to go. She would have to protect the young
girl and try to keep her out of her brother's way.

In the days that followed the funeral, Edward was
busy with matters of the estate and had little time to
seek Brianda out. As the weeks and months passed, he
only searched for her when he was drunk or angry, and
only to take great pleasure in mistreating her. Life took
on a new pattern, as Edward began destroying everything around him, including his only living relative.

5

Old Megan followed Mrs. Brady's broad back down the hall to the study. She couldn't help but stare at the beautiful wall tapestries and paintings. Manseth Manor was rumored to be the richest manor in this part of England, and it appeared to be true.

As she entered the large study, she noted the many volumes of books on the beautifully polished oak shelves. The furniture was crafted of the plushest leathers and the finest wood. This was a man's room, with pleasant odors of rich tobacco and cedar. With her eyes she looked around, trying to get a feel for the man from the possessions he displayed. She would need all the information she could get, to help her in gaining details about Brianda. The gentry were not in the habit of taking odd old village women into their confidence.

It hadn't taken long for word to reach Old Megan's ears that Brianda was either ill or injured, and was now in residence in the house of Lord Fauxley. All of the servants in the county knew of the relationship between Brianda and Old Megan. When the girl caused the ruckus the night of the storm, one of the lads from the manor made sure that Old Megan knew about it.

Standing still and resolute in the middle of the room, Old Megan faced the door and waited. The door opened, and she braced herself for the fight. Her breath stopped when she saw him. He was the most handsome man she had ever laid eyes on, so tall and broad he resembled a Viking god, only this man had hair as black as a moonless night. His eyes were deep blue, as if they had once been sapphires in the earth's crust. His body was lean with strong shoulders, a tapered waist, and long, well-muscled legs. Instead of demanding to see Brianda, as she had planned, she simply stared at him.

"You wished to see me, Madam?"

"Yes, my Lord," she said, her voice not nearly as forceful as she had intended, "I was told that you have a guest here. A young woman that may have had a mishap."

"A mishap? Hardly a mishap. What do you know of this situation?" he demanded. When she did not respond, he stood towering directly before her. "Who told you that I have a guest who may be of your acquaintance? I wish to know why you presume to come to my home seeking this or any other information," he stated firmly.

Old Megan held her head high, so as not to show any fear. "Let me introduce myself, my Lord Fauxley," she said. "I am Megan Sloan, and I have lived on the edge of your property all of my many years. I am the Medicine Woman. It is possible you knew my mother, Clarisa, as she was Medicine Woman before me. Brianda Breedon has been my friend for many years now. She is the only daughter of the late Lord Breedon." Old Megan paused to see if there was any recognition in his eyes. She could read nothing there. She continued, "She is like a daughter to me. I found her in the woods nine years ago. She was a very lonely child. Her mother died when she was born." Megan stopped abruptly, certain that she sounded like an addled old woman who could do no more than ramble on.

John studied her. He had heard rumors of her skill in healing. He waited for her to continue.

"I will not tell you, sir, who it was that told me that the lass was here. I do not wish to bring trouble to any of my friends. It was a friend who came to me and told me that the lass needed me, that she had become ill or . . ." Megan looked him straight in the eye, "that she may have been injured. I want to see her for myself—perhaps I can help her."

John continued to study her without comment for a few moments. He was impressed with her boldness.

His silence worried Old Megan, and she began to fear that the imposing Lord Fauxley intended to throw her out.

"Please follow me, Megan Sloan," John said, turning to lead her out of the study. He walked toward the main entrance, and Old Megan was sure he was going to show her the front door. She had to walk quickly to keep up with his long strides.

She was therefore surprised when he turned and led her up a huge staircase. At the top of the staircase, she passed a marble statue of a seated man and huge windows interspersed with oil portraits and sweeping landscapes. She wished she had time to examine each one, but now there was someone much more important for her to focus her attention on. She was so intent on her mission that she almost ran right into Lord Fauxley's back, when he stopped in front of a closed door. "Oh, excuse me, my Lord," she mumbled as she righted herself.

"Yes, well . . . Lady Breedon is in here. As you probably know, since you seem to know everything and everyone, I am a physician. This young woman is now my patient. You will do as I order and nothing more. You will not disturb her. My colleague, Dr. Martin, is with her now. Is all of that clear?"

"Yes, sir, quite clear. May I see her now?"

John opened the door quietly. Motioning toward the still figure on the bed, he said, "I am afraid that she is gravely ill."

With her hand on her heart, Megan stepped into the room. "Oh, good God," she whispered, when she saw her lovely young girl laid out on the bed, so still, as if she had already been welcomed by death. Old Megan moved quickly to Brianda's side and looked down at her face. Great tears filled her eyes and fell onto Brianda's chest. She rubbed her fingertips along the length of Brianda's arm, hoping that some of the love she felt would pass from her fingers into the body of the one she loved so much. After a moment she turned and looked at the faces of the two physicians as they stood together watching her. She felt her throat swell with emotion, and hatred seemed to clog her voice as she asked, "Tell me, doctors, has he gone and killed her this time?"

John took a step forward, his eyes hard and staring. "What did you say?"

Megan regretted the words the moment they had left her mouth. She took a deep breath. "I am sorry. Please forget what I said, my Lord. I am just an old woman saddened by this sight. I said nothing of importance."

"On the contrary, Madam, I think you said exactly what you meant to say. You look ill. Would you like to sit down for a moment?" John pulled a chair over to Megan and helped her sit down.

She stared straight ahead, unmoving.

John knelt in front of her. Taking her hands in his, he asked, "Who were you referring to a moment ago? You must tell me, for how can I help her, if I don't know the identity of her torturer? If I must, I will use any and all power that I have at my disposal to make you tell me what I need to know. Do you doubt me, Madam?"

"No, sir. I hope that you, in turn, will understand that I am from these parts." She looked up at him with powerful intensity. "Sir, I have made a blunder, a grave social error. If word should get out that I have spoken aloud against one of the gentry, my life could be endangered and, even worse, the lives of others much more important than mine."

"Your word is protected in my house. There is no one within earshot, except for Dr. Martin and myself. I guarantee you that not one word will leave this room. Now, tell me what you know."

Old Megan looked over at the still form, then back into the deep blue eyes of the earl. "My lassie's name is Brianda Breedon. She is an orphan. As I told you, her mother died when she was born, and her father died about three years ago. She lives with her brother, Edward, the Lord of Cliffshead Manor."

Megan continued, "Brianda's mother's health had always been very delicate. She bled to death after the lass was born. Her father blamed Brianda for his wife's death. Her older brother, Edward, has loathed Brianda all of her life, and has been known to treat her very badly on occasion."

"Was this one of those occasions?"

"I cannot be certain, sir, but it would appear so."

"Please come over to the bed." Turning to his friend, John said, "Paul, help me turn our young lady, so that the Medicine Woman can see her back." As the two men gently lifted and turned the young woman, Old Megan felt her stomach contract. She pressed the back of her hand to her open mouth to stifle the bile that rose in her throat. She could see how badly infected the wounds were. Her lovely little one was going to die.

Megan felt her knees go weak. Her vision began to blur, and suddenly she felt strong arms grab her elbows and lead her to the chair. She sat down gratefully.

"This time she will die, won't she?" She couldn't stop the tears that flowed from her eyes. She had seen so many horrible accidents, had seen the young die needlessly. This was the worst.

John leaned over and looked into Megan's emotion-filled eyes. "We are doing everything that we can to save her life. Can you offer us assistance?"

"I have powders that may help with the fever. I can make salves to heal the wounds. But I do not have the power to save her life." She leaned forward and sobbed.

John put his arms around her and held her for a moment. "Megan, tell me everything you know. Perhaps I will be able to help her. Trust me."

Sitting back in the chair, Old Megan dried her eyes and began relating the story, as she knew it, of Brianda Breedon. As her tale unfolded, the doctors looked from one to the other, sickened.

"Edward has been violent with her many times, but since her father died it has gotten worse. It is as if Edward would like to kill her, but doesn't, so that he will have her around the next time he wants to be cruel. She has no one to protect her. The servants try, but they can only do so much. Be on your guard with Edward, my Lord. He will be furious when he finds out that she is here."

"Thank you for telling me all of this. Rest assured, these secrets will stay within the confines of this room." Then he asked gently, "Do you think that you will be able to fetch your powders and salves? We could use them."

A light lit in Old Megan's eyes, and she reached for her traveling box that she took with her everywhere. She searched inside and finally pulled out a small glass bottle. "This is a secret recipe that my great grandmother invented for wound infections." She washed her hands and waited for the men to lift Brianda onto her side. She applied the salve and the three of them put clean bandages on Brianda's back.

John called to Mrs. Brady to ready a room for Old Megan, who accepted the invitation of a room for the night with all the grace of an honored guest. The three healers worked side by side, spelling one another as they broke only for short naps.

At dawn of the next day, as both physicians slept in chairs near the bed, Brianda's eyes slowly opened. Her vision was blurred, and she didn't know where she was. She lifted her shoulder to turn herself and was assaulted by searing pain. She gasped.

Awakened by the soft cry, John sat up and looked at his patient. She was moving!

He jumped up and awakened Paul. He leaned over Brianda and called out to her, "Good morning. How are you feeling?"

"Water, please," was all she was able to respond.

"Just a small sip for now. You can have more in a few minutes."

The water felt wonderful in her dry mouth, and when she finally swallowed it, she asked for more.

"No, not just yet," said the man. There was something familiar about the voice, but she couldn't place it. She was too tired to respond anyway. She closed her eyes and fell back asleep.

"It is a good sign, John," said Paul.

"Yes, a very good sign, indeed. Let's try to get some more sleep ourselves."

"All right, but it is time to put more of Old Megan's salve on the wounds." Paul reached for the bottle.

John lifted Brianda and turned her. He held her in his arms as he would a small child, looking down at her face and admiring the long dark brown lashes curling against her cheek. Even in illness, he found her exceedingly beautiful. With his left hand, he gently smoothed the hair back over her temple and let it fall behind her ear. Her hair felt like the finest silk, belying the toughness of her soul. Small as she was, she fought like a tigress against her brother's brutality.

"Let's hurry and get her settled again, Paul."

"Yes, I am just now finished. These welts look much improved, John. It seems that the Medicine Woman may have an answer in her salve."

"Whatever the answer, I will take it," said John, his voice determined.

Paul glanced up to look at his friend. It was unusual for John to get involved emotionally with anyone, let alone a patient. Yet, Paul knew his friend too well to respond. He just turned his head and smiled. It seemed that the young lady had made an impression on his Lordship.

The next few days passed in much the same manner. Brianda would awaken and drink water, and then a few sips of broth. Old Megan stayed at the house and tended to the wounds. They were healing well.

Paul was near when the fever broke. Brianda was restless, turning her head from side to side, moaning low in her throat. Alarmed, Paul moved closer to the bed and noticed the beads of sweat over her upper lip and on her forehead.

Brianda opened her eyes and looked around. Only a few feet away from her was a strange man's face! She was startled and tried to speak, but all she could manage was a croak. "Water, please," she rasped.

Paul put the glass to her lips and let her swallow a small amount.

She looked at him and asked, "Who are you and what are you doing here?"

Before Paul could reply, John stated, "Well, not even a thank you, just an imperious demand."

Brianda knew that voice! "You!" Her eyes followed the sound and found the blurred shape of the man who had spoken. She still couldn't focus very well, but she could see how large he was! "What are you doing in my room?" Brianda's voice was regaining some strength. Swallowing, she said even more firmly, "Get out immediately, or I shall call for help!"

"Is that a fact? It hardly seems proper that you would wish to throw me out of my own house, Miss Breedon."

"Your house?" she demanded. She looked around, only to find that she was staring at furniture and surroundings totally alien to her, then looked down at her body and saw a chemise that she didn't recognize. "Why am I here? Whose clothes are these?"

No one answered. The two men just looked at her.

"I am so thirsty. Please give me some more water," she requested in a much softer tone.

Paul passed a small glass to her.

When she tried to sit up, unspeakable pain seared her back. She drank slowly.

Now she remembered. The horror of it made her shiver. Edward, their confrontation over Dakota. Unable to look at either man, she asked in a voice that trembled with fear, "What time is it, sir? I have to get home." Gritting her teeth, she tried to rise, but felt so weak that it was impossible. She looked at the two men still standing silent, unmoving. "Where is my cloak?" she uttered, all the while trying to sit up. Suddenly she began to feel dizzy.

"Whoa there, little one. You cannot move like that yet. The fever has just broken. Lie back and rest," said Paul in his kindest voice.

Brianda looked at him again. "I remember you, sir. You offered me brandy tonight."

Paul smiled, "Yes, I offered you some brandy. In addition, I am a doctor who is advising you to rest now."

"You don't understand, sir," she pleaded, "I have to get home before . . ."

"Before what?" John demanded softly as he approached the bed.

"Oh, nothing, my Lord," she answered demurely, unable to look him in the eye. "I am sorry if I am not making sense. My mind seems disjointed." She looked at Paul. "Did you say I had a fever, sir?"

"Yes, a high one. You are very weak and need to rest. No more questions for now, just lie back and try to sleep. I will ask the housekeeper to bring you some soup."

"I cannot stay here! I have to get home. What time is it? Have I been here all night? Is it dawn yet?" she asked, her eyes searching for a window. The curtains were drawn, making it impossible to tell whether it was day or night. Maybe she could get home before Edward awoke. She swung her legs as hard as she could and let them fall over the side of the bed and muttered, "My brother. I have to get home before he finds me missing. He'll . . ."

"He'll what?" John asked.

She refused to answer. Instead, she looked away, staring at the wall.

"Brianda, what will your brother do? Tell me."

"He'll . . . He's very strict with me. Especially since my father died." She tried to stand again. "Now move back so that I can return home before he discovers me missing," she ordered, and tried to push his massive weight up and away from her.

"It is too late, I'm afraid," he said softly.

Cold fear grabbed her. "Too late? Why?"

"Brianda, you have been here for five days."

She felt herself go limp and fall back onto the pillows. Mute, she watched him, a terrible hopelessness claiming her.

"Paul and I have been caring for you. Old Megan has been here helping us for the past four days. You have been very ill, so ill that we thought you might not live. No one was notified of your presence here."

"Then you know. You've seen my back."

"Yes."

Tears filled her lovely eyes and slid softly down her cheeks. She made no sound. Her eyes darted about the room nervously as she wrung her hands in the sheets. "Five days," she said, almost as if she were talking to herself. "He may kill me for this. I have to think. I have to think about what to do," she finished, her voice thick with emotion.

"You need not worry. Nothing further is going to happen to you."

"You do not know my brother, sir." Brianda felt slightly nauseated. Edward would kill her now. She looked again at the doctor. "I have heard about how powerful and well-connected you are, sir. I thank you for everything, but you have no way of aiding me further. Edward is not as rich or as powerful as you are, but he can do whatever he wishes with me. I am totally in his power." Brianda continued to twist the sheets while she spoke. "He is going to be very angry. Now I am in real trouble. I don't know what to do . . ."

"Are you going to tell me what happened to your back?"

"No."

"Ah, I see. A family matter, I suppose. But you realize that your physician is like your priest. You can tell him anything without fear. I want to help you," he said, taking her trembling hands in his.

"Thank you, sir. I appreciate all that you have done for me. I would like to think that I will be able to repay your kindness one day. I would like to remind you, however, that I did not choose you as my physician. That is a role you took on yourself. Therefore, I have no desire to discuss the matter with you."

"Well stated," he said, a small smile on his face. He was surprised at her ability to express herself. Then, looking at her sternly, he admonished, "You were not able to ask for anything when you fainted into my arms, young lady. Paul and I responded to your needs, as we would have done for any person. But, as Earl of Manseth, I feel it is my responsibility to be aware of the needs of all those who live under my jurisdiction, including your brother and you. Your brother may be a lord, but he answers to me." Seeing that she looked exhausted, he said, "You must rest now, you look very tired."

Just then, there came a knock on the door. "Who is it?" answered John.

"It is I, sir, Mrs. Brady. There is a gentleman here demanding to see you. He states he is Lord Breedon, and he has urgent business to discuss with you."

Brianda's gasp was audible.

"Show Lord Breedon into the library, Mrs. Brady. I will meet with him in a few moments."

"Oh God, help me!" cried Brianda. She looked into Lord Fauxley's eyes, pleading with him.

"Don't worry, little one. I will be back soon. I am going to lock your door and station my personal assistant, Angus MacKenzie, outside. I guarantee that no one will get past him!" he said, as he smiled at her and gently stroked her cheek. "Stay in that bed, or you will have to deal with another angry man," he warned, his tone kind and gentle.

"I will stay here until you return. May God help us both."

The last thing she heard before falling into exhausted slumber was the sound of the key as it turned the lock firmly into place.

6

Edward Breedon paced back and forth across the length of the library, as if it were a jail cell. After spending the evening with Fauxley the other night, he realized that all that he had heard was true. The earl was a man to be reckoned with.

Edward would have to be very careful. It would be terrible if a scandal were to erupt now. His illegal transaction had almost been uncovered last month by the king's special guard; only by a stroke of luck had he and Biff been able to escape detection. At the last minute he had been able to arrange for alternate transportation for his contraband. He had arranged to stow the goods under the wooden planks of a small fishing boat that belonged to an old school acquaintance. It was a perilous voyage across the channel at that time of year; and Edward had had to pay an outlandish fee. Now he was not going to get anywhere near as much money for the opium as he had planned.

On top of that, his bloody sister had disappeared. If anyone had discovered the extent of her injuries, the blame would most certainly fall on him. He stopped his pacing and wondered again if he could have killed her this time. He seemed to remember that he had been particularly brutal with her.

If she was dead, then all the better. She was nothing more than a thorn in his side anyway. Things would be better with her dead. He could sell off the country estate and be done with this area forever.

He had spent enough time waiting for the blasted girl to turn up, and Nellie was driving him crazy with all her inquiries. He decided the most appropriate action would be to make a formal request for help from his Lordship, the Earl of Manseth. The earl was the highest ranking nobility in the county, and Edward knew it would look good if he sought Fauxley's aid. If no trace of his sister was ever found, at least he would have done what was expected of him.

Just then, the library door opened. Edward turned and saw Lord Fauxley enter. He felt a strange pull in his stomach. The man had an unpleasant effect on him. Another man entered the room behind his Lordship, and Edward wondered who he was and why he was accompanying the earl. He didn't have to wait long to find out.

"Breedon. How nice to see you again." John gestured with his arm toward a chair opposite his desk. "Please sit down. It has been a week or so since we played cards at your home. May I introduce you to my friend and colleague, Dr. Paul Martin?"

"It is my pleasure, Doctor." Edward tried to keep his facial muscles relaxed and his smile natural. He felt uneasy. Even though Lord Fauxley's words seemed cordial enough, Edward sensed the underlying coldness. He had been addressed as "Breedon" and not "Lord." It was hard to imagine that Fauxley would make such a social blunder.

"What can I do for you this afternoon?" asked John, his eyes veiled, alert.

Edward directed his gaze to John.

"I have a grave problem, sir. Five days ago my young sister disappeared from our home. We have looked everywhere, but no one has seen her. She is a decent young woman and a homebody. I am afraid that she has met with some grave misfortune." When John said nothing, just sat at his desk with his hands clasped in front of him, Edward continued, "As you are the highest ranking member of the nobility here in the county, I thought it best to come to you for aid and advice. How lucky we are to have you back in the country once again . . ."

"Mr. Breedon, excuse me for interrupting you, but I, too, have a grave matter to attend to at the moment. I have, upstairs, a patient. This patient has been critically ill, but it seems now that recovery is a possibility. As the physician in charge, I am bound to do all that I can to ensure that my patients receive the best care and have the best chances for survival. Would you not agree with that?"

"Oh, yes, of course! I am sorry if I am taking up your valuable time. It is just that I am so worried and I don't know what to do about my sister. I am at my wit's end!" Edward tried to sound panicked, and was secretly pleased with his acting ability.

"Ah, yes, family does come first, doesn't it?"

"Nothing is more important than one's blood relations!" Edward replied earnestly. "And we men have to be sure that our women are well taken care of and protected."

"Just so." Straightening in his chair, John nodded toward Edward. "You may be interested in this case of mine."

Edward felt uncomfortable under the earl's scrutiny. He had no interest whatsoever in the misfortune of some sick dolt, but knew he had to feign concern. "Please go on, my Lord."

John rose slowly from his chair and walked around the desk. He came straight toward Edward and stopped just in front of the chair. "The patient I have upstairs has been badly beaten." He let the last word settle like the hangman's cloak on its hook.

Edward shifted in his chair.

"It seems that whoever perpetrated this foul deed must be formally punished in the royal court. The authorities must be notified. Everyone knows that a lord has certain rights over his subjects, but this is an atrocity. In all my years in medicine, I have never seen such vicious wounds. I want the criminal to spend many years in prison in retribution for this heinous deed."

Edward was sweating now, his stomach queasy.

"I have a problem, though. I am not sure who the beast is that abused this person. Saving this patient's life was a battle that came within inches of losing the war, sir." John stood straight. He seemed to be concentrating on a thought. "As earl and highest ranking lord here in this parish and community, I guarantee you that I will discover the identity of the bastard, and when I do, I am going to use all my power and connections to see that the man receives what he deserves." John watched as Edward's breath caught and sweat beaded copiously on his forehead. "Is it too warm in here for you, Mr. Breedon?"

"No, my Lord, I am fine, thank you," answered Edward, unable to look Fauxley in the eye.

John grabbed a chair and dragged it across the carpet, leaving narrow trails where the legs bit into the fabric. Edward watched the progress of the chair as if it were the most fascinating thing he had ever seen. The chair was placed directly in front of him, and Edward watched as the earl seated himself. Even sitting down, Fauxley's sheer size was oppressive.

John leaned forward and put one hand on either side of Edward, holding firmly to the arms of the chair. "My patient is a young woman, Breedon. She has been here for five days. I am not totally sure of her identity. She almost died. As a matter of fact, she has just this day recovered enough so that she is now able to take a little water and speak a few words. She is much too weak to do anything else. She will need special care for some time to come. You know your subjects and those who live around here much better than I do. Do you think you know who this woman might be?" John never took his eyes off Edward's face.

"Is it Brianda?" he asked quietly, knowing that it could be no one else.

"Yes, it is your sister, Mr. Breedon. Do you happen to know what happened to her?"

"She has said nothing?"

"No, she refuses to speak about it."

Edward stood up and forcefully pushed his way out of the cell formed by Fauxley's arms. He walked quickly to the far side of the room. He caught his breath and forced himself to relax a little. "I am relieved to know that Brianda is here and alive. The criminal who has done this to her must be found and severely punished!" Edward put his hands to his head and swayed from side to side. He paused and said sadly, "I thought she might be dead."

"Did you leave her for dead the night of the beating?" John demanded, staring at Breedon, his face a picture of outrage and disgust.

"What are you implying, sir?" Edward stood rigid, feigning shock at what he had heard. "You think I had something to do with her condition!" Edward tried to sound extremely indignant. His knees had begun to shake, and he struggled to keep from showing his fear to the earl.

"I am very tired, Breedon. I have had precious little sleep these last five days. Do not evade my questions.

We both know what you did to that helpless young girl upstairs. You are beneath contempt. I have half a mind to turn you in to the authorities and let them do with you as they please. I could make sure that you never draw another breath of free air."

Edward stared out the window, trying to calm his panicked heart. It was racing so fast that he felt dizzy. If he ran, surely Fauxley would catch him, and something warned him a bribe would make matters worse. He waited for the earl to continue.

"I have been thinking about this matter, and after careful consideration, I feel that it would be better for Brianda if I did not turn you over for imprisonment. As low as you are, you are all the family that she has in this world. It would be too damaging for Brianda if you were sent to prison. She has already suffered the terrible loss of both her mother and father at a young age. Added to that, your public disgrace would be devastating for her. She has suffered enough." John paused to consider his next words carefully. "I am going to make you an offer. Consider it well. Refuse it, and you will regret it. You will be in custody before dinner is served. I have an employee and close friend who weighs near twenty stone of solid muscle. He will take you to the local authorities this very afternoon."

Without facing John, Edward asked, "What are you proposing?"

"You will depart at once. You are to leave England and never return. You will not be allowed to take anything from Cliffshead Manor. You will leave directly from this house. I will arrange passage for you on a ship leaving for the continent at midnight. How you survive is your problem. I have had my solicitors run a check on you . . ."

"How dare you, sir! You have no right . . ."

Lord Fauxley's face turned dark with rage. "Sit down and listen to me!"

Stunned, Edward sank into the chair near the window and sat down.

"In the three years since the death of your father, you have managed to squander almost all of your holdings and lands. Judging by the way you gamble, it will not be long before the manor, too, is lost." John rose and walked to his desk. He took out a sheaf of papers. "You will sign these. I had them drawn up by my attorneys, making me the full legal guardian of Brianda."

Edwards eyes lifted slowly to John's face. "Never."

"Oh, you will do it all right. Not only will I be her guardian, but you will also sign papers giving me the authority to oversee her property, Cliffshead Manor and adjoining lands."

Edward felt himself go cold. Fauxley knew everything! The bitch had told him every detail!

"You will go out to my carriage and leave for London. You will be out of the country by midnight."

Edward Breedon felt his gut twist and grab. The bastard was kicking him out of his own home! "Do you mean to say that I cannot see my sister before I leave?"

"That is correct. The sight of you would only make her suffer further. Brianda will never have the need to see you again. She will be told, when I think she is ready to handle the information, that you have left the country on business, and that most likely you will not return, that you have decided to make your home abroad. I will tell her that you requested that I, as Earl, accept her as my legal guardian. I will even tell her that you wished that she be well cared for."

"She will never stand for that."

"By the time she finds out, it will all be completely legal. There is nothing she can do about it."

"What is she to you, anyway? Have you a prurient interest in country virgins?" Edward smiled at the thought, his face contorted in a malicious sneer. "She is a stranger to you, yet you want to help her. I don't believe that you, the great and just local master, would take on the life of a young girl, unless there were something in it for you."

"I would advise you not to anger me further, Breedon." John rose and stood with his arms braced on his desk. "I have managed to control myself thus far, but cannot assure you that I will continue to do so, if I have to spend much more time in your presence. You had better sign these papers before I change my mind and let you rot in a London prison for the rest of your days."

Furious, Edward approached the desk. "I have no choice, do I? I warn you that someday you will live to regret this action. As far as Brianda is concerned, you are welcome to her. She is a pain in the ass, undisciplined, uneducated and bull-headed. It is too bad that she did not die." His eyes narrowed as he recalled the night of the beating. "It was a pleasure to watch her squirm and scream as I beat her." Turning to face John head on, he spat out, "Now, where are the papers to sign?"

John had to use all his willpower to keep from jumping over the desk and killing the young man in front of him. Instead, he walked to the door and summoned his two lawyers, who were waiting in the adjoining room. In a few minutes, the papers were signed and witnessed by the solicitors.

Edward forced himself to smile. He walked around the room for a moment and turned to John. "I am again asking that you allow me to see my sister for the last time. I want to give her a brotherly kiss good-bye." Edward threw his head back and laughed; the sound was unnatural and chilling.

"Absolutely not. Do not contact Brianda again. If you do, I will see that you will pay for the crime that you have committed. One set of papers that you signed was a full written confession with a complete description of what you did to your sister. I will guard it well and use it if I must. Go now and remember my words."

John watched from the second story window as the carriage carrying Edward Breedon, accompanied by Angus MacKenzie, pulled away and made its way toward London. Relieved, John walked back into the hall and went immediately to Brianda's door. He unlocked it and slipped quietly inside. He had his patient to care for and he had been away too long.

Biff Blanders was agitated. Edward was supposed to have been back in London by late afternoon. It was well past that now, and Biff had business to attend to, but he had to talk to Edward before he could leave.

He downed another mug of ale and thought of the young girl he had waiting in his room. The thought of her made him adjust his pants. Maybe he would forget the business for today and just go to his room and have a piece of that girl! He pushed his overweight body up from the table, knocking it over as he rose. The tankard clattered to the floor. Not a soul in the bar even turned to see what had happened. Biff was well known in this seamy part of London. No one dared to step in his path. Biff could break a man's neck with one hand. It was better to let the giant do just as he pleased.

They could hear him snorting and calling out the girl's name when he was halfway down the block. There were some who knew she would not live through the night.

7

Brianda had awakened to find the sun shining on her face. The sky was blue and clear, the way it always looked after a storm. Usually, a day as beautiful as this would make Brianda's heart sing.

However, that was not meant to be as Brianda now sat in shocked silence in Lord Fauxley's library. Her feet swung back and forth, and her fingers opened and closed repeatedly as she listened to John explaining quietly about Edward's decision to leave England. She learned that Edward had an opportunity to begin a new business on the continent and the likelihood of his returning to England was remote.

Brianda was stunned. A small part of her rejoiced at the thought of never seeing Edward again, but what was to become of her? She looked at John.

"Brianda, you know that I am Earl of Manseth. That makes me responsible for all the subjects who live within this parish and county."

Brianda nodded that she understood.

"Your brother asked me to become your legal

guardian, and that has been accomplished. I am now trustee of the Breedon properties and holdings. This legal act will remain in effect until you marry. Since your father stated in his last will that no woman could inherit his family estate, I will administer the properties as I do my own."

A dizzy sensation overcame her. She didn't know whether it was caused by shock or if it was due to her weakened condition.

She looked at him, sitting so regally in his high-backed chair, his fingers interlaced beneath his chin. She wanted to smash his face! How could he sit there so calmly and tell her that he had just taken over her life?

"Are you well, Brianda? You look pale, and your hands are shaking. Shall I see you to your room?"

"Don't you come near me! I have questions that need answers immediately!" Brianda heard herself shouting at him.

"You will calm down! If not, I will refrain from relating one more detail, and you shall go straight to bed. Is that clear?"

"Yes, sir. I will not shout. I want to hear everything." She sat back and did not feel much discomfort as her back touched the plush pillows.

John explained how Cliffshead Manor was being closed and boarded up. The servants, except Nellie, were now working members of John's staff. Nellie's ailing and newly widowed sister had begged her to come and live with her. Nellie had told John that she would visit Brianda when she could. At Brianda's persistent questioning in regards to her brother, John simply repeated what he had stated earlier. "Now, Brianda, listen carefully to me. I am going to outline to you the routines and schedules of my household. You will abide by them."

Brianda stared at him with unveiled disgust as she rose and walked to the front of his desk. She placed her palms on the polished wood, leaned forward and looked straight into his eyes. "Sir, thank you for taking your precious time to explain all of these recent events. I appreciate, very much, all that you have done for me, helping me when I was sick and talking to my brother for me. But I am afraid that I will have to turn down your offer. I don't want to live here or have anything to do with you. I have my own home, and I am old enough to run the estate myself." A wave of exhaustion washed over her, and she turned and walked about the room in an effort to shake the feeling. Unable to look him in the eye, she stated, "I do not know how you managed to attend to all the business required to close a home in such a short time, but it seems that all your work was for naught. I am capable of reopening Cliffshead Manor again and I shall."

Fauxley remained silent, his face unreadable.

"If, for some reason, I am not able to accomplish the reopening of my home immediately, I will live with Old Megan until I am able to do so. She is like a mother to me. Do you, by any chance, know where Megan is? I haven't seen her of late," she said, her voice weakened by fatigue.

"Sit down, Brianda. You look tired. You should not have left your sickbed just yet."

Brianda walked back to the chair and sat gratefully in the plush, overstuffed piece of furniture. She had to fight to keep her eyes open, and struggled for control.

"The day following the beating, Old Megan appeared at my door. She spent a fair amount of time telling me about your childhood, and I was appalled to learn how difficult it was. For the next five days she worked side by side with Dr. Martin and me applying a special salve for your wounds. She has been called away to attend a birth. She will return as soon as she can."

John watched her face carefully. She was swinging from one emotion to another, and he decided that the straight facts were the best course. "With regard to your not staying here, you have absolutely nothing to say about the matter. Just as I have the legal papers that show ownership of Dakota, I have papers that prove that I am your legal guardian." He paused to let the next sentence sink in. "I can do whatever I want with you, my dear. Right now I choose to keep you at Manseth Manor and see if we can drum some of the social graces into that hard head of yours. You will do as you are told, either by me or by any of the other adults in this house. That includes Angus. Your days of running around like a waif are over."

Brianda looked as if she were about to crumble.

"We will discuss the details later, as you look tired now and are in need of rest."

Summoning the last of her strength, she retorted, "Just like that, my Lord? I am supposed to accept what you have just told me and go off to bed like a good little girl? Well, I am truly sorry, but you can go to hell!" She tried to push herself into a standing position, but could not. Taking a deep breath, she stated, "I wish to see the legal papers, and I insist on being allowed to speak with one of your solicitors."

"All in good time. At the moment you are going to bed." He rose from his chair and walked around the desk. Without a word, he slipped his arms under her shoulders and knees and lifted her into his arms. "You are thinner than you were the last time I held you. I will have to watch what you eat more carefully. You need to recover some of your weight."

She tried to push herself away from him, but was unable to move very far. His arms, powerful and secure, carried their load easily. Halfway up the stairs, Angus offered to carry Brianda to her room, but John declined and proceeded down the upper hallway with his precious cargo.

Oh, how she hated him. She tried to push against his chest, but he held her fast and she was forced to suffer the heat of his body and inhale the masculine scent of him. As much as she would have liked to find the intimate contact distasteful, she couldn't. She had never really noticed the scent of a man before. Even in her agitated state, she found the sensation intriguing.

The physical stress and emotional shock were finally too much for her. Awash with fatigue, she let her head fall slowly to the side and come to rest on his shoulder.

As he was laying her onto the bed, her eyelids fluttered and then closed, shutting out the world, accepting the offer of temporary peace.

John remained bent over her as he watched her fall asleep; he smiled at the firm set of her small mouth, defiant even in sleep. He marveled at her beauty. Then he pulled the silk coverlet up over her body, so that she could sleep without the chill of the crisp fall morning.

The next week passed quietly with Brianda growing stronger every day. She was eating well, and some color had returned to her cheeks.

Old Megan returned the morning after Brianda's confrontation with John. The old woman sat and listened as Brianda tearfully recounted the earl's discussion, demands, and dictates. She became angry all over again at the thought of being forced to do whatever his Lordship decided.

"Calm yourself, girl," Old Megan entreated. "I was badly frightened when the lad came to tell me that you were here at Manseth Manor. However, the earl welcomed me here, Brianda, and he asked that I work with him and the other doctor to care for you. Then, when

Edward presented himself, demanding to know where you were, I waited to see what would happen. His Lordship obviously dealt with the matter. I think you are safe now. That is what matters."

At the sound of Edward's name, a cold wave of fear washed over her.

"Listen, Brianda, I know you are not going to like hearing this, but your living here under the watchful eye of his Lordship is a good idea."

"How can you say that? He has taken my freedom from me!" Brianda could not believe that Old Megan was taking the earl's side.

"Now don't be giving me that look, girl!" Old Megan shook her finger at Brianda. "I wish I knew how Lord Fauxley acquired guardianship over you so quickly. But he is a powerful man, and I am sure he gets whatever he wants, and speedily at that." Old Megan rose and wandered about the sumptuous room. "This is the life that you deserve. You will have opportunities here that you never would have had at home. You will be taught how a lady behaves and conducts herself. You will have pretty clothes, and there will always be good food on the table."

Brianda sighed and turned her head so that she could look out the window of her prison cell.

Old Megan continued as if she had not heard Brianda's sigh. "Your life with your father and brother was hard and cruel. I am an old woman, and I don't know how much longer I will walk on this Earth. I have thought about what would happen to you, should I die. I am content now, knowing that you will be well cared for."

"I hate it here, Megan, I want to go home, or live with you!" Brianda cried out, her eyes searching for compassion in the old woman's face.

"We can sit here and argue all day, but it won't make a bit of difference. The die is cast, and we will have to live with it. Now I want you to behave yourself!"

Two huge teardrops fell onto Brianda's cheeks. She felt rage at her impotence. She would get her revenge one day. The earl was not going to rule her life forever; she would make sure of that!

As the weeks slowly passed, Brianda felt more at ease. Her recovery was steady, but prolonged, and John spent most daylight hours away from Manseth Manor, conducting his estate business.

Mrs. Brady was in charge when his Lordship was absent. She made Brianda as comfortable as she could in her new surroundings. In her quiet, authoritarian way, she introduced Brianda to the day-to-day life of a young woman of the gentry. Brianda learned about proper dress, the use of utensils, and how to address other members of her class. Privately, she thought that the rewards of one's station were absurd and silently plotted her escape. Outwardly, she was the perfect pupil.

One bright, fall afternoon, Mrs. Brady informed Brianda that she could sit out on the balcony overlooking the gardens. Ensconced in a high-backed arm chair, she thrilled to the fresh air and gentle breezes. A soft white shawl barely covered her simple pale yellow dress, and her silky hair lay loose and smooth on the woolen fabric.

How glorious everything looked! The gardens were enjoying an unusually warm autumn and the late-blooming flowers that survived the rainstorm were still lovely. When Brianda could stand it no longer, she glanced over her shoulder, and seeing no one nearby, stood up and blithely kicked off her slippers, then stripped her stockings from her feet. Suddenly free, she walked down the steps and into the gardens. Although still somewhat weakened from the fever and the aftermath of the massive infection of her wounds, she meandered slowly through the rows of bushes and flowers. Each breath was a joy, filled with the fragrances of nature's beauty. How she had missed being outdoors with the fresh air and the breezes wafting onto her face and through her long hair. She let her fingers trail along the faces of the flowers, while her toes toyed with the sun-warmed blades of grass.

She was walking more this afternoon than she had in all the days following the beating. His "greatness," the doctor, had given strict orders as to how much physical activity she was allowed, and Mrs. Brady and Old Megan followed those orders exactly. Well, now she was following her own orders, and she felt wonderful.

She had to admit that she was tiring, though. Her legs felt heavier and were suddenly sore, but she continued on. She was determined that the joy of the walk overshadow the pain, but inevitably knew she must give in to her body's demand for rest. She looked up, and realizing that a huge tree was right in front of her but a few yards off, struggled to make her way to its shelter. Within its reach she tilted her head back and gazed at the broad expanse of the branches. The tree seemed to be opening its arms and asking her to join it. She stepped up to the trunk and leaned against it, admitting to herself that she was really tired now. She wasn't quite sure how far she had walked, and knew that getting back to the chair on the balcony was going to take all her strength. She closed her eyes and sighed.

"It is obvious to the dullest of souls on this Earth that you are incapable of following orders!"

Brianda's eyes flew open to find John standing not two feet from her! She hadn't heard him approach. Ignoring his comment, she said, "Good afternoon, Doctor. It is beautiful here, is it not?" Not waiting for his reply, she pushed herself off the tree and began walking back toward the house.

John fell in beside her. If he had been irritated by Brianda's calling him "doctor" he didn't show it. She was waiting for his lecture, but instead he said to her, "What do think of my gardens, Brianda?"

"They are so beautiful, sir!" she exclaimed, her face changing instantly from the wary look of a child discovered in mischief to animation. "They are so well tended. The gardens at Cliffshead Manor were as beautiful once. Megan tells me that my mother loved horticulture, and that she worked side by side with the head gardener." Brianda turned her head and gazed off at the distant trees. "I don't remember those days, because I wasn't born yet. But Nellie and Old Megan have told me all about my mother and her love for nature. Sometimes my father would call Edward into the study, and I would overhear him tell him stories about my mother and the way life was before my birth."

Once again, John was taken with the beauty of the girl. The afternoon sun played on her hair as it swung around her shoulders. When she smiled, he felt as if Cupid's arrow had struck deep in his heart.

"Why were you not invited to hear the stories?" he asked gently.

She frowned and looked up into his eyes.

"I suppose I can guess. You were as well behaved then as you are now, and were welcome anywhere," he said smiling down at her.

Her eyes crinkled, and she almost laughed. "I tried so hard to be just what my father wanted of me. But I could never please him. He blamed me for my mother's death. All told, I suppose he lived up to his responsibilities. I was fed and I had clothing, but I never had lessons or any training in the social graces. I have never been to a party or a gala ball," she said wistfully as she gazed out, once again, across the vast expanse of Manseth Manor.

"How was Edward treated?"

"Father gave Edward everything, a good education, clothes, money, freedom. Even with all of that, Edward still hated me. What he enjoyed most was punishing me, and Father gave that duty to Edward when we were just little children. The servants tried to protect me, but they didn't really discipline me much, for they felt they couldn't take the liberty. They didn't want to lose their jobs and homes. I suppose I was a lot of trouble, now that I think of it."

"No doubt."

"Well, actually, Richard, the stable master, spanked me once when I was seven years old!"

John could not help but smile at the seriousness of her face.

"I cannot imagine the heinous crime you must have committed for such a punishment," he stated seriously, while turning his head to hide the smile that played on his lips.

"Oh, I deserved it. I spilled a vat of vinegar all over the hay Richard had just stacked for feeding the horses. He was really mad, and he took me over his knee and gave me several hard swats. Then he stood me in front of him and wiped the tears from my face and told me I was never to be so careless again. After that I had to help him pull new bales of hay to replace the ones I ruined."

"The punishment seems just." When Brianda's quick retort didn't come as he expected, he looked down at her face. She looked pale.

Indeed, she was feeling very tired. In an effort to hide her fatigue, she looked away from him and tried to think of something to comment about.

"Are you feeling tired?" he asked, his voice soft and mellow.

"Why, no! I feel fine. The sun on my skin feels so good."

"And do the bare feet feel good on the dirt?"

Good God! He'd noticed her bare feet! What possible explanation could she come up with to warrant her excursion without shoes?

"What, no quick rejoinder? I rather like it when you are at a loss for words, Brianda."

Not knowing what to say, she just looked straight ahead and kept walking. Her steps faltered slightly, slowing, for her legs just didn't want to move any farther.

John noticed her slowed pace and knew that she must be exhausted. He leaned over and lifted her up into his arms. She didn't try to resist.

"It seems that if we are together for more than a few minutes, sir, I end up in your arms," she said in a small voice.

"That does seem to be the case, doesn't it? I would wager that if you did what you were told more often, you wouldn't find yourself being carted around so much. I know what is best for you, Brianda, and you will have to follow my advice, if you want to heal quickly and return to a normal life."

With her head resting on his shoulder, she closed her eyes. "Normal life, my Lord?" she quipped. "What is normal about losing my home, discovering my brother has deserted me, and acquiescing to a stranger who is suddenly in complete charge of my life!"

"I must admit that you have a point, there. I am sorry that these changes have taken place in your life, but I truly believe that they are for the best. You will do what I order, whether you think it advisable or not. I am sure that as you grow stronger, you will not feel so negatively."

"I have no choice, either way, do I?"

"No."

"That is why I hate you, my Lord, and hope that you fall on bad times," she said, with as much vehemence as she could rouse.

"For your sake, you'd better hope that I put you down first, before I take that fall," he teased, as he climbed the few steps up to the balcony. He leaned over and scooped up her shoes from under the chair and carried her into the house.

Mrs. Brady and Old Megan were just reaching the bottom of the stairs as Old Megan muttered to herself and no one in particular, "We have to find her before his Lordship finds out that she has gone and disobeyed him again!"

"Yes, indeed, Megan, that girl is going to be the end of me."

Then they heard his Lordship's voice. "Just what has happened this time, Mrs. Brady?"

The two women exchanged startled glances.

"Well, Mrs. Brady?"

"Oh, nothing, my Lord. All is well. Old Megan and I were just discussing how tiresome young Miss Brianda can be, that's all. Don't disturb yourself further, sir. I am just going to see that she gets her afternoon nap." Just as the last word left her mouth, John rounded the corner with his cargo securely in his arms.

"Oh, dear!" was all that Mrs. Brady could manage.

"Where has she gone this time, my Lord?" asked Old Megan.

"I found her in the garden, barefoot."

From her post up in his arms, Brianda widened her eyes and just looked at the two women.

"Augh, Brianda, it's no wonder you're always in trouble, lass. You have such a hard head!" Old Megan exclaimed.

"See to it that Miss Breedon is fed her tea and biscuits in her room this afternoon, Mrs. Brady. You will have to use the key, as I am going to lock her in. By the way, please see to it that she receives an extra biscuit or two. She is far too lean." John mounted the stairs and once again transported his ward to her bedroom.

"Yes, sir," said both women in unison.

8

All the while plotting strategies for escape, outwardly Brianda tried very hard to behave herself for the following few weeks.

For her efforts, John allowed her to take a few walks, but never alone. She was either accompanied by John, Old Megan or Angus. When the chore fell to Angus, Brianda cut her walk short. She couldn't stand the silent giant.

Her lessons took up much of her day. She studied history, French, writing composition and mathematics. Her tutor, Mr. Totter, was a kind, portly older man, who drummed the boring material into Brianda's head.

A seamstress from London, Madame Vibert, came to Manseth Manor and personally took charge of making a complete new wardrobe for Brianda. Brianda hated the hours she had to spend standing while her form was carefully plotted, and she wondered how Madame Vibert would feel if she knew Brianda preferred trousers and a simple blouse to any of these fancy clothes. But when the wardrobe was finished, even she was pleased with

how she looked. The seamstress had a gift for choosing
colors and fabrics that were a perfect match for Brianda's
skin and hair color. The fabric had been chosen carefully
so as not to detract from the startling beauty of the
young girl's violet eyes.

John was pleased with the changes he noticed in his
ward. She was lovely in the new dresses and seemed to
be learning quickly and well. Even though Brianda
protested hotly how much she hated the boring lessons,
he insisted that she continue. She had a bright mind that
needed to be challenged.

She had walled herself off from him emotionally
since the day of their walk in the garden. She no longer
spoke freely to him and answered only when a question
was put to her. He assumed it was her defense against
his many new rules and mandates. Her present behavior
was acceptable to him, however; he let her pout. John
knew that when he wanted her to reenter the ring with
him, all he needed to do was challenge her. She would
inevitably respond.

Fall was fully upon them, and Brianda could not
stand listening to old Mr. Totter ramble on about poli-
tics for one more minute. The trees were losing their
leaves, and the ground had a carpet of yellow, orange
and red patches. She longed to run barefoot and kick the
leaves up into the air.

"Mr. Totter, did you know that Lord Fauxley gave me
permission to end our class early today?" she asked in
her most coy and feminine voice.

"Why, no, my Lady, he did not tell me of this."

"I am sure he just forgot. You know what a busy man
he is. Thank you for such an interesting lesson today,"
she said, as she quickly gathered his books and note-
books and handed them to him. "I will see you next

week and thank you," she said as she ushered him out the door.

She smiled to herself as she hurried to her room to change out of her day dress and into the pair of boys' pants and the shirt that Old Megan had fetched for her from the now abandoned Cliffshead Manor. Without pausing a second she headed quietly down the servants' stairs to a door at the back of the house.

She trembled with excitement at the thought of being with her beloved Dakota. For weeks she had only been allowed to see him from her bedroom window. John insisted that she wasn't strong enough to ride him yet. She had the whole afternoon to herself. His Lordship wouldn't be back until evening, as he had been called to a distant manor to assist in an emergency surgery there.

Brianda slipped into the stable and rushed to Dakota's stall. It was a wonderful reunion. She wept softly with joy and had to shake her head to force the tears away. She began talking quietly to him, telling him everything that had happened since the last time she had seen him. He stood unmoving, as if he were understanding every word. All the while she talked, she rubbed his velvety nose and scratched his stubbly chin. She finally ran out of tales to tell Dakota and found herself winded. She sat against the wall of the stall and continued stroking the shiny black coat, running her hand through the coarse long hairs of his mane. How shiny and clean he was! Someone had been taking very good care of him, and she was grateful.

The horse nuzzled her, and Brianda laughed out loud. "You're as restless as I am, aren't you?" She shook her head at her folly and decided that she wanted to walk with him outside for a few minutes. If her luck held, she could get him across the pasture without being caught.

No one was in sight, so she led him quickly into the

woods. She didn't try to ride him. Her back muscles were still too sore to hold her comfortably erect on his back. Anyway, he was too full of energy for her to handle, and he seemed content to walk along beside her, her right hand buried in his mane as they moved through the trees.

At times, Brianda would stop and throw her arms around him and hug him with all the strength she could gather, and he would bring his head down over her shoulder and rest his chin on the small of her back.

John was galloping along the road when he spied the small carriage coming toward him. He wondered who could be leaving Manseth Manor at this hour. He raised his hand for the driver to halt. It was Mr. Totter!

"Good day to you, my Lord."

"Good day, Totter."

"If you don't mind my saying so, sir, I don't think it is a good idea for you to allow the young lady to have entire afternoons off from her studies. She has so much to learn, and she is not the most interested pupil. She is apt, that is certain. But she lacks concentration. I think it is folly for you to allow her free time like this," he finished breathlessly.

"When I want your opinion, Mr. Totter, I will ask for it. Just what time was it that you were dismissed by Miss Breedon?"

"One hour ago, sir. I asked for a spot of tea from one of the servants before I left your house, my Lord," he answered, flustered by the earl's tone.

"I see, Mr. Totter. Please contact my assistant, Mr. MacKenzie, and present your bill for your services. We will no longer be in need of a tutor for Miss Breedon. Good day."

"Yes, sir, good day, sir," was all that Totter could manage as John spurred his horse to a gallop.

John couldn't help but admire the boldness of the girl. She was indeed unique. He couldn't remember when he had been so challenged by a woman, and he found himself smiling as he tried to guess what she was up to on her stolen afternoon.

Dakota heard the rustling of the foliage first. He quickly raised his head from his grazing, and his ears shot straight up. Brianda's eyes were closed, however, as she let the sun's rays warm her skin, and she was unaware of the intrusion until it was too late. Her eyes popped open at the sound of the horses greeting each other, and at the sight of John Fauxley, her heart turned to lead.

She remained seated on the ground and waited for him, her eyes looking at the dirt beneath her toes.

He dismounted and stood at her feet, saying not a word. Several excuses jumped into her mind, but not one of them would help her out of this heap of trouble. She looked up at him and said nothing, and to her utter surprise, he let go of his horse's head and sat down next to her! He had some of his finest trousers on, and he was sitting on the grass!

She was at a loss for words as he turned his face to the sun and sat back resting on his arms.

"The sun feels wonderful on this beautiful afternoon. How long have you been here?" he asked lazily.

"About two hours," she answered warily.

"Dakota looks happy grazing on those young grasses, doesn't he? He and my horse, Sebastian, are stable mates. It isn't often that two stallions get along so well together." He let himself lie down completely on the ground and closed his eyes. Brianda couldn't imagine what had come over him! Uneasy, she lay back on the grass next to him and waited for his next move.

"You look exceptionally beautiful this afternoon, Brianda."

"Why, thank you, my Lord," she stammered, now wondering if he were drunk.

"Seeing you in those clothes makes me wonder why I spent so much money on your new wardrobe. I must admit that a man gets a completely different impression of a woman when she is wearing britches, though."

Brianda quickly turned and looked at him. The sun shone full on his face. He was extremely good looking when he wasn't scowling. His eyes were still closed, so she let her eyes roam over his body. His hair, thick and black as pitch, shone brilliantly in the afternoon sun. Her eyes wandered from his chin to his broad shoulders, then down to his well-muscled chest. His silk shirt fell lightly onto his skin, and where his ribs stopped she could see the slope of skin that fell to his perfectly flat abdomen.

The tight riding breeches that revealed his well-toned abdomen also revealed the masculine bulge between his thighs. Taking a quick breath, she let her eyes move quickly down to his powerful upper legs. They seemed unusually large, as if they had been used in arduous labor and had become rock hard from years of toil. From the vantage point of his knees, his calves seemed long and well toned, his feet extremely large.

So involved was she in her slow perusal of him, she did not notice when he opened his eyes and began watching her for several minutes. At last she lifted her head to look once again at his face and found him appraising her, his cobalt blue eyes unreadable.

Her cheeks burned fiercely, and she fervently wished that her newfound color was the fault of the sun, and not because she had been caught gaping at him, a victim of her own curiosity.

John was moved by her innocent assessment of his body. The instant blush had spread over her cheeks. There were many things he would like to teach this young beauty.

He turned on his side then, and leaned over her, slowly lowering his head. His eyes never left hers as he gently laid his lips on hers.

She jumped at the intimate contact. His mouth felt warm and slightly moist as his lips moved gently. Her lips did not move at all. She had never been kissed before, and she did not have the faintest idea what to do. Her heart responded on its own, increasing its rate rapidly, and, in turn, her breath quickened. There was a strange sensation in the depth of her stomach, both pleasant and unpleasant at the same time.

He increased the pressure of his mouth slightly and let his tongue slip between his lips and gently outline the contours of her mouth. He felt her shiver, and knew that this was enough for now. It wouldn't be long before he tasted the nectar of those lips again. They were too sweet to forget.

He lifted his head from hers and looked into her eyes. Pushing himself up to a sitting position, he said, "It is time we return home. It grows late, and the forest becomes less friendly as darkness approaches."

"I have no bridle for Dakota—we walked here from the stable. I will be unable to ride him. . . . I have ridden him with just a halter in the past, but he has not been well exercised of late and is full of energy. . . . I would have my hands full with him—and I don't want to pull at him. . . . My back is still sore when I stretch the injured muscles too far. . . ." she said, rambling, the words pouring from her as fast as she could speak them. Talking was better than thinking about what his kiss had just done to her.

"You will ride with me, then, and Dakota will follow along." John called to Sebastian, and both horses galloped over to them. John mounted his horse, and Brianda gave Dakota a hug.

"Let's go, young lady," he said, as he pulled her up into the saddle in front of him. She had to sit firmly against his chest. He let his left arm go around her waist to steady her. The heat of his arm penetrated her clothes, warmed her skin. She liked the feeling.

As they rode at an easy canter back to Manseth Manor, their bodies moved in perfect unison with the animal's. Dakota pranced alongside them, nibbling at Brianda's leg every so often.

It had grown colder, and Brianda sought the comfort of John's chest and shoulders to ward off the chill. When they arrived, Thomas and his men tended to the horses, while John hurried Brianda into the house.

"You had best get upstairs and into the bath quickly. You are expected at dinner in a short while," he said, looking into her eyes with a look that mystified her.

"Yes, sir." Brianda ran up the stairs and rushed into her room, almost knocking Billie, one of the maids, onto the floor. With the quickest of apologies, she slammed the door behind her and leaned against it.

Now that she was completely alone, she caught her breath and allowed the feelings of wonder and excitement to return. She could not come up with one reason why John would have done such a strange thing! She shrugged her shoulders and decided that she had not been injured in any way and, besides that, she had enjoyed her first kiss. Smiling, she called to Billie to come and help her with her bath.

When the master was at home, dinner was served in the formal dining room with fine china and silver serving pieces that were a testament to the longevity of the Fauxley tradition. Dinner was served at eight o'clock.

Brianda entered the dining room at the stroke of eight. She had taken greater care with her dress than she usually did, and her efforts had been well worth it. She looked beautiful in an evening gown of pale violet, with accents of deep purple ribbons. Her hair had been washed and hung loose about her shoulders, surrounding her face with a halo of spun gold.

The effect was well appreciated. Mrs. Brady smiled when she saw her, and Angus, who had stationed himself just outside the door in case he was needed, had to look twice to be sure the vision he was seeing was truly Brianda and not a visitor.

John looked up as she entered the room, stood stock still, and stared. Never had she been more beautiful. His groin stirred at the mere sight of her. As she walked shyly toward him, he smiled.

She felt her chest tighten, her knees wobble.

"How pleasant for you to be on time tonight, and to look so lovely, Brianda."

She squared her shoulders and lifted her chin at the compliment. "Thank you, my Lord. After your comment this afternoon with regard to my britches, I thought you might like to see that your money was well spent."

"How considerate of you."

Brianda raised her eyes to his face, to see if he was making fun of her.

His smile reassured her. He looked magnificent himself, dressed in tight black pants, white silk shirt with a thin black tie, and an emerald green velvet dinner jacket.

"You, too, look elegant this evening, my Lord."

"Thank you, Miss Breedon. Now will you do me the honor of allowing me to escort you to your place at the table?" He offered her his outstretched arm.

She accepted and hoped that he didn't notice that her hand was shaking slightly. He was behaving so strangely, so different from his usual gruff, deprecating self.

Dinner was wonderful. Mrs. Brady had prepared a feast of roasted chicken in herbs and wine. They ate in contented silence.

"Brianda, I would like you to join me in the study after dinner. There are several things I would like to discuss with you."

Brianda's face fell. So, it was back to business as usual. "Yes, sir," she said, her eyes bent on the carpet, certain that punishment would now be exacted for her behavior this afternoon.

"Meet me in the study in five minutes."

"Yes, sir."

For Brianda the five minutes seemed to last five hours. She thought of every possible punishment he could dole out to her. The palms of her hands were wet by the time she entered the study.

John was standing, gazing out the window with a glass of sherry in his hand, and when he heard her enter he said, "Please take a chair, there near the fire."

"Thank you, sir," she said in her most contrite voice.

"What happened to the confident young woman with whom I had dinner a few moments ago? Why the slumped shoulders and lowered voice?"

"That young woman wasn't thinking of all the rules she had broken or liberties she had taken," she responded, eyes still on the floor.

"I see."

"Which of the many errors are we going to discuss first, sir?"

"None at the moment."

That brought her eyes to his face in an instant, searching for some clue as to what he could mean.

"I have some news for you. Tomorrow we are going to London for a visit. I would like you to be packed and ready to leave immediately after breakfast. Take enough clothes for two or three weeks, and don't forget to have the maid pack your evening gowns, as we will most likely attend a ball or two."

Brianda sat staring at him, her mouth slightly open.

"Are you all right, Brianda?" he asked with mock sincerity.

"Yes, sir. Did you say that *we* were going to London? You and I? I am to accompany you to London? I am going to a ball?"

"Which question would you like to me to answer first?"

"All of them!"

"So be it, the answer to all of your questions is yes."

"I cannot believe it!" She jumped to her feet, her face bright with excitement. "I am thrilled! I have never been away from this countryside in all of my life!"

"Go now and begin packing."

Brianda turned and started for the door, her feet barely touching the carpet.

"Oh, and by the way, Brianda, if you ever again dismiss one of my staff, or leave this house when you have been forbidden to do so, you will face consequences. Do I make myself clear?"

"Perfectly," she said, though her heart sank and her skin prickled as she backed out of the study. She then turned and ran all the way to her room and closed the door. She fervently hoped that he wouldn't carry out his threats. Quickly, she began packing, letting the excitement of the trip lessen her worries. She did, however, keep one ear tuned to the sounds from his adjoining room and was ready to hide at the sound of his opening the door that connected their two suites.

9

The day was born full of sunshine and light breezes. Brianda was up at dawn, the thrill of the trip just too much to allow her to sleep any longer. She deliberately made as much noise as she could, slamming drawers and closet doors and stomping her feet, so that John would not be able to sleep either. She hoped that if he rose now, they could be on their way to London earlier! All she got for her efforts was a loud, "Be quiet, Brianda!" from the room next door.

Disgruntled, she finished her bath, got dressed, and hurried downstairs to breakfast. She was delighted to see that the earl had also arrived at the dining table. He looked rather owlish, though, so she didn't start a conversation with him.

Looking up from a sheaf of papers that had been scattered all about his end of the table, John said to Brianda, "I will forgive the ruckus. I understand your excitement, but you must learn to control your emotions. Do not interfere with my sleep in the future."

"Oh, please don't be mad, sir," she cajoled. "I am sorry if I disturbed you. I will do better, I promise."

John said nothing, just searched her face with his inscrutable eyes.

She bowed her head and paid very close attention to her hot cereal. "I have made that promise before, haven't I?" She turned her eyes to the side and peered up at him. "I have had a bit of trouble keeping those promises, but I am going to try very hard to do better."

She looked so earnest that he had to smile a little. "I certainly hope so. If this trip turns into a fiasco, you will be an old woman before you see the lights of London again."

"Yes, sir." She paused, trying to decide if it was the proper time to bring up questions that were plaguing her. Cautiously, she asked, "Sir, are we going to take Dakota with us? Oh please, I would love to ride him in the lovely parks there. Mrs. Brady told me that in the afternoons, all of the gentry go to the park to ride their horses. I would love to do that!"

"Brianda, you know nothing of life in the city. You are used to getting on Dakota and galloping across the moors, are you not?" Brianda nodded. "You will be quite disappointed, then, because the women who ride in London either ride sidesaddle or walk their horses to show off their latest riding outfits. The men accompany their women to enjoy a social afternoon, and some men use the afternoon outing for courting purposes. Those who ride for exercise and pleasure do so in the morning, and the vast majority are men, not women. There are a few women, of course, but even they do not go galloping through the park. You would look odd indeed, even cantering your black stallion. Most of the women ride mares, and usually choose older horses." He thought for a moment. "No, Dakota will be staying here. He is much too valuable to take on such a long trip, and he would not like the city." When he saw her crestfallen face, he added, "Upon our return, you may ride him daily. While in London you will be accompanied by a groom or myself, and I will make it my duty to grant you permission to ride each time you wish it."

Just after breakfast, Brianda was allowed to go to Old Megan's house to bid her farewell. Brianda threw her arms around Old Megan and held her for a long time. Then she started off for the main house, smiling over her shoulder and waving at the woman she loved as a mother. This was a happy day indeed!

The carriage ride took many long hours. They spent the night at an inn where the earl was well known. The accommodations were the best available as one traveled the road, and the food was excellent.

They spent the long hours getting to know each other. John felt his stomach tighten as Brianda recounted more horror stories from her childhood, telling them with a curiously detached demeanor as she gazed out the carriage windows, pulling the curtains to the side so she could see everything.

In turn, she asked him all kinds of questions. She was most curious about his choice to attend medical school in defiance of his parents, and loved hearing the stories about his patients, especially the tales about the rough and tough lower classes. The stories about the knives and guns used by the sailors and harlots on the back streets of London fascinated her. She begged him to grant her permission to visit his office.

John shook his head and explained that the area where his office was located was too rough and unstable for a young girl, and he didn't trust her to stay out of trouble for one minute. Brianda reminded him that she needed to thank Dr. Paul for all he had done for her, and how surely he would love a surprise visit from her! Fauxley countered that she would be able to thank Paul when he visited them in his London town house. Eventually she ran out of arguments to convince him otherwise, so she just closed her mouth and thought . . . and plotted.

John Fauxley, the tenth Earl of Manseth, owned a beautiful town house in London. It was in the most exclusive area and was the largest of the three London homes that John inherited. Made from large stone, it was three stories tall and had eight bedroom suites. It could not compare to the size of the country manor, but it had its own charm. John had lived in this house since he had come to London to study medicine. It spoke well of his taste and his fortune. He had the finest fabrics for the window coverings, and the furniture was also of the finest woods and construction. Displayed on the walls were exquisite pieces of art and tapestries.

John and Brianda were met at the door by none other than Stevens who had traveled from the country several days earlier to open the town house.

"Stevens! How did you get here before we did?" exclaimed Brianda.

"I left to open this house several days ago, my Lady. I trust your trip was enjoyable."

"Oh, quite enjoyable, really. We rode through beautiful countryside and spent the night at an inn! Do you know that our dinner was served in a large room where several parties all ate, but at separate tables, of course."

Seeing that the staunch Stevens was smiling at her, she continued, "When we neared this great city of London, I was standing in the carriage leaning out the window, trying to get a good look at the city! His Lordship," Brianda looked quickly over her shoulder at John, "made me get back inside the carriage and sit down when we actually entered the city. I couldn't see nearly as much, but he wouldn't let me lean out the window any longer." Whispering, she asked Stevens, "What does 'behaving beneath my station' *mean?*"

John caught Stevens's eye over the top of Brianda's head and waited to hear his reply. "I will explain it to you later, Miss, as I am sure that you are tired from your trip and would like to see your bedroom suite."

"All right, Stevens, but you must tell me soon! I think behaving beneath my station might be fun!"

Stevens and John shook their heads in unison.

"The rooms are ready, just as you ordered, my Lord. I will see that the valises are taken up directly. I have ordered water heated for your baths. Trays of tea and scones shall be brought to your rooms immediately, as I am sure that you are in need of refreshment after your long trip."

"Thank you, Stevens. I am pleased that all is in readiness."

"It is my pleasure to serve you, sir. A letter came by post today . . . from Lady Susana Smythe."

Brianda turned and looked at Stevens's face. There was something about the tone of his voice when he said that name. He looked composed as usual, but something was different. John, however, seemed perfectly composed as he ushered her up the stairs and showed her to her bedroom. It was, once again, the room adjoining his.

John sat at the teak desk in his bedroom and read the heavily scented note from Lady Susana Smythe. He smiled, marveling at Susana's gift for gathering information. He had been in town only a few short hours, and already Susana was inviting him for dinner! He sent a return note back via messenger, stating that he would be unable to attend the dinner this evening, but would be happy to see her one day soon. Standing and walking to the window, he thought that it had been too long since he had enjoyed the company of a woman. He was in need.

Brianda had unpacked and now had nothing to do. She wandered around the big house, checking out all of the doors that led to the outside and silently cursing the earl for cooping her up like this for hours while he went to his office.

The servants were all pleasant to Brianda, but kept a proper distance from her, not at all like the country servants. As she walked slowly through the library, she thought about how much she missed Mrs. Brady and Old Megan. Now that she had been alone for several hours, she even missed Angus, who had accompanied his master.

She crossed the threshold of John's study and she could tell immediately that it was his favorite room. Here the furniture was well used, and the room smelled like he did, masculine. Brianda sat in his chair behind the desk and put her chin in the palms of her hands. She had thought about the stolen kiss in the forest many times since that afternoon, and each time she remembered it a little differently, but it was always with warmth, excitement and anticipation.

She found herself browsing through John's papers. He would probably be angry if he caught her looking through his private correspondence, but it would serve him right for leaving her all alone on her first afternoon here. She heard the front door knocker and hurried toward the door, just as Stevens was entering the room. They barely missed running into each other. Straightening himself quickly, he announced that Lady Susana Smythe had arrived and was demanding to see his Lordship.

"Stevens, you know he is not at home."

"Yes, my Lady, but when Lady Smythe heard you were here, too, she demanded that you offer her an audience."

"Me?"

"Yes, Miss Breedon. Shall I show her in or not?"

"Why, I suppose so. Please have some tea sent in. That is the proper thing to do, is it not, Stevens?"

"Quite so, miss. I will see to it."

Stevens opened the study door and motioned for Lady Smythe to enter. The most beautiful woman that Brianda had ever seen floated into the room. She was tall and softly rounded in all the right places. Her auburn hair was piled high upon her head and was arranged so that it framed a face that looked as though it had been chiseled in alabaster. Her dress was a deep shade of blue, and she had gorgeous jewelry in her ears, around her neck, and on all her fingers.

Brianda was spellbound. "Eh, won't you please come in, Miss Smythe."

"It is Lady Smythe. I am a widow. And who, my dear, are you? Another of John's trollops?"

Brianda did not know what a trollop was, so she did not know quite how to answer. "I am Brianda Breedon, Lord Fauxley's ward. Won't you please sit down? I have ordered some tea."

"Ward? Did you say 'ward,' my dear?" Susana asked in honest disbelief.

"Yes, I am his ward."

Stevens entered the room with the tea, and Brianda silently rejoiced at the interruption, as she needed a few moments to gather her thoughts. She was glad now that Mrs. Brady had spent so much time teaching her how to pour and pass the tea. She did it quite well and secretly hoped that the lovely Susana Smythe did not know she was a country bumpkin!

After taking a few sips and studying the young beauty

over the rim of the delicate china cup, Susana tried desperately to figure out just what John was up to this time. Susana felt a strange pang in her chest. This young girl was so beautiful that Susana was genuinely worried. She had not considered that there might be serious competition for John's affections.

Brianda smiled at the older woman, whom she guessed to be in her mid-twenties, and tried to think of something clever to say. She was sure that this woman would not be interested in horses or herbal healing.

Susana reluctantly admitted to herself that even though Brianda's hair looked ridiculous in that style, it was gorgeous, flowing down her back as light and graceful as a feather on the wind. Her dress was fashioned in the current style, and she seemed to be of the same social class. "Tell me, my dear, just how long have you known John?"

Noting the use of his Lordship's first name, Brianda answered, "We have been acquainted for quite a while, Lady Smythe, but he only recently became my guardian." She was careful not to let any inflection enter her voice. She would not want anyone to know how much she resented Lord Fauxley's intrusion in her life.

"I would love to know all the details, my dear. Please tell me everything."

"Well . . ."

"Exactly which details do you think are any of your business, Susana?" asked John from the doorway.

Flustered, Susana jumped up, ran across the room, threw her arms around John's neck and kissed him on the mouth.

Brianda was shocked. She sat silently, her back as stiff as a board.

John pulled Susana's hands from around his neck and then gently pushed her away from him. "Susana, did you not receive my note?"

"Yes, darling, but I couldn't wait. You said you were only going to be in the country two weeks, and you ended up staying in that dreadful place more than two months! And not even one note!" she scolded him.

Ignoring her comments, he left her side, walked over to Brianda and took her hand in his. "I see that you have met my ward, Lady Breedon. She is beautiful, is she not, Susana?"

Susana was furious, and barely concealed her anger. "How dare you, John? You are acting as if you did not hear one thing I just said."

John continued on as if Lady Smythe had not spoken. He turned and asked Brianda to pour him some tea. Brianda knew that something important was happening, but she was not sure what it was. Knowing better than to ask, she poured John a cup of tea and handed it to him.

Susana pulled herself together, ready for a civilized battle. "Yes, I have just had the pleasure of meeting your ward, John. She is a lovely young thing, isn't she? She will be the hit of the season, someone new and beautiful to fill the hearts and dreams of all of the eligible young men of the Ton. Surely you will allow her to attend the gala balls, John."

"She will attend some of them, accompanied by me, of course."

Susana's eyes flew to John's to see if she could read anything possessive there. Not being able to detect anything specific, she continued, "I can't believe that this is the same John Fauxley, Earl of Manseth, whom I have known for so long, actually showing interest in the welfare of a young woman. So possessive. I am surprised."

"That will be enough, Susana."

Turning to Brianda, Susana said, "You must beg your guardian to let you attend all of the balls, my dear, so that you can meet the young man who will steal your heart."

"Thank you for your interest, Lady Smythe, and yes, I would like to attend a ball or two, but what I really would like to do is visit John's medical offices. I have a keen interest in medicine myself. As a matter of fact, I have treated the ill and infirm for many years and have studied with a well-known scholar in the art of healing. But here in London is where the most modern techniques are used. John has promised to take me tomorrow to see the office," she stated boldly, briefly casting a glance his way.

"Why, yes, I did say I would take you to see my offices," he stated, his eyes warning her. Facing Susana directly, John said, "I would like to thank you for visiting us this afternoon, Susana, and I hope that we will be receiving invitations to some of the balls soon. Now if you will forgive us, we have just arrived and are feeling the fatigue of the trip," he said, summarily dismissing her.

"B-But John," she stammered, "will I see you later tonight?"

"Possibly. Good evening, Susana."

"Thank you for your visit, Lady Smythe." Brianda rose and walked toward the door. "I hope that everyone I meet here in London will be as kind as you are." Brianda slipped out the door and walked briskly up the stairs.

John took Susana by the arm and escorted her to the door. Susana knew that her bed was going to be as cold again tonight as it had been for the past two months. She had to think of a way to get John back to her breast again, and then to the altar as soon as possible.

At noon the following day, John invited Paul to join him at his private club for luncheon. They left a very busy Dr. James Stovall in charge of the office. After they had been seated, John took a deep breath and looked at his oldest friend. "I have given a great deal of thought to what I am about to say to you, Paul. It is not without serious and directed soul-searching that I have come to the following decision. I want to become a limited partner in our practice . . ."

Paul sat erect in his chair and began to protest.

"Wait! Hear what I have to say first, and then we will discuss it fully."

Paul nodded his head in agreement.

"I was quite pleased when I saw how smoothly everything was running at the office. I am impressed with our new physician, Dr. Stovall. He is a good man and an able surgeon. I have been in contact with our colleagues at the hospital, and Stovall has been well praised. I have no doubts that you and he can carry on without me. I want to remain a partner, but only on a part-time basis," John said as he looked out the window at the winter sky. Turning to Paul again, he continued, "During these last couple of months, I came to realize the extent of my responsibilities at Manseth Manor. I have not fulfilled these obligations well since the death of my father. Now that I have seen the people who depend on me, I understand how much there is to be done. Furthermore, I feel that I must take a more personal interest in overseeing all of the Fauxley enterprises."

"I am not surprised to hear this, John. I thought that you would be unable to continue on as you had in the past. We will miss you, and so will the poor folk we treat. Stovall is a good man, but the office will be different without you. I have never known anyone as bright as you are, and I know that you will handle the new tasks with the same good judgment and fairness that you used in our medical practice. I will miss you, my friend."

"As I will miss you, Paul. I will be spending more time in the country, but I will visit London often. We will remain friends."

They ate in companionable silence. Later, over coffee, they discussed how John could better the health of his subjects. They entertained themselves with thoughts of small clinics throughout the county that the poor could utilize, a better system of schooling for the children, and how John might be able to improve the lives of those dependent upon him.

"This is all very noble talk, John," said Paul with a twinkle in his eye, "but would there be the chance that a high-spirited, outspoken, blonde lass has anything to do with these decisions?"

"What? Of course not! What an absurd notion! Paul, she is just a girl."

"She's old enough to marry, and you know it. She is hardly just a girl. She is as beautiful a woman as I have ever seen, and with her temper and character, I can understand why a man might change a plan or two for her."

"Well, I have not."

"Fine." Paul had seen that look on John's face many times. It meant that one should be careful in addressing his Lordship, and indicated that a change of subject would be a good idea, too. "It must be very different for you."

"What?"

"Having a ward. From what little I know of the lass, she must give you a run for your money!" Paul laughed out loud. A few members of the elite club turned toward the source of the mirth.

"I am doing just fine, thank you. She is difficult, but I am wiser and more experienced than she is, thank God. I have everything in hand. Brianda is here with me in London. I know how much you would like to see her, and she has mentioned how much she wants to see you again, so I am inviting you and your lovely Miss Elizabeth Ingram to dinner tonight at eight o'clock."

"Very good! We would love to come. I want you to meet Elizabeth, John. She is everything I have always wanted in a woman and a wife."

"Wife? You're going to do it? Don't you remember that the two of us swore never to marry? The good life, if I remember it well enough, was to have as many young ladies as we could, but never a wife."

"That was a long time ago, John. I am much older, and now that I have met Elizabeth, I want to be her husband, and I want children. Lots of them!" Laughing at the astounded look on John's face, he clapped his friend on the back. "You will understand when you meet her."

"This is a woman I definitely want to meet! I am sure that Brianda will love her, too. She is in need of a friend here in London. I cannot abide most of the young women of the Ton. They are so filled with airs and snobbery. Please tell Elizabeth that Brianda is not yet well-versed in manners and comportment, and that she might say or do something quite unusual!"

"I will tell her. Don't concern yourself, Elizabeth will love her."

"I also hope that you two will accompany us to some of the gala balls this season. You know how I hate the boring affairs. I promised Brianda that if she behaves, I would take her," John said with a deep sigh.

"We will go, and gladly. But, old friend, what are you going to do about Lady Susana Smythe?"

"You won't believe this, Paul. I received a handwritten note from her the minute I returned to London yesterday. How she manages, I will never know. I sent a response stating that I would see her at my earliest convenience, but she showed up the same afternoon at my door! I was not at home, and I assure you that she was not at all happy to discover Brianda ensconced in my study. When I arrived, I found her badgering the lass for details. You can imagine! Brianda was definitely out of her league. I am glad I arrived when I did. I finally escorted her to her carriage. Tiresome woman."

"I warned you before you left for the country that Susana had her sights set on you, old boy. She wants to marry that title of yours, and the Fauxley fortune!"

John scowled darkly. "Aren't all women the same?"

Paul did not answer, but just smiled broadly at him.

"I will not allow her to cause trouble for me!"

"This will be an interesting situation to follow," Paul said, "you have my condolences. I don't think Susana will say good-bye to you without a fight."

"Thank you very much, old friend, I'll manage."

10

Brianda was heading for the stairs, when she heard John call to her. Quickly she turned and ran to the study door. "Yes, my Lord?"

"How proper! You answered without shouting or crashing into the door frame. Come in. I have something to tell you. Sit down, please." When she was seated and not fidgeting, he said, "I have invited Dr. Paul and his fiancée for dinner this evening. I expect you to be on your best behavior. Understood?"

"Oh, yes, sir! And you *know* how I wanted to visit with him! He was so kind to me when I was ill. He was the kindest one of all!" she stated with a nod of her head.

John did not respond, he just looked at her.

Flustered, Brianda tried to think of something to say to smooth things over, but nothing came to mind. "Well, sir, let the truth be known. He has a better way with people than you do, sir," she said, trying to read the look on his face.

He remained silent.

"If I may be excused now, I am going to go up to my room and try to decide which dress to wear for dinner. Oh, I am so excited! May I leave now, please?"

"Yes, Brianda, you may go. Be in the drawing room at seven forty-five."

"You can count on that, sir!" she said as she sailed out of the study and up the stairs.

John let a smile break the smooth lines of his handsome face. Just listening to her wore him out.

"I see the carriage! They are climbing down right now!" cried Brianda from her post at the window. She had scrutinized every carriage that passed in the past forty minutes, sure that each one had brought Dr. Paul and Elizabeth.

John was sipping wine and watching Brianda over the rim of the glass. She was beautiful and wasn't even aware of it. Her dress was dark green, with simple lines that were perfectly shaped to her lithe, young body. She wore her hair loose, except for one small section pulled up on the right side with a multicolored silk scarf. She had been out in the sun, and her golden hair shone as if it had an inner light of its own.

Brianda was suddenly very nervous as Paul and Elizabeth were escorted into the drawing room. She couldn't think of a thing to say, and stood stock still, her hands clasped behind her back, as she stared at Elizabeth and Paul. Elizabeth had an angelic quality about her, as if she were incapable of ever getting flustered.

Paul scanned the room to locate his little waif. As his eyes found her, he was stunned into silence. He could not believe what he was seeing! Brianda was so gorgeous! Elizabeth pinched his elbow, finally, bringing him back to the present. "Elizabeth, may I present my oldest and dearest friend, John Fauxley, the Earl of Manseth, and his ward, Miss Brianda Breedon?"

"It is my pleasure, Lord Fauxley, and Miss Breedon," Elizabeth answered in her soft, lovely voice.

John walked over to Elizabeth and took her hand in his. He lifted it to his mouth and kissed her hand just above her knuckles. "I can see why you have fallen in love, Paul. She is, indeed, quite beautiful."

Brianda then walked over to Elizabeth and Paul and extended her hand, just as Mrs. Brady had taught her to do. "It is an honor, Miss Elizabeth. It is so good to see you again, Dr. Paul," she finished, giving Paul a truly warm smile of welcome.

"Brianda, I cannot tell you how glad I am to see you looking so well. The last time I saw you, you were still abed, and as white and frail as that orchid in the vase," he said, pointing to the delicate flower perched in the crystal vase that John's mother had bought in France. "I hope you don't mind, Brianda, but I have told Elizabeth that John and I cared for you in the country, and that you were very ill." Paul looked into Brianda's violet eyes, and she knew immediately that he had not told Elizabeth the cause of her illness. Brianda's smile conveyed her thanks.

Elizabeth took Brianda's hands in hers and looked down at the smaller woman. Brianda felt the warmth of her smile and hoped she would be able to form a friendship with Elizabeth. She had never had a female friend so near to her own age.

"I am sorry to hear that you were ill, Brianda. At least you had London's two best physicians at your side. I hope that your illness has not left you debilitated in any way?" Elizabeth asked with concern.

"Oh, no. Thankfully, the whole matter is a thing of the past. I am feeling quite well, thank you. I only wish that his Lordship would permit me a little more freedom," she uttered, her eyes finding John's in the candle-light. "He is still quite strict on matters of my physical activity."

Brianda impulsively took Elizabeth's hands into her own and looked at her quite sincerely. "Maybe you could invite me to go somewhere with you. Anywhere will do! Surely his Lordship will know that a lady like you would watch over me carefully," she finished, imploring Elizabeth with her eyes.

John, Paul and Elizabeth burst into robust laughter at Brianda's undisguised attempt at bribery. Brianda frowned slightly, thinking that they were making fun of her.

"Come now," said Elizabeth, putting her arm around Brianda's shoulders. "I am sure that I can talk Lord Fauxley into a day trip or two."

"Don't count on anything with him!" Brianda replied candidly. Her response only brought another round of laughter.

Stevens announced that dinner was served. The men offered the ladies their arms to escort them into the dining salon. After a scrumptious dinner of roast pork, boiled potatoes in garlic butter and various fresh vegetables, the four of them adjourned to the drawing room to enjoy the fire.

Elizabeth excused herself and left to find the bathroom. Paul stood and walked over to stand in front of Brianda's chair. He took her by the hand and, pulling her to a standing position, gave her an affectionate hug.

Brianda was surprised by Paul's outward expression of affection. She was pleased, however, and hugged him back.

"Brianda, seeing that Elizabeth has left the room for a few moments, would you allow me to see how your wounds are healing? John tells me that Old Megan's salve has continued to work wonders."

Brianda looked at John, silently asking that he offer his opinion. He nodded to her. Although Brianda was very self-conscious about the scars, she felt comfortable with Paul. She knew that he only had her best interests at heart. Still, she felt uneasy. She looked, once again, at John.

"What do you say, sir?"

"This is a decision that is entirely yours, Brianda. I think it wise to remember that Paul spent many hours caring for you. He is interested in any new treatment that he may use on his future patients. If it does not make you feel uncomfortable, let him examine your back."

Brianda turned her lovely eyes to Paul and said in a soft voice, "To be honest, Dr. Paul, I haven't seen my back in a long time. I have avoided looking at the scars. Mrs. Brady and Old Megan told me that they aren't so bad, but I really don't know if that is the truth. If you tell me that they are not too awful, then maybe I will look myself."

Paul was unable to speak for a moment. He and John exchanged glances, both men remembering the rainy night when they first saw the wounds. "Come, Brianda, closer to the fire where the light is better," Paul said as he took her by the hand and led her to a spot where the light was brightest. John helped Paul as they undid the buttons and opened her gown at the back.

To the two physicians, the wounds looked marvelously healed, but to a casual observer it would not have appeared so. The superficial wounds were now only barely visible. They remained as half-inch marks of a slightly darker color than the fairer hue of her normal skin. The deeper, more vicious wounds had healed by the granulating process, from the inside out, forming a rougher, darker scar tissue that was easily visible to the eye.

So involved were the two doctors in examining the wounds that none of the three heard Elizabeth return. As was her way, she moved about very quietly. She heard the muttered voices as she entered the room and became curious when she saw the men looking at Brianda's bare back! Without a word she hurried across the large room.

At close range, she saw the devastation that was the young woman's back. Unable to stop herself, she let out a cry. Even though she tried to muffle the sound with the back of her hand, the scream cut through the air sharply.

Brianda turned about quickly and saw Elizabeth's horrified face. She put her hands behind her back to try to close the fabric of the dress over her bare skin.

John and Paul rose quickly, and one look at Elizabeth sent Paul rushing to her side. "What happened to her?" Elizabeth cried, grabbing the lapels of Paul's coat.

Mortified, Brianda bolted from the room. John remained just long enough to see Elizabeth led safely to the sofa where Paul sat down with her, then left the room and headed upstairs.

Paul held Elizabeth close to him and slowly told her the entire story of Brianda Breedon. Elizabeth listened and wept uncontrollably on his shoulder.

John found Brianda's door locked from the inside. Without a word, he entered his room and walked to the door that joined his room to Brianda's. That handle, too, was locked. Turning back into his room, he made his way to the wall safe. It was well hidden behind a fake inlaid piece of stonework. He opened the safe and extracted the key that would unlock the door. Slipping the key into the lock, he turned it and entered her room.

Brianda was crying so hard that she did not hear the door open. She looked small and vulnerable on the big bed. Her heart-wrenching sobs tore at his heart. He sat on the bed and pulled the resisting girl into his arms. She pushed against his chest, but to no avail. Finally she collapsed into him, letting him hold her head cradled on his chest.

She was overcome with shame; a stranger had seen her scars. Everyone had lied to her; the scars were awful, and she knew it now. How she had hoped that the scarring would be barely noticeable one day!

The dressmaker had not said anything while she was making Brianda's new gowns and clothes. Of course not. The dressmaker would not want to incur the wrath of a client! Brianda guessed that perhaps, having seen the scars, the seamstress had made all of Brianda's gowns with high backs, or had fashioned a new style to cover her shoulders and back. How foolish and naive she had been to think her dresses were designed in the current style. Hot tears of fury and pain flowed from her eyes in small rivers that stained John's velvet coat.

Much later, John looked up when he heard a timid knock on the door. Elizabeth and Paul were standing in the doorway.

"May I come in, John? I want to talk to Brianda," Elizabeth asked shyly, her face pallid, her heart aching for the young woman.

"Brianda," John whispered into her hair, "listen to me."

Brianda wrapped her arms around him even tighter and burrowed in closer to his body. She didn't want to hear anything.

"You cannot let this one bad moment affect you like this. Yes, it was awful when Elizabeth came in unexpectedly and saw your injured back, but it is not the end of the world. She was taken by surprise. It does not mean that she doesn't like you."

"How can I face her now?" she whispered hotly against his skin. "Every time she sees me, she is going to think about it. Has Paul told her that it was my brother that did this to me?"

"Yes, I am sure that he has told her the whole story. There had to be an explanation to account for what Elizabeth saw. She knows that you were the innocent victim of an evil act of cruelty, and you can depend on her keeping the incident to herself. Elizabeth is a good person, Brianda. She would not do or say anything to hurt you."

Brianda lifted her head and looked into his eyes. "No man will ever want to marry me now," she whispered brokenly.

"Why do you say that?" he asked, still holding her.

"Because of the scars. What man is going to find that attractive? I wasn't much to look at before Edward beat me, but now I am doomed to a lonely life!"

He held her chin and looked into the violet pools of her eyes. "You are not ugly. You are beautiful. Always remember that."

At John's nod, Elizabeth walked quickly over to the bed and sat down. She put her hand on Brianda's shoulder.

Brianda shrank away from the touch, trying to find shelter in the security of John's arms. He would not permit her to hide again, and instead held her by the shoulders and turned her toward Elizabeth.

"Brianda," Elizabeth said softly, "everything that John has just said to you is true. I have only just met you, and already I feel as if I have a very special new friend. Forgive my ignorance, I only cried out when I saw your back because I couldn't imagine that a human being was capable of inflicting such cruelty on another. Forgive me."

Brianda's eyes were puffy and red. She was sniffling every other breath and taking in large gulps of air. She searched Elizabeth's face for any signs of falsehood, but saw none.

Elizabeth took the young girl's face between her two hands. "A man who truly loves a woman loves her as she is, and for what she has become. Superficial marks will not matter. You need not worry—there is a man for you who will love and cherish you just as you are. When you are loved thus, you will know it in your heart. I feel that way about Paul. He is the man I want to spend my life with."

Elizabeth turned and looked at Paul, and for a moment he was the only thing that existed. Paul came to her side and leaned down and kissed Brianda on the forehead. "Elizabeth's words have value, Brianda. We all love you."

John smiled at his friends and then took a long look at Brianda. "This little lady needs to sleep now. I would bid you both good evening. We will look forward to joining you in three days' time for the gala ball at Haley Hall."

The notices regarding the gala ball at Haley Hall were read with great interest. They heralded the first grand ball of the season! Fall was decorating London. The trees were dropping their colorful presents all over lawns, parks, and the streets. Chilly winds picked up the leaves and swirled them through the air, only to let them find a new spot to color for a short while. With all its gaiety, fall knew that soon on her heels would come winter to blanket the ground in white and cold.

All members of the Ton were agog over the prepa-rations for the gala affair. The seamstresses were working frantically to complete the exquisite gowns. Each one had to be the most beautiful dress presented that evening. The gossips were just as busy, spreading the word that the Earl of Manseth had arrived back in London, and the most exciting bit of news was that he had a ward with him! No one had known he even had a ward. Those who had been fortunate enough to be at the hairdresser when Susana Smythe was there also heard that the young ward was beautiful, too. But Susana was sure to add that it was her opinion that the earl's ward was not too bright, coming, as she did, from the country. Everyone was bursting with curiosity.

By far the most interesting bit of news was that the earl was not going to be accompanying Susana Smythe to the ball! That came as a great surprise, and all of the single ladies decided it would be the most advantageous time for one to look one's absolute best. The Earl of Manseth would be the catch of a lifetime!

A pair of filthy hands brushed the lines of print on the flyer announcing the Haley Hall Gala Ball. The man took a long time in studying the details of the ball as they were described in the announcement. Of special interest was the account of the return of Lord John Fauxley to his London town house. The gossip sheet was even kind enough to enlighten its readers as to the exclusive area of London where the earl made his residence.

Chuckling, he brushed his long, grimy hair back off his face, stretched his legs out in front of him and looked around at the dingy hotel room. He smiled.

Finally his luck was beginning to change. It had been a hard few months, but with careful planning, things would be looking much brighter. He laughed to himself and slapped his thigh. Edward was willing to wager that he was the only person in London, outside of Fauxley's immediate circle, who knew the true identity of the mysterious ward.

He rose quickly and left the squalid building in search of Biff Blanders.

11

Brianda woke at ten in the morning. She could not believe it. Never had she slept so late. She stretched in her bed, letting all her lazy muscles awaken. It had been two days since the awful experience with Paul and Elizabeth. During that time, Brianda and Elizabeth had had tea together in the main salon and Brianda had told her all about her life at Cliffshead Manor. When she had finished, the two women had hugged for a long time. Brianda had a friend, and she hadn't been ashamed to tell Elizabeth anything.

The night before, Brianda had been up very late trying to decide which gown to wear to the Haley Hall Gala Ball. Elizabeth had been wonderful, helping her with ideas for her hair and suggesting the appropriate jewelry. When Brianda announced that she did not own one piece of jewelry, Elizabeth hurried home and returned with a beautiful necklace and earrings fashioned from a perfectly matched set of pearls.

Brianda was thrilled. Real pearls! Why, she had never even seen pearls before. They felt so cool when they touched her neck. She tripped on the carpet as she walked over to the mirror to see how the pearls looked on her, and Elizabeth laughed and told Brianda that she had to practice walking in the new slippers with the high heels.

It took her a long time to master walking in the high-heeled slippers, and when she was able to glide lightly and not look as if she had drunk too much champagne, Elizabeth announced that she was going to teach her to dance. They giggled as they practiced all the steps to the latest dances. Elizabeth had to hum the music, because when Brianda tried to hum, she began laughing so hard that she could not continue. They fell to the floor in gales of laughter as they imagined all of the men at the ball limping around after their dances with Brianda.

Below, John could not help but hear the sounds of laughter and the creaking of the furniture as it was moved across the floor. He could not imagine what the two young women were up to, but from the sounds of things, they were having a terrific time.

Women! He shook his head to clear away those thoughts and tried to concentrate on the legal papers in front of him.

At midnight, he went into the salon and informed the two women that it was quite late and time for both of them to be abed. "I cannot believe that Paul would allow you to be out traveling the streets of London at this late hour, Elizabeth," John said sternly.

"Oh, he doesn't know anything about it, sir!" Elizabeth said gleefully. Seeing the look on John's face, she added quickly, "I mean he is performing emergency surgery tonight. He thinks that I am safely tucked into my bed at home. I did not tell him that I planned to spend the evening with Brianda. You are not going to tell him, are you, John?"

"Do you two think you can pull me into your small deceptions?"

"Please don't tell Paul. He will be very angry and might not even take me to the ball tomorrow night! You wouldn't want Brianda to have to go without a close female friend, would you?" she beseeched him. Brianda looked absolutely stricken.

"You are asking me to begin lying to my best friend?" John responded with mock severity.

Not knowing quite how to answer, Elizabeth thought for a moment, absent-mindedly chewing at the tips of her fingernails. Brianda was very worried. She had seen that look on John's face before, and it usually meant trouble for someone.

"John, er, sir, of course I don't want you to lie to Paul. If you could just refrain from saying anything at all. That isn't lying, sir," Elizabeth said as sincerely as she could.

John had to turn away for a moment so that the two guilty parties would not see the smile he had to hide. Composed, he turned back to them. "Elizabeth, you will spend the night here. I will send my driver to your home with a message that you will be returning home in the morning. I will also send a similar message to Paul at the surgery wing of the hospital."

Both women appeared vastly relieved.

"Lastly, I require your close attention."

Brianda and Elizabeth looked like toy soldiers, at attention, unmoving.

"Neither Paul nor I will allow this kind of behavior. It is inexcusable. Were it not for the gala ball tomorrow night and the excitement that it has generated within you two, I would not be inclined to be so forgiving. I will overlook it, but just this one time." He paused to let his warning sink in. "Have I made myself clear?"

Both heads nodded in rapid agreement.

"Then I bid you both a good night."

Before he could say another word, both women were hurrying from the room and disappearing up the stairs.

Smiling, John called to his driver and dispatched the notes. He then returned to the unfinished work that awaited him in the study.

Clara was reluctant to draw the bath water for Brianda, as it was only one o'clock in the afternoon. "It is way too early to bathe for the ball, Miss!"

Brianda scowled at Clara and tapped her right foot furiously.

"If you bathe now, miss, you will have to sit around all afternoon in your robe, for you certainly wouldn't want to wrinkle your gown by putting it on too early. You refused your breakfast and lunch, so why don't you go down and have a spot of tea and a small sandwich? That will help pass the time, miss."

Brianda turned her back on the servant. "Clara, if I have tea and a sandwich now, it is possible that my dress won't fit later. It fits perfectly now, so I am not going to take a chance that I will become fat by this afternoon."

"Oh, really, miss! You are not going to gain weight in one afternoon. Now, his Lordship is going to be angry if you don't eat a bite or two."

"His Lordship will not know, if you don't open your big mouth, Clara! You are always running to tell him every small thing about me. Why?"

"Those are his orders, miss. He is the master, and we all do as we are told, not like some people I know!"

"If you are referring to me, Clara, I refuse to jump when his Lordship gives orders!"

"Then you are in for some rough waters ahead, my girl. I will be downstairs if you need me. I do have other duties around here." Clara started for the door.

"Clara, please don't tell him that I haven't eaten! I am too excited to eat. Tonight is my first ball! Please!"

Brianda was so young, and she looked so excited. "All right, miss, but just this once. I care for you, Brianda, but I am not willing to incur the wrath of the master."

"Thank you, Clara. I will try not to be a pest."

When John returned in the late afternoon, he was met with a near-hysterical Clara, who, when she saw him, simply threw her arms toward heaven and stomped off toward the kitchen. *Brianda must have been more than a handful today,* he surmised, as he closed the large entry door behind him.

At the sound of the great door closing, Brianda rushed from her room, her hair flying behind her, and bounded down the stairs two at a time to greet him. Dispensing with all the formalities, she began dancing around him, asking so many questions that he simply stood still and waited for her to run out of breath.

"Well, sir, at what time are we leaving? What time?" she repeated breathlessly.

"Have you been this hyperactive all day, Brianda? I am sure the staff is ready to strangle you," he answered, grimacing and shaking his head from side to side.

"Oh, no, I have been fine all day! Ask anyone! Well, maybe not Clara. She is a little put out with me at the moment."

John bit his lower lip with his upper teeth to stifle the smile. "What have you done to Clara? When I came in, she looked as if she belonged in an asylum!"

"I may have been a bit insistent about having my bath a little too early and a few other minor things." Brianda placed her hand on his arm. "But please answer me, sir, what time do we leave for the ball?"

"We shall depart for the ball at eight-thirty. We will eat our dinner and then get dressed."

"Dinner! We are going to have dinner here?" She stomped her small foot. "I thought that dinner would be served at the ball, sir."

"Sometimes dinner is served at gala balls, but this affair is the grandest of the season. There will simply be too many people there to serve dinner. Tonight, all of the gentry will dine in their own homes before going to the ball."

"Oh. Then we are going to eat here?"

"Yes, Brianda, we eat dinner here every night."

"I am not going to eat dinner."

"Why not? Did you eat a late lunch?"

"Ah . . . no. I am just not going to eat, that's all."

"Why not, pray tell?"

"Because I am not hungry!" Seeing that John did not believe that—her hearty appetite was notorious—she added firmly, "Besides, I might not fit into my dress! It fits me perfectly now and I don't want to gain any weight and have the dress look horrible!"

"That is absurd, Brianda."

"I am not eating!"

"So be it. Then you are not going to the ball."

"What!"

"It's a real shame. I know how important this ball is to you."

Brianda could tell by the look on his face that he really meant what he said. "All right. You win. But you use unfair tactics, your Lordship," she said, setting her jaw and clenching her teeth together in fury.

"I always get what I want, Brianda. Don't you ever forget it. Now tell Clara that we are ready for dinner."

Brianda strove for perfection. Elizabeth had given her a small bottle of perfume as a gift, and Brianda was beside herself with excitement. Clara and a sweet young servant, Ellie, fashioned her golden hair into a soft bun, and from the center fell long strands that had been curled with a hot iron. She looked as if she had a crown made of sunlight, cascading down her back in swirls of perfect light.

When, at last, she was ready, Clara and Ellie stepped back and sighed. Surely Brianda was the most beautiful woman in London tonight. Brianda walked over to the long mirror, and she, too, was surprised. Why, she almost looked pretty!

John heard her descend the stairs. "Come into the library, Brianda," he called out to her.

She felt suddenly shy as she walked through the door. Her breath caught in her throat when she saw him standing near the fire. He was devastatingly handsome, dressed all in black, except for his crisp, white shirt. Somehow, he looked even taller than usual, and his shoulders seemed broader in his evening jacket. When his face wasn't set in an angry glare, he was dashingly attractive.

John was expecting Brianda to look beautiful, but not this beautiful. He couldn't take his eyes from her face. He saw a different woman, now entirely feminine. The effect was stunning. When he moved his gaze from her face, he saw the pearls, luminescent on her creamy skin, and the gentle swell of her breasts. Her gown was a lovely shade of violet that matched her eyes perfectly. The silk fabric fit exquisitely around her tiny waist and fell softly over her slim hips to cascade in shimmering layers to the tops of her feet. The gown was perfection. John looked into Brianda's eyes and asked, "Where did you get those pearls, Brianda?"

"Elizabeth lent them to me, sir. Why? Don't they look appropriate with the gown?" she asked, concerned.

"They look beautiful, but not as beautiful as you do."

Brianda looked deeply into his eyes for signs that he was teasing her. What she saw there caused her to take a step backward. She felt a slightly disturbing, but strangely enticing sensation.

John took both of her hands in his. He lifted them to his mouth and kissed them, never taking his eyes off hers.

She did not move, drawn to the magnetic sapphire blue of his eyes.

He slipped his hands to her elbows and gently pulled her to him. The scent of her perfume beckoned. Drawing a deep breath, he leaned forward and kissed her mouth.

Shocked, she could not move. The memory of the last kiss flooded her mind. Her knees felt unsteady.

His kiss grew more insistent, and she felt her mouth opening under the pressure from his lips. He slid his tongue gently past her teeth, and tasted the uncharted waters of her mouth.

She felt her knees give a little, and she swayed backward. His warm, sweet breath bathed her face.

He steadied her with his hands and quickly put his arms around her, holding her securely against him. He wanted her, right there and then!

She was having difficulty breathing, but the sensations from the kiss were too wonderful to worry about a silly thing like breathing! Tentatively, she put her arms around him, amazed at how firm the muscles of his back felt under her fingers. Slowly, she slid her hands up toward his shoulders, thrilling to the feel of him. She found herself responding with feelings altogether new to her. It was both wonderful and frightening. She wanted him to invade her mouth further, so she opened her lips wider.

He ran his tongue around her teeth and over her tongue, then gently probed the contours of the roof of her mouth.

A small moan escaped from deep in her throat. She heard the sound but wasn't sure where it came from.

"Pardon me, sir," came a voice from the other side of the closed library door, "but the carriage has arrived, and Dr. Martin and Lady Ingram are waiting for you."

"Thank you, Stevens," John said, as he took his mouth from Brianda's.

She looked up at him with such innocence that he had to force himself to remain in control of his growing passion and not ravish her right there on the library floor! "Come, Brianda, the ball awaits us."

He took her arm and reached for her dark purple satin cloak, placing it onto her softly, letting his hands brush her shoulders.

She shivered and closed her eyes, trying desperately to cool the flush that had invaded her cheeks.

Smiling behind her back, he turned her and, taking her arm in his, led Brianda toward the main hall, then out into the chilly night.

Paul and Elizabeth were anxiously awaiting the arrival of their friends. Paul, also dressed in the black formal attire of gentlemen, looked at Elizabeth and sighed.

She looked so lovely in her gown of white satin. The bodice was covered with seed pearls. A deep red sash was tied at her waist, and the full skirt of white satin fell to her ankles. Her dark hair was pulled up to one side, where her maid had fashioned satin ribbon about her naturally dark curls.

Paul had a maddening urge to kiss and kiss again the spot where Elizabeth's hair lay gently on her soft skin. Their wedding was set for a fortnight hence, and it promised to be a long two weeks.

Elizabeth, too, was thinking of her wedding. There were so many things to be done! Her mother had seen to hiring the same dressmaker John had chosen for Brianda's new wardrobe. The woman promised that the wedding gown would be ready on time, and that Elizabeth would surely be the most beautiful bride of the season!

Secretly, Elizabeth hoped to conceive promptly. She wanted many children, even though Paul was worried about their financial status and had expressed the wish that they wait for a time before beginning their family. Elizabeth had simply smiled and assured him that she concurred with his decision, but deep in her heart knew that she was going to deceive him.

Biff Blanders had everything planned just as Edward had ordered. There had been one small problem, though. He had had to kill that old bloke two nights ago when he robbed him. But he did get all the documents that Edward required. He hadn't meant to kill the gentleman, him being a government official, but things had gotten out of control, and Biff often forgot just how powerful he was.

Born thirty-four years earlier in the slums near the waterfront, Biff was an orphan at two minutes old when his mother had died giving birth to the enormous baby. Biff was bounced around from one house to another as he grew up. His bad temper and dim wit were too much trouble for the people who had taken him in. His huge size made him clumsy and awkward. At eleven years old, he was thrown out into the street, and there he remained. He ate from the garbage, slept in filthy alleys and learned quickly the art of thievery and the benefits of maiming his victims.

It was in one of the seediest bars at the waterfront that Biff Blanders first met Edward Breedon. Biff couldn't believe his good luck when he spied a real gentleman coming through the door! The gentry never ventured into this area of town, especially alone. Why, he would be easy pickings. Biff salivated at the thought. He watched as the gent sat down and ordered a drink.

It wasn't long before Edward noticed the giant of a man sitting in the corner. The man seemed to be staring at him, and seizing his opportunity, Edward rose slowly from his seat and made sure his jacket was open in the front—he didn't want the man to think he might have a concealed weapon. He approached him and offered to buy him a drink. Biff accepted warily, wondering what it was that the gentleman really wanted. Whatever it was, it gave Biff the opportunity to better assess his prey. Edward sat down, and after only a few minutes, realized that this fellow was mentally deficient. He smiled and began an easy conversation with Biff, who was soon telling Edward all about himself. In an hour, Biff agreed to become a business partner of the fine gentleman, making it clear that he had no compunction whatsoever about handling the dirty side of their business.

Edward had entered the seamy world of drug smuggling in his first year away at university. One night, well past midnight, a classmate had offered him a smoke that he guaranteed would obliterate Edward's foul mood. It worked, and Edward wanted more. Soon he was using heroin once in a while, too. His classmate was himself an addict and had begun smuggling heroin to make money for his own habit.

It was well known among his schoolmates that Edward was a spendthrift and a womanizer. He often sent word home to his father that he needed additional funds, and his father always sent the money immediately. Edward would laugh when the money arrived, giving thanks that he happened to look so much like his dead mother.

All was well until his father died, when he suddenly had to concern himself with his supply of cash. He was unable to halt his nightly visits to the gaming halls, and fell deeper and deeper into debt. Soon the managers refused to advance him any more credit. He sold as much as he could from his father's estate, but finally ran out of money. He was desperate.

Edward was convinced that providence had introduced him to his new friends. Smuggling was perfect for him as he had neither conscience nor a sense of honor. All he wanted was to pleasure himself, no matter the expense to others. After seeing what was happening to his friend, it did not take him long to stop using the drugs himself, and soon he took over the business completely. Six months after Edward started his new venture, his friend used a tainted dose of heroin and died on the filthy floor of a vacant building in the slums of London. Edward then had to do all the work himself, but he was making a small fortune.

In Edward's eyes, Biff Blanders was a gift from heaven. He had been without a helper, and this stupid goon was perfect. Edward learned early on that Biff had a terrible temper and could be completely unreasonable when angered. Not wanting to die at Biff's hand, he began winning Biff's loyalty by providing the giant with a few small things he craved, and in return won a loyal henchman who would do anything that was asked of him.

Biff liked women—he liked women more than anything else in the world. His problem was that he could never get one. Stories spread fast about the way Biff treated women, and even the worst whores in London shunned him as if he had the plague.

After some intense dealing, Edward bought a young girl who had been kidnapped from her home in the country. He brought her with him to his small apartment in London, tied her to the bed, and forced her to take heroin. After a few days, he presented the girl to Biff as a gift, as a thank you for all of his good work and all the good work to be done in the future.

Biff was beside himself with joy. In three months, the poor girl was dead, dead from Biff's abuse and the heroin that it took to keep her under control.

But in those three months, Biff worked for Edward like a man possessed, so grateful was he for his gift. When the poor girl died, Edward simply bought Biff another girl, and so their pattern was established. Biff never was much interested in money, leaving all that for Edward.

And so it was that Biff panicked when he received word that Edward had left for France. He feared that Edward might never return, and he would have to resume the life he had known before. Edward's message had told him to wait, and wait is just what Biff did, just as he always followed the orders of his master.

When Edward returned to London, he was ready to kill someone. He walked the familiar streets of his neighborhood, kicking at the stray cats and rats that lived off the garbage strewn in the gutters, and smirking at his thoughts of revenge. So the rich lord had gotten the best of him. Well, Edward was going to get even, and in doing so, was going to get his sweet little sister back in his clutches as well.

She would be a great girl to give to Biff, a virgin and so young and tender!

12

As the carriage drew close to the Haley mansion, it seemed as if the sun had set itself within the confines of the house and was generously, gloriously spilling its rays through every opening.

Brianda couldn't control herself any longer, so she stood up and peered out the window at the wonderful sight. "Just look at that!" she exclaimed, pointing out the carriage window. The three other passengers smiled at one another and said nothing.

There were many carriages with magnificent, matched teams of horses lined up along the private drive, each one displaying the family crest and colors of its owner. Brianda sighed as the carriage of the Earl of Manseth made its way to the front of the line. She could see many of the ladies in their sumptuous gowns and finery being taken into the ball on the arms of their escorts.

As she stepped down from the carriage, Brianda noticed the pair of beautiful black geldings harnessed to the carriage just behind theirs. A sharp yearning for

Dakota pierced her heart, but she shook the feeling away. Her time in London would be short, and before she knew it they would be reunited. Suddenly she was shaken from her reverie.

"Why, Brianda," Elizabeth exclaimed. "I see that John has allowed you to use some lip coloring this evening! It looks so pretty."

Brianda was puzzled, then quickly turned her head and looked away for a moment. John had not allowed any such thing.

John smiled inwardly, also well aware of the cause of the color on Brianda's lovely mouth. He stepped forward and guided his ward toward the door, having decided that no comment was better than trying to explain the reason for the color on her soft lips. Let Elizabeth think what she wanted. It was of little consequence.

The uncomfortable moment was quickly forgotten as Brianda entered the main hall and looked around her. Everything was spectacular! There were distinctive flower arrangements in every room and streamers of ribbon were hung from the ceilings, creating the illusion of rainbows softly waving in the sky.

The men were all dressed in black, with colored cummerbunds and neckties. The women were attired in gowns fashioned from the loveliest of fabrics. And the array of colors! Brianda had never seen such a spectacle. It was a glorious sight!

Suddenly her heart caught in her throat. She cast a furtive glance at John, but he seemed not to notice that everyone had stopped what they were doing and gazed at them. Little did she know that she had been the talk of the town ever since the word had spread that the earl had brought his ward to London! John, however, was composed as usual, and looked the picture of the perfect English gentleman. Brianda drew courage from his strength, and felt safe and secure near him. She lifted her chin and offered a small smile to all there.

John smiled down at her and escorted her through the receiving line. She was introduced to so many people that her head was spinning, but she kept smiling and curtsied to everyone.

John avoided answering the questions about his new ward by expertly changing the subject or directing the conversation to other topics. The only information obtained about Brianda Breedon that night was exactly what he wanted people to know.

All about them, uniformed servants walked silently, offering glasses of wine and assorted finger sandwiches. Music floated in and around each chamber, filling them with beauty.

Brianda kept an eye on the servant with a large tray of crystal glasses, some filled with wine and others with champagne! When John was suddenly surrounded by a small group of friends, she found her opportunity to slip away. She was short enough to pass quickly through the crowd, and when at last she spied the bearer of the wine, she stopped directly in front of him.

"May I offer you some refreshment, miss?" he asked formally.

"Yes, thank you," Brianda answered, as her hand went quickly to the crystal goblet on the front of the tray. She lifted it off and with a curt "thank you," hurried off to find a spot where she could enjoy her first taste of champagne!

In an adjoining room she found an unoccupied corner and turned into it so that her back faced the room. Slowly she lifted the glass to her lips, enchanted by the bubbles that magically rose from its bottom and floated in orderly rows to the surface before disappearing into thin air. She held the cool rim of the glass to her lower lip, then tipped it upward, closing her eyes in anticipation of the special moment.

Nothing happened! She tipped the glass again.

She looked down at the stem of the glass and saw the reason why. Several large fingers were holding it secure!

Her heart sank. She looked up from the glass directly into the imperturbable face of the Earl of Manseth!

"There is a very good explanation for this, sir . . . I just cannot seem to think of it at the moment," she finished feebly.

John's face remained impassive. "I can wait."

"Oh . . . well then, the truth is, sir, that I have asked you on many occasions to allow me to have a glass of wine. You have always refused. It is my opinion that as I am of marrying age, I should be allowed to have a little wine."

"Really? Well, you are considered by the Crown to be a minor. Therefore, you are subject to my rules and must abide by my decisions. I do not think it is necessary for one so young to imbibe liquor."

"But, sir, it is supposed to be fun! We are at a party, are we not? People are supposed to have fun at parties!" she reasoned.

"Considering how you do everything to excess, Brianda, I think that you would not find drinking *fun*."

"Will you allow me to find out for myself?" she asked hopefully.

"No."

"Can I change your mind, sir?"

"Not a chance."

"Very well, but I want you to know that I consider this an unfair barrier to my learning and maturing."

"I will keep that in mind. Now we are going to find Paul and Elizabeth. The dancing is about to begin again."

Slightly mollified by the thought of dancing, Brianda let him take the glass from her hand and lead her through the crowd to where Paul and Elizabeth were waiting.

Elizabeth was glowing from the excitement of the evening. Brianda hugged her and whispered into her ear, "You look so beautiful tonight, Elizabeth, has something special happened?"

Elizabeth's gaze went to Paul. "Shall we tell them, darling? Let's do—let's not wait!"

Brianda's eyes flew from one face to the other. "Tell us what? Oh what is it? Please tell me at once!" Brianda begged.

Paul took Elizabeth's hand in his and looked at John and Brianda. "We are to be married in two weeks' time. All is arranged. We have decided that waiting would be a waste of precious time. Time that we could be sharing together."

"This is news that I welcome with a glad heart, Paul! I wish you both the greatest happiness," John said.

"I, too, wish you all possible happiness!" Brianda hugged her friend fiercely. "Oh Elizabeth, I am thrilled for you!" Brianda said, her eyes glistening with tears.

"Now stop those tears, Brianda, or soon I will be tearful too, and what will everyone think?" Elizabeth said as she kissed Brianda's cheek.

Paul disappeared for a moment and returned with four crystal glasses. "Here, I've brought champagne so we four best friends can toast together for the success and happiness of our marriage!"

Brianda beamed and took the glass of champagne that Paul offered her. She kept her eyes directed at Elizabeth.

John scowled, but took his glass without comment.

Brianda had her first taste of champagne and laughed out loud as the bubbles tickled her nose.

Several heads turned at the sound of the delightful laughter. The young girl was ravishing, and when she laughed, even more so.

There was one person in the crowd who was especially interested in the laughing girl. In his instructions from Susana Smythe, Jeremy Bristol knew that he was to make the girl fall in love with him, toy with her for a couple of months, bed her if he could, and then drop her. Bedding virgins was the part of his work that he enjoyed the most, and to make it even better, Susana was going to pay him one hundred pounds to do it! For that much money he would bed an ugly scullery maid! But one look at Brianda Breedon convinced him he was in for a run of good luck!

Jeremy Bristol's conceit was ignited during his adolescence, when he had attracted women without even trying. His striking good looks and his tall, trim, athletic body were inherited from his parents. But his suave, self-confident manner was the product of many long hours of practice and experimentation. He knew how the ladies loved his dark blond hair and gold-flecked, green eyes, and used both to their utmost advantage. He trained his body every day, knowing that this too was part of his meal ticket. He had made a profession of living off rich women, either as a live-in lover or as a kept man, and he enjoyed his roles to the fullest.

Jeremy had known Susana Smythe for several years. He had been the man sharing her bed until Lord Fauxley came on the scene to take Jeremy's place. Susana had dropped all of her lovers when she decided that it was time to marry again and that the Earl of Manseth was to be her husband. Jeremy had been quite put out by the new development, for he had enjoyed the plush life Susana provided for him, but he was a realist and knew better than to cause a scandal.

Now was his chance to exact revenge on the famous earl. How sweet life could be! He was going to seduce Brianda Breedon right out from under Fauxley's nose, and when he was done with her, not one man of the gentry would speak to his ward, much less marry her!

Jeremy watched and waited for the right moment, irritated that Lord Fauxley was never more than a few feet from Miss Breedon. When it was beginning to seem that he would never get his chance at her, the earl gave Brianda permission to dance with some of the young men who had been crowding around her. Now was his chance, and from across the room he waited for Brianda's first partner, a very nervous young man, to sweep her rapidly around the dance floor. Within moments Jeremy cut in. Surprised and somewhat disgruntled, the young man relinquished Brianda to Jeremy.

Brianda, almost breathless with excitement, looked up to see the face of her new partner, and drew in a deep breath, her eyes widening.

Jeremy smiled down at her, pleased with the response he saw on her face. "Good evening, my beautiful lady. May I present myself, I am Jeremy Bristol, at your service."

"Good evening, sir, I am Miss Brianda Breedon. I am pleased to make your acquaintance," she said, mesmerized by the intensity of his green eyes.

"I have been attending gala balls and social functions in London for some years now, and I have never seen you before. I thought I knew everyone, but here you are, a beautiful stranger. This must be your first ball! To overlook a woman as enchanting as you are would be impossible!" Jeremy put his fingers to his forehead and pretended to be thinking. "I know! You are a fairy, you are not real, you have been sent by the angels to make this ball bearable for me!"

Brianda laughed gaily at his silly words and found herself blushing. "I am no fairy, sir, I have just arrived with my guardian from the country, where I reside. I am happy to say that he is going to take me to several balls this season!"

"What fabulous luck for me and for all of the single young men of the Ton. I hope that you will allow me to dance with you at all of the gala balls."

Brianda smiled up at him, her violet eyes shimmering with delight at his compliments.

Jeremy smiled back, happy that things were going so well. The music ended, and she stepped back from him. "May I have this next dance, Miss Breedon?" he asked. "We have just met, and I want to have a little more time to get acquainted with you."

"Why, yes, sir, I would so enjoy another dance with you."

"Please call me Jeremy. I like informality. It brings people together faster, makes them feel more comfortable."

"All right, Jeremy it is."

The music began, and he took her into his arms again, this time pulling her slightly closer to him. He was trying to judge how fast he could move in on his naive quarry.

At the feel of his breath on her cheek, she pulled back slightly, and he let her go, acting as if nothing had happened. Brianda relaxed once again and gave in to the rhythm of the waltz. As her breathing quickened, Jeremy Bristol leaned close to her ear.

"Your face is flushed, Brianda. May I call you Brianda?"

"Yes, of course."

"Why don't we step out on the balcony for a moment to get some fresh air?"

"What a lovely idea!"

The air was decidedly cooler on the terrace and felt wonderful to the skin. Brianda was enchanted by the gardens. Even in autumn, there remained some flowers. She said nothing as she gazed out at the tranquil night.

"What are you thinking about, little one?" Jeremy asked as he placed his hand on the middle of her back.

His touch made her suddenly uneasy. Brushing the feeling aside, she answered, "I am thinking of my home. When I was a little girl, I would walk outside in the evening and smell the flowers and look up at the stars."

He said nothing, thinking that gazing at the stars was boring and totally absurd, but it mattered not to him what this inexperienced girl enjoyed. She was feeling vulnerable, and he was sure he could use her loneliness to his advantage. He moved in a little closer and smiled sweetly, as if to say he understood her feelings.

"I guess I am feeling lonely—for my home, my best friend and my horse," she continued in a small, wistful voice.

"This is no time for homesickness, Brianda!" he admonished gently. "You are attending your first ball in London and should be enjoying yourself."

"You are absolutely right, sir . . . I mean Jeremy," she said, and made herself smile at him.

"That is better," he said as he stepped up to her and gently grabbed her upper arms. He pulled her toward him, piercing her with his intense green eyes.

Brianda placed her hands on his chest to stop her forward motion. "What are you doing?" she demanded.

"I only wanted to see the color of your eyes. The light here is poor, and I couldn't make them out."

"You will be able to see the color of my eyes inside, sir, for that is where I am going. Excuse me," she said as she tried to pull away from his hold on her.

"Don't be angry, little one. I can see now that you are unused to dealing with grown men."

The comment had just the effect that Jeremy intended. She lifted her chin and stared him in the eye. "I have had plenty of experience with men, thank you. It is just that I am . . . thirsty!"

"Oh, please pardon me. How remiss I am. If you will

excuse me, I will go now for drinks for both of us. Will you wait right here for me?"

"I suppose so, but I should get back inside." Chiding herself for letting thoughts of the earl interfere with her fun, she said, "I will take a glass of punch."

"As you wish," he said, as he turned and walked toward the salon.

Brianda wrapped her arms about her and sighed. The night air was much cooler now and she wished she could go inside, but decided that Jeremy would never be able to find her in the crowd. She moved back from the rail and stood closer to the corner of the house to escape the bracing tendrils of the breeze.

Just then she was grabbed roughly, a hand was placed over her mouth, and she was pulled backward deep into the shadows. Frantically, she tried to free herself, but she could neither scream nor move.

"Stop that squirming! Stop it or I will break your pretty neck," said a voice, harsh and very low.

She stopped moving, and stood still, her chest heaving with fear.

"That's better. Now listen to this. I want you to give a message to his Lordship, the Earl of Manseth. I am only going to tell you once, so you'd better get it the first time. If you don't relay it proper, I'll be back for you. Do you understand?"

She shook her head up and down as hard as she could to tell him that she understood.

"Good. Now tell him that he will receive a letter in the post. He is to follow the directions exactly, or he will pay a higher price than he can imagine. Got that?"

Once again, she nodded her head. The man's arm around her waist was hurting her. Breathing was difficult.

"Don't tell nobody else. Nobody. I'll know it if you do, missy, and you'll pay."

There was something about the way he said those

words that made Brianda's skin crawl. She shook her head from side to side, indicating that she wouldn't say anything to anyone.

"I am going to let go of you now, and I want you to walk straight ahead. Don't turn around, or I'll stick my knife in that pretty face of yours." He loosened his grip and repeated, "Walk straight ahead and don't turn around."

Trembling, she waited to be released. He pushed her hard from behind, and Brianda fell forward, struggling to keep her balance. As she righted herself, she turned and looked behind her. There was nothing there but the empty darkness.

Jeremy was just rounding the corner when Brianda flew into him. The crystal glasses made a terrible racket as they crashed to the ground.

"What the hell!" exclaimed Jeremy angrily, but the look on the young girl's face startled him. "Brianda, what is wrong?" he asked, as she grabbed his arms and looked up at him, her eyes wide with fear.

She was so frightened that she couldn't speak. Vastly relieved to see someone who could help her, she threw her arms around him and held on.

He pushed her back and looked at her face. She looked exquisitely vulnerable, like a deer trapped in a hunter's snare. He bent over and kissed her full on the mouth.

Just at that moment, John came through the door.

13

Instantly filled with fury, John walked toward the pair. So intent was he on watching their mouths that he did not notice Brianda's struggle.

Jeremy Bristol had suffered many a blow from angry husbands and lovers, but never had he been struck with such force as the Earl of Manseth administered. He was forcibly yanked away from Brianda, spun around, and hit squarely in his stomach. The wind was knocked out of him, and he gasped with his mouth wide open, unable to draw another full breath. It was a frightening sensation. The next thing he knew, he was flying through the air over the railing and landing on the cold earth of the garden, barely conscious.

Both blows gave John great satisfaction; it was a pleasure to strike the bastard.

When John turned to Brianda, he looked as if he were about to coldly murder someone. His eyes were as hard as steel balls that had been frozen in a glacier. She stood immobile, afraid to move. Breathing became difficult for her, and she reached out into thin air for support.

Several guests who had been enjoying the evening air gathered at the rail and searched the garden to see what had become of the gentleman who had landed on the grass.

In one stride, John was at Brianda's side. She started to open her mouth to explain, but the look on his face stopped her cold. He grabbed her right wrist in a vise-like grip and turned away, pulling her along after him. He was moving so fast that she had to run to keep up with him.

Brianda tried to pull her arm free, but he held her fast, his fingers biting into the tender skin. She put her free hand on the hand that held her captive and tried to pry his fingers off her. It was useless.

They were almost at the door, and she could not believe that he was going to drag her across the main salon! He wouldn't make a fool of her in front of London's best!

The musicians were playing a beautiful melody that Brianda had never heard before, and the music floated out the door to greet them. The entire situation seemed unreal. She had to stop him!

John turned into the main salon without breaking stride. Brianda was almost airborne trailing behind him. Dancing couples stepped aside, shocked as Lord Fauxley left a wake of astonished guests behind him and his young ward. He veered right toward the main entrance and shoved a slightly drunk man out of his way. The man reeled, hit the wall, and slid into a sitting position on the floor. From the corner of her eye, Brianda caught the horrified look on Elizabeth's face.

"Sir," Brianda entreated, "Please, sir, you are humiliating me."

John stopped, turned, and impaled her with his steely eyes. Speaking with controlled fury, but in a voice that only she could hear, he replied, "Not another word from you, not another word."

He then headed for the main entrance, Brianda still in tow. He called to a servant to fetch their cloaks. Without bothering to put them on, he pulled her into the night and summoned their carriage. The footman opened the door, and John put his hands around Brianda's waist and lifted her off her feet. He almost threw her onto the carriage cushion. She sat quickly on the seat and stared at the carriage's wooden floor.

John seated himself across from her. He studied her a moment and then handed her the silk cloak. His hands were steady, his jaw set.

Brianda put her cloak on slowly, grateful for something to do with her hands and needing an excuse not to look at his face. With trembling fingers she hooked the fasteners around her neck and wondered if she should try to explain to him what had happened. One quick peek at his countenance was enough to put any questions about talking to him to rest. He looked as if murder would be an easy task, and she was the only one close by! She shrank back into the seat and studied her feet. It was going to be a long ride home, and only God knew what was awaiting her when they arrived.

It was a long ride, too, for John. He sat and stared out the carriage window and reflected on his actions. He had surprised himself; never had he done anything quite so scandalous in public before, and furthermore, he hadn't even cared that he was probably causing the scandal of the season! He glanced over at Brianda and saw that she was still examining the tops of her slippers. Feeling that he had overreacted, he shrugged his shoulders uneasily.

How he detested that little worm Bristol. His reputation was the lowest. It was his amazing good looks that won him his bed and board, and he cared not whom he hurt in the process. The tales of his conquests were long and sickening. There were young women now living in convents for the remainder of their days, shunned by their families, alone with only the memories of those green, faithless eyes to keep them company. Well, the bastard wasn't going to come near Brianda again. If he tried, John would kill him.

Stevens was waiting at the manor's massive front door as John and Brianda came up the walk. One look at his master's face, and Stevens knew better than to say anything. Hearing the commotion in the entry hall, a surprised Angus appeared at the top of the stairs and quickly assessed the situation. Everything appeared to be in order, except for Brianda's face. It looked a mile long. There must have been trouble, or why else would they have come home so early from the ball?

Brianda stood just behind John, awaiting her fate. Her head was hung low, her chin on her chest.

"Go to your room, undress, and prepare yourself for bed. Now!" he ordered.

Lifting her gown with both hands, she fairly ran along the hall and up the stairs. She passed a silent Angus in a flash and was in her room in less than a minute. Breathing heavily, she hurried out of the lovely gown and laid it on the back of the wing chair, overcome by sadness. It looked so empty and forlorn, the way her heart felt. She walked slowly to her closet and took her night chemise off its hook, thinking about what this evening could have been.

She pulled the chemise over her head and walked across the cold floor in her bare feet to wash her face from the porcelain pitcher and bowl. Then she carefully put all of her lovely clothes away. The dressmaker had made a special hanger for her gown, and Brianda hung it so that it would not be pressed against the other clothes and wrinkle. She put the pearls in a safe place on top of her cabinet, intending to return them to Elizabeth. Then she sat on the bed and waited.

*   *   *

"Stevens," John said to the butler.

"Yes, sir?"

"From this moment forth, Miss Breedon is not allowed to entertain or receive mail from a Mr. Jeremy Bristol. There will be no exceptions. Understood?"

"Perfectly, sir."

"I, however, am to be notified if mail arrives from him, or if the bastard presents himself here at my door. He is not to be shown into the house, no matter the reason."

"You will be notified at once, should either of the two situations present themselves, sir."

"Thank you and good night, Stevens," John said as he began walking upstairs. Seeing that Angus was waiting for him at the head of the stairs, John said, "You may go back to your room, Angus, there is nothing for you to do this evening."

"Very good, my Lord. Until the morning, then."

"Yes, good night."

John entered his room and took off his evening jacket and silk tie, leaving his white silk shirt open at the neck. There wasn't a sound from the adjoining room. He took a sip of brandy from the decanter that had been placed on the small table near his closet, fortifying himself before turning the door handle and walking into Brianda's bedroom.

The room was lit by a solitary candle. Brianda was sitting on the bed with her hands in her lap, watching him. He crossed the room slowly and ended up standing directly in front of her. She sat deathly still, her eyes now on the floor. He did not say a word.

"May I speak?" she whispered.

"No. I am going to speak, and you are going to listen to every word. You will not interrupt."

"Yes, sir."

"The man I saw you kissing this evening . . ."

"But, sir . . ."

"Brianda!"

"Excuse me, sir," she said contritely.

"This man—I cannot call him a gentleman—is Jeremy Bristol, a notorious seducer of women. He lives off wealthy women for as long as he can, and when he is finally thrown out, he simply finds another woman. His reputation is well known all over London. He is a scoundrel and a thief. How he found out about you so fast, I'll most likely never know." John put both of his hands on her shoulders and shook her slightly. With his right hand, he tipped her chin upward, forcing her to look at him. "But I will tell you this, my dear, you have seen the last of him. You are forbidden to receive him as a guest in this house, receive mail from him, or acknowledge his presence should you come across him at a future social function. Am I well understood?"

Unable to take her eyes from his, she felt the icy appendages of fear wrap around her body. She hugged herself with her arms and nodded that she understood.

At her frightened look, he removed his hands from her and took a step backward. "Brianda, I realize that you are very young and inexperienced with men, and that this rogue is an expert at turning the heads of females. However, these are not sufficient reasons for me to excuse your shocking behavior tonight."

"May I explain?" she asked, full of desire to convince him of her innocence.

"What is there to explain? I saw the two of you kissing each other on the terrace. Your telling me how Bristol was able to conquer you so fast will not help assuage my anger, I assure you."

"But, it wasn't like that . . ."

"Oh, and how was it then? You seduced him? With all your worldly experience?" he asked, his eyebrows raised in mock surprise.

"Of course not! But you needn't look so smug, sir. I am not totally without experience in affairs of the heart," she answered, her chin slightly raised.

"You don't say! You could have surprised me. It is too bad for you that when you lie, Brianda, your cheeks take on a brighter hue, and your eyes cannot stay locked with mine."

Unconsciously, Brianda put her fingers to her hot cheek. Gathering strength, she took a deep breath and looked him straight in the eye. "My cheeks are flushed from the anxiety you instilled in me." She saw the momentary tightening of his facial muscles, and knew she had won at least one point. In a flash, it was gone, and the hard veneer returned.

"Anxiety? You have every right to feel anxiety. I have never been angrier at you. You came very close to being the public scandal of the season."

"I may already be just that, sir. I am grateful that you were able to control your anger and bring me home before deciding on a stricter course of action." She did not like the look on his face at all. Deciding that changing the topic was definitely in her best interests, she continued, "Please, my Lord, listen to me. If, when I have finished, you still feel that I deserve the beating, at least I will feel that you will have been just in hearing all the evidence before the sentence is carried out." She saw him purse his lips to contain the smile that threatened to emerge.

"Speak, Brianda, I only hope that you will not further incriminate yourself." He crossed his arms on his chest and set himself to listen to her.

Carefully, she continued, "Mr. Bristol was trying to get close to me, and I did not enjoy it. I found his odor

. . . unappealing. To get him away from me, I asked that he bring me some fruit punch. I was going to leave to find you, when I was grabbed from behind and a horrible, stinking hand was forced over my mouth . . ." She paused for effect.

It worked, for John had squared his shoulders and was listening intently. "Go on," he ordered.

"The man dragged me back into the bushes at the corner of the house. He stayed behind me, and I could not see his face. I could smell his breath, though—it was awful. His voice was disguised, it seemed, for it did not sound natural to me. He told me that I was to give you a message, and that I was to tell no one else. Also, if I did not give you the message, he would find me, and I would be sorry."

"What was the message, Brianda?" he asked in that deathly quiet manner of his.

Squaring herself so as not to forget a single detail, she said, "Sir, you will be receiving a letter in the post in the next few days. You are to follow the instructions exactly and do as the letter says. If you choose to ignore the letter, you will pay a greater price than you ever imagined," she finished, her eyes clouding over.

"Was there anything else?"

"He told me not to turn around, and then shoved me forward very hard. I almost fell. When I righted myself, I turned and looked back, but there was no one there. I was so frightened that I began running, and I ran smack into Mr. Bristol, who was returning with the fruit punch. The glasses fell and made a terrible clatter as they hit the porch. As I had almost knocked him over, I grabbed onto his coat, and we were unbalanced for a moment. He must have misinterpreted my actions, for he grabbed my shoulders and pulled me to him and kissed me. I tried to push him off, but I couldn't. It was at that very moment that you came out onto the terrace."

John said nothing, but began to pace up and down the room. "Did the man who grabbed you call you by name, Brianda?"

"I don't remember, sir, I was so frightened."

"Try to remember, it is important."

"No, I don't believe he did. He called me 'Missy,' that is all."

"Think back, no matter how unpleasant it is to recall what happened, and tell me if you have forgotten any part of the message."

"No, I remembered it all. I had to, for he threatened me with a knife and said that I would pay. I remembered it all."

"A knife?"

"Yes, he told me that if I tried to turn and see who he was, he would cut my face. I believed him." She shivered.

"Why didn't you tell me this immediately?" he yelled at her.

"You would not allow me to speak. You looked so angry in the carriage that I . . ."

"Good God, am I that much of an ogre? In the future, should a matter of urgency arise, I want you to tell me immediately," he said in a more restrained tone.

Brianda sat, wringing her hands, obviously upset.

"Brianda, I do not want you to worry about this. When the letter arrives, I will take care of the situation. You are completely safe here. Angus is aware of all that occurs in and around my home, and he will see to it that you are well protected. This whole unpleasant situation may have been a foolish prank by some person who doesn't like me," he added to further convince her.

She smiled wanly. They both knew it wasn't a prank.

"I feel safe with you, sir, but please tell me that you believe I had no desire to kiss Mr. Bristol."

"What is a single kiss to a woman with such experience in affairs of the heart?"

"Are you mocking me, sir?"

"Certainly not. You told me yourself that you are experienced with men, did you not?"

To save face, she replied, "That is correct, quite experienced."

"I recall Old Megan telling me that you had a rather lonely childhood. Never once was a beau mentioned."

"Not all matters are discussed with virtual strangers, sir."

"Quite so. Then, all during the time that you spent with Mr. Bristol, you were aware of his intent?"

"Yes." As Brianda had no idea what the earl was referring to, she thought it better not to say too much and give herself away.

"You were not taken in by his touches, his words of love?" he asked, moving closer to her.

"Taken in? Me? I saw right through it, sir," she answered happily, sensing that he wasn't going to ask her for details.

"I see." He turned and walked to the window, now frosty with the evening chill. "Come here, Brianda, and look at the night. The moonlight is like a path of stars across the gardens, leading up and over the trees and then peacefully on to a secret place," he said. She came gladly, relieved that the other discussion seemed at an end.

Peering out of the window, she saw the lovely sight. Content, she stood next to him and felt the warmth of his body. They stayed that way for several minutes. She hardly noticed the touch of his hand when it rested on her shoulder. Were it not for its warmth, she would not have known that it was there. This touch was oddly comforting.

John stepped behind her and pulled her back against his chest. She could feel the length of him along her whole body. He bent forward and rested his chin on the top of her head, drinking in the floral fragrance of her. He slipped his hands under her arms and let them encircle her rib cage.

She could feel his hot breath on her scalp. Somehow it warmed her whole body, and she drew in a deep breath.

His fingers tightened slightly, and Brianda felt like a field mouse held in a hawk's talons. But strangely enough, she felt no fear. Slowly, he let his hands move down the sides of her body, barely touching her, and at her waist they stopped, and once again she felt the slight pressure of his fingers. She took another deep breath, not really knowing what was happening.

With his chin, he tipped her head to the side, exposing her neck, now open and inviting. He kissed her just behind the ear, and then moved slowly down, laying small, quick kisses all the way down to her shoulder.

She shivered against him.

Twisting her easily with his hands, he turned her to face him. There was a peculiar look on his face, but she had just a moment to notice it before his mouth fell on hers, demanding entrance. She opened her mouth without hesitation, and his tongue sought all the sweet places.

Brianda felt an uncontrollable urge to hold him, to be closer to his body. She put her arms around his waist and grabbed his shirt. Intertwining her fingers in the material, she held on as if she would never let go.

As his tongue ran over her teeth, his hands began their ascent, stopping under her arms. There, his thumbs began a slow, deep, circular motion, catching her breasts underneath and moving upward along the soft outer curve, causing a sensation so new, so wondrous that she caught her breath and waited for it to begin again. All the while, his mouth continued its unrelenting need for discovery.

At the intimate contact, she felt uneasy and instinctively tried to move away from his offending fingers. But he held her securely, and all she accomplished in her movements was to expose more of her breasts to him.

His tongue demanded her attention once again as she felt him slide it along the roof of her mouth. Tentatively, her tongue reached out to meet his. It was as if two waves met, one small and hesitant, the other masterful and knowledgeable, joining to become one for a timeless moment.

The kiss made her knees go weak, and she felt her balance waver from a delicious bliss engulfing her. She grasped his shirt more tightly, pulling herself up against his body. He was firm and rock solid everywhere. His fragrance was wonderful, so different, so appealing. Inhaling his manly scent with every breath, she reluctantly surrendered to her own mounting passion.

John, sensing the change in her, slipped his hands up onto her shoulders and hooked his thumbs under the small, round straps of her chemise. By moving his thumbs outward and over her shoulders, he caused the chemise to fall to the floor in a silent heap of ivory silk.

Brianda stood completely naked in front of him. Holding her slightly away from him, he let his eyes roam over her entire body, reeling with the sensual delight of her.

Brianda was too shocked to move. She stood like a statue, her eyes locked with his.

Unhurriedly, he slipped his arms behind her back and knees, lifted her into his arms, and carried her to her bed. He slowly and gently laid her down. She wanted to cover herself but could not move.

He stood next to the bed and stared down at her. Quickly removing his shirt, he joined her there. His weight was surprising on the bed, and she found herself rolling toward him. She put her hands on his chest to stop the motion, but he moved forward at the same moment, forcing her back into the mattress where he loomed over her.

His chest was covered with thick, curly black hair that felt slightly abrasive to the palms of her hands. Although she was no stranger to nakedness, having attended many sick men, she had never touched a man's chest before. Never before had she had the chance to feel the hairs on a man's chest as they slid between her fingers. Never before had her hands known so intimately the strength in a man's muscles.

John watched her face as she touched him, her eyes filled with wonder and curiosity. She filled him with an unusual desire, one he definitely wanted to investigate.

14

Deep inside, Brianda warned herself to put a stop to what was happening. But in truth, she didn't want to stop. It was all so new and exciting. Never before in her short life had she felt so wanted by anyone. John's hands were masterful instruments of love playing an intricate, lovely melody on her body.

John lifted his mouth from hers. Then, as his tongue passed over her supple upper lip, she felt its hot wetness and in its wake a path of cool liquid lingered sweetly. He kissed the tip of her nose and the tip of her chin. Down in a trail of heat he went, kissing her neck, then hesitated to survey the terrain there before moving down to explore her chest.

Brianda was breathing slowly and deeply, discovering with every new touch that John was setting her further afire.

He moved to her nipple quickly, taking it fully into his mouth and sucking softly. So shocked was she by the sensation that both of her hands flew to his head and grabbed his hair. She tried to pull him off of her. He ignored her, pulling more ardently on her areola and taking its firm tip between his teeth. Her fingers curled in response to the slight discomfort. His hand came up and gently massaged her other breast. The contrasting sensations were driving her mad, one almost hurting, the other soothing and gentle in its application. He moved his mouth to her other breast and made wet circles around her nipple, causing it to become erect and responsive.

"Please stop this!" she implored in a voice that didn't seem like her own.

He acted as if he had heard nothing and continued moving back and forth from one breast to the other, leaving one hot and wet for a moment of bliss, only to let it become cool in the night air, as the other was suckled and made warm again.

She shifted beneath him as she felt her whole body begin to respond to his assault. A strange, alien sound slipped from her lips.

Acknowledging the age-old sign, John slid his hand down slowly over her abdomen and then let it move in a large circle as he traced the contours of her hips, thighs and abdomen once again. Acutely attuned to her responses, he let his fingers enter the downy triangle of dark-blond hair between her legs.

She froze, and then, as if shot with an arrow, tried violently to move away from his touch. "No! Leave me. Do not do this!" she cried.

"Hush, love, all is well" is all he said, as he brought one leg up and over hers and held them pinned down on the mattress. His upper body was positioned so that she could not turn or twist away. His fingers continued downward over the soft mound of her pelvis and along the furry outside folds of her womanhood.

Brianda moaned deep in her throat. "Please, please, no more."

Well-experienced fingers rose over the outer swell and entered the velvet chute of the inner lips. He reversed his course and moved straight up to find the hard nubbin that was the core of her womanhood.

She let escape a cry that declared her as woman.

He moved his finger in tiny circles, using slight pressure.

Brianda arched against him, unable to breathe. Never had she experienced such a feeling, never had she known a woman could feel like this. Her hands were frantic, moving over his back and arms randomly, as if searching for a safe hold.

Lifting his mouth from her bruised and tender lips, he let his tongue drag along her breast bone and down between her breasts. He continued on until he reached her navel and stopped to taste her there. All the while, he softly touched her, causing her hips to undulate slowly.

Just when she thought she could not bear any more, and surely there could be no more new sensations, he moved his finger down and carefully and slowly entered her tight sheath.

Panicked, she cried out and tried once again to get away from him.

"Don't be frightened, don't fight me. You cannot get away, so stop trying and let yourself enjoy what you are feeling," he said, his voice husky with desire.

"I want nothing further, John. I cannot bear more."

"You will bear all that I wish. Let yourself relax."

"I cannot!"

"Stop talking and let yourself feel what my finger is doing to you right now," he urged, as he began to move his finger in and out of her. Upon entering, he was stopped at the barrier of her virginity and silently gave thanks that this prize awaited him.

Brianda was all but lost in the passion and let her body move and respond as it decreed. She stopped trying to fight him, and gave in to the all-consuming pleasure.

Suddenly John pulled his finger from her, pushed her away from him and got up off of the bed.

Brianda was stunned by his sudden departure. Confused, she looked up at him.

His face was hard, unyielding. "I have just proved my point, miss. You have no more experience than a twelve-year-old milkmaid. I, on the other hand, have a great deal of experience with bedding women, and you have been one of the easiest to conquer. You will require close watching." With that he turned, grabbed his shirt and left the room.

Brianda felt as if she could not draw a normal breath. Her chest did not want to expand fully. She sat up and stared at the closed door. It loomed at her like the face of a gravestone.

She pushed herself up into a sitting position on quavering arms, feeling her heart turn cold. A chill, like the icy fingers of death, spread down her body and through her limbs, leaving her vulnerable and unable to move.

She wanted to die. How could she have let herself be used so? How could he have done those things to her without an ounce of feeling, of caring?

She was ashamed, humiliated. He had destroyed what small amount of pride she had built for herself over the last months.

As if from another body, she saw herself naked on the bed in the cold night air. She felt she did not deserve the warmth of the blankets and coverlet. *Maybe I will die if I stay thus, naked and exposed to the extremes of the night and the cold,* she thought. *It would be better than setting my eyes on him again.*

The hatred welled within her, bringing some warmth from deep inside her abdomen. It stretched up and touched her heart. She felt the muscle flutter, then resume its normal beating. As her hatred grew, tears came from the deepest part of her soul. Hot and burning, they blurred her vision. When her sad violet eyes could contain them no longer, they spilled over onto her cheeks, leaving tracks like lava flowing down from the rim of a volcano after erupting out of the inner core of the Earth.

She beat both fists on the mattress in a futile attempt to vent her rage. She did not want to cry, for his cruelty did not deserve her tears, but she could not stop the flow, nor her agony. Giant, wracking sobs rose from her lungs. To silence them, she threw herself onto her pillow to muffle the clamor of their pain.

Brianda woke late the following morning. Her eyes burned from the aftermath of her tears and from her lack of sleep. She had lain awake well into the night, unable to grant herself the temporary peace of sleep. She tortured herself by remembering and reliving every sensation, the heat, the desire . . . the ultimate humiliation.

Suddenly, she came to the realization that she was lying under her blankets and coverlet! For a terrible moment, she thought he may have returned and had covered her naked body during the night. The thought brought a wave of nausea, and she had to take some deep breaths to alleviate the awful sensation. She shook her head and vowed to use all her strength to put those memories out of her mind. She never wanted to recall what had happened between them again.

Brianda rose and walked naked across the room to pick up her chemise from where it fell the night before. Mechanically, she pulled her chemise over her head and cringed as it floated down, caressing her body, just as he had.

The wash water in her heavy white china basin was quite cold. She splashed it over her face and neck to shock herself. She stood shivering, letting the droplets fall on her chest. It didn't matter that her chemise was dampened, too. With resolve, she went to the closet and pulled out a heavy wool navy blue dress. It was plain, its severity matching her mood.

Completely dressed, she sat in the straight-back chair and looked out her window at the gardens. They looked as barren as her soul felt, the flowers now gone and not to return in the face of the approaching winter.

The realization that she had to live with John made her want to die. There was no way to change her current situation. She was trapped with him and now had the added degradation of accepting what he had done to her.

Death seemed preferable to facing him. After all of Edward's unspeakable cruelties, she had never felt this violated. She wondered how one could kill oneself.

She walked to her bedroom door and hesitated. Her hunger was less than her dread of encountering him in the hallway. She put her ear to the door and strained to listen for movement. There was only silence. Forcing her head high, she left her room and ventured out into the hall. She saw no one, and slipped quickly down the stairs and hurried into the kitchen. There, she sat at the huge wooden work table and asked that Cook serve her some lunch.

"Excuse me, miss, but you know that his Lordship has forbidden you to eat in the kitchen. He wishes that you eat in one of the two dining halls."

"I don't give a damn what he ordered. I am hungry and I want to eat here in the kitchen. The food is ready, Cook, so please make me a plate."

"His Lordship is not at home at the moment, Brianda. I will serve you here this one time, but you must know that I will not disobey him in the future."

"All right, Cook. I understand that it is not fair to ask that you disobey your master, but some of his rules are absurd! What difference could it make if I choose to eat a meal here in the kitchen instead of in a formal eating salon?"

"I do not question the decisions of the master, Brianda! If you had any sense, you would do the same!"

"I will never live under the thumb of any man, Cook. Men live with the misconception that we females are helpless, flighty, dim-witted and incapable. Yes, I admit that I am somewhat ignorant of the world, but that is only because I have not had the opportunity to explore."

Cook rolled her eyes at heaven. "You are going to need the help of the Almighty if you hope to see your twentieth birthday! Here, child, eat your food and let's talk of something else. This topic is raising my inner pressure!" She placed the plate of steamed fish and boiled potatoes in front of the slender girl.

Cook smiled at Brianda, secretly admiring the girl's gumption. Cook knew men who would not stand up to the earl as this young girl had done. It was going to be very interesting living with Brianda in the house!

After eating much of the fish and a sampling of the potatoes Brianda smiled up at the large woman and pushed at her plate.

"Brianda, is that all you are going to eat? In a strong wind, you would blow away!"

"Thank you, but this city life does nothing for my appetite. It was delicious, and I promise to eat more at dinner!" Brianda stood and planted a big kiss on Cook's cheek. She turned and pushed open the door leading to the hallway.

Angus stood outside, his arms folded across his chest, and Brianda realized that he must have heard every word she said.

"You ought to be more circumspect, Brianda. One never knows who will overhear your words."

"Don't you know that eavesdropping is rude? Oh I suppose that is your role, spying on me. Well I don't give a damn what you heard or didn't hear. I meant what I said, and you can run right off and tell the earl anything you choose. Now get out of my way! I am going to my room. I am sure you will have a boring afternoon waiting outside my door, but one must follow orders, right?" With that, Brianda pushed past Angus and walked upstairs.

"You would have a more tranquil life, if you followed your orders, young lady." Angus held her gaze and didn't seem in the least bothered by her hostile look. "You have a lot to learn, and I think it will be a rocky road for you."

"Stop thinking, Angus, it might strain your brain."

John cast his partner a weary look over the brim of his cup. They had been in emergency surgery most of the morning and were just now relaxing after the trying operation. A man's leg had had to be amputated after it had been crushed by a heavy crate at the docks. They had almost lost the man, but their skill and quick action had saved his life.

Seated in the well-cushioned leather chairs, John and Paul took long sips of the hearty tea that their nurse had brought them. Still dressed in their surgical garb, they began to discuss matters other than medical cases. Both men were smiling broadly, and every so often John reached over and slapped Paul on the back.

"So, married it will be, and in two weeks' time! After all we have been through, I find it difficult to believe that you are really going to wed! How many women have we dallied with, only to be rescued at the last minute and saved from a life of drudgery?"

"Ah, yes, John, but Elizabeth is different. This is not an affair that has been influenced by alcohol and the comfort of a warm body in the night. Elizabeth is everything I have always wanted. She will be the mother of my children, the only woman of my bed. I am happy, content and excited. Who knows? One day you may feel the same way."

"I sincerely doubt it, Paul. Marriage isn't for me. I like my life as it is, uncomplicated by the whims and demands of a wife."

"We shall see. I must say that I was surprised by the scene you provided for all of London last night. Yours were the actions of a jealous man, the way you punched poor Bristol and then dragged little Brianda out of there like an angry husband. So unlike you," Paul said with a smile on his handsome face.

"Laugh if you choose, my friend. I was not about to let my ward be molested by that bastard. You know very well what his reputation is, and I am afraid that an innocent like Brianda would be clay in his slimy hands."

"So these actions of yours were to save her virtue. Jealousy was not the catalyst?"

"Certainly not. I found the worthless sot, Bristol, kissing her! As her guardian, I had the responsibility to protect her from his advances," John answered haughtily.

"Of course, but in times past, when you had the opportunity to watch a bastard like Bristol try his wiles on an innocent young woman, you sat back and watched, amused. I even remember your waging a pound or two on how long it would take the rake to make his conquest."

"You cannot compare Brianda to those other young ladies! If those young women had no one to watch out for them, then it was their misfortune. Brianda is my responsibility, and I shall see to her honor."

"What a different story it is, then, when the prey is a relative or ward."

"I am through discussing this topic with you, Paul.

We will either discuss your wedding plans, or I will return to the work at hand."

"Very well, your Lordship," Paul said, standing and bowing toward John. Seeing that John wasn't at all amused, he continued, "You are my best friend, and Elizabeth and I want you to serve as my first witness. And Elizabeth would like Brianda to serve as maid of honor. Will you both accept?"

Still frowning slightly, John replied, "I am honored that you have asked me, and I accept gladly. Brianda will have to answer for herself, but I am sure she will be thrilled." John rose and hugged his friend. "I know you will be happy, Paul. Elizabeth is a wonderful woman. I like her very much."

15

Four days following the ball, Elizabeth sat in the Earl of Manseth's library and waited for Brianda. She had not heard a word from her new friend since the embarrassing episode and imagined all sorts of horrors that could have befallen Brianda. When she had asked Paul if she might call on Brianda, he told her that she must wait a few days. He refused to give her any further information, no matter how hard she begged him. At last she was here, waiting to see her little friend.

Hearing of Elizabeth's arrival, Brianda put her book away and flew down the stairs and into the library. She threw her arms around Elizabeth who stood up to greet her and they hugged each other.

"I have been worried about you, Brianda. Are you well?"

"Yes, I am fine. I am so happy to see you, Elizabeth! Please, let's sit down."

"Why haven't you sent me a note or come over to visit me?"

"John is not happy with me at the moment. I thought

it better not to try to visit you at your home until I knew he would allow it."

"Oh, I thought it must be something like that. Paul told me I had to wait several days before I could come over to visit. What on earth happened?"

"It is something that I would prefer not talking about, Elizabeth. You are my dearest, my only, friend here in London, but still I think it would be wise not to discuss this matter. Will you forgive me?"

"It is not a matter of forgiving, Brianda. I simply hope that all is well."

"Yes, suffice it to say that I am always finding trouble right in my lap!" Brianda laughed and hoped that Elizabeth would let the matter drop.

"I am happy that all is well, little friend. Now I can address the topic I came here to discuss with you."

"What?" Brianda sat forward in her chair expectantly just as Stevens interrupted with tea. After he had served, he nodded and left, and Brianda could hardly contain herself. "What, Elizabeth? Tell me!"

"It is not 'tell,' actually, it is 'ask.' Brianda, Paul and I would like to ask that you act as my first witness at my wedding."

Tears of joy filled Brianda's eyes. Jumping up from her chair, where she had been trying hard to act just as lady-like and genteel as her dear friend was, she threw her arms about her confidante. "Thank you, Elizabeth! No one has ever asked me to perform a duty as important as this one. I am honored. I am thrilled and happy to accept." Just then, a frown passed over Brianda's beautiful face.

"Why so worried, Brianda?" asked Elizabeth, genuine concern in her voice.

"Oh, Elizabeth, I don't know if John will allow me to be in your wedding!"

"Why wouldn't he? He could not refuse a request like this from the future wife of his best friend! In addition, he is going to be Paul's first witness. As he will be an official in our wedding, you will, too, my darling little friend. Now, let's dry those tears and forget these small worries and drink our tea. We have so much to talk about. I have the most important day of my life to plan, and I want you to help me do it!"

Elizabeth led Brianda back to the tea table, where the two young women were soon deep in discussions of flowers, fabric, food, and, in the most hushed of tones, the advancing wonder of the wedding night.

The mysterious letter never arrived, and Brianda began to think that it must have been a nasty prank by some of John's friends. As John never mentioned it again, she chose also to let the matter drop.

When forced to be in John's presence, she would not look into his eyes. If he noticed, he said nothing. He spoke to her only of the affairs of the household. As he was frequently gone from the house at meal times, she found herself eating alone often and was glad of it. When they did share the dining table, there was an awkward silence. John did not seem at all uncomfortable in Brianda's presence, but he did not initiate conversations with her as he had in the past.

He allowed Brianda to leave the house with Elizabeth for shopping trips and fittings for their gowns for the wedding. They made forays into many small specialty shops and bought everything they needed to make the wedding perfect.

Jeremy Bristol made the colossal error of calling on Brianda one week after the disaster at the ball and was met in the library by the earl himself. He had thought it well worth his while to give Brianda one more try, as

Lady Smythe's reward still stood and the chit was the ward of one of the richest men in England. However, seeing the look on the earl's face, he thought to himself that this prize was not worth dying for.

"Please excuse the disturbance, my Lord Fauxley," he began in his most polished tone. "I came to offer my apologies."

John's face remained as if carved from solid rock.

Hurrying along, Bristol continued, "I offer my sincere apology for kissing your ward without your permission, my Lord. I am afraid that I lost my good sense when I found myself face to face with her beauty." He looked up to check on the response that his unctuous words produced.

His Lordship looked even more stern.

Bristol felt a shiver of fear crawl up his back. Except for the beating he took the night of the ball, Jeremy had never before been this close to the famous Earl of Manseth. He hadn't realized how tall and broad the earl was, nor how good his physical conditioning was.

Sweat broke out between Jeremy's shoulder blades. He felt it trickle, cold and wet, down his back. "Your ward is lovely, and I assumed by her presence at the ball that she is of courting age. I would like to ask permission to call on her, sir. I assure you that I will behave with the utmost propriety in her presence. Should she someday accept me, I will come directly to you to ask for her hand," Jeremy finished grandly, thinking that he had stated all that very well.

After what seemed an eternity of utter silence, John took a few steps toward Bristol. Jeremy retreated to a safe distance, feeling as if a tall tree were about to crush him. Then out of the corner of his eye he noticed the library door open and a huge man enter the room. Jeremy had heard stories about the earl's bodyguard, but he had never seen the man before. It was a sobering sight.

"Mr. Bristol, the only reason that you are still alive is that you chose to try your wiles on my ward at a well-attended social affair. I find it hard to believe that you have the nerve to present yourself to me like this . . ."

"But your Lordship, it was only a kiss . . ."

"Interrupt me again and your words will lie as dead in the air as your body will on the floor! Understood?"

Unable to respond verbally, Jeremy nodded vigorously. The sweat ran down his back and from his underarms.

"My ward is a decent young woman. She will have nothing to do with slime like you. If you ever come within thirty feet of her again, I will see to it that you will be food for pigs and rats in the slums of London. Do I make myself clear?" John said, taking another step toward Bristol.

"Yes, quite clear, sir."

"You may be lucky enough to leave this house unscathed today, Mr. Bristol." John was rewarded with the glimmer of fear in Bristol's eyes. "You see that man just inside the library door?" John knew that Bristol had seen Angus enter the room. He wanted to reinforce Bristol's fear. "He gets very agitated when he thinks that I am disturbed. I have seen him break a man's neck like a twig and then throw him fifteen feet into the gutter. So as not to irritate my friend any further, I suggest that you depart immediately. After you have left my property, never consider returning. I repeat that not even a nod in Brianda's direction will be tolerated. Any questions?"

"None. May I leave now?" Jeremy asked in a whisper, a definite green tint to his complexion.

"Immediately. And walk swiftly."

Jeremy Bristol fairly flew out of the room and out of the house. He was running hard by the time he reached the street and he did not wait for a carriage, but just kept on running.

John and Angus watched the retreating figure with amusement.

"I beg your pardon, sir, but may I comment on one thing?" Angus asked.

"I would be glad to hear your comments, Angus. Go ahead and speak."

"Forgive me if I was eavesdropping, sir, but I did overhear you tell that man that you saw me break a man's neck and throw him fifteen feet into the gutter?"

"Yes, those were my words."

"I want to apologize, sir, I did not think that you had seen me do that. It was several years ago, and I want you to know that I can control my temper completely now and am always in your service."

"Angus, I have complete trust and confidence in you and your loyalty to me. I told the slime that story to convince him that he had best never consider visiting this house again, or to try to see Miss Breedon under any circumstances. You are to keep that in mind, Angus, and if you should see him, feel free to take whatever steps you must to keep him at bay and away from Miss Breedon and me."

"Consider it done, sir. Is there anything else?"

"No thank you, Angus. Go about your regular duties now."

"Yes, my Lord." Angus bowed his head slightly and left the library. He headed straight for the kitchen. Talking about matters such as Bristol made him very hungry. He knew that Cook had made a couple of apple pies that morning, and he wanted to talk her out of a large piece.

The day of the wedding was cool, crisp and full of winter sunshine. Brianda woke early, so excited that she couldn't sleep another wink.

Upon her return from the wedding rehearsal the previous night, she had put on her new dress twice to make sure it was perfect. And perfect it was. The gown was the palest of blues, almost white, and there were rows of tiny silk roses of a slightly darker shade all over the bodice. The seamstress had fit the dress beautifully over her small breasts and had made her waist look as if a man's hands could encircle it with ease. The imported fabric floated to the floor, where her pale blue slippers could just barely be seen.

John had presented her with a set of two-carat sapphire earrings and a single strand of perfectly matched sapphires for her lovely neck. They had belonged to his mother, and Brianda knew she would have to return them as soon as the festivities were over. They were the most beautiful stones she had ever seen, and they were exquisite with her gown.

As the morning sun peeked through her window, she desperately wished the hours would fly by so that she could dress for the wedding. Suddenly, her eyes widened and she covered her mouth to hold in a giggle. She had the perfect solution to the empty morning.

Brianda knew that John had been out quite late celebrating with Paul on his last night of bachelorhood. He had come home with more than a few drinks under his belt, and she was sure he would sleep late, rising only in time to get ready for the wedding. That meant she had several hours to do as she pleased without worrying about her warden! She put on her oldest riding outfit, hurried from the house and headed for the stable.

Entering through the small side door, she saw the young groomsman, who was busy with his morning chores feeding the animals and cleaning the stalls. Quickly she slipped into a stall with a gentle little roan mare, and in a few moments had her bridled and saddled. Waiting until the groomsman had left the barn for a moment, she led the small horse out the main door and jumped up onto her back. Off they went out the back gate and headed at a brisk trot toward the largest park in

London. There, several men were exercising their horses, and no one paid any attention to her as she eased the mare into a canter. She rode through the park for two hours, careful not to come too close to any other riders. She did not want anyone to recognize her face and tell the earl that she had been riding!

The mare liked the young girl, and together they enjoyed their outing. When the sun had risen high overhead, Brianda decided that she had better return home. She had to be ready to leave at two o'clock.

Turning its head toward home, she let the horse advance from a canter to a gallop for a short while. She loved the way the wind felt as it rushed through her hair. She missed Dakota so much!

As she neared the house, she halted and dismounted, walking the mare the rest of the way home, so that the animal could cool down and resume her normal breathing. Once again within the confines of the earl's property, she was careful to stay close to the tall hedges until she reached the barn. Sneaking into the stable was easy, and she had the horse in her stall and the tack put away in a flash! No one would be the wiser.

Kissing the mare on her velvety nose, Brianda slipped from the barn and headed for the house at a dead run. The servants' door was just as she had left it, unlocked. She hurried up the back stairs to her hallway and entered her room quietly and rang for Ellie.

"I came up about a half an hour ago or so, miss, but I guess that you had fallen asleep again, for you did not answer me when I called out to you," Ellie said.

"You did not disturb your master, did you, Ellie?"

Ellie looked very startled for a moment and answered, "No, miss, I was careful not to bother Master at all."

"That's good, Ellie. Now draw my hot water. I must dress for the wedding now."

"Yes, miss, all is ready for you."

Brianda spent the next two hours bathing, dressing and having Ellie prepare her hair. When she was finished, Brianda looked like a princess. Her blond hair was up on her head like a crown, with small flowers and beads woven into it. Brianda put on the perfume that Elizabeth had given her, and, for the final touch, the sapphire earrings and necklace.

At the stroke of two, John, knocked on her door and inquired if she were ready to leave.

"Come in, my Lord. I am ready," she answered.

John opened the door and nodded his head in her direction. "You look so beautiful that I fear you might outshine the bride, Brianda."

Those were the first personal words he had spoken to her in two weeks. Brianda blushed at the compliment, but still couldn't look him in the eye. "Thank you, sir . . . do you think your mother's gems complement the gown?"

"They look as lovely on you as they did on my mother. Now, we must leave. The carriage is waiting." He lifted his arm, and she slipped her small hand under his elbow to rest it gently on his arm.

Paul and his parents were talking quietly when John and Brianda entered the huge church. All three were struck dumb for a moment when they saw the pair walk into the vestibule toward them, John looking elegant in his black morning coat and black silk cravat and on his arm the petite, beautiful Miss Breedon.

Paul's parents, Mr. and Mrs. Gaylord Martin, were especially honored to have the Earl of Manseth at the wedding of their son. Even though John and Paul had been friends for many years, it was still a showing of marked preference to have a member of the nobility attend a function outside of their circle.

"John, you look more handsome than I have ever seen you before," said Priscilla Martin, taking his hands in hers and lifting her face to receive his kiss on her cheek. Turning to Brianda, she said, "I have been waiting to meet you, my dear. Elizabeth has told me so much about you. You are even more beautiful than she described, Brianda. May I call you Brianda?"

"Yes, please do! I, too, am very happy to meet you, Mrs. Martin. And to meet you, Mr. Martin," she replied, extending her hand to Paul's father.

"The pleasure is mine, Miss Breedon. You are definitely the prettiest young woman I have seen in many a year. And may I add that you are in the best of company. John is a very special friend," he said, nodding toward the earl.

Brianda smiled at the older man and said nothing. How could she tell these nice people that the earl was a rat?

John shook Mr. Martin's outstretched hand, smiling at both of Paul's parents. They had been wonderful to him for many years. He only wished that they would forget his title and accept him as an equal.

Paul stepped forward to hug John and kiss Brianda on each cheek. "I am so happy to see you both! Brianda, please go to the bride's dressing room and tend to Elizabeth. She gave strict instructions that you were to be sent to her immediately upon your arrival."

Brianda smiled brilliantly at everyone and then hurried off to find Elizabeth. John and Paul began checking on the last minute details, while the excited Martins trailed behind them, offering opinions and advice.

At the first strains of the music the assembled guests hushed. All heads turned as the bridal attendants made their way up the aisle. Each young woman was beautiful in her own right, but there was no question as to who was the most stunning.

When Brianda reached the altar, she took her place across from John and looked straight at him. He was watching Elizabeth walk toward Paul on her father's arm. Brianda mused that there couldn't be a more handsome man on the Earth than John. She studied his profile, which she found to be as stunning as the rest of him. For a moment, she felt an intense longing but quickly made herself stop thinking such thoughts that only reawakened feelings of pain and shame. Then she, too, turned and watched the bride walk toward the groom.

Elizabeth looked truly beautiful. Her wedding gown, tiara and bouquet of baby white roses were all designed to enhance her beauty, but nothing could match the radiance of her face, or the way her soft brown eyes emitted love when they locked with Paul's. She proudly took her place next to him, turned and smiled at Brianda and John, then looked once again to Paul and did not take her eyes from him again until they were pronounced man and wife.

The reception following the lovely wedding ceremony was filled with laughter and love. Paul and Elizabeth were the best of hosts, spending precious time with each guest, enjoying their company and thanking each one for sharing in the glory of their day.

The champagne flowed like water in a brook, and everyone overindulged themselves on the plentiful and sumptuous food. The hall was filled with music and dancing couples.

Brianda drank two glasses of champagne while John was engaged elsewhere, and thought she might truly be floating on air. Several young men asked her to dance, and she accepted. It was glorious to be held in a man's arms and guided artfully over the dance floor. The relaxation she felt from the bubbly wine made her carefree and gregarious. Her laughter was sweet and lilting, like a playful flute. There were many men who thought she was the most beautiful thing they had ever seen, and each of them begged a chance to dance with her.

Toward the end of the evening, John asked Brianda to dance, and he stayed as her partner the remainder of the night. She felt uneasy at first being so close to him, but as the music played on and the alcohol continued to relax her, she pushed her thoughts of humiliation and embarrassment to the back of her mind and let herself revel in the music and the fun. Relaxing, she let her head fall softly on his chest.

It was finally time for Paul and Elizabeth to depart, to take their leave of their friends and family and to begin the private life of marriage during a week-long honeymoon trip. Paul had made all the arrangements, and they were a well-kept secret.

Elizabeth hugged Brianda and promised to call on her as soon as she was back in London. Brianda felt a tear fall from her eye as she said good-bye to her dear friend. She was harboring the fear that as a married woman, Elizabeth might not have much time for her anymore. Mad at herself, she wiped the tear away and hugged Elizabeth and then Paul. Holding onto John's arm for moral support, Brianda waved gaily as the young married couple got into their carriage and rode off into the night.

Soon after the newlyweds had departed, John informed Brianda that it was time to leave for home. She was disappointed, as she was having a splendid time, but knew better than to argue with him. She said her farewells to the bride's parents, hurried for her wrap, and waited for John as he said good night to all. He joined her at the main door and helped her into their carriage.

Brianda was gaily babbling away about the wedding, when John said abruptly, "Brianda, did you enjoy your ride this morning?"

Brianda froze in her seat.

"Perhaps you did not hear me. Did you enjoy your ride this morning?"

What could she do? He had found out, so it was useless to deny it. "I had a wonderful ride this morning, sir." Squirming uncomfortably on the carriage seat, she looked at him through the darkness of the unlit carriage. "How did you find out?"

"This morning, when it was discovered that you had taken the mare out without telling anyone, the groomsman quickly saddled a horse and followed you. He was riding just behind you the entire morning. When I arose, I was informed of your outing."

"What has become of the groomsman?"

"Why do you ask?"

"Because you had not given your permission for my ride, I assume that the young groomsman will have been held responsible for letting me leave without your permission, sir."

"He has been replaced."

"What! That is not fair, sir!" she cried out at him, slamming a fist into the seat cushion. "I am the one who broke the rule. I hid from him and slipped out when he wasn't watching. He had no way of knowing if I had your permission or not. Firing him is totally unfair. I should be punished, not him!"

"In my household, I decide what is fair and what is not, young lady."

Brianda said nothing, just clamped her lips together and stared.

"What am I going to do with you, Brianda? I make decisions for your well-being . . ."

"In your opinion . . ."

"Yes, it is my opinion that counts where decisions on your health and state of well-being are concerned."

"One of these days I will make my own decisions, and

no man will have the right to countermand them," she stated firmly.

"Should that day arrive, you will have my blessings. Until then, you will abide by what I say, and if not, you, my dear, will have to learn the hard way that I rule all that is under my care."

"Of this, you keep reminding me. Maybe your rules are too strict and unyielding, sir, and maybe that is why I try to find ways around your dictates."

John had to smile at her bravado. "It is a continuous battle between us, is it not?" he asked, still smiling at her as they rode on in the dark carriage.

Brianda couldn't really see his face, but she thought she could hear the amusement in his voice. This infuriated her even further. "I demand that you inflict your punishment on me, and that the poor fellow get his job as groomsman back. You cannot be that unjust! For all in you that I find unsavory, I have never witnessed your being unjust to any soul, except for me, of course," she finished strongly.

John laughed out loud and kept on laughing.

Brianda felt herself stiffen. How dare he be so amused when she was discussing a matter of serious importance! She wanted to bash his gorgeous face, but it was too dark to spot her mark well. She bunched her fists and pretended to smash his jaw.

"If you recall my earlier words, Miss Breedon, I said that the young man had been replaced. I said nothing of firing him," he answered, as he controlled his mirth.

"You mean he's not fired?"

"I have decided that he is too young for the responsibilities of groomsman, or he would have used better judgment this morning. He is working for me in another capacity. You need not worry any longer about his future." John leaned forward, his elbows on his knees. He was uncomfortably close. "As for you, Brianda, for the next several weeks you will not leave the house, not even for walks in the garden. You will receive no social callers, nor will you attend functions in the evenings. If you disobey me again, I will not hesitate to use physical means to convince you that I mean what I say."

Brianda sat mute, staring out the window. There was no response that wouldn't grant her immediate punishment, so she sat quietly and concentrated on the thought that she had to plan a permanent escape.

16

The carriage smelled like a spring garden, even though it was late fall. Paul had ordered the inside of the bridal carriage to be laden with fresh flowers, for he knew how Elizabeth loved them, and giving her something she loved gave him great pleasure. He had expressed this wish to John a week earlier with regrets that he could not afford the expense of this extravagance, and John offered to provide the flowers as a wedding gift. Paul accepted gladly, knowing this gift would be one of the happiest memories offered Elizabeth on her wedding day.

Elizabeth leaned over and kissed Paul sweetly on his mouth. This was all so very special. When she had climbed up into the fragrant carriage she had entered her own private wonderland. The wedding had been perfect, filled with love, family and friends, and now they were on their way to a new life.

The thought brought her a moment of worry, for she wasn't sure that she could be the wife Paul wanted and needed. She hadn't voiced this concern to anyone, but it troubled her. She had thought of discussing it with Brianda, but she was so young and inexperienced, what would she know of these things? Elizabeth's mother was a sweet, dear woman who never gave much thought to anything more serious than what to serve for dinner. No, Elizabeth had to face this problem alone, learn all she was able and do everything she could to make him content and happy.

Paul looked down at his new wife and felt a new and overwhelming sense of responsibility wash over him. He was no longer accountable for only his own life, now he had a woman who would depend on him and need him for all the years of their lives together. One day they would have children, and what tremendous responsibilities they would be! Their needs would be just as pressing and necessary as Elizabeth's. He wondered if he were capable of the task. He smiled to himself and knew that whatever came along, with Elizabeth at his side, they would conquer all challenges and disappointments. He turned his head and kissed her forehead.

After two hours of travel, the carriage turned onto a private road and jostled gently on down a tree-lined lane. The ground was partially frozen, and the carriage wheels made crunching noises as they passed over it. It was a beautiful night, with the moon shining through the bare branches, casting willowy shadows on the frosty earth.

The carriage slowed and stopped at the door of an enchanting cottage. It was small but well built with large rocks and mortar. Ivy grew all over the walls. Nature's insulation, Elizabeth dreamily mused, to keep all the love and warmth inside and the cold and unwanted outside. The interior of the cottage was well lit, with candles throwing their glow all about the rooms. There were two huge candles with large glass chimneys on either side of the heavy wooden front door. Everything about the cottage welcomed them.

"Have we arrived at our resting spot for the night, Paul?" Elizabeth asked.

"Yes, darling, this is the first of my surprises. This cottage is one of many that John owns. He had it readied for us, and there will be a fire in the fireplace waiting to remove winter's chilly cloak from our backs. There are, however, no servants. Tomorrow morning, the couple that lives here as caretakers will return to prepare our breakfast and help us ready ourselves to continue on our trip."

"Where are we going tomorrow?" she asked excitedly. "Why is it a secret?"

"Why are you so full of questions?" He kissed her cold nose, and without giving her time to answer, jumped from the carriage and helped her to the ground. It had grown quite cold, and she shivered. He turned and walked to the door, pulled a key from his pocket and opened it. Then he scooped her into his arms and carried her inside. They looked around and smiled at how lovely it was. Paul carried his bride directly in front of the roaring fire and held her close. Instantly, she felt warmed and content.

After a few tender moments, Paul returned to the carriage for their valises and gave instructions to the driver to return at ten o'clock the following morning with the provisions they would need for the continuation of their journey. He carried the bags into the house and into the large bedroom. There, another fire was dancing brightly with several large logs that would surely last the night through. A large fireplace screen protected them from falling embers. Everything was perfect.

Paul returned to the main room to find Elizabeth still warming her hands in front of the fire.

"How about some tea?" Paul asked as he reached out to her and pulled her into his arms.

She smiled tremulously up at him and then pushed herself gently away from his embrace. "I will find the kitchen and put the kettle on. It is a cold night, and we both could use some hot liquid to warm us."

She hurried off in search of the kitchen. It was just off the main salon, and was unusually large for a small cottage. It was well-equipped, too, with a big stove and large metal pots hanging on hooks. Several long, large knives were stored in a wooden holder, and as Elizabeth lit the burner, she surmised that this must be a hunting cottage.

She made her way to the walk-in closet and looked around. The kettle boiled and the tea steeping, she wandered out into the hallway and looked in another closet. Rifles, handguns and outdoor clothing were stacked neatly. John had once mentioned that his father had been an avid hunter. Elizabeth went back to the kitchen to check on her tea and thought how lucky the caretakers were to have this special place to live in all year round. It must be glorious in the spring and summer, she thought, as she opened cupboards and looked for sugar. Cups and small china plates had been left out on a small wooden table, along with freshly made biscuits as if their need had been anticipated.

Paul was sitting in a large leather chair with his feet resting on a small stool, gazing at the fire and thinking about what a lucky man he was. He looked up and saw Elizabeth enter with the tray and his heart skipped a beat. She looked so beautiful in the firelight.

He wanted her right then, but knew that he had to control his desires and let things happen slowly. This was not a woman for the night; this was his wife, his woman, and he wanted her to enjoy every minute of her first night with him. So he took the cup that she offered him and sipped while they sat and talked about the wedding and their future. Elizabeth avoided any conversation that pertained to children.

They laughed and held hands. Paul kissed her mouth, and she kissed him back. They sat on the floor and held their feet up to the fire, waiting to see who would be the first to let their feet fall back to the floor. Laughing, Elizabeth gave in first and jumped on Paul's out-stretched legs to knock them to the floor. Paul howled his mock protest and grabbed her, and they wrestled for a few moments, ending up with Paul hovering over her, clearly the victor in the match of physical strength. Exhausted, he leaned against her, and watched the flames lick at the logs.

Elizabeth felt herself grow sleepy and let her head fall gently onto Paul's shoulder. He stood then, and lifted her into his arms, and carried her to the bedroom. Instantly, she stiffened, and he gently placed her on the bed.

She sat up quickly and nervously wrung her hands in her lap. "Your valise is over there, Elizabeth. Would you like me to bring it to you?" Paul asked quietly.

"Yes, please," she answered, unable to look him in the eye. Her eyes were cast to the handmade rug under her feet. Paul carried her suitcase to the bed and placed it beside her.

"Darling, I am going to check the fireplace to be sure that it is well screened for the night. Is there anything else that I can get for you?"

"No, thank you, Paul," she whispered, looking at him at last, her eyes huge with uncertainty.

He smiled at her and then turned and left the room.

The time had arrived that Elizabeth had been dread-ing all day. She knew she was supposed to feel nervous, but she felt more than nervous. Cold terror might not be too much of an exaggeration. Her mother had told her nothing, just waved her hands at Elizabeth and told her that she would perform her wifely duties as she should, but refused to elaborate further. Elizabeth knew nothing. She felt awful.

Paul returned and took one look at her sitting forlornly on the bed and knew that it was going to be a long night. He would have to be a master of patience. She hadn't changed her clothes or washed her face. Instead she was sitting like a statue.

"Elizabeth?" he asked softly.

Her eyes shot up to meet his. "What am I supposed to do now?" she asked, fingers trembling in her lap.

"Why don't you change into your night clothes. It grows a little colder. I will do the same."

"All right," she answered. She rose as if she weighed three hundred pounds and walked behind the dressing wall. She removed her traveling clothes, and then couldn't decide where to put them. Finally she laid them in a neat pile, making sure all her undergarments were well hidden underneath. She kept telling herself that Paul was a physician and had seen many naked bodies in the course of his work. She was sure that hers couldn't be that unusual.

Eventually she emerged in her white silk chemise specially designed by the seamstress. It lay softly over her well-rounded breasts, and three wide, white ribbons crossed and tied at her small waist before the fabric fell straight to the floor. The chemise had a matching robe that Elizabeth was holding together at the middle with both hands. She looked up at Paul and stopped in midstride. He was dressed only in a pair of silk pajama bottoms! She had never seen a naked chest before, neither on a woman nor a man! She felt faint.

Paul took her hand and led her to the side of the bed where he leaned toward her and kissed her. She put the tips of her fingers on his lips and looked into his gray eyes. "I don't know what is expected of me, Paul. Please tell me, and then maybe I won't be so nervous," she pleaded.

At her beguiling innocence, he felt for a moment like a lecher. "All that is expected, my darling, is your love."

"Oh, I do love you, Paul. You know that."

"Yes, I know. I want you to feel comfortable with me, Elizabeth. We will do nothing that makes you feel ill at ease. We have a lifetime to share, and I want you to feel safe and secure, not nervous and upset."

"I do feel ill at ease, but I love you so much, Paul Martin, and I want to be the best possible wife for you. It is just that no one has ever told me what a wife does. Well, you understand, the private things that a man and wife do." She had to look away. She couldn't keep her eyes on his face a second longer. Pushing away from his arms, she stepped away and said, "I have heard stories, but they all sounded awful. I cannot believe that people who love each other as we do, Paul, would be expected to participate in an act that sounds so degrading."

"Your mother has told you nothing?"

"No, she said my husband would teach me all that I needed to know. I am sorry that I am so uneducated in these matters. I don't know anything!" she pleaded, looking to him for direction.

"There is nothing to be sorry about, love, and your mother is correct. Together we will find our secret pleasures and they will remain ours and only ours."

He walked slowly to her, tilted her head up and kissed her. He felt her lips respond to his. They remained standing, kissing for a long time, letting their lips do the silent talking.

He slid his hands up and down the silky fabric and felt her skin, even smoother, underneath. She did nothing to stop him when he lifted the robe from her shoulders and let it fall to the floor.

She was experiencing a sensation of heat, but it wasn't from the nearby fire. She didn't know where it originated. It worried her a little, but she trusted him.

He kissed her neck and let his hands explore her back. Tentatively, she put her arms around him and explored his back in turn. A man's muscles felt so different. They were hard and corded, not soft and pliable like hers.

When he picked her up and laid her on the goose-feather bed, she did not feel afraid. She ran her fingers over the lines of his face, the face she had loved for so long now.

He pulled the chemise from her shoulders and let it glide over the contours of her body as it left her naked in its wake. She felt embarrassed as she lay completely exposed before him. Her legs clamped together, and her arms hugged her sides, as if they were pinned there. She found a spot on the ceiling and stared at it with all her concentration.

"Look at me, Elizabeth."

"I cannot, Paul."

He leaned over her so that his face was only inches from hers, nose to nose. She laughed at the absurdity of the situation. Her eyes found his, and he kissed her.

"I will always want to look at you naked, Elizabeth, as you are now, as you will be when your womb is large and heavy with our child, and even as you will look when you are an old woman, my woman. We will give the gift of our bodies to each other, and they will be received and revered, no matter their shape or condition."

"Yes, Paul. I wish to give you my body, now and always," she answered, looking into eyes that held total love and respect.

Soon he was completely undressed and lying next to her. He studied the length of her, finding delight in all of her hills and valleys, her broad expanses and narrow inlets. She was not yet able to let herself explore him, but she was beginning to enjoy the special and tender touches of his hands and fingers.

When he kissed one of her coral-colored nipples, she felt herself go rigid. He continued his sweet suckling, first one nipple and then the other, and soon she was writhing under him, turning to offer one breast. When the other nipple began to ache, she would twist again, showing him that she needed him to ease the pressure building there.

Paul was aware that she was completely absorbed in his feasting on her precious breasts, and he knew that this was the time to carefully slip a long finger into her moist depth.

She cried out at the surprise intrusion and asked him to stop. Never before had she felt a sensation close to this invasion.

He lifted his head from the honey of her breast and whispered, "Elizabeth, it is all right. Let me touch you like this," he whispered as he glided his finger in and out of her.

She felt herself grow wet around his finger, and the moisture slipped from her body. A strange heat was forming deep and low in her abdomen. Her breathing was becoming ragged. She held onto his shoulders, afraid that if she let go she might rise off the bed and disappear.

He raised himself over her and slid one leg between hers. As his leg advanced upward, her thighs parted, opening the panorama of her private beauty to him.

"Don't look at me down there," she cried out, trying to squirm away from him.

"Why, my beauty?"

"I don't want you to. Please, look at my face and kiss me," she whispered, her voice weak and quavering.

Planting both legs between hers, he leaned forward and kissed her, his tongue reaching all the secret, untouched places inside her mouth. She relaxed a little, and he eased her legs farther apart even as she tried to close them. Then, lowering himself down, he hovered over her, adjusting himself so that the proof of his love and need for her was resting at the entrance of her warm moist opening.

He slipped the tip of his manhood into her. It was uncomfortable for Elizabeth, and she tried to wriggle away from him. Taking command, he moved his hands to her shoulders and held her firmly.

"Elizabeth, I love you and I am sorry if I am going to cause you discomfort. Know that I love you," he said, as he pulled back a little and then plunged straight into her, tearing the fragile membrane from its moorings and continuing on until he was fully embedded within her.

Elizabeth screamed and tried to pull away from the shattering pain, but pushing against his chest did not help. She could do nothing but endure it as tears filled her eyes.

Paul held her and did not move, because he wanted her to become accustomed to the feel of him within her. He kissed the tears from her cheek and cradled her head in his hands. "Shh, Elizabeth, it is all over now. I promise no more pain."

"Why did you hurt me?" she choked out, feeling betrayed.

"I have broken the barrier of your virginity, darling. I am fully within you now, do you not feel me?"

"Yes, and I feel the pain," she cried out to him.

"Do you still feel the pain, now, Elizabeth?" he asked softly.

Concentrating, she discovered that the pain had faded and that all she could now feel was the hardness of him completely filling her. "No, I cannot feel the pain any longer, but I remember it. Why did you hurt me? Is that what loving is?" she asked, afraid to hear the answer.

"The pain of the loss of virginity is inevitable, but once felt, it is lost forever, my darling. You will feel only pleasure from now on."

"I trust that it may be so, sir, for if it is not true, then I will not look forward to our mating in the future," she said stoically.

He smiled and kissed her face, lapping up all traces of the tears. "Let us discover what wonders lie in store for you, Mrs. Martin," Paul said, as he began to move within her. She braced herself for more pain, but felt none. As he began to increase the pace, she felt the return of that hot sensation in her abdomen. His hands were fondling her breasts, and his delicious lips were kissing her mouth, as he continued to stroke the velvety insides of her body, softly and then with fervor. Her breathing quickened. She grabbed his upper arms and held on, knowing that he would guide her where he wanted her to go.

Suddenly, the heat in her abdomen became fire, and it spread as if it were an explosion, traveling through every nerve fiber she had. When she was totally engulfed in the sensation, she stopped breathing for a moment. As it spread upward through her body and out along her arms, she heard herself call Paul's name. Her breathing was so strange, so deep, and her voice so far away that she thought she might have died.

Paul looked down at her and saw that she appeared to be asleep. He envied her this, her first orgasm, and was pleased that he was able to give her this ultimate pleasure. He had been so young when he had his first orgasm, a mere teenager, and it had been over so quickly. Since that experience, he had been with many women, but none had been as fulfilling as Elizabeth. He had been so intent on giving her the ultimate pleasure that he had neglected his own, but knew they had a lifetime before them.

As she slept, Paul cleaned her inner thighs with a warm, wet cloth, so that she would not be frightened in the morning by the sight of the blood. When he was finished, he, too, fell asleep, satisfied and content.

*   *   *

The next morning, they shared their bodies again, and this time Elizabeth felt the hot spray of Paul's seed spill within her. Now she understood the miracle of conception and hoped that she would soon be with child, Paul's child. She had never been happier. She now knew what it was to be a woman.

As they dressed in their warm traveling clothes, each in his own way thought of the days and years ahead of them, and smiled. This marriage was a good one, one that would endure with love and respect.

The Browns arrived that morning and gave the young couple a country feast for their first breakfast as man and wife. When their coach arrived, Mrs. Brown handed Mrs. Martin a basket of food for the day's journey. The young woman smiled as she accepted the gift, glowing with love and pride. Soon Paul and Elizabeth were in the carriage, bundled in warm blankets, and waving good-bye as they started on their day's adventure.

The old couple held hands as they watched the carriage draw away down the lane. Together they walked back into the cottage that had been their love nest for forty years, happy to have shared it, but equally happy to have it to themselves once again.

17

Paul and Elizabeth had been gone for four days, and Brianda was so bored that she could hardly stand it. She had checked every book in the library to see if reading it would be worthwhile and not too time-consuming. Digging through the dictionary every few words certainly took the joy out of reading! She pulled out a couple of John's medical school textbooks and rummaged through them, amazed at how much information John must have in his head.

Soon giving up on that diversion, she turned to the window at the gardens and longed to go to the stable. Even if she were not allowed to ride, she would enjoy grooming the horses, running her hands through their coarse manes and over the velvety softness of their noses.

Desperate, she even took to sitting in the kitchen on the high white stool and watching silently as Cook readied the food. When the older woman could not stand Brianda's sadness any longer, she asked her to fetch something from the potato cellar, then to go and find one of the servants to help her. Brianda was quick to oblige and even offered to help prepare the food. Cook rolled her eyes to the skies and asked what Brianda thought his Lordship would say if Cook allowed his ward to work like a servant in his own house! Finally, Cook shooed Brianda out of the kitchen altogether, as she was not getting anything done with her in the way.

Brianda hadn't spent much time with John; even though he had relinquished much of his medical practice, he was busier than ever with demands of his other business interests.

She noticed, though, that Angus was watching her more now than he ever had in the past. The man rarely spoke to her, but he always seemed to be close, no matter what she was doing.

Just when Brianda thought she could stand the monotony no longer, the door knocker sounded. She ran to the door and waited impatiently for Stevens to get there. His slow, elegant gait drove Brianda crazy, and she wanted to get a pig prod and stab him in his very proper behind. She giggled at the thought and put her hand over her mouth, pretending to cough so that Stevens would not see her laughing at him.

"A letter has been hand delivered for the master, miss, so if you will excuse me and move your small body out of my direct path, I will take it to him," Stevens announced in his most tolerant tone.

"Oh, how wonderful. Maybe it is an invitation to a ball!" Brianda moved to the side to let Stevens pass, then followed on his heels right into the library. John did not see her enter, and as Stevens passed the large brown leather chair, she slipped behind it and hid there, just dying to know what was in the letter.

John took the letter and dismissed Stevens, who closed the door behind him and returned to the loathsome job of polishing silver. He did not give a thought to where the young mistress had gone.

John opened the letter and read it in complete silence. After a few moments, she heard his foot stomp down on the wood floor. She jumped, but silently.

"Bloody hell," he swore quietly. "Angus! Come in here," he ordered. Angus was in the door and standing in front of John's desk within seconds, so anxious to answer his master's call that he failed to see Brianda hiding behind the chair.

"Yes, my Lord?"

"I have just received a very disturbing note. It was hand delivered a few minutes ago. I am to meet someone at ten o'clock tomorrow morning on a very important matter. I have been instructed to attend this meeting alone, but I want you to go ahead of me and station yourself inside the tavern. Be sure to conceal your identity as you have in the past. I will tell you the name of the establishment and directions to the tavern tonight after dinner. Brianda is not to know anything about this, understood?"

"Clearly, sir. But who will watch over her while I am gone, sir?"

"That is a good question. It is not an easy assignment, is it?"

"Sir, it is astonishingly difficult!"

"Yes, well it is too bad that Elizabeth is still off on holiday, or I would ask her to come over while we are both away. I must be careful, for the little vixen can charm just about anyone! I will have Cook see to it."

"Yes, my Lord. I will talk with Cook myself and make sure that she understands just what she needs to do to keep an eye on the lassie."

"Thank you, Angus. You may go."

"As you wish, sir."

Following Angus's departure John got up and paced

around the room. Brianda, terrified that he would see her, pressed herself as close to the back of the chair as she could. John, however, was concentrating so hard on the content of the letter that he did not notice her.

Brianda was worried. She had to find out what was happening! She heard John go to the desk and pull open one of the drawers. It seemed to her that he had slipped the letter into the top desk drawer. That was a break; she could wait until he left, go to the drawer and read the letter.

Just then, John gathered his papers, placed them neatly on the corner of his desk, grabbed his coat and left the library. She heard him call to Angus and heard the big man's footsteps as he hurried to join his master. Brianda ran quickly to the window and pulled the drapery back enough to see them as they walked down the path toward the stable to get their horses.

Brianda immediately ran to the desk and pulled on the drawer. Locked! Damn him! She pulled and pulled, but still could not budge the drawer. Frustrated, but undaunted, she left the library. She would have to keep her eyes and ears open tonight at dinner to see if she could uncover a clue.

At dinner that evening Brianda sat quietly and ate her food. She was surprised to see that Angus had joined them. It was a rare event when he joined them for dinner, and he considered it the highest of compliments, attending in his best clothes. John smiled at the show of formality, but respected his friend too much ever to let the Scotsman think that his master had been amused at his expense.

The two men discussed estate business for most of the meal. It occurred to John that Brianda had been exceptionally quiet, and he looked over at her to see that she was sitting upright, just looking at her plate.

"Are you ill this evening, Brianda?"

"Why no, sir, why do you ask?"

"You are extraordinarily quiet tonight and I must say it is disquieting. Have you perpetrated some escapade of which I am not yet aware?"

"What could I have done, sir?" she asked with wide, innocent violet eyes.

"Just thinking of the possibilities is enough to take away one's appetite."

"I have done nothing. I was just listening to you discuss the matter of the new stock for your properties in the north."

"Really?"

"Yes, I find the whole thing quite interesting."

"Since when have you found mundane estate matters interesting?"

"I have decided that as I will be the lawful owner of Cliffshead Manor when I come of age, I had better pay attention when you discuss such matters with your consultants."

"I see."

"Have you learned any new information that could contribute to your decision regarding the purchase of three new brood mares for Manseth Manor?"

"No, I am inclined to think that it remains a good purchase. What is your opinion, Brianda?"

"One needs to think of the future, and keeping a well-defined stock is of great importance," she answered haughtily. She raised her chin and looked at each man, and noticed that Angus hid his face behind his napkin so she would not see his smile.

"That was very well stated, Brianda. I wonder if you came up with that idea all on your own," John responded, one eyebrow raised.

"Well . . . to be truthful, those were almost exactly

the words that my father kept repeating to my brother Edward during their evening talks. I listened at every opportunity, so that if my father ever questioned me, I would be ready with a good answer." Brianda gazed softly, living in her memory. "He never asked me though . . ."

"I am grateful that I asked your opinion, and I will consider doing so in the future, if you continue to show interest in business matters."

"Truly, sir?" she asked, amazed.

"Most truly, Brianda. Now ring the bell and tell Cook that we would like our dessert."

Brianda rang the bell and asked the uniformed servant to serve their desserts. It was one of her favorites, bread pudding, and she ate it with gusto. Never before had John shown any interest in her opinions, and she felt as if she had grown a few inches.

On finishing dessert, John turned to Brianda. "Will you please excuse us, Brianda? Angus and I have some private matters to discuss. You will go to your room now. Thank you for your charming company this evening."

"The honor was mine, sir, sharing the company of two elegant gentlemen," she said demurely, as she placed her empty tea cup on the tray and left the room without another word or glance at either of them.

Angus and John exchanged bewildered looks and returned to the business at hand. Brianda had reached the stairs and started up. She knew that John could see her from where he sat in the dining room, and she caught him looking at her out of the corner of his eye as she walked up the steps. Her plan was to walk sedately up the stairs, and then quickly double back and listen at the dining room door.

She heard the chairs as they scraped on the hardwood floor. They were getting up and leaving! Craning her neck, she could just barely see them as they walked toward the library, entered and closed the door firmly behind them. Fine, this change was not going to stop her! She would wait a few moments, then slip down the stairs and find a spot very close to the library door. She stood at the top of the stairs and made herself wait until she counted to one hundred, then headed down to find the perfect spot to spy on her guardian and his confidant.

"Ah, and there you are, lassie. I have been looking for you," said Cook, slightly out of breath. "Would you like me to draw a bath for you tonight? All the other servants are busy with a special project for the Master, so I was asked to see after you."

Brianda drew in a long breath to stave off her irritation. Smiling up at the old woman, who Brianda knew was not to blame for foiling her plans, she said, "No, thank you, Cook, I won't be bathing this evening. I think I shall read a little, and then go to bed."

"I will just see you to your room then, miss. I want to know you're all settled in before I go to my room."

"No one else is this thoughtful, Cook. I can see myself to my own room."

"Oh, no, miss. Master's orders. Come along now, dear. I am tired and have much to do in the morning," Cook said, holding out her hand to Brianda.

Defeated, Brianda grabbed the outstretched hand and walked to her room. She reached up and kissed Cook good night on her leathery cheek, then pushed open her door, undressed and hurried into bed.

It was a cold night. Huddled in the center of her bed, covered with blankets and her comforter, she set about making her plans for the next day. It was definitely possible that she could glean a bit of information from one of the servants. She would try that, and maybe she could find the key that would open the locked drawer.

* * *

Angus left the house at nine o'clock in the morning, and John left at nine thirty. John had taken breakfast in his room and had remained there until he was ready to leave. He had tied a small revolver to the inside of his right ankle, as he was certain that this meeting was not going to be a pleasant one.

Brianda had knocked on John's door and had been politely shooed away. He had cupped her small chin, assuring her that he would meet with her upon his return and would be happy to discuss anything that she had on her mind then. He had noted the concern in those incredible eyes of hers, eyes that appeared almost purple in color when she was worried. He had smiled to reassure her and had then gently closed the door in her face!

Doubly frustrated, she had stomped off only to run straight into Cook.

"What, you again, Cook?"

"I am afraid so, miss. Master has asked that you stay with me in the kitchen this morning. You are not to leave the kitchen and are absolutely forbidden to leave the house. Now do you understand, girl, for I am not in any mind to be dealing with any of your shenanigans today. I have a lot to do, and have never yet been late with Master's dinner. Let us go to the kitchen now," Cook announced as she began her way down the stairs.

If Brianda had a nail, she would have bitten it in two, she was so angry. Now she had a fifteen stone cook for a nanny! Furious, she followed Cook's ample bottom down the stairs and into the kitchen.

John arrived at the Quail's Feather Inn at exactly ten o'clock. It was a run-down, dirty tavern in the slums of

London, just like a hundred other hellholes where watered-down liquor and very young, used girls could be had at any price.

John pushed the door open and stepped inside, then had to wait until his eyes adjusted to the dim light. He scanned the room and let his eyes pass right over Angus as if he weren't there. Angus was well disguised. The only thing he couldn't hide was his size, and that was the one factor that kept the curious away. Not seeing anyone he recognized, John went to the bar and waited. After a few minutes, he was tapped on the shoulder, and a rough, raspy voice invited him to join the party in the back room.

John followed the large man into a small, foul-smelling room at the back of the tavern and spied Edward Breedon waiting for him at a small, broken-down table.

"So it is you who sent that very interesting note, Breedon. I must say that I was intrigued. I am anxious to hear the news that is guaranteed to arouse my ire."

"Won't you sit down, my Lord, and have a drink with me and my friend, Biff Blanders? I have been waiting for quite a while for this meeting, and I am relishing the moment. It isn't often that one of you aristocrats gets a nasty surprise, is it?"

"I'll decline the drink, thank you. It is too early for me, but please, enjoy yourself. I am most interested in hearing what you have to say," John said with undisguised distaste.

"What's the hurry, old man?" Breedon snapped, and let his eyes lazily scan the earl's attire. "Before we get into it, how is my little sister? Biff tells me that she has developed a sweet, young body. Biff liked having his arm around her waist, wanted to touch more of her, didn't you, Biff!"

"Yes, sir! I would like to have a hand at that one,

Edward!" Biff smiled an evil grin that allowed dark-colored spittle to run out of the corner of his mouth. He wiped it away with the sleeve of his filthy coat.

John regarded the large man with disgust. Turning his attention back to Breedon, he stated, "Your sister is fine, Breedon. She remains my ward. Now what is it that you wish to tell me? If there is nothing, I will be on my way." John stood up.

"You will not be wanting to leave before you hear what I have to say. It affects my sister, too," Edward said with a smirk.

"Speak then, man."

"All right. It is going to give me great pleasure to watch your face when you hear this," Edward said, rising from his chair and striding across the small room. "You know many things that I don't know, sir. Why, you are a fancy, rich lord. You have done wonders with the country properties. I have heard all about it. But there is one thing that you don't know." He stopped speaking and stared at the earl. "My father loved and respected only one woman in his life. That was my mother. When she died, my father swore that no woman would ever own his properties. I have the only copy of his will, and it states that if there is no male heir—and I do not qualify, thanks to your interference—the property will be sold before a female can inherit. Furthermore my father put a time limit on the transfer of ownership. That time is up this Saturday coming, my Lord. Cliffshead Manor will be sold on Saturday, and I have friends that have already made inquiries regarding price and disposition of the property. There is also a clause that states that the land will not be sold to any member of the Fauxley family, my Lord. You see, my father did not like his neighbors, either!" Edward burst into a raucous, harsh laughter. "Too bad, old man, all the trouble you went to, you won't ever get my lands. Only by marrying my sister could you get control of my father's properties." Edward walked to the table and stood a few feet from John. "Too late to marry her now, not that you would want the snit any-way, but even the high and mighty Earl of Manseth could not pull off a wedding in three days' time! Oh, and there is one more small matter you will find of interest. I have gone to the local magistrate and con-fessed to having had some . . . wild younger days. I have convinced him that I have repented and found God. In my personal turmoil, I lost all my lands. Now after suffering these tragedies, all I desire is to be reunited with my orphaned little sister. I am now able to provide for her and want to care for her until she reaches majority. The magistrate felt compassion for my plight. He thinks it was wonderful of you to take over her care while I rehabilitated myself, but now he is in agreement that I can care for Brianda. I will have all the legal papers the day after tomorrow, relin-quishing her to me, and there is nothing you can do to stop it."

"I find this all very interesting, Breedon. I will believe you when I see the legal papers."

"Have Brianda ready to leave with me on Friday morning. I will be at your London town house to pick her up. I will have all of the legal papers at that time. You will be sorry that you put your nose in my business. By the time you are able to get legal help, I will be out of the country with my sister and her new husband, Mr. Biff Blanders. You see, Blanders here may not look like much, but he has a great deal of money and he has offered me a large sum for her. She had better still be a virgin, or I'll have you up on morals charges, my Lord," Edward spat at him with hatred. "Revenge is sweet, sir, and I have enjoyed immensely arranging all of this behind your back."

"You have been very clever indeed, Breedon." John sat back comfortably in the small wooden chair. He did not appear upset.

"It is too late for you and for sweet, little Brianda. Now that you have heard me, get out of here! Have my sister ready for me, and don't try any tricks, as I will bring the authorities with me. The law is on my side, Fauxley. Get out!" Edward sneered.

Blanders had risen and stood menacingly in front of John. "I can't wait to taste the honey of the girl, my Lord," he said slowly. Edward and Biff burst into laughter and threw their arms about one another.

Without a word, John got up and left the room, closing the door on the two men still overcome with mirth. Signaling to Angus, John then left the tavern. On the way home, John gave Angus a long list of things he needed done, and Angus at once hurried off to do John's bidding. John then entered the house and sent for Brianda.

Brianda ran down the stairs and rushed into the library. All excitement died on her lips when she saw the grim look on John's face. Fear flooded the pit of her stomach. Something was terribly wrong. Frightened, she sat down and waited for him to speak.

"Brianda, we have shared serious conversations in the past, but this will be the most serious. You must listen without interrupting me," he stated, looking straight at her.

"As you wish, sir."

"Two important factors have become known to me today. The first is that Cliffshead Manor is to be sold in three days' time . . ."

"It cannot be sold! I am the rightful heir. I just have to wait until I am eighteen, and my birthday is in only a few months!" she wailed.

"I was informed today that your father placed specific instructions in his will regarding heirship. No matter your age, you could never be the legal owner of his properties."

"That is a lie! Who told you these lies? My father was never kind to me, but he would not do such a thing to his own blood!" she said, disbelief fueling her anger.

"He has done just so, Brianda. They were his properties to do with as he saw fit. This decision cannot be challenged."

"I don't believe a word of this. Who told you these lies?" she repeated, standing and taking a step toward him.

"Sit down, Brianda," he demanded.

She remained standing, challenging him.

"If you wish to hear another word, you will sit down. Now!"

Brianda sat.

"These things were told to me by your brother."

Brianda grabbed the sides of the chair. "Edward? I thought he had left England. What does he want in this? He is no longer eligible to take my father's lands, is he?"

"No, criminals by their own admission forfeit their rights to own lands. He is back for another reason . . ."

Brianda felt lightheaded for a moment. She had lived for so long without the threat of Edward's brutality. Now that he had returned, the threat of his cruelty was a reality once again. "Please tell me the rest," she pleaded, looking at her hands in her lap.

"Edward has paid an official of the court to allow him to regain guardianship over you, Brianda," John stated in a quiet, calm voice, watching her carefully. "The legal papers confirming his rights over you will be ready on Friday, and that is when he intends to come for you."

Brianda tried to stand, but her legs would not hold her up. She sank back into the chair. "Are you going to let me go?" she whispered, still not looking at him.

"There is only one solution, Brianda, and that one solution will solve both problems."

"And what might that be, my Lord?" she asked, half afraid to hear the answer.

"Marriage, Brianda."

18

"*Marriage? Whose marriage,* sir?" she asked, genuinely surprised.

"Your marriage, Miss Breedon."

"Me? And why would marrying anyone help me?" Brianda sat back in her chair and thought for a moment. "Well, I can see that if I were married, Edward would not have any claim to me. I would be the responsibility of my husband, correct?"

"Correct. Also, were you to marry, then all properties that you are entitled to would become the property of your husband. Cliffshead Manor would remain yours, yours and your husband's. Edward has arranged some shady deal with friends of his, and they are going to try to buy Cliffshead Manor on Saturday. I am sure that Edward plans to conduct some of his illegal business there." John's expression remained grim as he considered the predicament. "The letter I received yesterday was from Edward and his friend, Biff Blanders. Do you know him?"

"No . . ." she said uncertainly.

"Perhaps he was the one who gave you the message," John suggested. "A large, odorous man? His voice is gravelly and rough," he went on, still observing her.

At the unsettling description Brianda jumped from her chair, startling both of them. Walking quickly to the window and back, she implored, "Oh God, what will become of me? What am I to do?" she cried out to him.

"Marry."

"Who on earth would want to marry me, and in two days' time?" she anguished.

"I will marry you," he stated calmly.

Brianda stared at him as if he had suddenly lost his mind. "I am so astonished. I do not know what to say to you, Lord Fauxley," she said, sitting once again and holding on to the chair for all she was worth.

"Say nothing. It is done. I have sent Angus to make the arrangements. We will marry Friday morning, at Manseth Manor. Your brother has underestimated my wealth, power, and connections. He will arrive for you here in London while you are marrying me in the country. Once you are my wife, he will never be allowed to see or visit you, nor will you ever have to live with the threat of his violence again. As soon as we are married, your properties become mine instantly. By law, Cliffshead Manor will be saved, and so will all of the villages and their people."

"There is one problem, sir. We do not love each other. I cannot marry under those circumstances," she finished hotly.

"I am afraid that you have no choice, Brianda."

"How can you sit there and discuss my future, my marriage, so coldly, as if it were a business deal?"

"Brianda, you have no other solution to this very grave problem. You are under age, you have no money, you will lose your family home, and you will be subjected to Edward's tyranny."

"No! I will not do it. You cannot force me. I . . ."

"We will argue no longer, Brianda. It is decided. We will leave for the country just after noon tomorrow. Go now and pack. I have affairs to attend to," he said, waving his hand and dismissing her.

"You can take me by force to the country and stand me up in front of the priest and witnesses, but you cannot make me say 'I do'!"

"Once again, Brianda, you will do as you are told. Now stop acting like a child, and go and start readying yourself for the trip," he said, piercing her with his dark blue eyes.

Bursting into tears, she screamed at him, "I hate you! I hate you! I will never do what you want me to do! I will make your life miserable!"

"Then miserable we will be. Go now before I lose my temper with you. I know that all of this has been a shock, but we simply do not have time to discuss it any further at this moment."

Unable to stop the flood of tears, Brianda ran from the room and up the stairs.

Much later, as she lay on the tear-soaked pillow, Brianda thought over all of the implications. As she had no choice, she would go through with the wedding. By sacrificing her future happiness, she would save Cliffshead Manor and all the people she loved in the village and throughout the countryside. Their lives would continue on as they had for decades.

As the wife of an earl, Edward would have to leave her alone, and that thought was reassuring. Though Brianda was not willing to live a life without love, she wasn't worried any longer. She had a plan. . . .

Brianda piled her hair on top of her head and fastened the flat bun with several long pins. She placed her plain cap over her head and dressed herself in the boys' clothes she had owned since her early teen years at Cliffshead Manor. Making her way to a small side door, she slipped out of the house and was at a dead run within seconds and on her way to the seamy side of London and the docks.

She hurried along the wharf, looking for signs that one of the huge sailing vessels was being readied for departure. Finally she spotted one, the *Maid of the Green*. She boarded her and asked to speak to the first mate. After she waited a long ten minutes, he approached her and introduced himself. Without standing on ceremony, she asked to book passage for herself and her horse.

"Are you fooling with me, lad? You want to sail by yourself, and you wish to bring a horse?" he asked suspiciously.

Lowering her voice and keeping her head down, she repeated her request. "I want to sail Saturday morning with you, sir, and I will be transporting my horse as well."

"As well as what, lad?"

"As well as myself, sir. May I ask what your first port of call is, sir?"

"We are going to make port in Edinburgh, Scotland first, lad. Is that where you are going?"

"Why, yes, sir, yes it is. Scotland. That is fine. How much will it cost for my horse and me, booking passage one way to Scotland?"

"That will be ten pounds for both of you, in advance. That will buy you a cabin and the horse a nice area below decks."

"How many weeks does the journey take, sir?" she asked anxiously.

"Depends on the winds. From a couple of weeks to more than I'd like to think about, lad. Do not fret, we'll get you there. Now, we sail Saturday at morning tide, just about daybreak. We'll not wait for you, lad. The captain's a tough one. He gets real angry when we are held up. Understand?"

"Yes, sir, I understand. Here are the ten pounds. May I have a receipt?"

"A smart young one. Are you sure you are old enough to be going off to a new land? Does your family know?"

"I have no family, just my horse, and being smart makes me old enough to go."

"Right you are, lad. I will see you before the sun rises on Saturday."

"Thank you, sir."

Brianda headed for home as fast as she could move. Oh, the earl was going to have a wife and his new properties to own and lord over, but the wife would never be his to own and lord over! She had taken care of that.

The household was in an uproar at the unexpected departure of the earl and his ward. Cook and Stevens would be traveling with their master, as they always did. All of the servants had been informed that they were to behave normally, so that to the outside world, life would appear to be continuing on as usual at the earl's home.

If Edward or Biff were watching the house, John wanted nothing suspicious to tip them off. Brianda was packed and waiting when John returned at Thursday midday. He ate luncheon. She did not. Finally, when John completed all of his paperwork, and his business associates had departed, he announced that the time had come for them to leave.

Their carriages were waiting for them across the park. Angus had taken great care to provide secrecy, and they reached the carriages without being noticed. Angus rode behind the carriages on his stallion.

Brianda spent the entire ride from London to Manseth Manor watching the road. John thought she was just trying to avoid talking with him, but in reality she was paying very close attention and making mental markers for her return trip with Dakota. She was trying to calculate how long it was taking them to travel from London to Manseth Manor, and how much time she would need to cover the distance on horseback. Brianda had never made a trip alone before, but that did not deter her. It was her only escape from this farce!

Arriving at Manseth Manor gave Brianda more of a thrill than she had thought it would. Old Megan and Mrs. Brady were waiting to receive them. Both women started talking at the same time, and Brianda had to laugh, hugging them in turn. They walked arm in arm into the house, chattering about London and the wedding! She couldn't tell them the truth about the marriage, so she played along with the lie that she was madly in love with the earl, and that they could not wait any longer to wed.

Brianda's wedding day arrived cool and clear under a brilliant blue sky.

At early daylight Brianda sneaked out of the house and hurried to the barn. She took Dakota from his stall and led him to the spot far from the house, where she tethered him for the remainder of the day. She made sure he had plenty of rope, so that he could graze and wander about during the long hours that he had to wait for her. She also tied to the tree several small parcels that she would be taking with her on her journey. Then she kissed her black stallion on the nose and hurried back to the house.

Old Megan arrived early, so that she could help Brianda with her bath. The old woman's eyes filled with tears as she watched Brianda bathe. She had become a woman in the last few months. Her body was beautiful, ripe and unspoiled except for the scars on her back. Most of the lash strokes had faded with the exception of two severe indentations, but they were far down near her waist. Megan handed her lovely girl a towel and chuckled to herself, thinking how the earl was going to have his hands full even though his lady was but a slip of a girl.

Early in the morning a servant brought a large box with a small envelope on the top to Brianda, but she showed no interest in opening it. Old Megan handed the card to her and Brianda slid her finger under the seal and pulled out a handwritten message.

May you wear this dress and be as beautiful in it as was my mother when she wore it fifty-five years ago. May you be as happy in your new life as she was in hers. Love, John.

Brianda's eyes filled with unexpected tears. How could he be so cynical, yet sound so sincere and caring in his note? What a hypocrite!

Old Megan lifted the lid off the top of the box and gasped in surprise and joy. Inside was the most beautiful wedding dress Old Megan had ever seen. She lifted it out and showed it to Brianda. Tiny seed pearls covered the entire bodice of thick white satin. It had long lace sleeves that stopped at the wrists with a double row of real pearls! The white satin skirt fit snugly to the hips and then fell gracefully to the floor, and from beneath trailed a train of gorgeous Irish lace.

Old Megan helped her with her underthings and held the dress as Brianda stepped into it. It fitted to her slender form as if it had been made expressly for her.

Looking at her form in the mirror, Brianda felt a rush of tears. She was glad that John's mother was not here to witness this farce, to see her cheapen the beauty and meaning of this lovely dress.

Biting her lip, Brianda turned toward the window under the pretext of checking on the weather and wiped the tears from her eyes. She wondered if she would ever marry again and be able to experience the joy of a bride who is marrying a man she loves. She doubted it. Those thoughts belonged only in fairy tale books.

"Come on, girl, stop that daydreaming! We have much to do and only a little time," chided Megan from across the room. "Come here and sit down, so that I can start fixing your hair."

Brianda slid the dress off and sat down in front of the mirror, waiting for Old Megan to begin.

"What's this look of sadness, girl? This is a special day, the most special in any young girl's life, and you look as if you were about to be led to the gallows!" Megan accused while brushing the long, golden strands of hair.

Brianda forced herself to smile. "I was just thinking of my mother for a moment, Old Megan. I am sure you understand."

Hugging Brianda from behind, Old Megan nodded her head in understanding. As she was arranging Brianda's hair, she tried to bring up the subject of the wedding night, but Brianda seemed totally uninterested. Old Megan felt a moment of alarm. Maybe his Lordship had already taken her! Why, the girl had never been shy in asking the most pointed of questions before, so Old Megan assumed that Brianda already knew what was going to happen between her husband and her that night. Old Megan watched the young woman's face in the mirror and decided that his Lordship could never have done such a thing. The girl was just nervous and wishing for her mother. That was only natural.

The truth was that Brianda had no intention of being within miles of her husband on her wedding night.

The whole village had been invited to the wedding. Large notices had been placed all around the county by John's staff. The neighboring gentry all arrived, thrilled to be invited. It was not often that an earl got married in the country!

By midmorning, the day was unseasonably warm and sunny. The estate's chapel was very old, with a high ceiling and beautiful stained-glass windows. For decades his Lordship allowed Father Whitesmith to use the chapel for Sunday services, holidays and occasional weddings and baptisms.

Volunteers from all over the county had come to help in the washing and cleaning of the old chapel for the wedding. When they were finished, the chapel shone brilliantly. Some of the women wove intricate wreaths from boughs of evergreens and used them to decorate the stone walls and floor. Father Whitesmith thought, as he looked around him, that in all his years tending his flock, the chapel had never looked more beautiful than it did this day of the earl's wedding to young Brianda Breedon.

The gentry were escorted to their places first, and then the doors were opened to the villagers. Those who couldn't fit into the chapel looked in through the doors and windows. This was an important day, indeed, when the common folk were invited to take part in their master's wedding! Many had come to share in Brianda's glory, for she was well remembered for all of the kindness and love she had offered to anyone in need.

*   *   *

At precisely eleven o'clock on Friday morning, Edward Breedon, dressed in the remnants of his best clothes, walked sedately up the stone pathway to the Earl of Manseth's London home. He politely lifted the door knocker and knocked three times.

Biff Blanders, hidden within the confines of the rented carriage, peered out the window at the stately home of Lord John Fauxley. He was salivating so much at the thought of the beautiful Brianda Breedon, that he had a hard time not letting the saliva run from the corners of his mouth and down his chin. Not wanting to scare the little thing off, he swallowed hard, but felt the stuff begin to fill his mouth again. She would just have to accept him as he was!

After waiting a decent amount of time, Edward let the knocker fall three more times, but with more force. Finally, the door was opened, and a slight wisp of a woman looked out from behind the large wooden door to ask, "Yes, sir, what can I do for ye?"

"Please tell Lord Fauxley that Edward Breedon is here to see him," Edward responded in his most cultured voice. He was fairly jumping out of his skin at the prospect of taking Brianda away and handing her over to Blanders while Fauxley watched!

"His Lordship, the Earl of Manseth, is not at home. Good day," the servant woman said, and began to close the door.

"Hey, wait a bloody minute, madam!" Edward yelled at her, pushing against the heavy door with all his might. The door swung open, forcing the woman to fall backward.

"Help! Matthew! Phillip! There's a bloke trying to break in here!" she screamed at the top of her lungs.

Within seconds, the two men came running, each holding a large rifle in his burly arms.

Edward raised his hands to stop their advance. They stood four feet from him with the rifles held at the ready. "Get out of this house before I bash your head in with the butt of this rifle, mister," Matthew growled at Edward.

"There must be some mistake. I am Edward Breedon, and Lord Fauxley is expecting me this morning. Please tell him that I am here. We have legal business to conduct."

"His Lordship is not at home and left no word that he was expecting anyone. Now leave, or we will shoot you in the legs and then drag you to the authorities," Phillip warned.

"I have important business with the earl!" Edward screamed. "If you do not fetch him at once, I will go for the authorities myself!"

"Please do so, sir. I am sure that they will be very interested in hearing that you forced your way into this house and refused to leave. Lord Fauxley has many powerful connections, sir, and he will not hesitate to use them when his home is threatened."

"Well, I have connections, also, and I will be back. Tell Fauxley that I will be back!"

"In that case, sir, we will be sure that his honor, Lord Heath, First Magistrate of the Royal Court, will be notified of your appearance here, and that you claim to have legal business with his Lordship. His Honor Heath takes charge of the earl's business personally when his Lordship is absent from home."

Edward blanched. He wasn't sure that his bribe to the local magistrate would pass the scrutiny of a first magistrate of the Royal Court. He backed out toward the front door. "No need to summon Lord Heath, gentlemen, I am leaving. When I have my papers in order, I will return. When is his Lordship expected back?" Edward asked as civilly as he could.

"We have not been authorized to give out any information, sir. When you return, give your name at the front gate, and one of us will meet you there. You will not be allowed in this house again until it is directly ordered by his Lordship."

"Very good," Edward said, raising his chin to maintain a modicum of dignity. He turned to leave and heard the large steel bolt slide into place as the door closed at his back. "Bloody hell," Edward spat. That damn Fauxley wasn't going to get away with this!

19

John Fauxley, the Earl of Manseth, walked slowly from his house toward the family chapel along a path bordered on both sides by identical evergreen bushes. He meant to enjoy his last minutes of single life walking the familiar ground that now led him to a new life.

He gave no thought to how handsome he looked as he towered over the men he encountered, stopping to shake hands with each and engage in the brief conversations. His black hair shone like polished onyx in the late autumn sun, and his eyes were the color of the deepest blue sapphires, flawless and rare. His black morning coat was of pure wool and cut perfectly for his body, and his black trousers fit snugly to his well-muscled legs. The black leather boots rose to midcalf, and his white silk shirt was tied at the neck with a black silk scarf that had just a hint of red flecks in it.

Several women felt twinges of jealousy as they watched him stride toward the chapel, and could not help but wonder what special charm the Breedon girl possessed to have conquered his heart. There were those who had predicted that he would never marry. Why, he was said to be past thirty, and no one had won him yet, even though many a good woman had tried.

John stopped just inside the double wooden doors to admire the beauty of the chapel. The sun shone through the stained-glass windows, creating a pastel hue that floated above the heads of all inside.

He continued on down the aisle, stopping to shake the hands of all those who offered congratulations. A few of the villagers curtsied and offered brief stories of their fondest memories of Brianda. He smiled and thanked them for sharing their treasures with him. When, at last, he reached the front of the chapel, he turned and smiled at all who had gathered there. A few young and hopeful hearts were broken at the sight of the handsome man standing so tall and strong, welcoming everyone there to his home and wedding.

With Elizabeth and Paul still on their honeymoon, Angus was chosen to represent John and hold the wedding ring. The two men stood at the altar, and as the music started, turned and looked down the aisle.

Brianda was ready outside the chapel's double doors. When the music began, she reached over and grabbed Stevens's arm. The very proper servant was magnificent in his role as substitute father. He walked her slowly, so that all could see her incredible beauty, her grace. The wedding dress flowed with her small steps, and the train floated behind her, as if she had angel's wings. Her violet eyes shone with a spectacular hue that drew all attention to them. In her ears and around her neck, she wore a matched set of emeralds and diamonds. John had given them to Stevens to take to Brianda before she left the house to make the walk to the chapel. They were her wedding present from John, and she steeled herself to remember that they would draw a good price when she needed to sell them to finance her new life.

Stevens stood with her as the priest asked who was giving this woman to this man. With his cultured voice, he proudly announced that it was he and the rest of the staff of the Earl of Manseth who offered this lovely young woman to the earl in the presence of God and all these witnesses.

At the words, guilt overwhelmed the young bride, making it difficult to control her emotions. Taking a deep breath, she forced herself to look up into John's eyes.

What she saw there unnerved her. It almost looked like love. Telling herself not to be a ninny, she smiled dutifully. He smiled back, and for a moment she was lost. He was so breathtakingly handsome that she felt her heart skip, and then noted a strange, warm sensation deep in her abdomen. She recalled the last time that he had made her feel that way, and she looked away from him in an effort to hide her weakness.

John took her hand and turned them both, so that they were standing directly in front of the priest. Father Whitesmith read from the Bible and the chapel fell silent.

Brianda didn't hear a word. When it came time for her to repeat her vows, John had to squeeze her hand to get her attention. She repeated the words mechanically.

Father Whitesmith then asked John, "Do you take this woman as your lawfully wedded wife?" John answered, "I do."

When Brianda was asked if she accepted John as her husband, to love, honor and obey, she froze. She couldn't say yes. She was silent. Here she was swearing this oath in God's house in front of all these people! Could she be such a liar? Troubling thoughts flew about in her head, making her dizzy. Everyone was waiting. The priest repeated his question. She swallowed, looked at John and at the priest and said in a whisper, "Forgive me, but," and then in a loud voice, "I do."

Smiling, Father Whitesmith said, "I pronounce you man and wife, and what God has joined, let no man put asunder. You may kiss your bride."

Brianda stood next to John in the grand salon of the manor and shook hands and kissed cheeks for what seemed an eternity. She was being congratulated by people she had known all her life, and she felt like such a traitor. Some had brought handmade gifts. How could she leave all that behind?

A huge feast was arrayed on several long tables. There were platters of roast beef, turkey and pork, trays of fresh fruits brought from London, and countless dishes of potatoes and salads. Cook had stayed up all night making the three-tiered wedding cake. There were places for each person to sit at elegantly draped tables. Wine and punch were available. All the guests ate and drank knowing that they would remember this day for a long time to come.

Brianda, however, did not eat one bite of food, nor did she drink any champagne. Thoroughly unnerved, she thought she would never survive the toasts and the cheers. Finally they cut their wedding cake and offered some to their guests.

The musicians began to play, and John danced the first dance with her. To the guests, they looked like a dream come true as he led her through the strains of the beautiful waltz.

Brianda was secretly getting very concerned about the time. The reception was taking much longer than she had anticipated. She felt herself becoming disoriented. Friends would ask her questions, and she would just stare. When the questions were repeated, she tried to think of an answer that would serve, but at the same time would cut the person off, so as not to have to talk any further. She was becoming very nervous, worried that she wouldn't be able to sneak away as she had planned. It was a long, hard ride to London, and the *Maid of the Green* would not wait for her if she were delayed. She began to perspire.

John left her side for a few moments to talk to Father Whitesmith. He was in deep conversation, when he was approached by Old Megan. "Forgive the interruption, Doctor, but I am quite worried about my lassie," she said in a low voice, so as not to attract attention. John turned his head immediately in Brianda's direction and studied her. Indeed, she did look very pale, almost ill. He excused himself to Father Whitesmith and began making his way to Brianda across the room.

Brianda was panicked. She was losing too much time. She began breathing fast and shallowly, and put her hand to her throat as if it would help her breathe more normally. She told herself sternly that she had to remain in control, now more than ever. Suddenly her legs wobbled. Blackness started from the outside of her vision and moved slowly toward the center, terrifying her. Her head fell slightly backward, and just at that moment, she felt John's arms go around her. As he lifted her up into his strong arms and held her close to his chest, the blackness took her completely.

Silence fell on the crowd as the young girl fainted into her husband's arms. John looked down at her beautiful face and said aloud, so that all could hear him, "Do not be alarmed. Brianda is fine. I am sure that she did not eat this morning, and as soon as I get some food into her, she will be bright once again. We will join you as soon as we can. Please excuse me now, while I tend to my wife. And please continue to enjoy yourselves."

John carried Brianda into the small breakfast room and laid her on top of the round wooden table. Old

Megan was right beside him and he ordered her to bring him some punch and cold towels.

Brianda stirred when a cold towel was placed on her forehead and another at the back of her neck. She opened her eyes and looked at John's face. She was confused. Where was she? Had they been married yet? Oh, yes, it all came back to her. She had to get up quickly, so that she could find the opportunity to get away! She tried to raise herself, but John held her down firmly. "I don't want you to try to get up yet, darling."

Darling? Who was he trying to fool? "I feel much better now, sir. I would like to sit up. I am so embarrassed, please," she begged of him.

"All right, let's try it slowly. If you feel dizzy, I will lay you down again."

John helped her into a sitting position. Her head swam a little, but she forced her eyes to focus.

"No dizziness?"

"I am all right, thank you," she lied. "May I have a small drink?"

"Old Megan has some punch for you. Drink it slowly. Did you eat breakfast this morning, Brianda?"

"I don't remember. I don't think so." Smiling her most innocent smile, she looked up at him. "That may be why I felt faint. I did not eat dinner last night, either. Jitters, I guess."

"This ought to put you right in no time. When you feel well enough, I will take you back into the main salon to prove to our guests that you are alive and well!"

"I feel well enough now, John. Please take me in to them!"

"Are you sure? Perhaps a few more moments of rest."

"No!" she fairly yelled at him, "I am ready now. Enough time has been wasted already."

"That is a strange way to put it—*wasted time,*" he said, searching her face.

"Forgive me, sir, it is just the excitement of the day. Let's go in to our guests now," she said, as she slipped down from the table and straightened her dress. "I would like to thank you now for the use of your mother's dress. I felt honored that you would think your mother would have been pleased to share this lovely gown with me. And the earrings and the necklace . . . They are much too beautiful for someone like me, but I thank you for them with all my heart. You cannot know how much they mean to me," she said as she walked away from him toward the salon where the wedding guests were waiting.

"You are welcome on both counts," he said to her back, as he followed her down the hall. "I wish my mother and your mother had been able to be here to celebrate this day with us."

Brianda felt as if he had stabbed her in the back. "What a nice thought, sir. I will long remember that you said that to me."

"You are speaking very strangely tonight, Brianda, and not really making much sense."

"This has been a day to be remembered, sir, and maybe I am trying to take it all in."

"I understand that, and you don't have to call me 'Sir' anymore. Call me John. I am, after all, your husband."

Brianda felt the hair on her arms prickle. "'Sir' fits you, sir. I will call you both names, depending upon my mood," she answered haughtily.

"So be it, Lady Fauxley."

Trying hard not to ruin everything, Brianda smiled at him through clenched teeth and made her way quickly around the room to see to it that everyone knew she was fine. The story that she hadn't eaten for almost twenty-four hours spread quickly and all were relieved that she was much improved.

Genuinely revived by the food, she joined in the merriment. The music played on, and couples began to dance. It was a strange sight, the poor and the monied folk all dancing on the same floor.

But it was late, and Brianda had to leave. John was busy talking with Stevens when she approached him. "I am going upstairs to rest for twenty minutes or so and change my clothes. I will join you here in a short while."

"I will look forward to seeing you again soon, my love," he answered, and before she could move away, he put his arms around her and kissed her soundly on the mouth. She couldn't fight him; too many guests were watching the newly married couple, and she was his wife. But she did not kiss him back, merely waiting until he was finished.

"Are you rejecting my kiss, Brianda?" he asked mockingly.

"Of course not, sir. I simply don't feel comfortable doing something so intimate in front of a large group of people."

Laughing, he sent her on her way upstairs. Once in her room, she had the wedding dress off in a few moments. She placed it carefully on her bed and put the train on top of it. Then she took off the jewels and lifted the loose board in the floor where she had hidden her money and important papers. Stuffing all of it into a small leather pouch, she tied it around her rib cage, where it would remain until she needed it. In a small satchel she put a few clothes. She put on the boys' clothes, put her hair up, tucked it into her hat and pulled on her boots. Looking about her room one last time, she sighed.

She was leaving people she had grown to love, and it was possible that she would never see any of them again. Tears sprang to her eyes, and she angrily brushed them away. This was no time for maudlin thoughts.

Being as quiet as she could, she locked her door and opened the window. Grabbing the rope that she had left there, she slid down the roof to the tree. On the ground in seconds, she ran toward Dakota and freedom.

Dakota was prancing about, anxious. First he smelled her, then he heard her. He whinnied his hello, and she called out softly, running to him. She hugged his massive chest, letting his strength and power give her confidence. "We have a long way to go tonight, boy, so let's go." Brianda jumped up on his back, secured her satchel and turned his head toward London.

Dakota ran at a steady pace, and she was careful not to overexert him. Every so often, they would walk a while before resuming the faster pace. He was a big animal, and young, so he was able to cover the distance much faster than the heavy carriage. She rode down close to his neck, so as not to make it harder for him to cut through the wind. She was so pleased with the amount of distance they covered, that she stopped at an inn and rested in its stable where she took an hour's nap.

By now, it would have been discovered that she was missing. She hoped that it wasn't too embarrassing for the earl to explain her absence to his guests, but she could not waste too much sympathy on him, not after what he had done to her. He could soothe his hurt pride looking at ownership papers for Cliffshead Manor. If all went well, she would be far from England before any of them had a clue to her whereabouts.

Brianda and Dakota arrived in London half an hour before sunrise. They made their way through the busy docks and found the *Maid of the Green* just as the sun was rising.

Cappy Bowles, the first mate, saw the young lad and his horse at the gangplank waiting for their turn to be boarded. He scratched his gray beard. He had been at sea since he was a young boy, and he had seen just about everything. This was another of those strange passengers. The lad sure looked young, and the horse was pure quality. Cappy hoped the animal wasn't stolen—that would be all he needed, having the young one sought after by the authorities.

He went down and supervised the loading of the horse. To Cappy's relief, the boy handled him well and he was convinced that the two belonged together. The horse was quickly settled into a pen and was content with his water and feed.

"Come with me, lad, and I will show you to your cabin."

"Thank you, Mr. Bowles," Brianda said in a low voice, keeping her head bowed as she followed him up to the next deck.

"This is your cabin, lad. Captain told me to give you this one. Don't ask me why."

"What is the matter with it? Is it awful or small or something?"

"Quite the contrary, have a look."

Brianda couldn't believe her eyes. The cabin was well-appointed, with furniture crafted from solid oak. It smelled like a man's room. "Whose cabin is this, Cappy?"

"No one in particular, lad. Make yourself at home. Your meals will be brought to the room. You wouldn't want to eat with the crew. They are a bunch of salty dogs and have no manners at all."

"Thank you, but do I have to pay extra for the service? If so, I will eat with the crew."

"No extra charge, Captain's orders. You may meet him in a day or so."

"Captain's orders? Why would the captain make special arrangements for a stranger, Cappy?" Brianda asked, for the first time looking up at the kind, older sailor.

"Don't rightly know, lad, but it is better not to question the captain when he gives an order. If you need anything, call on me. I bunk just a few doors down. See that door with the carved half-moon on it? That be mine."

"Thank you for your kindness, Cappy."

"Aye, laddie, you're welcome. I'll be off now."

Cappy walked off scratching his beard, thinking that it was strange indeed that the captain had taken such pains with the small passenger. But it wasn't his place to question, and he headed topside.

Brianda had only her small satchel and small leather pouch, so there was nothing much to unpack. She had thrown a simple dress, underclothes and shoes into the bag. She would need feminine things when she looked for work in Scotland. She had no idea what she could do to earn a living, but knew how to care for animals and could clean a house if she had to.

After a half hour or so, the ship set sail. She had been aware of the gentle swaying of the ship ever since she had stepped aboard, but this was different. Her stomach rolled and then settled down, and she prayed to God she wouldn't be seasick.

She sat in the middle of the mattress, hoping the bed would sway less than the floor, and raised herself up on her knees to look out the porthole. It appeared that they had not yet left the harbor. Then the huge ship lurched again, and Brianda fell back to the mattress. Exhaustion finally claimed her, and she curled up in a ball beneath the coverlet and drifted off into a deep slumber.

Brianda didn't know how much time had passed, but she awakened with a start. The ship was swaying steadily now, but that wasn't what had alerted her.

She had heard something! It was the scraping of metal on metal. She sat up and listened intently. Some- one was turning a key in the lock. She still clutched the key that Cappy had given her. Were there two keys to her cabin, and, if so, who was trying to get in? She wanted to scream, but paralyzed with fear, she sat and watched the handle of the door move down. Without another sound, it swung open, and standing in the doorway was the silhouette of a large man!

Brianda felt herself turn cold. Catching her breath, she asked, "What do you want here?"

There was no response. The man stood there silent, unmoving. She could not see him clearly, for the late morning sun was shining through the portholes and casting a strong glare. Why was he just standing there?

She didn't know what to do. Suddenly her folly dawned on her. She was a petite woman, alone on a ship filled with men. God knows what they might do to her. She shrank back against the wall. "Who are you and what is it that you want?" Fear was evident in her voice.

"Have you forgotten me already, Lady?" the man asked, as he stepped into the cabin and closed the door behind him. She heard the sickening sound of the key turning in the lock, sealing her inside with him.

20

"*You! What are you* doing here?" Brianda cried.

"I missed my wedding night . . . and so, I have come for you now," he answered in velvety soft tones.

"This cannot be! How could you possibly have found me?"

John did not answer, but walked toward her, stopping at the side of the bed. She couldn't take her eyes off his face.

It was an unreadable mask, and tentacles of fear wrapped around her heart. He reached down and pulled the cabin key from her fist.

"I will keep both cabin keys, Brianda, as I don't want to wake and find that you have locked me in the cabin," he said, pocketing the keys in his heavy winter cloak and hanging it in the closet.

"Please answer me, sir. How did you find me? How did this happen? I must know," she pleaded, dropping her eyes to the coverlet.

"After all our time together, Brianda, you continue to underestimate me. Do you not remember that I told you that you were not to leave the London town house without my permission or without someone to accompany you?"

Defeated, she replied, "Yes, I remember your orders."

"On the day that I informed you of my meeting with your brother and our impending marriage, you left the house dressed in boys' clothes and went to London harbor, seeking a ship to take you away."

Brianda stared at him, shocked.

"Angus was returning from an errand and saw you leaving the house. Without hesitating, he followed you to the ship. There, he watched you make your deal with the first mate and then leave again for home. As soon as he was sure you were safe in my house, he returned to the ship and inquired about you. Afterward he returned and informed me of your plan. I also came to the ship and spoke with the captain to make further arrangements. That is why you are now quartered in the captain's cabin, your food will be delivered, and you are safe."

"I would just love to know how you accomplished all of that, sir! I don't think ship's captains just give up their own quarters because some gentleman asks them to," she said, her voice dripping with irony.

"They do when the gentleman owns the ship, Brianda."

"What!"

"I own this ship and several others. When I explained to the captain that I had an eccentric young wife, and that I needed him to go along with all of your plans, he willingly agreed. He also offered us this cabin on our voyage to Scotland."

"Our voyage! You plan to travel to Scotland, too?"

"Yes."

Brianda clapped her hand to her forehead. "I don't believe this. You bastard! You knew all about this since Wednesday!"

"I'd watch your mouth if I were you, young lady."

"What for? How much farther into a mess could I get? You let me make a fool of myself at the wedding, and all the while you knew my plan. Tell me, if you knew everything, why did you permit me to leave Manseth Manor and make a fool of you in front of your friends and all the guests at the wedding?" she demanded.

"I was curious to see how you planned to carry out your escape. At first, I thought the fainting spell was contrived, but then discovered that it was genuine. Have you eaten today, by the way?"

"You are abhorrent, sir, feigning interest in my health."

Ignoring her caustic statement, he continued, "After you had gone upstairs to change from the wedding gown to other clothes, I ascertained immediately that you had left the bedroom. I waited for half an hour and then made quite a show of calling all of our guests together to tell them that you and I had planned a secret honeymoon getaway and that you were, at that very moment, waiting for me in my carriage. With a huge smile, I told them that we were about to run off to an undisclosed place for a week or two of holiday, and that we both thanked them all for doing us the honor of attending our wedding. All the guests were offered our home for dancing, food, drink and merriment until daybreak, and everyone thought it was the most romantic thing they had ever heard," John said, as he pulled his wool jacket from his shoulder and hung it on a rack in the closet.

He turned back and looked at her. "Angus and I followed you, I on horseback and he in a carriage. He needed the carriage to transport our luggage. I was on horseback, as I didn't want you to get too far ahead of me. I was afraid that something might happen to you on the road, and I wanted to be close behind. I caught up with you at the inn where you stopped to rest. I had to hide in the forest, so that you would not see me, and when you mounted to leave, I was right behind you. I must say that your stallion is a magnificent beast. He is very fast and has amazing stamina. You two beat me here by a good half hour."

"This must have been some funny joke to you, my Lord. I feel like a complete fool. I thought I was well rid of everything to do with you," she said resignedly.

"It was no joke, Brianda. You have a great deal of spunk and determination. Had I not been aware of the whole plot, had I not discovered you missing, and then found you, I guarantee you that my attitude about this would have been very different."

She did not at all like the tone of his voice. "If I had had better luck, you would not have found me."

"I would have found you, Brianda, no matter where you went, or how far you traveled, and when I did, I am not so sure you would have been happy to see me," he said, his voice hardening.

At his threat, she drew away from him. "Indeed, I am not happy to see you now, sir."

"I am not happy with you, either, my dear."

"Well, what are you going to do? Beat me? It is well within your rights as my husband."

"I am well aware of my rights," he said, as he approached her and sat down on the side of the bed.

"Then get on with it," she said with courage that she really did not feel at all.

John raised his hands to unbutton his shirt and Brianda cowered, raising both hands to her face in an attempt to shield herself from the blow.

"Brianda," John said, his voice softening, "it is not my right to beat you that I am interested in."

"What then? Surely you are very angry with me," she said, coming out from behind the shield of her hands and looking at him expectantly.

"There are other things that a husband can demand from his wife. Do you know what I am referring to?"

"Yes, I think so, but those rights do not apply to us, sir," she stated flatly.

"Oh? And why not, may I ask?"

"I thought this was to be a marriage in name only. I did not want to agree even on those terms, but you showed me that I had no other choice. I think that your marrying me to help the villagers was a kind thing to do, but you did gain all of my father's properties as recompense, sir. However, you will not have access to me as you do to my family's lands," she said, pushing herself off the bed and brushing past him. She walked to the center of the room and, with her back to him, said, "I want to leave this room now. Please open the door."

"No."

"What do you mean, no?"

"Brianda, you are my wife and you will do as I wish."

"I will not be ordered around for the rest of my life, wife or not!"

"You will do as I say and that is that. Come here."

"No."

"Will you come here, or do I have to come over there for you?" he said confidently.

"If you come for me, I will fight you. I warn you now that I will not come willingly," she said, backing away from him.

John stood, noted the determination in the young woman's eyes and walked slowly toward her.

Panic rose in her throat. What could she do? He was so much bigger and stronger than she. Her words had no effect on him. She was a small animal that was cornered, and she was going to have to fight for her life! Backed into a corner, she stood ready to fight him with her fists.

He stopped when he saw the small hands raised in defense. "So, you feel the need to protect yourself from me. Am I so threatening, unjust and cruel? What I have done in the past has been for your own good, and I have no intention of changing the ways in which I deal with you. We are married now, and we should try to make a good life together." His calm manner served only to infuriate her.

"You hypocrite!" she yelled at him. "I would rather die than give myself to you. I was taken under your spell once, and you humiliated me. That will not happen again!" she shrieked as she watched him with wary eyes.

He stopped advancing and started to remove his shirt. "What are you doing?" she demanded.

"Getting ready to bed you," he replied, throwing the shirt into the corner.

"You are despicable. None of this has any real meaning for you. It is all just a lark. Well, I am not willing to play along."

He stood, half naked, not saying anything.

She could not help but look at him. He was dressed in his tight riding britches and tall black leather boots. His shoulders were broad and muscular, and his chest was covered with a mat of black curly hair. He looked the way she imagined a pirate would look, and pirates were decidedly dangerous and untrustworthy.

He started toward her again, watching her every move. She backed up until she touched the wall. Frightened and angry, she had no choice but to try to get around him. She dashed to the right, but his arm caught her and pulled her to him. She cried out as her body slammed into his. Fighting and kicking, she tried to free herself. Even so, he managed to lift her into his arms, all the while trying to keep her feet away from his body. When they reached the bed, he threw her down forcefully. The free fall startled her, but in just a moment she was rolling quickly to the right to try to get off the bed. He grabbed her and pulled her back to the center of the bed, and then sat on her! His hips straddled hers, and soon her hands were pinned over her head.

Looking up, she spat at him. "I hate you! I wish I were a man. I would kill you for this!"

"You will not hate me for long, sweetheart."

He transferred both of her wrists to one hand and with the other grabbed the top of her boys' shirt. With one strong yank, he split the shirt in two halves and threw it to the floor.

She gasped at the violence of the action.

He unraveled the wide piece of elastic that she had wound around herself to flatten her breasts. She was naked to the waist, and he feasted his eyes on her. She closed her eyes and thought of all the ways she would like to torture him. She felt him undo the top button of her long pants, felt him slip his hand down inside until he was able to lift and remove her pants and pantalettes in one motion. Her shoes and socks were flipped up into the air, landing in odd spots all over the floor. He raised himself off her hips and lay alongside her so as to inspect her whole body.

She felt her cheeks grow hot and clamped her legs together, swearing to herself that she would rather die than open them to him. "I will never be yours willingly, you bastard."

"Such words from such a beautiful mouth," he said as he leaned over and kissed her. At her attempt to bite him, he squeezed her jaw, forcing her mouth open. The pressure of his fingers hurt her fiercely, and she moaned a low, sad protest.

He kissed her slowly, slipping his tongue into her mouth, exploring. The stiff short hairs of his chest rubbed against her nipples, causing them to harden and ache. She tried to pull her hands from his grasp, but gave up after a few moments, knowing that her efforts were futile.

She wanted to die. Tears sprang, hot and heavy, and slipped down her cheeks to run into his mouth.

At the taste, John raised his head and looked at her. "I wish these were tears of joy," he said, as he kissed them off her cheeks. "As I know they are not now, I know they will be soon."

She couldn't respond, wishing she were somewhere else. But there she remained, captive, unwilling.

Softly, he nibbled on her bottom lip, then moved his lips and tongue down over her chin and onto her neck. He stopped and nuzzled her there, drawing circles with his tongue in that sensitive place at the base of her throat.

Brianda forced herself to remain still, not wanting him to know that he was affecting her, but she could not stop the clenching and unclenching of her hands.

Then, when he moved his head to her breast, she moaned aloud. He opened his mouth and drew the rosy nipple into the wet warmth. He sucked gently, immediately creating a spot of intense heat deep in her abdomen. She writhed under him, trying to move away. He moved his mouth to the other breast and circled the areola with his tongue, slowly moving inward until he was making tiny circles at the tip of the nipple.

She bucked beneath him. Unable to retreat from his tongue, she cried out in a husky whisper, "Please, stop. Don't do this to me."

As if deaf, John continued his exploration of her. He moved his free hand swiftly down and traced the spectacular landscape of her chest and rib cage. The maddening hand then dipped down to her waist and made large circles over her abdomen, as, all the while, he transferred his mouth from one begging breast to the other.

Brianda was beside herself. Once again, he was lighting the fires that she had hoped would remain banked forever.

She waged a fierce battle against the sensations, concentrating on ugly thoughts to distract herself, but when John would touch a new place, a spark would ignite and burn hotly.

John felt her respond to him and knew she was losing her inner battle. He had all the time in the world, and knew that eventually he would win. Her heart, beating regularly and rapidly under her ribs, was just beneath his mouth, revealing to him her true state of arousal.

He lifted his tongue from her breast and dove immediately into the tiny pool of her navel. There he tasted the delicious ring and caused the heated spot deep within her to erupt. He slid his hand down and played with the triangle of dark-blond hairs, pulling softly on them.

"Please, no more. This is unfair! I don't want you to do this to me," she implored.

"I know, but I cannot resist you and I won't," he replied, his need for her evident in his deepened voice.

"My feelings . . ."

"Hush, love, concentrate on my touches, nothing else."

As he finished his sentence, he slipped one finger into her tight, warm sheath. Brianda moaned deep in her throat. Carefully, he slipped a second finger into her, and she tensed at the uncomfortable sensation.

"You are tense, love. Don't tighten your muscles against me. It will be less uncomfortable."

She cringed at the intimacy of his words, and a sob of helplessness escaped from her throat.

She was dry still, so he moved his fingers in and out of her, his mouth alternating between her breasts and the swollen lips of her tender mouth. She tried moving from side to side to stop his invasion, but she was unable to impede him.

He let go of her hands then and lifted himself up to straddle her again. Braced on his arms, he moved backward, so that he was kneeling at her knees. With his hands, he pushed her legs apart and placed his knees between them. Immediately, she tried to clamp them together, but they were held apart by his strong thighs. Very slowly, he spread her apart.

Oh, God, he is looking at my body, there. I will die from the humiliation! Please, God, take me now, before anything more happens, she begged silently.

He watched as his fingers rode within her and felt himself grow harder than he had ever sensed before. He had to wait longer. She was not yet ready. Keeping his fingers within her, he lowered his head and placed his open mouth at the top of the mound of her womanhood, and with his tongue found the small bud of ecstasy. He took it between his teeth and sucked ever so gently.

Brianda's hands flew to his head and grabbed large handfuls of his hair. Pulling upward with all her might, she tried to get him off of her. He did not try to stop her. Faster and faster he circled and sucked on her, causing her to cry out, to arch her hips against him. He kept up a fast rhythm with his hand and felt her wetness seep through his fingers and slide out of her.

The spot deep in her abdomen was more than hot now. It was aflame, and the blaze was growing. She was confused and frightened. Overwhelmed by all the new sensations, she was unable to sustain further resistance.

His fingers repeatedly hit the barrier of the taut but delicate membrane that declared her virginity. When it did not give against the pressure he exerted, he knew that he was going to hurt her, but he could do nothing to prevent it.

He rose and stood at the end of the bed. With fear-filled eyes, she watched him as he pulled off his boots and then his britches. He stood straight and magnificent, revealing to her his obvious desire, as his manhood rose stiff and bold in the cool air of the winter morning.

The sight of it terrified her. She roused herself from forced acquiescence and pushed herself backward with arms that had barely any strength left in them. "Please, do not come near me again. I can stand no more. You are too tall, too broad . . . too large for me, sir."

John could see the fear on her face. He looked down upon her with a gentle understanding of her plight. It was not fair to allow her to suffer her fears any longer, and he moved quickly onto the bed and pulled her beneath him.

She tried desperately to push him away as she clamped her legs together and held them so, with all her might.

He inserted one knee between her legs and began forcing them apart. She groaned aloud as she exhausted the last of her strength. He was too strong for her. Her legs gave way and parted. Soon he had them spread wide, then he lifted her knees to make her more open to him.

Brianda cried out from deep within her. With his body looming over hers, she felt as if she were about to die. She scratched wildly at his chest as she tried to maneuver her body out from under him.

John raised up on his arms, holding himself over her. He felt himself rub against her wet, velvety lips to moisten himself for entrance, then slipped inside her ever so slightly. Brianda bolted at the intrusion. It was too big. He moved his hands to hold her hips and entered her further, stopping at the gate of her innocence.

She looked up at him, fear distorting her beautiful face, pleading with him to halt.

"Forgive me, love," he said, as he withdrew and then thrust forward, rupturing the delicate membrane and forging forward until he came to rest at the depth of her femininity.

Brianda screamed. Her hands pushed hard against his abdomen as she tried with all her strength to force him out of her, to lessen the awful, searing pain.

She was convinced that her body would not be able to expand sufficiently to hold him without being damaged. In a state of panic, she beat her fists against his chest and scratched at his face, trying to hurt him as he had hurt her.

John held her and did not move within her, knowing he had to wait for the pain to subside. "Brianda. Brianda. Hush, love, do not fight so. It is just hurting you further. Stop, now," he said softly into her ear.

She was afraid. His tender words confused her. Why would he speak thus, if he only wanted to cause her harm? Overwhelmed, defeated, and exhausted, she could no longer hold back the tears. They flooded her cheeks as great, wrenching sobs came from deep within her. Too weakened to resist, she let him cradle her in his arms and sought comfort in what seemed to be the haven of her tormentor.

He held her close and whispered loving reassurances into her ear. She felt him hard and unyielding within her, but the pain was receding. As her nostrils filled with the wonderful scent of him, she wondered, vaguely, if it were finally over.

John felt her relax somewhat and slowly began to move again. She tensed, and her fingers dug into the muscles of his back. "It is all right, Brianda, the pain is over, and it will not return. There is still more for you to learn about making love, and I want to teach you all of it," he said, his voice still heavy with desire.

It had been so hard for him to wait, but he had controlled himself. He was well experienced in the art of lovemaking and knew that he had to give it more time. He took command of himself, as his desire mounted anew and he felt the need to take all of her.

Brianda thought she could not stand any more. How could he make her suffer so? With the strength she had left, she called out to him, "Leave me. Have you not done enough?"

"Not quite enough, darling, but soon you will discover what it is to be a woman, to know the pleasure that a man can give a woman, and it will have been worth your momentary discomfort."

"I hate you," she spat at him.

"Still? I think soon you will not."

Any passion, any tenderness that she had felt was instantly gone. The hot rose of passion in her abdomen had changed to ice, cold and unforgiving. She felt him move, sliding back and forth in the slick wetness of her inner sheath. If there was pleasure there, she did not feel it. Her mind was closed.

John, finally overcome with his need to have her, began moving more quickly, thrusting deeply, long and hard. Faster and faster he went, until he was beyond stopping, until he felt the fiery tingle of confirmation. Within seconds, he was spilling his seed deep inside her. The first contraction, the second, the third, all glorious. He cried out his pleasure and fell heavily on top of her, his breathing still rapid and rough. He felt as if he couldn't move, so great was his satisfaction.

Brianda lay beneath him as would a corpse. She felt the warm fluid as he filled her, and coldly, hoped it signaled the end of this horrible experience. And when he collapsed upon her, she knew that, at least for now, his lust was spent.

21

John rolled over onto his side, carrying her with him. Still inside her, he wrapped one leg over her, proclaiming his ownership, and fell soundly asleep. She reached for the tousled sheet and pulled it up over both of them. By the angle of the brilliant sunlight pouring through the portholes, Brianda assumed it was midday. She could hear the shouts of the sailors as they went about their tasks on the decks above them. The *Maid of the Green* was well under way.

Brianda was trapped in the cabin of a ship at sea with a man she detested! He had brutalized her and now he slept as a child would, completely relaxed, his powerful hands curved into soft fists. The helplessness of despair fell upon her, and with the burden of her feelings came the temporary relief of sleep.

When the young bride lifted her head once again from the pillow and looked about the room, the sun was much lower on the horizon. She cautioned a glance at her husband. He was breathing slowly and deeply, obviously in heavy slumber. She watched his nostrils flare with each breath. Sudden warmth suffused her entire body, and for a brief moment she wished she could love him. She traced the outline of his face with her finger. It was so smooth over his temples and so rough where his beard began. Then her eyes settled upon his jaw, and recalled the steely, unyielding set to it whenever she confronted him. And she was going to have to spend her whole life under his authority! *This cannot be,* she cried silently to the ceiling of her prison.

Carefully and extremely slowly, she extricated herself from him. He moved in his sleep, pulling the sheet with him, and her heart almost stopped when she thought he would awaken, but he settled down into slumber once again.

Searching, she located all of her clothes where they had been thrown so carelessly to the floor. She could use everything except her shirt, which had been torn in two. His fancy shirt would have to do.

Sitting up, she inched her way to the side of the bed. She was sore deep inside, and moving her legs caused her discomfort. She looked down at her inner thighs, and her eyes widened and her stomach constricted. Her flesh was streaked with dried blood! This was not her time of the month. Something terrible must have happened to her when he abused her.

At that moment, her spirit gave way. Her brother's beatings had been bad, but now she was damaged in her very core. Dispirited she slipped onto her feet and grabbed her clothes. In a moment she was dressed in the boys' pants and her boots, then she found his shirt and pulled it on. It was so big that her fingers didn't even stick out at the cuffs. She rolled up the sleeves and went in search of the keys to the cabin door.

Suddenly, there was a major shift in the ship. Brianda was thrown down to the floor and slid on her bottom all the way to the wall, where she landed with a thump. She glanced quickly at the bed to see if the noise had disturbed John. He slept as before.

Heavy winds were buffeting the ship. She pulled herself up and looked out the porthole. A winter storm had come up, and the ship was rocking violently over the cresting whitecaps. Brianda stood for some moments, watching the awesome power of nature. For some strange reason, the thought of a storm did not frighten her. Instead, it gave her more confidence.

In the closet, she found the keys at once, just where he had left them in his cloak pocket. She tucked her long hair into a bun and put on her cap, not wanting to draw attention to her gender. Satisfied that she was well enough disguised, she turned the key and felt the lock give. The first step in freeing herself was accomplished!

She opened the door slowly, casting a furtive glace over her shoulder at the still sleeping earl. Then she looked up and down the corridor, and seeing no one, closed the door silently and locked it from the outside. Now she had both keys, and the bastard rogue was locked inside!

As she moved along the corridor, she could hear the shouts of the sailors as they toiled against the powerful swells and the cold whip of the wind. A deep, resonant voice could be heard above all the others, yelling orders one after the other. Their preoccupation with the storm had a strange calming effect on her soul; they would be too busy even to notice one small boy jump to his death in the raging sea.

Carefully, she climbed the stairs that led the way to the top deck. As her head left the shelter of the stairwell, she felt the wind slap her face with an enormous force. With logical precision, she considered the direction of the wind, wanting the strong wind at her back, so that she would sail out far past the ship and well into the water. Surely she would drown before anyone could get to her. It was a sobering thought, death, but it was preferable to her fate.

On the upper deck was a small opening in the railing where she could slip through. The wind was accommodating as it blew fiercely and relentlessly in that direction, and she began her journey along the deck, slippery from the salt water slicing over the wooden planks. She held steadfast to the railing, as the ship's response to the undulating waves was so unpredictable, jolting and sudden.

By the time she reached the rail, her hands were so cold that she could hardly move her fingers. It hurt to grab and grip the wooden railing for support, but she forced herself to do it.

The ocean was churning, the waves reaching up to lap at her feet and legs. The water was frigid. She would die quickly in the cold water, she thought to herself, and found it a strangely comforting thought. She pushed herself straight against the wind and looked out into her graveyard. A fierce gust whipped the cap from her head and loosened her hair, so that it flew in front of her face like a warrior's shield.

Calmness pervaded her last moments as she wondered if she would see her mother again. Then she gathered the strength she needed for the leap.

John heard the lock turn and was out of the bed and at the door in a flash, but it was too late. Brianda had locked him in the cabin! Reaching for his clothes and pulling on his boots, he began yelling for Angus. The trunks had not yet been delivered, so the only clothes he had were those he had worn when he boarded the ship. He found his pants but could not find his shirt anywhere. With an oath, he sprinted to the door and began beating his fists against it, calling for Angus at the top of his lungs. There was such a din from the storm and the shouting of the crew that he feared no one would hear him.

Angus, who had stationed himself on the middle deck, was enjoying watching the skill of the sailors as they fought their oldest and least equitable enemy, the weather. Something caught his ear, and he strained to determine whether he was imagining hearing his Lordship call for help, or if it were the wind playing tricks on him. The racket was deafening, as Angus's face was pelted by drops of water hitting him at gale force. He realized that he couldn't trust his ears and concluded that he had better go to see if his master needed him, just in case.

Once under the deck, he could move easily. It was then that he heard the calls for help, and they were from the earl! The huge man moved surprisingly fast along the corridor. "What is it, my Lord?" he called from outside the door of the cabin.

"Angus? Angus, help me quickly! Get an ax and break down the door! Brianda has taken both of the keys and has slipped off somewhere. Get me out of here, fast!" John yelled.

Before his master's last words were out of his mouth, Angus was running to the wall where the ax was stored. He ripped the ax from the ropes that held it and ran back to the door, flipping the head of the ax over and hitting the door at the top and bottom hinges. Several times he hit those spots with all of his force. "Get back, my Lord. I am going to knock the door inward!" he shouted over the roar of the storm.

"Go ahead!"

The heavy door fell inward on the fifth blow. It slammed to the floor with a thud that could be heard throughout the entire ship, but none of the busy crew noticed it, as they were too busy with their own battles to heed an isolated noise.

Angus stormed into the room, looking for John. "Are you all right, sir?"

"I am fine, Angus, but we must find that blasted girl. I cannot imagine what she is doing this time. Come, there is no time to waste!" John shouted as he bolted from the door, Angus right on his heels.

As John reached the top of the stairs leading to the upper deck, he was met by Cappy Bowles. The first mate had a look of deep concern on his face, and most of the crew members were staring aft. With dread in his heart, he turned and looked in the same direction. Ice filled his veins when he saw the figure of a small woman standing on the edge of the railing, looking down into the sea.

Captain Eric Bennett was thirty years old. In all his years he had never met a woman like the wife of the Earl of Manseth. She had been an enormous amount of trouble so far, and now, to top it off, she was about to fling herself into the stormy sea!

He was sure she would jump, as she had about her the singular purpose of a person on the brink of suicide. And if she were to see someone coming up from behind to stop her, there would be no hesitation. So carefully, warily, he slipped over the rail and made his way along the outside of the ship toward Lady Fauxley. The greedy water tried to claim him by drenching his body with icy droplets, and his numbed fingers did not want to grip the safe-holds, but he forced himself onward. Foot by foot, he advanced, keeping his head below the railing so he could remain undetected.

He was ten feet from her when he saw the earl move in behind his wife. Eric hoped the earl was as astute as he had been told he was, and would not do anything to cause his wife to jump before he could get to her.

Brianda was ready. She took one great breath and then another. Everything was so tranquil, even in the face of the storm, for in her present frame of mind, there was peace. She felt nothing, not the icy water, not the rush of the wind, only the compelling idea that they beckoned her to join them.

There was an eerie silence among the crew as they all watched, their breaths suspended. The sailors saw the large man approach and stand behind the young woman.

John stood several feet behind his wife, not knowing what to do. The whole situation seemed ludicrous. Brianda's hair had come undone and was blowing at the whim of the winds. Her clothes were soaked and clung tightly to her body, outlining the form that had been his only a short while ago. Her stance was steady, her manner unafraid.

"Brianda!" he called out to her.

She didn't move, and it appeared that she did not hear him.

Louder he called, "Brianda, you must come away from there. It is so cold out here, don't you wish to be warm?"

Brianda heard someone. Someone was talking, and it sounded like her name was being called. Curious, she turned slowly and saw him. Instantly her tranquillity was gone, replaced by an adrenaline surge. She raised her arms, fists closed. "Stay away from me! Stay away!" she yelled at John over the roar.

"I will not come any closer. But please tell me, why are you doing this?"

"I owe you no explanation! Leave me alone! Go away!" she yelled as she turned back and looked at the water.

John's heart leapt to his throat. He was too far from her. If she jumped, his hands would grab only the thin air, and she would be gone forever.

He inched forward.

She turned and saw him, and prepared to leap.

"Wait, I will back up to where I was! Don't jump, not yet!" he pleaded.

Brianda stood straight and looked at him over her shoulder.

John saw the captain edge closer to Brianda, and his hope surged. He tried to keep his face impassive so that Brianda would not realize that Bennett was close to grabbing her.

Captain Bennett tied a rope around his waist, then secured it to the railing. When he felt certain that the rope would hold, he began to move in closer to the girl.

Brianda sensed a change in her husband. Something was different, she could tell! These men were up to something. They wanted to stop her! She looked back and forth from the turbulent water to John's face. She was suddenly confused, and didn't know what was happening.

Then she saw him! A strange man was only inches from her! In her panic, she lost her balance and swayed in the wind. She made a grab for the railing but it slipped from her grasp. Her feet went out from under her, and she felt herself falling.

Eric Bennett sprang up and outward with all the strength of his powerful legs and threw both arms around her waist. Together they plummeted toward the icy water and waited for the furious ocean to consume them.

Just as they were about to be swallowed by the turbulent water, the rope that Eric had tied so well held, went taut and jerked them to a halt. They swung crazily, barely a foot above the icy water, buffeted about like a kite on a windy day.

Instantly, John and several crew members began pulling on the rope, lifting Brianda and Eric up and away from the welcoming arms of death. With great effort, the two were hoisted onto the deck.

Brianda was furious, her chance to end her life foiled. She began swinging her arms in all directions. Muffled groans and oaths resulted from the blows landed on whoever was unfortunate enough to be within arm's reach. She felt herself being roughly bundled up and thrown over someone's shoulder, and she immediately began pummeling the man's body with her fists and feet.

John made sure the captain was safe before he lifted Brianda onto his shoulder, and when he saw that Eric was well, he made haste in taking his wife off the deck. She cursed him with language fit only for sailors' ears and beat on him with her fists, but he paid no attention. He was far more concerned with keeping his footing on the slippery deck.

Angus had fashioned a door for their cabin by the time John carried Brianda down below decks. She grabbed the door frame to stop him from taking her inside, screaming that she was not going to enter any room with a randy tar like him! John ducked down, then quickly rose up again, causing Brianda to lose her hold. Once again she was confined to this room with the man she had grown to hate!

"Put me down, you bastard!" she screamed at him.

"You are hardly in a position to demand anything, you brat! Now be quiet and stop hitting me on the back! I need to get you out of these wet clothes," he said as he lowered her down to the floor.

Brianda wasted no time. As soon as she was standing, she swung at him with all her might, her right fist catching him just under the chin.

John staggered backward, his head reeling. He fell back against the wall, and his feet slipped out from under him. Slowly he slid down the wall and ended up sitting spread-eagled on the floor.

Angus had had enough of this troublemaker. "With your permission, sir, I think it is time that someone takes the lassie in hand."

John looked up at Angus, who was hunkered down on his knees directly in front of him. "You have my permission, Angus. I, for the moment, am unable to tackle her," he answered, slightly lightheaded.

Brianda backed away from Angus. "You . . ." she said through clenched teeth, pointing a finger at him, "Keep away from me. Don't you dare come close!" she threatened.

The big man did not even slow his step, grabbing Brianda around the waist and pulling her along the floor after him. Brianda screamed and fought with all her might as he sat down calmly on the large captain's chair and pulled her across his lap. She yelled obscenities as he pulled down the soaking wet pants and brought his mammoth palm down smack in the center of her buttocks. She screamed in pain, and Angus lifted his hand again and again, the smacks loud and sharp as he brought his hand down on her tender skin. She tried to twist away from the blows, but his other hand held her securely on his lap.

She was humiliated, raging until the pain was so overpowering that she finally burst into tears and stopped fighting. Angus stopped then, pulled her pants up, and laid her gently on the floor in front of him. Without a word he got up and walked over to John. "How are you now, sir?"

"Rested, thank you. Angus, you have done well. Your assistance in this delicate matter is much appreciated. I must warn, however, that you are not to discuss this with anyone, ever. Understood?"

"Yes, sir, I understand. I will be happy to help you out in the future with this little hellion, if you forgive my choice of words, sir," Angus whispered to John.

"Thank you, Angus, but I think I will be able to handle her."

"Yes, sir, good evening."

Brianda lay in a heap, just as Angus had left her. She cried as if her heart were breaking, and perhaps it was. Her face remained covered by her trembling hands.

John stood a few feet from her, contemplating what in the world he was to do with her. She was so beautiful, so precious . . . and so difficult. Absently, he rubbed his chin where she had hit him, thought he should never love a woman as he loved her. He knelt down next to her and touched her shoulder. "Brianda?"

"Don't touch me!" she managed between great gulps of air. She pulled her shoulder from his touch, then looked at him, an aloof coolness glazing her eyes. "You, sir, are like my father . . ."

John was stunned that she would say such a thing. He stared at her, silently.

"But you are worse than he ever was," she hissed venomously. "My father did not love me or care whether I was alive or dead. When he decided that I needed to be punished, he gave the task to my brother, Edward. You are aware that Edward performed those tasks with much pleasure. You, on the other hand, have professed to have some feeling for me, and you swore in front of God and witnesses that you would love, honor and cherish me. And just now you allowed an overgrown tree-trunk of a man to unclothe me and then beat me in your presence!" She spat at him, disgust in her eyes.

"I would hardly call a spanking a beating, Brianda."

"You were not under the hand that dealt the blows, sir," she countered, her voice laden with resentment.

"A point well taken." John grabbed her chin, forcing her to look at him. "All I know about your life before we met is what you and Old Megan have told me. From what I have heard, you were unjustly and wrongfully treated. Those odious deeds are on the conscience of those responsible. However, the punishment that you received was less than you deserved for your actions. As your husband, I am duty bound to control you . . ."

Brianda spat at him, but missed.

John shook his head and continued, "Angus aided me because I was momentarily incapacitated from your blow to my jaw. Had I not been stunned, and had I been clear of mind when I carried you into this room, I assure you that I would have dealt with you personally, and I very much doubt that I would have stopped the spanking as soon as Angus did." His gaze did not waver from hers.

She looked away first. The tears returned and she could say no more as she gave in to her anguish.

Ignoring her feeble protests, John lifted her into his arms and cradled her there. Crying too hard to fight him, she fell against his shoulder, permitting him to hold her, rock her slowly back and forth. After a few moments, he carried her to the bed and laid her gently on top of the covers. "Brianda, we have to get these cold, wet clothes off. You will get a chill if you remain in them."

Brianda only rolled onto her side and cried. John went to the door and gave several curt orders to Angus, who hurried off to see to them. By the time John returned to the bed, Brianda was shivering, her teeth chattering in her closed mouth. Without another word, he began stripping the clothes from her body, and she did not resist as John pulled a heavy blanket over her.

There was a brief knock on the door. John answered and then opened the door as wide as possible. Angus had arrived with several other sailors carrying a bath tub filled with steaming water into the room.

Brianda hid from curious eyes under the blanket. As soon as the men had departed, John picked Brianda up and carried her to the tub. He lowered her slowly down into the hot water, and she jumped as it touched her cold skin. She struggled to resist, but John held her firmly and lowered her completely into the water.

Once submerged, Brianda's body felt wonderful and warm again. She savored the heat. John raised a small metal cup and let the warm liquid spill over the top of her head. Her hair was matted and sticky with sea water, and John repeatedly rinsed her hair until it straightened into clean strands. He rubbed soap on a cloth and raised each limb to wash it, then washed her back and chest. She felt no sexual touches, only kind and gentle hands helping her wash the horror of the night away. A towel had been warmed near the fire, and soon Brianda was wrapped snugly within its softness.

The storm was easing now, its winds only playing with the ship. Carrying Brianda quickly across the room, John pulled back the covers with one hand and gently laid her down on the bed, pulling the sheets and blankets over her. Then he wrapped another smaller towel around her wet hair, so that all that could be seen of her now was her small face. She closed her eyes and allowed her muscles to relax and fell asleep immediately, oblivious to the cold chill in the cabin.

22

John was reading a book when a knock took him to the door. He was handed a small white envelope and after reading it, he woke Brianda.

"We have been invited to join Captain Bennett for dinner in one hour. We shall accept."

Brianda raised up on one arm. "I am not going!"

"You will go, if I have to take you as is from that bed," he stated flatly.

Horrified, Brianda looked under the covers at her naked body. "You wouldn't!"

"I would, believe me."

"Have I not suffered enough embarrassment in front of the captain and the whole crew, and now you would drag me stark naked from this room?"

"Your embarrassment is solely of your own making. You must learn that we are all responsible for the consequences of our actions. Now, I have business with Angus. Get up and find a suitable dress in your trunk. I will be back to collect you in one hour, and you will go in whatever state I find you." He nodded curtly to her and left the cabin. She heard distinctly the sound of the key turning in the lock.

She roused herself and began to dress quickly in her underclothes, as the night air had a definite chill. She found a simple, dark blue dress, some heavy stockings and a beautiful white shawl. After she had dressed, she began to repair her face and hair. She put a cold cloth to her puffy eyes, to reduce the swelling. She brushed her long hair until it was completely dry and shining, then pulled it back and tied it with a piece of blue satin ribbon.

With a critical look in the mirror, she decided she looked good enough, if she discounted the somber sadness in her hollow eyes. It served as a stark reminder that she should have been quicker in jumping into the ocean.

Eric Bennett was waiting for his guests. He, too, had bathed and was dressed in evening clothes. This was the first time he had ever entertained an earl and his wife, and he wanted all to be perfect. The table was set with china and crystal, and the food was ready.

Cappy knocked on the door and announced that the Earl of Manseth and his wife had arrived for dinner. Eric welcomed them with a smile. "Come in please, and do sit down." He was amazed at how beautiful the young girl looked, and had the feeling that she had no idea how gorgeous she was. Feminine attire revealed her stunning beauty. Indeed, he couldn't take his gaze from her violet eyes. Her lids were noticeably swollen and puffy, but that did not detract from their mesmerizing beauty. He smiled in appreciation and caught her husband's eye over the top of her golden hair. John acknowledged the silent compliment with a nod of his head.

"Won't you sit down, Lady Fauxley?" Eric said with a slight bow.

"Don't you think you could call me by my name, 'Brianda,' sir, since we have been intimately close to one another?" she asked with unmistakable sarcasm.

"Thank you for the honor, Brianda," he said, gesturing toward the table. "Won't you sit down, Brianda? John?"

John sat down to the right of the captain's chair. Brianda walked slowly to her chair and hesitated.

"Have you a problem, Lady Fauxley?" Eric asked sincerely.

Brianda shot him a look that stopped him cold.

Eric struggled, so as not to smile at her. "Perhaps a feather pillow for the seat of your chair?"

Brianda straightened her shoulders and raised her chin. Through narrowed eyes, she stared at him with obvious distaste.

"Defiant, aren't you, my Lady?" Eric commented, privately impressed with her bravura. Brianda continued to stare him down. "May I say, Brianda, with your permission, sir," Eric added, looking to John for consent to continue, "that were you my woman, at the moment I discovered you on this ship, dressed in boys' clothes and flirting with countless dangers, I would have blistered your bottom then and there, and in front of whoever happened to be present."

Chin held high, Brianda lowered herself into her chair. With utmost dignity, she replied, "It seems, Captain, that you exhibit your lack of breeding by broaching a subject that is none of your business. I do not recall hearing my husband ask for your opinion in the matter. As you are an employee of my husband's, I would think it prudent for you to confine yourself to matters within your province."

Eric moved behind her and pushed her chair in toward the table. When his eyes met John's, each man had to look quickly away to avoid bursting into laughter. "Touché, Madam," he quipped.

John looked at both of them and said, "Shall we eat?"

Eric returned to his chair and sat down. The food was served forthwith, and the two men attacked the delicious fare with relish. Brianda toyed with her food, her appetite flagging. But the hot tea was ambrosia, and she concentrated on savoring its flavor. John noticed that she wasn't eating, but thought that making an issue of it tonight would be a mistake. It had been an extraordinary day for all of them.

Soon the men were deep in conversation about John's shipping business. John was seriously considering adding import and export to his line and wanted Eric's opinion. As Eric talked, John found himself drawn to the man. Not only was he an accomplished sea captain, he was astute in business matters as well. He was loyal, honest and his bravery could not be questioned. He seemed interested in advancing in his career, and John made a tentative offer that he retire from the sea and consider taking over the responsibilities of John's shipping enterprises. Eric agreed to think it over and they shook hands.

John glanced over at Brianda and found her sound asleep with her head cradled on her crossed arms. Eric's gaze followed John's, and they turned to smile at each other. She had an angelic beauty while she slept. Eric motioned his head toward his bed and John nodded in agreement. While the captain pulled the heavy coverlet back, John carried Brianda over to the bed and laid her down. Eric looked down at the beautiful girl who was sleeping so profoundly. "She is a bewitching thing, sir, but, if you don't mind my saying so, she's a handful."

"You have no idea! Look at her! Except for the last few minutes, she has been awake for forty hours or so with only a few minutes' sleep here and there. She is still gorgeous, even after a suicide attempt and a well-earned punishment from Angus. You should also know that the only reason that I did not administer the spanking personally is because Brianda belted me in the jaw and I was too light-headed to stand up at the moment!"

Eric reared his head back and howled. John laughed, too, as they sank back into their chairs.

John put his hand on Eric's shoulder and said, "Seriously, Eric, I owe you a debt that I cannot repay. Your bravery saved Brianda's life this afternoon, and I will never forget it. I never want to come that close to losing her again."

"It would be very difficult to lose something that precious, sir. You will have to be constantly alert where she is concerned, I'm afraid."

"There are other factors of which you are not aware. Brianda has an older brother, a no-good bastard, Edward Breedon. He'd sell his own soul for the right price. He lost the family fortune in just a couple of years after his father died, and when he tired of gambling, he beat his sister for fun. . . ." John clenched his fists in brief frustration before continuing the sad, sordid, twisted and very complicated tale of how Brianda had become his wife.

"What a confounded situation! The best part of this whole thing is that you have a beautiful, spirited wife that you love."

"The problem is that Brianda did not marry me willingly. That is why she ran away and tried to escape on your ship. Even now, she thinks I married her for the Breedon estate, but that is not true. I will just have to let time prove that my feelings for her are genuine. If I can just keep track of her long enough!"

Eric walked about the cabin scratching his head. "Is there no way that this brother of hers can be put in prison?"

"I explored all avenues with regard to putting him away, but without more evidence against him, it is hopeless. The only concrete evidence I have is the last beating he gave Brianda. It almost killed her, but men are rarely put in prison for beating their women. Edward Breedon, however, was such a coward that the mere possibility of legal action was all it took to intimidate him into signing. Everything else is not substantial enough. He has threatened my life and Brianda's, too, but the threat was made in private and would have been impossible to prove." John took a sip of his cognac and stared out at the night.

"I should think that it would be dangerous for you and Brianda to be anywhere near her brother, once he discovered what you had done," Eric stated thoughtfully.

"When I discovered that Brianda had planned this escape, I rejoiced. I had wanted to take her away from England for a while anyway to avoid any contact with her brother, and then I found that she had planned almost the whole trip by herself!" John said, rising from the table and walking to the bed to gaze down at his wife.

"You love her, then. The marriage wasn't all just to help her and stop that ruffian?" asked Eric as he filled his snifter with cognac.

"Yes, I love her. I never realized how much until I saw her standing on the edge of the ship ready to jump off. She has been so troubled and angry that I have found myself angry with her most of the time! She needs to learn to trust me, to know that my love for her is genuine. This will take time. Yes, she is a handful, but I have big hands, Eric, and plenty of patience."

Eric smiled at his employer. "Sir, it is late, now, and you, too, have not had much sleep. I will consider your business offer, and we can discuss the details when you return to London."

"Good enough. Open the door for me, please, and I will take my little troublemaker to our bed."

Eric hurried to open the door and watched as John lifted Brianda into his arms, carried her down the hall and disappeared into his cabin. Eric then went up to check on his ship. She was his true mistress, and, like most women, needed constant attention and vigilance.

Had it not been for the cough, Brianda would have slept until noon. She was so exhausted that it took the full force of her lungs' raspy barking to rouse her from her deep slumber. She heard the rough, coarse sounds in her head and wondered vaguely where they were coming from and why someone did not do something to halt the annoying noise. Brianda opened her eyes to the realization that she was having difficulty drawing a normal breath. She could not fully expand her lungs. She pushed herself into a sitting position to see if that would help, and it did, a little, but she felt herself growing panicky, and she shoved the inert body of her husband as hard as she could to waken him.

"Brianda, what is wrong?" John asked, forcing himself awake. Brianda did not answer, alarming John. In no time, he was fully awake. He turned and looked at her sitting up against the backrest, mouth partially open, struggling to breathe. He was on his feet in a second and had his pants on before he reached the door a second later. He shouted an order to Angus, who was in his cabin next door.

John hurried back to the bed and looked at Brianda, his trained eyes taking in all the abnormal signs. Her warm forehead indicated a high fever. Her cheeks were unusually red and her lips had a bluish hue. He counted her breaths and noted that she was breathing thirty-six times a minute. Her fingernail beds were also blue. He pulled her chemise up and placed his ear on her chest just over her right breast and listened. He moved and listened over her left breast and then under her breasts on both sides. Gently moving her forward, he placed his ear on her back and carefully listened. She had crackling noises at the base of both lungs and congestion throughout her chest.

Pneumonia. Her wide eyes revealed her fear.

"Brianda, try not to be frightened, darling. Angus is going to bring us some steaming water, and I want you to lean into the steam and breathe. Do you understand?"

Brianda nodded. It felt good to have him there.

Angus came in with the water, and she leaned forward to let the steam enter her lungs and surround her head. Almost immediately, she felt her lungs expand a little more.

John hurried to his trunks where he kept his medicines and instruments. He found what he wanted quickly and mixed the medicines. At the taste, Brianda made a momentary face. He smiled and insisted that she finish all of it.

As he watched her drink, he thought of Old Megan and the conversation they had had the day before the wedding. She warned John of Brianda's tendency to become ill easily and her difficulty in fighting off infections. The old woman gave him some special herbs mixed just for Brianda, in case she should become ill on the trip, and John did not hesitate to administer the herbs along with his medicines.

Brianda was gravely ill for five days, during which time John never left her side, caring for her as he did once before. She was a fighter when she was ill, as she was with every other challenge, but John was beginning to think that she may have inherited her mother's frail constitution.

On the sixth day, when she announced that she was not going to swallow any more of the bitter medicine, John knew Brianda was better. "Angus!" John called,

"Please come in here and sit on Brianda. She is refusing to take her medicine, and I need someone to hold her down, so that I can pour the stuff down her throat."

"Coming, my Lord!" answered Angus, rising from his chair and heading for the bed.

"Whoa! Hold on, now," Brianda said firmly. Looking at John, she implored, "You can't mean that, sir! You wouldn't have that huge giant sit on me!"

"I will, if that is what it takes to get the medicine down that lovely throat of yours."

"You are such a bully!" she railed at him, coughing with the exertion.

"You will take the medicine, by force or otherwise."

"Oh! . . . All right! Give me the noxious slop. I will drink it, but only because there are two of you and one of me. That would not stop me normally, but I have been sick and cannot fight as well as I could were I at normal strength."

"Fine. Just swallow this medicine and save us the lecture." John held the medicine in front of her. She took the glass and downed the green liquid. "That is awful! You should have to take it. Do doctors have to try the medicines they prescribe for their patients?"

"Not unless they, too, are ill."

"They should be made to try everything they prescribe, so that they can know how their patients suffer."

"Write a letter to the head of the Council of Physicians in London and offer your opinion, if you feel that strongly, my Lady."

There was a knock on the door, and Eric poked his head in the door and smiled at Brianda. "How is my woman passenger? You had us worried for a day or two, my Lady."

"Won't you come in, Captain, you look ridiculous standing half in and half out of the room," Brianda said matter-of-factly.

Eric entered and nodded good morning to John and Angus. Looking at the wan girl in the middle of the large bed, he said, "You are lucky that your husband is so well trained, Brianda. You might not have made it through this illness had he not been on board. We are all happy to see you so greatly improved."

"Thank you, Captain. If you are truly so happy to see me better, you can do me the favor of swallowing the awful medicine that my husband is forcing me to take four times a day!" she said, smiling her mischievous smile.

An old sailor came into the room bearing a large silver tray with wonderfully aromatic tea and muffins that seemed to be just out of the oven. The old man had an ancient cap on his silver hair that he touched when he looked at Brianda. "I am Bill Sanders, my Lady, and I am the oldest member of the crew of the *Maid of the Green*. I ain't good for much work anymore, so the captain lets me cook once in a while. I am the day-watch lookout, too. Anyway, I thought you might enjoy my muffins! I learnt the recipe in the West Indies many years back."

"Why yes, thank you, Bill! Won't you sit and join me in eating one?"

Bill looked uncertainly at Eric, who smiled and nodded his permission for the sailor to share tea with Brianda. Bill sat down and smiled at Brianda, and she smiled back.

Eric looked affectionately at Brianda. "You are much too slender, Brianda. We must not let the word get out that our food is not good, or I will have trouble attracting paying passengers!"

"Thank you for your interest in my weight, Captain Bennett. Now I promise not to tell anyone about the quality of your food, if you will take my husband out of here for a while so that I can get some peace! Anyway, Bill and I have a lot to talk about."

"Done! But, Lady, I have news that you will like to hear before I take John away."

"What?" she asked, looking up expectantly.

"If the wind holds, we will dock in Edinburgh, Scotland, in two to three weeks' time."

"Really? That is wonderful!" she exclaimed. Turning to John, she said, "I will be well enough to leave the ship by then, won't I?"

"You sit and enjoy your tea and your conversation with Bill now, and we will discuss the trip later. I have some business with Captain Bennett, so I will be gone for a while. I am going to leave my wife in your capable hands, Bill. If she misbehaves or tries to leave that bed, you are to notify Angus immediately."

"Aye, sir. The lassie will be fine. Once she hears my many stories of the sea, she won't want to leave."

"You behave, Brianda! Do not get out of that bed! Do not try any of your tricks on Bill. You wouldn't want to begin a friendship that way, would you?"

"Oh, no, sir. I am very anxious to hear Bill's stories. I want to be well enough to leave the ship in two weeks' time, too," she announced, as she sat back against her pillows and turned an innocent face to the old sailor. He began his story when the three men left the cabin and quietly closed the door behind them.

When John returned to the cabin late in the afternoon, Brianda was sound asleep, curled into a small ball on the huge bed. Bill Sanders was sound asleep, too, in the adjoining chair. John smiled at both of them. What an unlikely pair!

As John moved about the cabin, Bill woke. Embarrassed, he rose, cap in hand, and began to apologize to the earl. John held his hand up to stop the man's words. "Bill, I am so grateful that you were able to amuse

Brianda. I hope you will find some time in the weeks to come to spend with her and free me to work with Captain Bennett."

"Aye, sir, it would be my pleasure."

"Excellent. Then I will count on seeing you in the morning, Bill, at about ten o'clock?"

"Aye, sir. If the captain gives his permission, I will be here at ten a.m. Good evening to you, sir."

Brianda woke for dinner, and ate with an appetite for the first time in a week. She and John shared a roasted chicken stuffed with wild rice, dipping crusty bread in the gravy. The white wine was slightly fruity, and Brianda loved it. It wasn't long before she felt the wine's effects, and giggled when she spilled some food in her lap.

"That is enough wine for you," John said as he pulled her glass toward his place.

"Just a little more, John. I promise not to become silly," she tittered, blinking her eyes and raising her eyebrows at him.

"You are already silly. I would prefer if you ate more food and forgot the wine. The cook has made some delicious fruit tarts for dessert as a celebration of your recovery. You will want to taste them."

"So be it. No more wine. I plan, instead, to get drunk on more of Bill's stories!" Brianda recounted a few of the old salt's tales, and when she was quite breathless, she asked, "When are you going to tell me where we are going on our trip?"

"I will tell you the details in the morning at breakfast, and no sooner. You really look tired, love," he answered, handing the fruit tart to her. Brianda enjoyed the cook's delicacy, delighting in the sugary treat after all the concoctions that John had forced down her throat these past few days.

When she couldn't eat another bite, she stood on shaky legs and slowly walked over to the porthole to gaze out at the sea. Cold winds whipped the waves, leaving the tops white for a moment, before they dissipated to join the black water. The ocean appeared at rest for the night, but could awaken with a fury that no man or woman could duplicate. Brianda sighed.

"It is time to return to bed, Lady Fauxley. You have been up long enough. Tomorrow you can get up and walk for a short while. Now off to bed."

Without objection, she hurried behind the screen and changed into her night chemise. She walked along the cold floor quickly, jumped into the bed, and pulled the covers up to her chin. It was cold at night, and she wanted no taste of the chill this evening. Brianda was tired from the exertion of the last few hours. Her eyelids were heavy, refusing to stay open.

John left his papers and walked to the bedside to look down at her for a long moment. Sitting down next to her, he leaned over and kissed her mouth. She was startled, but did not respond. Then as his lips coaxed hers, she kissed him, too, putting her arms around his shoulders and holding him close to her. He smelled like wine and the salty air. He held her close to him, too, happy that she was well and his once again. She soon slept in his arms, and reluctantly he laid her back on the pillow.

He joined her in bed soon thereafter, but did not sleep immediately. Troubled thoughts were his companion.

23

During the weeks since Brianda had disappeared with her new husband, Edward and Biff had tried every avenue open to them to learn the couple's whereabouts. Edward's rage and hatred for Fauxley and the little chit gave him the will to live, to put up with life in the slum. He would get his revenge, and Fauxley would pay. Then Brianda would pay, but with her it would be different. He was going to enjoy watching her scream for mercy.

After his visit to the London town house, it didn't take Edward long to figure out that Fauxley had taken his sister to the country, and he and Biff pursued them directly, arriving at noon on Saturday. When their coach pulled into the way station, Edward disembarked and was drawn immediately to a posted notice declaring that the sale of the Breedon Estate had been canceled! He was livid, and went directly to the office of the county recorder, where he was informed that the Breedon Estate was not going to be auctioned, as it had become part of the estate of the Earl of Manseth. Edward hit the poor old clerk, knocking him to the ground. He then held a knife to the throat of the terrified old man and demanded details. As he listened, his stomach contents rose in his throat. The beautiful young Brianda Breedon had wed his Lordship, the Earl of Manseth, in a stunning ceremony held at the chapel at Manseth Manor.

It was impossible! How could Fauxley have arranged a legal wedding so fast? Edward was beside himself. He had counted on using his family's beachfront property as the landing spot for his deliveries of opium, and now Fauxley would forever own his lands and his manor!

Later that day, Edward watched as the carriage occupied by the would-be investor of Cliffshead Manor and properties disappeared around the far bend under gray clouds. Edward flexed his fists in impotent exasperation. He had had to mollify the fellow with a cut in the opium business. Now he was out even more money and had lost his family's property, too.

Furious, he and Biff returned to London to wait, and to formulate plans. Sooner or later, he would find Fauxley and his bride, and then he would strike. No one was going to deprive him of his lands and his sister!

The *Maid of the Green* entered Edinburgh's harbor at midday, three weeks out of London. Brianda had spent the final hour peering out of the open porthole at the huge city. The busy docks, smoke-belching factories and crowded streets reminded her of London. Brianda's head was cold, as the wind whipped her long hair about, but she did not care. She was so anxious to set her feet on land, she could hardly bear it.

"Come in from that window immediately, Brianda!" John yelled at her as he entered the cabin. In her haste to comply, she slammed her head into the edge of the porthole. She stepped down off the chair, rubbing the spot that was already swelling. "I was just trying to see Edinburgh," she explained quickly, as she noted the hard lines around John's mouth.

"Are you packed and ready to leave?"

"Hours ago!" She gestured toward her trunks, all lined up and ready to be picked up. "Will you finally tell me now where we are going, sir?"

"We are going to travel to a place nestled in those snow-covered mountains you saw in the distance, Brianda. All of Angus's family lives there, and they own a large portion of land. I am sure you will love it."

"Angus's family? He will be going with us?"

"He goes wherever I go, as always." John gave her a warning look. "Angus is thrilled to be seeing his family again after many years' absence. You will be on your best behavior, won't you?"

"How could I be anything else, what with you and Angus constantly watching every move I make?" she said peevishly.

"What is bothering you, Brianda?"

"Well . . . I want to know if Angus will have the same privileges on land that he had at sea, my Lord."

John smiled at her. "When Angus performs a special service, it is always on my direct orders. He would only take independent action in a dire emergency, and if I were incapable of taking care of the matter myself," he explained, watching her face contort with each new sentence. "Angus is trustworthy. He would not abuse his privilege."

"Oh no, sir, all he would abuse is my backside!" she answered testily, turning to look out the window. She did not want to see his smirk one second longer.

John laughed out loud. "Brianda, you challenge me constantly! See to it that you behave, and you will have nothing to worry about, either from Angus or from me. I am going out to talk to Captain Bennett regarding the details of our departure. Stay away from the porthole! I don't want you getting another chill." John turned to leave.

"Wait! Sir!" she called out to him.

"Yes?"

"What about Dakota and Sebastian? Will they be unloaded first or last? They are going with us, aren't they?" she asked, worry evident in her tone.

"When the horses are unloaded is a decision for Captain Bennett and his crew to make. Yes, they are going with us. Now, excuse me. The ship is drawing near, and I have urgent business with Eric."

Brianda pulled the chair over to the porthole again, so that she could stand on it and look out. As soon as she was sure John was safely gone, she stuck her head out the porthole and contemplated what was to become the land of her new adventure.

It took several hours to unload all the ship. Brianda was hurrying up and down the dock, looking at everything and asking a million questions of anyone who would give her an answer.

The December chill whipped off the ocean, and she was careful to keep the hood of her heavy overcoat pulled far over her face. For all her clothing, Brianda felt as if she could hardly move, but found that she was toasty warm.

Sebastian had been unloaded and tied to the back of the carriage, but Dakota was skittish and ornery after his weeks at sea. The crew was having a devilish time getting the stallion down the loading ramp. Brianda watched in dismay as one sailor yanked on his halter. Running at full speed, she was up the ramp in seconds and bashing the startled sailor with both fists like a prize-fighter. "Get your slimy hands off my horse, you lame excuse for a man!" she yelled at him. The sailor jumped back and stared at the small girl. Brianda grabbed Dakota's halter and spoke soothingly to him. The great animal quieted. Rubbing his nose, she led him slowly down the ramp.

John, Angus and Eric all watched the scene in dismay from the top deck.

"She fights very well, my Lord. She landed some excellent punches," Eric said, nodding his head up and down, as if agreeing with himself.

"She is very protective of her horse," was all that John could say, he was so astonished.

"Needs discipline, the little hellcat," was Angus's contribution.

"Thank you, Angus. Please see that all of our luggage is correctly loaded on the carriage," John commanded.

"Very well, my Lord," Angus answered as he headed off to count the trunks. He was so happy to be on his native soil that he forgot his irritation with young Lady Fauxley. She was his master's responsibility, after all.

John said good-bye and farewell to the crew, then departed the ship. He found Brianda still leading Dakota about. "Angus, tie the animals to the carriage and let us begin our journey. We want to get there before midnight."

Reluctantly, Brianda left the horse and looked up at the *Maid of the Green*. Standing at the top of the ramp was Bill Sanders. He was waving slowly at Brianda. They had said farewell earlier, and he had reassured her that they would see each other in a month or so, when the ship returned for the journey back to London. John had offered the old sailor a job at Manseth Manor, and Bill had accepted gladly. He wanted to be useful, and he would be close to his precious little friend.

With a final wave, Brianda turned to John, who took her hand and helped her up into the carriage. He placed a colorful blanket over her knees and without a word offered her his handkerchief for her nose. He then called out the orders to move on.

The carriage was much more uncomfortable than the ship, as the roads leading from the port city of Edinburgh to the countryside were old and not well tended. The carriage hit ruts and bumps, knocking the three passengers about inside like rag dolls. Angus pointed out places of interest along the way to help pass the time.

However, by late afternoon, Brianda was bored to distraction and asked if she could ride Dakota for a while. Surprisingly, John agreed, and he, too, had his horse saddled. In a few minutes the two were astride their mounts and riding at any easy canter in front of the carriage.

Even though the air was bitter cold, Brianda was happy. It had been so long since she had ridden, and the feel of Dakota beneath her gave her a thrill.

John watched her as she rode, free and confident. How was it possible that she was more beautiful each day? Even covered head to toe against the freezing air of Scotland, she looked fresh and light.

When there was less than an hour's ride to their destination, it began to snow. Large, wet flakes struck their faces, lingering just a moment before they faded. Brianda laughed heartily and spurred Dakota on a bit faster. Her cloak was black, and she blended perfectly with the horse. With the copious white snow falling harder and faster, she appeared to be a graceful black mirage in the middle of a frozen, white desert.

Angus's yells caught Brianda's attention. She strained her eyes and saw the lights ahead! John caught up with her, and they rode together though the sturdy

wooden gates that welcomed all visitors to Loch Inver-
stook, the home of Angus's family.

Great shouts of welcome were heard as the horses
and the carriage approached the main house. A large
group ran off the porch and rushed into the night snow
to greet them.

Angus jumped from the carriage and ran smack into
the middle of the group. First he kissed a stout, middle-
aged woman and then lifted her into the air to swing her
about. There were hugs from each member of the family,
and everyone seemed to be talking at once!

John and Brianda had been totally forgotten for the
moment. Brianda felt her eyes fill with tears as she witnessed this outpouring of love. Angus turned and smiled
at John as another set of arms wrapped around him.
John smiled back, as he dismounted, happy that his most
loyal friend had come home at last.

Wiping tears away, the stout woman approached
John and Brianda. "You must be his Lordship, the earl. I
am Rebecca MacKenzie, Angus's mother," she said,
curtsying and bowing her head toward the ground.

"Yes, I am John Fauxley, and this is my wife, Brianda.
It is a pleasure to meet you, Mrs. MacKenzie, and we are
honored that you have invited us into your home. Your
son has been a great friend to me," John said over the
din of the reunion.

Smiling up at the handsome man, Rebecca stammered, "W-Whatever is the matter with me! Please follow me inside, so that you two can get out of this cold
night. I will have one of my sons come to care for your
animals," she said, gesturing to Colin, the youngest of
her four sons, to come to her.

Brianda slipped from Dakota's back and grabbed his
bridle. "Mrs. MacKenzie, it is a pleasure for me, also, to
meet you. Forgive me, but I would prefer to accompany
my horse to the barn. Dakota is very sensitive to

strangers. He will feel more secure, and so will I, if you will allow me to lead him to his stall."

"Why, yes, my Lady," she faltered. "Of course you can go to the barn if you wish." Rebecca was so startled by the request that she couldn't say more.

"My wife makes many unusual requests, Mrs. MacKenzie. I, also, will walk with my wife and your son to the barn."

"As you wish, my Lord," Rebecca responded politely, though from the look on her face she obviously found the request quite peculiar.

Brianda gazed up at John, astonished at how well he could extricate her from socially awkward situations.

Colin MacKenzie, the youngest son, came quickly to his mother's side. "Take his Lordship and his wife to the barn and show them where they can stable their horses, Colin."

"Yes, Mother." Looking directly into John's eyes, the tall young man said, "Won't you follow me, please, my Lord, my Lady?" He turned and led them down the long path to the barn. The snow continued to fall around their feet, and they were up to their ankles in several places.

Once inside the barn, Brianda and John were impressed by the sturdy, clean structure. Colin showed Brianda and John which stalls were to be used for their horses. Brianda grabbed a curry comb and gave Dakota a quick brushing, then toweled him off. Making sure that his feet were dried well enough, she looked around the stall and noted that Dakota would have a bucket of oats and plenty of fresh water. Rubbing his extremely soft nose, she leaned forward and kissed it, then ran her hands up and down his strong neck. "I will see you in the morning, Dakota. Have a good evening. I have missed you, my friend." The horse answered by nibbling gently at her shoulder.

Smiling, Brianda turned to John, who took her hand and led her toward the friendly lights of the house.

Rebecca MacKenzie held her second-oldest son, Angus, in her arms. She wanted to memorize the feeling, as she knew he would leave again one day soon. It had been five years since she had held him so, and simply touching him was a joy.

Angus had thought that he might never see his mother again, so their reunion was precious and sweet. After several minutes of hugging, Angus led his mother to the hallway that led to the back of the house, where there was less din from the revelers. Holding her shoulders and looking into her pale blue eyes, he said, "Mother, I have missed you and thought of you every day. It is so good to see your smile and to see how happy the whole family is. Father looks robust, and I can see that you are feeding my brothers and sisters well!"

Rebecca smiled up at Angus. He looked over his mother's head at the ceiling for a moment, and then looked deep into her eyes. "Mother, tell me please, what has become of Mary Carmichael?" he asked, the pain obvious in his voice.

"Mary Carmichael married one year after you left, Angus," she answered carefully and slowly. She knew the news would bring added sorrow to her son.

Angus leaned back against the wall, his eyes gazing off into space. He didn't speak for a few moments. His mother waited. "I thought that might have been the case, Mother. I cannot tell you how often I have wondered what became of her. Is she happy?" he asked, emotion clogging his voice.

"I do not know if she is happy or not. Mary disappeared from our lives as soon as she married. It is best to forget her, son. So much time has passed since you were last with her, things have changed."

Michael MacKenzie found his wife and son huddled together in the hallway. "Here you two are! I have been looking everywhere for you. Come, we are all waiting to see you." Michael ushered them back into the main living room.

Angus's sisters had grown into women in the five years that he had been gone. As Alison and Margaret walked toward him, smiling, he noted how beautiful and healthy they looked. He pulled them to him and kissed each one. Andrew and Ian joined them, and they stood united, five of the six children of Michael and Rebecca MacKenzie.

Colin opened the front door to allow the lord and his lady entrance, and the joy of the homecoming poured out to meet them. John and Brianda stepped inside to find Rebecca carrying out trays of food. Placing a large platter of vegetables on the dining table, she went to fetch the newest, and the only titled, of her guests. Angus, too, had seen John, and left his siblings to show John and Brianda to their seats at the dining table.

There were twenty-two friends and family celebrating at the MacKenzie house, and they all fit comfortably at the dinner table! Michael MacKenzie had built the table by hand when Rebecca was pregnant with their first child. When asked why he was cutting wood pieces so large, the very young Michael had announced that he was going to have at least six children and lots of friends. He intended that not a single person be without a seat at his table.

John sat at Angus's right, and Brianda sat next to him. Brianda, for once, was silent, absorbed by the events of the evening. She loved the atmosphere, and ate hungrily. The flavors were new and hearty, and when she was finished, she looked up and smiled at everyone.

"Do you not find the food wonderful, sir?" she asked John.

"Maybe not quite as wonderful as you have found yours," he answered, leaning over to kiss her cheek. "I am happy to see you eat so well. You are too thin now, but if you continue eating like this, I will have no worries!"

Brianda frowned at him, and then burst into laughter. She felt warm and welcome, and she wasn't going to let John goad her into a verbal duel.

Alison and Margaret helped the other women clear the dishes. A few minutes later, they brought out steaming cups of coffee and several cakes that were quickly cut and served to all that could fit another bite of food into their mouths. Brianda had her hands outstretched, ready for one of the first pieces, while John shook his head with mock sadness, patting his already full stomach.

Angus was just putting the first piece of cake into his mouth, when there was a knock on the door. Ian rose and went to see who had arrived, and hesitated a moment before opening the door.

When the door was open wide, there, silhouetted by the black night, stood Mary Carmichael! She carried a woven basket in her arms and offered it to Ian without a word. He took it and bade her enter. All eyes in the room were on the pretty young woman. All conversation stopped.

Rebecca rose, walked to Mary, and led her toward the table. The woman took a few tentative steps, but stopped. She stood without moving, staring at Angus. He rose and walked to her. She was a tall woman, five feet and eight inches, but she had to look up to see his face.

She turned to go, but he grabbed her arm and turned

her back to face him. "How are you, Mary Carmichael?" he asked, his voice barely above a whisper.

"I am fine, Angus, and you? Are you well?" came her response, hardly audible.

"Come in and join us for cake. It is cold and harsh outside. The coffee will warm you," he said as he urged her forward. Her doe-soft skin was quite cold to the touch.

Michael stood and pulled a chair out for Mary, and she sat, head down, eyes on her lap.

"Welcome, Mary," Michael said clearly, and several voices from around the table called out their welcome, too. Mary glanced up and saw friendly faces, not judging ones. She forced a small smile for all those gathered there, and then looked once again at her lap.

Alison brought her a cup of coffee and gave her a hug. "It has been so long since we have seen you, Mary. I have missed you. Maybe we can talk together later?" Alison asked, her heart breaking at the sight of her brother's old love.

Michael stood and offered a toast to the return of his son and to their distinguished guests, the Earl of Manseth and his wife. Mugs were held aloft as all cried out their personal welcome. Everyone returned to their conversations regarding the upcoming Christmas festivities.

Brianda's head began to bob softly up and down, and her eyes drifted closed. Michael nudged John, and then signaled to Rebecca to come to him. "The lass is tired, woman. Show the earl and his wife to their room," he ordered softly.

"Brianda. Wake up, it is time to go to bed," John whispered into her ear.

Brianda woke instantly and announced that she was fine and wanted to stay for the party. Everyone at that end of the table laughed good-naturedly at her attempt to convince her husband to let her stay.

Brianda looked at John. He had that look on his face that said he would not change his mind, so, with a sigh, she rose from the table and said good night to all assembled. She was met with friendly farewells and promises of more enjoyment the next day.

Brianda felt drawn to the eyes of Mary Carmichael, and for a moment, she felt a strange communion. This, too, was a woman who had suffered. Brianda smiled at her and said, "I hope I will have the opportunity to converse with you in the future." The woman smiled back and then looked down, the moment lost.

Brianda followed John and Rebecca into the hallway. All at the table watched as the handsome lord and his beautiful wife left the room.

As everyone was saying good night to the couple, Mary Carmichael took the opportunity to slip away from the table and out the door before anyone noticed she was gone. Angus turned to look at her, but her chair was empty. He saw the front door standing slightly ajar and ran to it, but when he looked out into the frozen night, all he could see was the blowing snow and the outlines of the huge trees in the forest. Disappointed, and with a sour feeling in his stomach, he turned back to the room.

"Sir . . ." Rebecca said to John.

"Please call me John, and I am sure that Brianda would like you to call her by her given name, also," John said. Brianda shook her head in agreement.

"Very well, John and Brianda, please put your coats on and follow me." Rebecca pulled her own coat over her shoulders.

"Is it so cold upstairs that we will have to wear our coats there?" Brianda asked, surprised.

"Oh, my dear, you think the silliest things!" Rebecca laughed as she hugged Brianda. "You and your husband are going to have a special place all to yourselves. Please follow me and watch your footing. The steps get icy this late at night." Rebecca led them out of the main house and down a path a short distance to a small cottage.

"Come on, sir . . . I mean John and Brianda. It is too cold to stand here looking at the guest house. It is charming, though, isn't it?"

24

Rebecca opened the front door of the lovely cottage and motioned for John and Brianda to come inside. She showed them around briefly, and after she was sure they were comfortably settled, she left, calling out, as she disappeared in the heavily falling snow, that breakfast was at eight o'clock and lunch at twelve noon.

John closed and latched the door, and the two of them explored the small cottage. It was lovely and inviting, with one bedroom, a small kitchen, and a large salon. A fire, recently tended, roared behind a metal screen. It would easily last the night without care. The furniture was crafted from solid walnut and beautifully upholstered by skilled hands that had made the cushion covers from bright sturdy fabrics.

Brianda entered the bedroom and removed her coat, testing to see if the fire was warm enough to heat the bedroom as well as the salon. To her contentment, it was. She carried the heavy coat to the wall pegs located near the front door and hung it there to dry, as it had become quite wet from the snow. She took

John's coat and hung it on another peg. Then, wishing to look outside, she walked to one of the windows in the salon and put her hands up to her face to shield the light.

All around the cottage were huge trees that looked like dancers, lifting their graceful branches to meet the falling snow that blanketed everything. Brianda was enchanted, certain that she had never seen anything so utterly beautiful. She imagined she was alone in the vast forest, and she relished the fantasy, so mysteriously lovely was the scene before her. Her warm breath made a circle of fog on the cold windowpane, which she wiped with her handkerchief so she could see more clearly.

John had pulled off his heavy sweater and boots and was standing in the bedroom doorway, watching his wife blow her breath on the windowpane and wipe it away quickly to see through the clearing she had made. She was so childlike in some ways, and so appealing as a woman in others. "Brianda, come to bed. It is late and we are both tired from our long journey."

"Yes, I'm just coming now," she called back to him, reluctantly dragging herself away from the magical scene. "Have you looked outside at the forest in the snow? It is so delicate and mystical."

"You are delicate and mystical yourself, little one. Come here."

She stopped and looked at him. She'd heard that tone in his voice before, and fretfully hoped he had no intention of forcing himself on her again. "I will be there in just a moment. I have to . . . use the facilities. Will you excuse me?"

"Certainly. I will wait for you here."

Brianda used the small room and found it to be exceedingly cold. She hurried out of there and into the bedroom, where she found John sitting in bed, the covers pulled up to his waist. Brianda stared at his naked chest.

Pulling her attention to other thoughts, she walked to her trunks and pulled out her heavy chemise. She turned to find the screen and there wasn't one! Tears sprang to her eyes, and she quickly blinked them away as she decided on an alternative. She walked to the bed, got under the covers and began undressing.

"Isn't that somewhat difficult, undressing like that?"

"Of course, but they forgot to put the screen in this room."

"They don't use screens in this country, Brianda."

"Why ever not?" she asked, mortified by the thought.

"They don't think married couples need to hide their bodies from one another."

"Oh." She was still struggling to maneuver out of her dress.

"Would you like some help?"

"Of course not! I can manage quite well, thank you," she stated firmly.

"But, madam, I am finding it much too difficult keeping my hands to myself. Your body entices me," John said in a low voice, his fingers lightly stroking the length of her arm.

"Controlling yourself, sir, is what you should strive to do. You are very tired. You told me so yourself!"

"Yes, I am indeed tired, but my heart and my body respond more to your presence than to my need for sleep." In one motion he was pulling her to him. He tilted her head back and kissed her fully on the lips. She tried to struggle, but her arms were entrapped in twisted material, and her legs were held by the confines of her skirt.

After a few moments the heat was too much for her. She opened her mouth and let him in, willingly.

He felt her resistance fail, and relishing the pleasure

he explored her sweet mouth once again and felt himself grow hard, his desire for becoming one with her stronger than ever.

Brianda felt him loosen her arms and pull the dress over her head. Part of her mind urged her to fight, but somehow she could not muster sufficient desire to resist him. His kiss was too stunning, too wonderful.

John knew that he still had to take time with her. She was wary and inexperienced. Their last encounter had been anything but fulfilling for her. He had inflicted pain, and now he must heal her wounded heart. Time and privacy were his allies.

Brianda lay still as John removed the rest of her clothing. The candles were plentiful, giving more than adequate light for him to see her clearly. She brought her legs together and covered her breasts with her hands.

"Brianda, why do you want to hide your body from me? Do you not remember that I have cared for you for days on end? Your lovely body holds no secrets from me."

"You were functioning as a physician then, not a lover, sir. It is my mind that hides my body from you," she said softly.

"The first time we shared our bodies, it was daylight. It was a prolonged period of time, and we could not have been closer to each other. Why is it that now you feel uncomfortable?" he asked sincerely.

His frankness embarrassed her. She didn't answer, but she didn't need to. A flush began on her chest and rose to her face and cheeks. She looked at the wall.

"Brianda, look at me. You are my wife. I want you to enjoy our private moments. The moments that we have shared, and that we will continue to share often, should be cherished memories that fade only when replaced by even better memories. I don't want you to fight me. Any time you wish to ask a question or discuss any matter with me, please do. I will be more than willing and happy to talk with you. You are still very young, and no doubt have questions. Who better to ask than me?"

"You expect me to be comfortable?" she asked, incredulous. "May I remind you that I have been an unwilling participant in this whole matter," Brianda responded in a soft voice, her eyes still locked on the wall. "I assure you that I did not find the last experience pleasant." He was silent, so she continued, "To be totally honest with you, I cannot understand why people enjoy the . . . act . . . at all!"

"Do you not remember a single moment of pleasure during our last time together?" he asked, watching her as she lay stiffly on the mattress, her eyes fixed on the wall near her side of the bed.

"Do we have to talk about this? Why can't we just sleep?" she said, turning her back to him.

"This discussion is important to our future," he said firmly, turning her toward him, holding her shoulders down on the mattress and commanding that her eyes meet his.

"Is this how it will always be, taking me by force?" she said, struggling against the hands that made it impossible for her to move. "I hate it when I cannot move! Take your damned hands off of me!" she hissed, as tears slipped from her eyes.

He immediately let go of her. Angrily, she brushed the tears away and felt herself go rigid.

"Brianda, I am going to show you, prove to you, that you can enjoy being a woman. A woman that is well loved by a man. I know that you do not believe me at this moment, but you will. I have no other choice but to make you join me now, so that I can prove to you that one day you will want me to make love to you."

"That day will never come!" she cried out, just before he covered her body with his and kissed her. She tried to bite him, but he simply pulled his mouth off hers, held her down, and lowered his lips to caress her breasts. She moaned as his wet lips pulled her nipple into his mouth and then slowly laved each pale mauve crest. How she hated being forced to respond to him! At the stirring in the core of heat that lay deep and low in her abdomen, she fought, trying to think of ugly thoughts. She vowed not to let him know how he affected her.

She made fists, digging her fingernails into her palms. Her nerve endings instantly rebelled, demanding release from the inflicted outrage, but she kept her fists closed tightly, forcing herself to concentrate on the self-induced pain, not the pleasure of his tongue.

At her tenseness, John lifted himself up, and then saw blood seeping out from under her closed palms. Grabbing her hands in both of his, he forced his thumbs against her coiled fingertips and pried her fists open. Eight small crescents of blood oozed from the injured palms. He held the palms to his lips and kissed each of the shallow wounds.

"That was foolish, love. You waste your time, for I have the whole night and all of the morning to delight in you, and you cannot hold me off that long. Why don't you let me show you the meaning of passion?" he asked, placing his head directly over hers and piercing her violet eyes with the sparks of blue embers emanating from his.

She could do no more than turn her head away to avoid the look in those eyes.

"So be it." He lowered his head and kissed her along the long lines of her neck as she strained to turn farther from him.

He insinuated his knee between her tightly closed legs and moved it upward, forcing the limbs apart. She used all the force in her thighs to hold him off, but gave up when her muscles began to burn with the ache of their useless exertion.

"I hate you," she whispered into the night.

"I hope that phrase is not going to be a permanent part of our lovemaking, darling. That is not what a man wants to hear when he is trying to please a woman."

"I hate you!" she cried out, choking on the words.

"I empathize with you," he replied, as his other leg joined the first and spread her open even further.

Brianda's hands flew to his back to dig her nails into his flesh and scratch him. He did not try to stop her. His mouth found its way to her navel, where it circumvented the lovely whirlpool a moment and then lowered further to the forest of crisp, dark-blond hair that protected the delicate valley below. This was where he wanted his mouth now, and he thrilled to the scent of her.

Brianda froze as she felt his mouth touch her. His large hands rested on the peaks of her jutting hipbones, making it impossible for her to move her hips. John knelt between her open legs and moved his nose slowly back and forth through the willowy branches of hair.

Desperately, she reasoned through a cloudy mist that at least his hands were on her hips, and maybe he wasn't going to do to her what he had done the last time. She suddenly remembered the feeling of his fingers within her, and the unwanted heat spread its fingers of tingly warmth throughout her whole abdomen. She moaned deep and low.

Moving quickly, he lowered his right hand and his mouth at the same time. While his fingers spread the slippery, satiny folds, his tongue found the exquisite hub of her womanhood.

Instant, hot, consuming fire engulfed her. "Oh God!" she cried out, her hands flying to his hair. She had to stop him! Her fingers grabbed handfuls of the black strands in an effort to dislodge him.

He opened his mouth and sucked, pulling in a circle of the most sensitive tissue, and his tongue flicked across the erect, tiny flower, causing her to gasp for breath.

"Stop! For the love of God, stop it!" she cried hoarsely, writhing beneath him, trying to move away from the marauder.

"It is for the love of woman that man extends himself. I will do whatever is necessary to bring you the ecstasy you deserve. Stop fighting me and let the sensations take you to a place of beauty you have not yet imagined," he responded, returning to his tender assault on her innermost core.

She could think of nothing else but the sensations he was delivering, as her hips rose and fell with a rhythm of their own, a rhythm as old as the tides of the sea. She could not control them, and she became overwhelmed with fear.

What was happening?

Beads of perspiration were forming on her silken flesh, creating a sheen of liquid heat. She felt as if she might explode.

Maybe she would die from this! Panicked, she gathered all her force, and in one major thrust tried to throw him off of her. But it was useless, she was so small, and he was so large. He would not stop. Her efforts against him were futile.

Strange, garbled sounds rose from her throat. Fire raged within her. She was burning. Her breathing was rapid and ragged. Her thigh and calf muscles tightened, her toes pointed like a dancer's. Her arms were straight and stiff at her sides, and the handfuls of sheet in her fists offered no solace.

John sensed the mounting tension, yet he continued the ever increasing assault. Forcefully, he thrust his fingers into her opening and slipped them in and out in sweet torture. Her hips moved in perfect counterrhythm, as if some force of nature directed them.

At the very moment of what seemed to Brianda her imminent destruction, the expanding fire exploded into a million tiny suns, spreading through her body at incredible speed, generating the most delicious, overwhelming pleasure known to woman. Brianda's head arched backward, her eyes open but unseeing. The gasping sounds of her breathing expanded to cries of joy, as timeless as they were inevitable. The tiny suns touched the outermost reaches of her being and then slowly dissipated and dissolved.

She felt him enter her then, so different from his fingers, filling her so much more, pushing deeper into her soul. Hard and insistent, he coaxed the cushioned softness of her opening, begging entrance into her core.

She could take no more. Her arms and legs flailed about aimlessly, her hands looking for some place of shelter.

"Bring your legs up around my hips, Brianda. Hold me with your arms, and we will move together as one," he cried hoarsely. He had exercised all the self-restraint he possessed to hold himself back. She was so beautiful and so innocent. His desire for her clamored for fulfillment. He had waited until he was sure that she had acquired her gift from him, and only then did he take her. He wanted her to know that he could deliver her to the heart of bliss.

Now she was truly his.

She did as he suggested and locked her legs across his buttocks. With slender arms she reached up and held him, feeling the sensuous movements of his muscular back. Attached thus, she felt safer somehow, as if she were part of his strength. Her body tensed again but the tension was sweet, and hopeful.

He thrust into her again and again, sensing the return of her anticipation. Suddenly, he began thrusting faster and faster. Nothing could stop him now.

The glorious explosion erupted within her again, more quickly than before. She called his name as he called hers. Spewing his essence and future, he showered her cervix in a warm bath, over and over.

Suddenly he lay atop her, breathing hard. Under the weight of him, she felt exhausted, her breath coming in short bursts as her heart and lungs raced to meet the demands for more air. The muscles that had held him within her contracted in involuntary spasms, as if she were trying to wring each drop of his precious fluid from him.

Suddenly she was awash with an overpowering emotion she couldn't place. It was wonder, it was awe. The power of the feeling was growing, overwhelming her, and she burst into tears, her hands coming up to cover the face that had already told him so much.

He rolled onto his side, gathering her into his arms, holding the back of her head as her face sought the comfort and relative privacy of his neck. Softly, he murmured into her ear, "The tears are an expression of release. They represent your surrender to the force of sensual pleasure. Let them fall. Cry for the joy of the first time. Cry for us, for you and me. Remember this night and what it has brought to you, Brianda, and swear that for you, it will be reserved for the expression of love."

She pulled herself closer to him and cried until she slept. He held her cradled against his chest all night.

The bright morning sun shone through the bedroom window. Brianda slept alone in the big bed, covered by a patchwork quilt. As the day grew older, the streak of sun lengthened and finally came to rest on her cheek, awakening her as she unconsciously rubbed at the heated spot on her face.

She was sore all over, every muscle feeling as if it had been in battle. Grimacing as she turned onto her back, she raised the cover and looked down at her body. At the telltale signs of their lovemaking, a rush of feelings overcame her. Her nipples tightened and her stomach rolled a little.

"Good morning, my darling. I have brought you some coffee. Would you like to drink it in bed, or would you rather come out into the salon and drink it in front of the fire?" John asked from the doorway, the steaming mug of coffee in his hand.

Knowing she would have to parade naked in front of him to get to her clothes, she motioned him toward the bed. He handed her the mug and sat beside her as she took her first sip.

She didn't know what to say. She certainly did not want to discuss what happened last night! Everything was so clear in the daylight. She wished he would leave, so that she could get dressed without feeling so vulnerable. She kept the mug at her lips and kept sipping nervously.

"You look beautiful this morning," he said, running his fingers through her hair. He loved the way sunlight made the blond hair seem almost to disappear, so light was its color.

She did not pull away from his touch, although she wanted to. Instead, she forced herself to remain still and prayed that this was not an overture to more physical intimacy. "Sir, I can see that the sun is shining, and it is no longer snowing. You said we might ride today. May we, or is the snow too deep?"

"Is that what you would like to do right now, ride?" he asked, his face so close to hers that his breath was warm on her neck and shoulder.

"Yes. I would very much like to ride."

"While you slept the morning away, madam, I checked with Angus. It is safe for us to ride. Shall I ask that the horses be saddled while you dress?"

"Yes, please do so! I will not be more than twenty minutes in readying myself. Where is some water to use for washing?" she asked, finally turning her face to his.

"See it there, on the small table? I brought it for you. By the way, Brianda, you are not to wear the boys' clothes that you seem to favor. You are to wear a warm riding outfit. Do not be fooled by the sunshine. The air is frigid. I will see to the horses while you get dressed," he said, as he quickly leaned over and kissed her, tasting the coffee on her lips. "You taste like coffee, and you smell like wildflowers. Quite a combination! Hurry along and we will go for our ride."

25

John kicked the snow from his boots as he stepped into the door of the cottage to find Brianda in the kitchen. She looked wonderful in a riding habit of deep crimson wool. Her hair was braided down her back, and her violet eyes sparkled with anticipation.

"I am ready! I am just rinsing out the mug," she announced, hurriedly drying the mug and placing it on the shelf.

"Come, then. The horses are ready and waiting for us," John said, holding the door open for her. She took his arm, and they walked along the slick path to the barn.

Dakota pranced around, held secure only by his strong leather tether. His hooves made hundreds of hollow hoofprints in the virgin snow. At Brianda's approach he began to whinny and throw his head up and down. Ian MacKenzie had to hold the leather strap with both hands as the huge animal pulled against his hold, trying to get to his mistress.

"Dakota! Behave yourself! I am coming!" she called

out to her horse to quiet him. At the sound of her voice, he settled and waited for her.

Ian watched as the small young woman ran to the stallion and threw her arms about him. Looking to the earl, he asked, "Are you sure it is safe for your wife to be so near to this stallion, sir?" his voice filled with concern.

"Thank you for your concern, Ian, but without her presence, we might be the ones in danger from the horse," John said calmly.

"Sir?"

"You see, that horse belongs to Brianda and only Brianda." John looked at his wife, so beautiful in the morning sun, and was not sure whether the sun or Brianda had more brilliance.

Looking back to Ian, he continued, "If it hadn't been for that horse, I would probably not have met my wife. I won him in payment for a gaming debt, and Brianda came to claim him, stating that I had stolen him!"

"I'm sorry, sir, but I don't understand."

"That's all right, Ian, it doesn't matter . . . If my horse is ready, would you call Angus and tell him that we are ready to leave."

"Yes, sir, immediately," Ian answered, as he broke into a run to find his brother. Minutes later, Angus emerged from the barn, his own horse in tow.

"Good morning, my Lord. Good morning, Brianda," Angus said as he mounted his horse. "If you will mount and follow me."

Brianda frowned. "Does Angus have to go with us? Even here in Scotland, does he have to watch out for your welfare every second?" she whispered to John with unveiled hostility.

"Brianda, this is Angus's home and it is to our benefit to have a guide. He is looking out for your welfare, too. Angus is near me, as he feels he should be. I would suggest that in the future, you think before you speak. I would be very displeased if you spoke out of turn and hurt someone's feelings. Am I making myself clear?"

"Yes." Disliking his superior attitude, she turned her back to him and pulled herself up onto Dakota's back, wincing as she let herself down into the saddle. Damn, but she was sore!

Angus led the way, and John and Brianda fell quickly in behind him. "We are going to Bott's Glenn, a small village a mile from here down the mountain. We are traveling on the one main road that leads to the village, although there are many small trails through the forest. The villagers know how to travel these trails, but I would strongly advise that you don't go off on any of them alone—you can get lost, and it is possible that you might never be found," called Angus over his shoulder.

"Did you hear that, Brianda?" asked John sternly.

"Of course, I heard him. I'm not deaf. May I infer from your statement that you will allow me to ride alone while we are here?" she asked expectantly.

"Absolutely not."

"Then why . . . ?"

"Brianda! You are not to ride alone, ever. You had the same restrictions in England, do you not recall?"

"Yes, I remember. All too well," she said defiantly.

"See to it that you continue remembering," he said flatly.

After a downhill ride through the evergreen trees and the pure white snow, they came to the edge of the small village. Small cottages were scattered throughout Bott's Glenn, and women could be seen hanging laundry in the cold air while their children played happily around their homes.

Near the center of the village were various small shops, and John suggested they look for a present for Rebecca. Just as Angus was dismounting, he saw Mary

Carmichael cross in front of a shop at the other side of the village and disappear down an alley. Turning to John, he explained, "Sir, I have something I must do. Do you think you could find your way home without me?"

"It is just straight back up the mountain. I anticipate no difficulty finding the way. Shall you return for dinner, or shall I inform your mother not to expect you?" John asked kindly.

"I shall be back for dinner. Now if you will excuse me," Angus said, turning and running down the street.

John was reflecting that Angus's behavior was indeed extraordinary just as an object in a store window caught Brianda's eye. At her exclamation of delight, he followed her into the shop.

Angus's long legs carried him quickly across the street and along the length of the small village. He found the building where Mary had made her turn and looked both ways, hoping to catch a glimpse of her. He saw nothing to the right. Scanning to the left, he caught a glimpse of Mary entering the door of a small cottage at the farthest edge of town. He ran back and fetched his horse, his heart pounding in his chest.

Mary Carmichael stood in her tiny kitchen and pushed the wayward strands of chestnut hair back from her face. With a sigh, she looked about at her small array of handmade crafts and hoped that she would have better luck tomorrow, as she had sold nothing for three days. She walked to the stove and lit a fire under the kettle. A cup of tea would be wonderful now, and she was pulling the mug from the shelf when she heard a knock on the door.

She stood frozen, unable to move. Not one person had knocked on her door in the last year. The last time someone had knocked . . .

Angus knocked again, harder this time, his concern raised by the sorry condition of the cottage. There were cracked windows, and paint was peeling everywhere. What kind of a husband did Mary have?

Mary wiped her hands in her skirt, a habit she had had since childhood, and walked slowly to the door. With a deep breath, she opened it. "Angus?" she said, the shock evident in her voice.

"Good morning, Mary Carmichael. I wonder if I might come in for a moment?" he asked. "I have just brought the earl and his wife to town, and presently they are shopping."

"Well . . . I-I don't think it would look proper . . ." she stammered, looking about to see if any of her neighbors could see Angus standing at her door.

"Oh, is your husband here, or is he working? My mother mentioned that you were married, but declined to tell me any more. I don't even know your married name, Mary Carmichael," he said, looking into her big, brown eyes.

"My husband . . . Angus, you can't stand there in the cold. Please come in and warm yourself," she said in that soft voice of hers that had haunted his dreams.

He kicked the snow from his boots and walked into her house. It was immaculately clean. She led him to the salon and offered him a seat. As he lowered himself into the old chair, he thought she was more beautiful in the daylight than she had been by candlelight.

"Excuse me while I prepare us some tea." Mary hurried out of the room and found that she had to put both of her hands on the kitchen table to steady herself. What if someone had seen him enter the house? *To the devil with them!* she thought as she poured tea into the mugs, put sugar in each, and carried them unsteadily to the salon . . . and to Angus.

He stood when she came into the room and took one

of the mugs from her trembling fingers. He sat, and she took a chair across from him. He noticed her fingers twisting the fabric of her skirt, but said nothing.

"Tell me how you have been, Angus. Is England exciting?" When Angus didn't answer immediately, she became flustered. "I suppose anything would be exciting compared to Bott's Glenn, would it not?" she rambled, embarrassed beneath his scrutiny.

Mary Carmichael did not have to look up at Angus MacKenzie to see him. His face was a permanent part of her memory. She saw the dark blond hair and hazel eyes, the broad nose, the full mouth, and the scar over his right eyebrow from the time he ran straight into a branch when he was seven years old.

"I have been fine, Mary," he answered at last. "I cannot believe that I have been gone from home five years. You look the same. My parents and brothers look the same. However I must admit that my little sisters are not little anymore. They have grown into young women and are courting now, I'm told."

Angus paused, remembering back when he had courted Mary. Forcing himself back to the present, he looked at her. "England is a marvelous place, Mary. I have seen things there you couldn't imagine. Someday I would like to tell you about it, but now I want to know about you."

"There's nothing much to know. Here I am, in Bott's Glenn. I'll most likely die here. My future holds nothing exciting—no foreign land, no new life," she said, the pain soft in her voice.

"Mary, I left for England five years ago because my father made me go. I had every intention of coming back."

"But you did not . . . You did not come back like you promised, Angus," she said, rising from the chair and walking to the window. Furious with herself, she blinked back the old, unwanted tears.

"Mary, did anyone ever tell you why I did not come back?" he pleaded.

"No. After three months of waiting for word from you, I asked permission from my father to visit your parents. I climbed the mountain and asked your father why you had not yet returned. He told me that he had heard no word from you, and that he would inform me if and when word arrived. He asked me not to bother your mother, for it caused her too much pain to talk about it. She was sure you were dead." She stopped talking, it was too difficult to go on.

"Mary . . ."

"Let me finish. When one year had passed, I returned to your house. Your mother told me simply that something had happened to you, and that you would not be returning home, ever. She cried, and I left and returned to my father's home. My world had been destroyed."

"Allow me to tell you what happened, please," Angus begged.

"What difference could it make now? So much time has passed."

"Please, Mary, let me speak."

"I am listening," she said gravely, looking at her lap.

"I arrived in London after weeks on a ship where gamblers and drinkers filled the lower deck. They tried to get me to join in their gaming, but I always refused. The sum of money I carried was the final payment on my father's debt, and he entrusted me with the honor of completing that transaction. The men never let up on me, and swore they would get my money one way or another. On the day we docked in England, I forgot about those men, too excited by the teeming streets and English voices. I never saw them when they attacked me from behind. One of them hit me in the head with a club, then they stabbed me fifteen times in the chest and abdomen. I was left to die in the gutter."

Mary sat ramrod straight in her chair, the tears falling unnoticed from her eyes.

"They took my money and my bag. Luckily for me, someone carried me to a local surgeon. I was barely conscious. He worked on me for hours, never left me for a moment until he knew I would live. He took me to his own home and cared for me. The physical wounds healed in time, but for many months—a year—I didn't know who I was, Mary, or even that I had left you behind," he said, his voice hoarse with emotion. "Eighteen months after my attack, I regained some memory. I remembered my father's debt that had gone unpaid and I remembered you. . . . I wanted to die. I had dishonored my father, and I had lost the only woman that I ever loved.

"The earl gave me reason to live, Mary. I owe him my life and my sanity. He gave me a job and, without my knowledge, paid my father's debt. He wrote to my parents, telling them of my misfortune and the fact that he didn't know if I would every fully recover. I suppose that is why my mother told you what she did." He stopped talking and reached over to take Mary's hand in his. He saw the thin gold band on her finger as she hastily pulled her hand from his.

"Don't touch me like that, Angus. It is wrong," she whispered.

"Forgive me. I had to touch you for just a moment." He rose and walked around the room, noting how plain it was. "I figured that I had lost you by the time I recovered my memory, and I knew I had to work to pay off my debt to the earl. I vowed that I would look after him always, that I would guard his life, as he had salvaged mine. It was his idea to return to Scotland.

"I was afraid, I didn't want to come home to find you married to someone else. That is, of course, exactly what I have found. Fate dealt us a nasty blow. I realize the most I can hope for is that you understand. If you cannot find it in your heart to do that, at least forgive me, Mary," he pleaded. Then he bent, a sob breaking from his chest like a clap of thunder. He put his hands to his face, overcome with grief.

Mary rose and went to stand behind him and gently put her arms around his waist, resting her head in the middle of his back. "I understand, *and* I forgive you. I thank God for the surgeon—his skill and his heart. You are well, that is all that matters."

Angus put his hands over hers and held them. "Tell me that you are happy, Mary."

She did not respond.

"Is he bad to you? Answer me, Mary!" he demanded, turning to face her.

"Come and sit down. I will tell you my story now. Fate, indeed, is a cruel taskmaster," she said, as she pulled her hands from his and led him to the chair. "I want you to listen and not interrupt me."

Angus wiped the tears from his face and nodded in agreement.

"One year after you left, a man came to my father's door and presented himself as Brian McCoy. He stated that he lived in Bott's Glenn and had a job working in forestry for the McIntosh Company. He asked my father for my hand in marriage. Though I had never seen him before, my father agreed immediately, telling me that he was not going to continue to feed me all my life, as it was obvious that you were never coming back for me. He had four other daughters to care for, and he was sure that, as I had reached the old age of twenty, this would be my last chance to get a husband. We were married two weeks later. I never spent one minute with him before the wedding. No one came to the church, just my family. McCoy did not have any family," she explained, her voice strange and flat. "He brought me to this house right after the ceremony. It was just before noon. He showed me each room and where everything was. He told me that he expected his house to always be perfectly clean. He told me what foods he liked and how he wanted them prepared. I made the noon meal. He left then, and did not return until dark. When he entered the house, he smelled of liquor. Without a word, he sat at the table and ate the dinner that I had prepared. Afterward, he went into the salon and sat while I cleaned the kitchen. He called me into the bedroom and told me to take my clothes off."

Angus felt as if he'd been punched in the stomach. Breathing was an effort.

"I started to undress, slowly. He stood and watched me, not saying anything. When I was completely undressed, I just stood there. In seconds, he was undressed, and he took me to the bed. He laid me down, spread my legs and thrust himself into me. I bit my tongue, but I did not cry out. In a very short time, he was finished. He rolled off me and told me that I had to do that whenever he wanted to, for he wanted a lot of children. . . ."

Angus stood up and ran to the door, flinging it open, then vomited into the snow. When the spasm passed, he walked back to his chair and waited for her to continue.

"I was not allowed to leave this house. I saw no one, and no one visited. I was told that McCoy had made it known to all in the village that we wanted no neighbors, no visits. He worked seven days a week. He came home to eat at noon and every night at dark. After six months, I still wasn't pregnant, so he decided that he would have to have me more often. After lunch, he would turn me over the kitchen table, lift my dress and take me there. He drank every night, some cheap liquor that made him smell awful. There was hardly a night that he didn't use me. After two years I still wasn't pregnant. That is when he began hitting me. Maybe he thought he could beat me into getting pregnant." Mary had to take a few deep breaths before she could go on. "Then one day, over a year ago now, there was a knock on the door. It scared me—no one ever came here. It was one of the men he worked with. There had been a terrible accident. McCoy was dead. A tree had fallen in the wrong direction and had crushed him. The man took off his hat and asked me where I wanted the body. I looked over his shoulder, and there were the men, with McCoy's body in a sling. They laid him out in the salon and left. I had him buried as soon as the church would allow. No one came, not even his fellow workers."

Mary stood and walked to a nearby table. Angus sat, unable to speak. She returned and put a small hand-carved ornament into his hand. It was delicate and beautifully painted. "This is what I started making after he died. My father would have no part in my returning home, so all I had was this cottage and myself. Now I make ornaments and go out every day to see if I can sell a few to make money for food. No one here in the village wants anything to do with me. I guess what McCoy told the villagers must have been pretty bad. I overheard some women talking one day, when they didn't know I was near. McCoy had told his fellow workers horrible stories about me, sexual things . . ."

"Oh my God, my Mary, how you have suffered!" Angus cried out to her, his heart breaking.

"When I heard you were coming home, I had to see you for myself, just once. I was sure you would have come with your wife and children. I didn't care. I have no pride, I just wanted to see your face to know that you were all right. Then I could go on with this long life until God calls me."

Angus raised his head and looked at her, to him, the

world's most beautiful woman. She sat staring straight ahead, not seeing him, lost in her own sadness.

He reached across the table and grabbed her hands. She tried to pull them away, but he wouldn't let her.

"You must go now," she cried. "I cannot stand any further alienation from these people, Angus. If no one buys my ornaments, I cannot eat. Thank you for your visit. It will be a sweet memory that will carry me through the long days and nights after you have returned to England." She smiled wanly at him and walked to the door.

"Mary, I would like you to take a walk with me on Saturday. Will you go?" he asked gently, tilting her head up with his fingertips.

"A walk? In the village?" she asked, worried.

"There is nothing wrong with a walk, Mary. You are a widow, and your husband has been dead one year. I am not married and never have been. It is perfectly acceptable. Will you go?" he asked again.

"All right. I will."

"Have you a pretty dress, Mary Carmichael? Please wear your prettiest dress and let your hair hang loose around your shoulders. It is so beautiful, but no one would know, the way you have it tied up back here," he said, patting the bun at the base of her head.

"It has been five years since I have had a new dress, Angus. But I swear to you I will look pretty for our walk," she said with a small sparkle in her eye.

"I promise to come for you at ten minutes before ten in the morning. Make sure you are ready for me, for I am not a man who breaks his promises."

"Yes, I remember," she said, thinking of the one promise that he had not kept. At least she knew now that he could not have kept it. "When will you leave for England?"

"Soon. We are only here on holiday," he said, bringing her hand to his lips.

"I see. Well, we were at least able to talk to each other a little, and now we will be able to talk more on Saturday."

"That is true. I will leave now and will return in three days, just before ten. Be ready," he said, opening the door and walking outside.

She watched as he mounted his horse. "I have been ready all my life," she whispered to him as she watched him ride up the mountain.

26

John and Brianda raced each other the last half mile up the mountain to the MacKenzie house. On the back of Dakota Brianda won easily. John bowed low and freely admitted defeat, for which Brianda gave him a wholehearted hug. John tried to remind his wife that it was he who had to carry the package they had bought in the village, but she just waved him off, stating that her horse was superior. Once they had walked their horses to cool them down, they put them into their stalls and walked hand in hand to the main house.

Ian's wife, Sandra, greeted them warmly and ushered them into the salon, where they could warm themselves before a fireplace so enormous it held two huge logs, ten feet long and two feet in diameter. Sandra brought her guests hot tea and biscuits fresh from the oven.

"I could get fat living here, sir," Brianda said contently. She had had a wonderful day.

"It would please me to see you gain some weight, Brianda. Maybe I should bring a Scottish cook home with us when we return to England. Then you would have no excuse not to eat."

"Surely you are jesting, sir! Why, you would break Cook's heart if you did such a thing!"

"My sweet, I was just teasing you. I would never do anything to hurt Cook's feelings."

"Are we returning to England soon?" she asked expectantly.

"Do you wish to?"

"No! I am enjoying my stay here. Everyone is so friendly and nice. I loved our ride today. Can we go again tomorrow?"

"You just want to beat me in another race," he said, smiling at her beaming face. "We can decide in the morning if we wish to ride. As for our departure, we will be returning to meet the *Maid of the Green* in three to four weeks' time. I, too, am enjoying our visit, but I have matters to attend to at home and cannot be gone any longer."

Angus burst through the door and, seeing John, walked quickly to him. "May I speak to you a moment, alone, sir?"

"Yes, of course, Angus. Brianda, please go into the kitchen and bring a cup of tea for Angus," John said firmly.

"All right." Brianda hurried off to find Sandra.

"May I take the liberty to discuss a personal matter with you, sir?" he said, his stance restless, his eyes afire.

"We had better find a private spot, then," John responded. "Where can we talk freely?"

"In my bedroom upstairs, sir. Follow me, and I will show you the way."

When they were seated in two chairs facing each other, Angus began pouring out Mary Carmichael's story. John said nothing. As the tale drew to a close, tears fell from Angus's eyes, slipping over the contours of a face wracked with pain.

"I want to murder a man who is already dead!" Angus said brokenly. "I want to bash his head in, break every bone . . ."

"I understand why you feel this way. If he were alive, I think I would like to have a go at him myself. You cannot change what is in the past. What matters is how you will handle yourself and Mary in the future. You know I will help you in any way that I can," John stated calmly.

"I know that you will, and I thank you. You are always there when I need you, sir. I have done some thinking. Here is my plan . . ."

Brianda carried the cup of tea into the salon, only to find the room empty. She considered trying to find the men, but then thought better of it. Recalling the tone in John's voice when he suggested she fetch some tea, she understood it as a request to leave the men to talk in private. She decided to return to the kitchen to see if she could help with the food preparations.

Katherine, Andrew's wife, and Judith, Colin's wife, were peeling potatoes when Brianda entered. Katherine, almost nine months pregnant, was balancing the unpeeled potatoes on her bulging abdomen. Judith was roaring with laughter. Soon Sandra and Rebecca came over to see what was so hilarious. Brianda joined them, and all five of them ended up laughing at Katherine's antics.

Sandra took Brianda with her to the counter near the sink and showed her how to mix freshly cut apples with cinnamon and sugar before placing them in a pie. Brianda soon forgot about John and paid very close attention to the art of pie-making.

Hours later, when Rebecca rang the dinner bell, Brianda's dress, arms and hands were covered with flour. She could not see her face, and had no idea that she looked like a clown. She had made two excellent pies completely unassisted, including the preparation and rolling of the crusts. Brianda had never done anything like it in all her near-eighteen years!

All of the MacKenzie women had praised her work and had added their own bits of advice as Brianda had worked throughout the afternoon. Each woman now smiled inwardly as they observed both her joy and the tremendous mess. Flour was spilled throughout the kitchen, but no one was concerned, because Brianda's beautiful face beamed with pride at her accomplishment.

John and Angus descended the stairs when they heard the dinner bell. Both came to a dead stop at the sight of Brianda.

"Hello!" she called out. "Wait until you see what I have done!"

"Have you destroyed the kitchen?"

"John Fauxley, don't you dare tease me!"

"I am completely serious. Will I have to spend a fortune repairing Michael's kitchen, or did you have a run-in with a baker?"

"You are just saying that because I have a little flour on me."

"Three loaves of bread could be made from your dress alone. How did you manage that glob of stuff on the tip of your nose?" he asked half seriously.

The six MacKenzie women, hiding behind the kitchen door, burst into laughter. Brianda turned and looked at the closed door and frowned. The MacKenzie men took one look at Brianda and had to pinch each other so as not to laugh, but at her defiant look they couldn't hold their mirth inside any longer.

Brianda stood her ground. "Go ahead and laugh. Maybe I do look like a mess, but I am quite proud of myself!"

Michael MacKenzie rushed over and swept her up in his enormous arms. "Girl, any woman who is proud of something she made in the kitchen is always welcome in my home. Thank you for making whatever it was you did make. I am sure everyone is going to enjoy the fruits of your labors. And don't pay a bit of attention to any of these laughing goons in this house." With that he lifted her straight up in the air and carried her out the front door. He stopped and gave her a few hefty shakes, and a pile of flour fell from her to the ground. "There, the flour will blend in with the snow and no one will be the wiser!"

"Why, thank you, Michael! And thank you for not making fun of me," she said, as her beautiful violet eyes found his.

"You are a beauty, a real English flower. Maybe a little too delicate for life here on the mountain top, but I think your spirit is great and full. Now, Lady Fauxley, will you do me the honor of accepting my arm as we go to the dinner table?" Turning to his guest, the earl, and the rest of his family he asked, "Will the rest of you please come to dinner before it gets cold."

Soon the ten members of the family and their two guests were sitting at the big table, ready to savor the delicious fare. John leaned over and whispered to Brianda, "I apologize for laughing, sweetheart. You just looked so comical. I, too, am proud of your efforts."

Brianda beamed. Life could not be better.

Early Saturday morning, Mary Carmichael McCoy awoke and examined the dresses she had pulled from her old trunk. They were old when she had packed them. Now they were five years older, and they looked it. Sadly, she noted that there wasn't a single pretty dress in the lot, but decided on a green dress that was the least faded and worn. She hung it outside to take the musty smell out of it, then she lit the burners on the stove and put three pots of water on to heat for a bath. What a luxury!

In the kitchen, on the top shelf of her cabinet, she found a very old, dusty bottle of rose-scented shampoo she had hidden ages before. There was enough for one more washing. She decided that she might as well go all out for her walk with Angus. She might never again have the opportunity.

She stepped into the old metal tub filled with warm water and shampooed her hair. She then found herself daydreaming while she luxuriated in the warm, scented bath water. She shook her head to clear those fanciful thoughts away and slipped out of the tub, then dried herself and looked at her naked body in the cracked mirror in the bedroom. Her face was thin, but still fairly pretty, and her tall body still looked firm and somewhat youthful. She leaned over to pull on her only under-clothes. Clean but shabby, they spoke of the way Mary's life had been, weary and sad.

The lonely young woman sat on a small stool near the window, so that the heat from the rays of the sun would help dry her long tresses. She brushed and brushed, and when she was done, her dark hair glowed with a red hue. Her mother had always said that her thick tresses were her nicest feature.

Tears threatened when Mary thought of her mother. She missed her so much. Before McCoy had died, her father had forbidden his wife to visit his oldest daughter. "There is something wrong with a woman who cannot have children. She is tainted," he had told his wife.

Shaking off the sadness, Mary put on the green dress. It was still early, but she had no way to tell the time, other than by guessing, so she did not want to be late.

Suddenly there was a knock on her door and she

ran to open it, but there was no one in sight. Baffled, she was closing the door when she spotted the box on the doorstep. She grabbed it quickly and hurried inside. It was a big box, and her heart beat fast with the excitement of it all.

Inside, wrapped with tissue paper, was the most beautiful dress that Mary had ever seen. It was cream-colored with pale pink ribbons on the sleeves, on the bodice and at the waist. She held it up in front of her and stroked the fabric. She had never felt anything like it before. It flowed through her fingers, soft as the heather on the mountain. There was an extra piece of ribbon at the bottom of the box, and to it was pinned a note.

> My Dear Mary,
>
> Please accept the dress as a gift from me. It will be more beautiful with you wearing it. Use this extra piece of ribbon for your hair, but wear your hair long, the way I like it, please. Until ten a.m.
>
> Love, Angus

She took off the green dress and pulled the new one on. It fit her perfectly, making her breasts look firm and her waist tiny. She turned around and around in front of the mirror, watching in wonder as the dress floated through the air. She tied the pink ribbon into her hair, and the overall effect was wonderful! The joy of the moment brought a rosy glow to her cheeks. She was still smiling when a knock on the door brought her from her reverie.

Angus stood at the door with a bunch of pink roses in his hand. Mary didn't know what to say, and thanked him with her eyes instead. Handing the roses to her, he stepped inside.

"You are the loveliest woman on this Earth, Mary

Carmichael. The dress is perfect. Are you ready for our walk?" he asked, his heart bursting with anticipation.

"Yes. Thank you for the dress, Angus. I should not accept it, as it is not proper . . . but it is so beautiful. I love it." Mary's eyes sparkled like diamonds. She looked up at Angus, and what she saw there startled her. Looking quickly away, she said softly, "Let me put the roses in some water before we go."

"Bring them with us, Mary. They smell so good, and they look just right in your hands."

"They're so beautiful, and I would hate for them to die from the cold. Will they be all right?" she asked, looking into his eyes.

"Everything is going to be all right, Mary. Where is your coat? It is time to go."

"All I have is this old coat. Does it matter that I have to put it on over the beautiful new dress?"

"My mother lent me this cloak for you to wear this morning. Would you do her the honor of wearing it?"

"Your mother's cloak? I thought she wanted nothing to do with me, Angus, just like all the rest of the people of Bott's Glenn," she said, looking away.

"You were welcomed in our home the other night, were you not, Mary?"

"Yes."

"Here, put on the cloak, and we will go." Angus put it on her and tied the front ribbons. He took her hand firmly and led her from the house, then began walking toward the center of town.

Mary pulled her hand from his. "Why are you going this way?" she asked warily.

"You will go with me wherever I choose to walk. We will walk with our heads high, Mary Carmichael. You have nothing to fear," he said gently.

Mary kept her eyes on the ground. She couldn't stand the thought of the prying eyes and wagging tongues, but she was so happy to be with Angus that she was willing to live with the consequences. They had been walking for five minutes, when she finally looked up and saw that they had almost reached the small church. The door was open.

Angus took a firmer grip on her hand and kept walking straight up the steps toward the open door!

"It has been a long while since I have been in the church, Angus," she said, as she leaned back and pulled on his hand in an effort to slow him down.

Angus kept walking, pulling her along behind him. Just as they reached the door, he turned to her and said, "Mary, my love, I am going to take you into the church and marry you. Father Brown is waiting for us. The earl is going to walk you down the aisle and present you to me. His wife, Brianda, will act as your matron of honor. Give me your left hand."

Wordlessly, she lifted her hand to him. He slipped the thin gold band off her finger, placing it into his pocket. Then he leaned over and kissed her.

"Wait! There are things to be said, questions to be answered . . ."

"Hush, love, there will be plenty of time to explain all the details to you later. Now everyone is waiting." He smiled at her with such love that she felt her heart skip a beat.

"But how did you get the papers so fast, how . . .?"

"Mary! I will tell you all you wish to know later. Suffice it to say for now that having an English lord as a friend helps." He ushered her into the church.

John and Brianda were standing at the back. Brianda ran up and kissed Mary on the cheek. The young woman looked wonderful in a dress of deep rose. She, too, had a bunch of fresh flowers for her bouquet. Angus walked to the front of the church and stood beside the priest.

Brianda started down the aisle when the organ began to play. John took Mary's arm and smiled down at her.

His arm felt strong and secure under Mary's hand, and his presence gave her courage.

As John began walking Mary down the aisle, he felt her trembling. Her fingers were cold on his arm, her gait unsteady. "Are you all right, Mary?" he whispered to her.

She looked up at him and gave him a brief smile, which he returned with a broad grin, letting her know that he was her friend, and that she was safe.

As they neared the front of the church, Mary saw the whole MacKenzie clan sitting on the left side of the church. Rebecca had tears running down her face and a handkerchief at her nose. They all smiled at her, and she felt their silent welcome.

All alone on the right side of the church sat Mary's mother! Eileen Carmichael, too, had tears in her eyes as she watched her oldest daughter walk toward the man she had always loved. This moment was an answer to her prayers.

Mary's hand clamped down on John's arm as she felt her knees go weak for a second. He supported her by slipping his left arm around her waist and taking her right hand in his. She smiled a tremulous smile at her mother, and they spoke of love with their eyes.

Angus stepped forward and took Mary to the altar. In twenty minutes, they were married. Then Angus gently kissed his bride, and the ice around Mary's heart broke.

The guests gathered outside the door of the church. Every member of Angus's family hugged and kissed Mary. "You are where you belong at long last, Mary," Michael MacKenzie whispered into his newest daughter's ear.

"Thank you, Mr. MacKenzie," was all Mary could say.

"It's father to you now, girl," he answered, hugging her to his massive chest.

Eileen Carmichael was the last person to leave the small church. Clutching a small white handkerchief in her hands, she watched as the MacKenzies welcomed her daughter to their family. She dabbed at the flow of tears that fell softly from her eyes, then descended the church steps and walked to the corner of the building to lean against it. The smooth stones were almost as cold as her heart. For four years she had been cruelly deprived of seeing her daughter. Now she gratefully watched her lovely Mary.

Mary turned just then and looked for her mother. Finding her in the shadows of the church, she ran to her with arms outstretched.

Clasped together, they said nothing, just holding each other was enough. Eileen held Mary's face between her hands and looked at her, trying to memorize every detail. From deep within her soul, she said to Mary, "My daughter, at last you will be happy. My prayers have been answered. I have thought of you every day and have kept you in my heart. When Angus came to me to tell me of the wedding plans, I wept with joy. He is, and will be, your salvation. This I know, for he loves you, girl, he always has."

"And I love him. As I love you, Mother."

"I have defied your father in coming here today. Indeed, he knows nothing of this wedding. I have never before done such a thing in the thirty years that we have been married. . . ."

Mary couldn't hold back the sob that came from her throat. "For all the pain Father has caused, I love him still, Mother. Please know, always, that your love means more to me than I can say."

Eileen held her daughter tightly in her arms and continued, "You are my child, and I love you. So do your sisters. One day we will all be reunited. Mary, your bad times are over now and Providence has offered you a chance at happiness. Know that wherever you venture, your sisters and I go with you in spirit and in love."

"Thank you, Mother."

"Angus promised me that when you two are settled permanently, he will write to Father Brown, and the good priest will see to it that I am informed. I swear that I will write to you often, my daughter. Be happy with your new husband. Now, I must go before your father finds me missing," she said, holding her daughter tight to her breast for one last moment before releasing her. "God bless you and Angus. I love you, Mary." Then with a long, last look, she turned homeward.

Mary stood frozen as she watched her mother leave, knowing that she might never see her again. Angus, standing just behind Mary, could feel her agony. He slipped his hands and arms around her waist and pulled her back to his chest.

"Come, Mary, it is time to go," he whispered softly into her hair, but Mary didn't move until she lost sight of the small figure, now high up on the mountain.

When Angus turned her and helped her onto the waiting wagon, Mary turned to him, her eyes glimmering with tears. "Angus, I must return to the cottage! There is something there that I must have," she implored, both hands on his forearms.

"I have already seen to it. All of your belongings have been packed up and transferred to my home. I have made arrangements to sell the cottage immediately to a single man who works in the forestry. You will not go back to that horrible place again, Mary," he said sternly, looking directly into her eyes.

"You don't understand! There is something there that means the world to me. Only I know where it is hidden." Facing him squarely, she continued, "I love you and I am your wife. I am begging you to allow me to go back to the cottage for just a moment to get what is precious to me."

"I swore that when I took you from that hell, you would never return. But, if this means so much to you, we will go now, but we will go together," he said, looking into the most expressive eyes he'd ever known.

"Thank you, Angus," was all she could manage.

As they rode through the village of Bott's Glenn, Mary Carmichael MacKenzie held her head high, holding the arm of her husband, her eyes straight ahead. She no longer needed to look to the side to see if hastily drawn curtains were falling back into place.

Angus opened the cottage door, and Mary passed by him. It was shocking to see the rooms empty, the cupboards bare. Taking a deep breath, she walked into the kitchen with Angus right behind her.

She reached up and pulled a brick from the chimney stack that vented the kitchen's oven. Hidden behind the brick was a small, old brown leather box. Tenderly, Mary pulled the box out of its hiding place and opened it. Inside were the rosary that her mother had given her at her first communion, and a necklace that Angus had made for her on her fifteenth birthday. It was fashioned from horsehair that had been woven tightly, and hanging from the center of the necklace was a polished blue-green stone. She put the necklace around her neck and held the rosary in her hand. Looking up at Angus, she announced, "Now, I am ready to leave."

Angus leaned over and kissed her. "I love you, Mary Carmichael, I always have and I always will. Let's go home."

Mary walked from the cottage and never once looked back.

27

The party was in full swing when the newly-weds arrived at the house. A joyous cheer welcomed them and they were soon surrounded by family and friends. Rebecca, her daughters, and the neighbor women had prepared a fabulous feast. Brianda had been assigned to the pie-making, and she was thrilled, as pie-making was now her specialty. No one mentioned that it was the only thing Brianda knew how to make.

Once the guests could eat no more, the men retreated to the main salon and drank coffee, and the women took care of the kitchen chores. Mary shyly offered to help but Rebecca shooed her off, telling her that no MacKenzie woman washed a dish on her wedding day!

Angus took Mary's hand and snuck her out of the house to go for a walk. It was late afternoon by then, and they bundled up in heavy cloaks to keep out the bitter cold.

But the cold did not bother them in the least as they walked to their favorite, secret place of years gone by. They had first come here when they were seven years old, and it had been theirs ever since. They both stood with their backs to the huge boulder and looked out across the forest and to the neighboring mountain tops covered with snow. This seemed to be an eternal place, untouched by time or worries, a place of solace.

"Mary, I have some important things to tell you," Angus said, holding her hands in his and looking down at her.

Suddenly fearful, Mary looked at him. "Tell me whatever it is," she declared bravely. "Nothing can tarnish the joy that this day has brought to me."

"I hope the news will not be too difficult for you to understand, Mary." Clearing his throat, his eyes unwavering, he spoke. "Soon the earl and Brianda will be leaving Scotland. I don't know when or if he will ever return. We will leave by ship for England. My life is dedicated to the service of his Lordship, and my responsibilities are exceedingly important to me," he concluded, trying to read the reaction on her face.

Grabbing her skirt in her hands and wringing the material fiercely, she bit her lip. When he said no more, she asked, "Am I to stay here?" Her look revealed the dreaded answer she anticipated.

"Of course not!" he almost yelled at her. Taking her by the shoulders, he gave her a slight shake. "You will never be separated from me again, Mary. Never again! Do you understand?" he demanded.

"Yes, I understand, Angus. But then, what is the bad news?"

"That we are leaving Scotland, maybe forever."

"Angus, I am ready to leave this land. I feel no loss leaving behind those who have treated me unkindly. Scotland is the country where I was born, and I love it. But I love you more and will go willingly wherever your life leads you." Mary looked around her, a look of sadness settling on her face. "I leave here a family that I can neither see nor enjoy, nor even love freely. They will always be in my thoughts, but my heart and soul go gladly with you."

Angus smiled warmly and lifted her into the air. When her mouth was even with his, he pulled her close and kissed her. "We have plans to make . . ."

"Angus." Mary put her fingertips to his mouth. "My love, we must speak about one very important matter. Our marriage has not yet been consummated, so you can still be free of it if you choose."

"What in the hell are you talking about?"

She once again placed her fingers on his mouth, and her eyes filled with tears. "Have you forgotten, sir, that I am unable to have children?" she asked quietly, her words breaking into a small sob.

"Oh, my God, Mary!" Angus cried out, pulling her close to him and holding her tight against his chest. "My dearest Mary, if God has decided that He will not bless us with children, then so be it. It does not matter to me. I have you, and you are all I need. If God chooses to bless us with a child, then we will have a child. But that will be His decision. As it is, I could not feel more blessed by God than I do now."

"Thank you, Angus," she whispered.

"Mary, what shall we do with the furniture, dishes and other small items from the cottage?" he asked, holding her to him.

"Offer whatever you like to your family, and whatever is left can be given to the church. Father Brown can distribute what he chooses to those who are in need. I want nothing except what I had saved in the small, brown leather box."

"Fine then, that is what we shall do. Let's go home. It is getting quite dark, and it is even colder now."

Arm in arm they walked back through the snow, turning to look one more time at their spot in the woods that they would most likely never see again.

*   *   *

It was late that night before Angus was able to steal Mary off to his bedroom. He took her to the door of his bedroom, picked her up and carried her across the threshold. He placed her square in the middle of the room and smiled at her. A fire had been set and the room was pleasantly warm.

Tired from the busy day, he stretched, and turning, took off his coat and placed it over the back of the chair.

Mary turned her back to him and began undressing mechanically and swiftly, laying her clothes on a blanket chest. Naked, she faced Angus.

To Angus, she was more beautiful than he had ever imagined. Many times he had dreamt of how she would look, but never would he have been able to conjure her up as she looked tonight.

Suddenly he realized that she was rigid, her face unreadable. His heart constricted and he reached out to her and smiled gently. "I wish you would have let me take your clothes off, Mary. You are so beautiful like this that it may be too great a shock for my heart!" he said as softly and sweetly as he could.

Mary did not know what to think. Wasn't she supposed to have done that? She smiled back at him, confused but reassured by his kind words.

He picked her up then and carried her to his bed. "Wait for me here. I will join you in a moment." Angus walked to the chair and quickly undressed, knowing how very uncomfortable she was. When he turned to her, she gasped loudly.

His desire for her obvious, Mary was shocked at the mere size of him. It hadn't occurred to her that because Angus was much bigger than McCoy, he would be that much larger there, too!

Unnerved, she pushed herself back and away from

him. All she had ever experienced in her wifely duties with McCoy had been painful and degrading. Now she considered that she might die from the sheer size of Angus!

Angus saw the apprehension in her eyes. Once again thinking that he would like to murder McCoy, Angus moved slowly toward her. He meant with all his heart to show Mary how much he loved her, he would demonstrate just how much with kindness and respect. He would teach her that their union was for their mutual pleasure, from which all good things would come in time.

He climbed into bed and pulled her gently into his arms. She felt like a piece of wood in the snow, frozen and unyielding. "Mary, do you remember when we were teenagers, and we would lie in the woods and talk about what making love would be like?"

Mary nodded and kept her head pressed safely on the strong muscles of Angus's chest.

"We wanted to make love, but we did not, knowing that we should wait for the blessing of the church first. Now we have that blessing. Tonight we will be those young teenagers, thrilling at the sights and touches of each other. We have loved each other secretly, silently, all through these lonely years. Tonight should be ours. Are you ready to be mine, Mary?"

"Yes, Angus, oh, yes!" she beamed, lifting her smiling face to his, kissing him with all the love she had stored for so long in her aching heart.

They took their time and came to know each other in ways that would have seemed unattainable only a day earlier. When at last he entered her welcoming warmth, she cried out, not only from the pain of the size of him but from the joy of finally holding him as only a woman can hold the man she loves. Later, calling out in unison, they clung together, wet with the extremes of love. She fell asleep in his arms, knowing the special peace that lovers share.

In the early morning, Katherine MacKenzie went into labor. It was her first child and the first grandchild for Rebecca and Michael. The men took Andrew out to work on their farm as they would on any other day of the week. Andrew was driving everyone in the house mad, and Katherine's contractions had only just begun.

She labored hard until midnight. The midwife was worried because the contractions were close together and hard, but the young woman's cervix wasn't dilating as expected. First baby or not, something was amiss. The continuous cries of Katherine's pain wrenched the souls of all those in the upstairs room with her. For she was a strong woman, and not given to hysterics.

Brianda had attended many births with Old Megan, and from experience knew Katherine didn't seem to be progressing as she should. Finally, when Brianda could stand it no longer, she went in search of John. Deep in her heart she knew that she shouldn't interfere with MacKenzie business, but Brianda was afraid that Katherine might die if someone did not do something to help her.

John heard Brianda enter the cottage and looked up expectantly from his book. He didn't like the look on his young wife's face.

"What is wrong, darling?"

"Sir, I am sorry if I am doing something wrong, but I am frightened. I think Katherine is in terrible trouble. You need to come and help her," she said, her voice quavering.

"All right, you go for my medical bag while I get my coat. You can tell me all the details while we walk to the house."

When they entered the main salon, the MacKenzie men were sitting together, trying to keep Andrew occupied while Katherine's cries permeated the house.

John went directly to Andrew. "Andrew, do you know that I am a physician and surgeon?"

Andrew shook his head no, worry written all over his face.

"I am a practicing physician in London. Do I have your permission to tend to Katherine? I think the midwife might object, so I need to know which course you wish to follow," John stated simply.

"Please help her, sir. Please help her!" he begged.

"Stay down here with your family until I call for you, Andrew. Brianda, you will assist me," John said, as he headed up the stairs.

Upon entering the room, all the women gasped at the idea of a man's presence in the birthing room. Brianda stepped forward quickly and explained that John was a physician.

The indignant midwife rose and announced that if her services were no longer required, she would leave. Rebecca walked the older woman out of the room, calming the irate woman with the explanation that John was an old friend of the family and was, after all, a doctor of medicine.

John sat on the side of the bed and took Katherine's hand in his left hand. With his right hand he felt the top of her uterus, near her navel. When the contraction began, he pushed lightly with his fingertips. At the intense tightening for the full duration of the contraction, he deduced that her contractions were powerful and spaced less than a minute apart. "Katherine, I am going to examine you. You need to try to help me, just do as I instruct if you can. All right?"

"Yes, doctor, I will try."

"Good girl." To Brianda he said, "Put the instruments

on the table next to the provisions left by the midwife."

John washed his hands and returned to the bed. He then slid his first two fingers into Katherine's vagina and, finding her cervix, discovered that it had opened only slightly and had not thinned out much from its donut shape. This was not a positive sign after all the hours Katherine had been in labor. When the next contraction started, the powerful muscles of the uterus squeezed down, forcing the child to put pressure on the cervix and open it. As the contraction reached its peak, John did not feel the bony skull. What he felt was soft, and the tissues gave in when pressed by his fingers.

This was a breech delivery! The baby had turned buttocks first instead of headfirst. That was the reason why the dilation of the cervix was going so slowly. John feared the prolonged length of this labor and its consequent toll on the mother and her child.

Unable to perform the surgery under the circumstances, he had only one option—to turn the child inside the mother's uterus. His biggest concern would be trying to turn the baby without compromising the umbilical cord, which could cut off the baby's supply of blood and oxygen.

Scrubbing his arms to the elbow, John told Brianda to get Andrew and bring him to help. Running down the stairs, Brianda called to the anxious young man to come upstairs immediately. All the MacKenzie men followed them to stand vigil outside the bedroom door.

Andrew entered the room, and to him it smelled like death. Ice gripped his heart. John called him to his side and explained that he was going to try to turn the baby within Katherine's womb. It was evident that Katherine was not going to deliver her baby buttocks first, and if nothing were done, the baby would be born dead, and Katherine might perish, as well. "I need your permission and your help, Andrew. Do I have both?"

"Yes," Andrew said, tears on his cheeks, hands spread open at his sides, a posture that bespoke how helpless he felt.

"Go to the head of the bed and talk to Katherine. Keep her as calm as you can, and when I begin to move the baby, try to keep her from moving around too much. When I ask, I will want you to press on her abdomen firmly until the contraction is over. When the contraction begins again, you will push until I tell you to stop."

Taking John's hands in his, Andrew looked into the doctor's eyes. "Please don't let Katherine die, sir," he begged.

"Let's save them both," John said, and turned to his wife. "Brianda, darling, just hand me the things that I ask for."

John slowly inserted his fingers and spreading the cervix, forced his fingers up inside the womb. Steadily, he began turning the baby, guiding the movement from the outside with his other hand.

Katherine's screams filled the house. In the hallway, Alison felt faint, and her brother Ian had to hold her upright. Michael stared grimly at the door. He had witnessed the birth of all six of his children, but never had he heard anything like this.

At long last, John was able to turn the baby around, so that its head was presenting at the cervix. He felt the umbilical cord; it still pulsed strongly with life.

"Andrew, go to the head of the bed, and when I tell you, put your hands on Katherine's abdomen and push—hard. We have to get this baby out soon."

"Yes, sir, I am ready." And to Katherine, he urged, "Hold on, soon this will be over."

The young woman could not speak, so severe was her discomfort, so weakened her condition.

At the next contraction John spread the cervix, and it gave way. Andrew pushed, Katherine called out for

God's help, and four contractions later, a baby boy was born, screaming bloody murder.

Katherine collapsed, breathing raggedly, and Andrew rushed to hold her. John delivered the placenta and attended to the task of suturing several small cervical tears. Katherine, beyond exhaustion, did not protest.

Brianda and Rebecca cleaned the baby and placed him in his father's arms. Andrew cried at the sight of the tiny infant, so dear and so precious.

John asked everyone to leave the room so that Katherine could sleep. Hearing his order, she waved to him and feebly stated that she wanted to hold her child in her arms before sleeping.

John placed the warm bundle in her arms, and she put him to her breast. His tiny mouth latched onto her nipple instantly. With a smile John closed the door and left the new mother and father with their son.

Brianda and John rode every day, exploring the mountains and filling their hearts and souls with Scotland's wild and rugged beauty.

John was well pleased that Angus and Mary would be returning with them to England, having thought that perhaps Angus would prefer to stay in his homeland. Arrangements had been made for Angus and Mary to occupy a small cottage on the grounds of Manseth Manor, and an old gatehouse on the back tract of land on his London town house property. John explained that they were welcome to live under the roof of Manseth Manor and in the London town house, but Angus felt that they should have their own homes and their privacy. It was also decided that Angus would administer a portion of John's business interests. John insisted that he did not need a full-time bodyguard any longer. He did, after all, have Brianda, and she was enough to put any ill-doer in his place!

John and Brianda spent a lot of time with Angus and Mary and their friendship flourished. Brianda remained a bit wary of Angus. She had not yet forgiven him for his taking her over his knee, but the two young women came to love each other as good friends.

Finally the day came for their departure. Everyone kept swiping the tears from each other's eyes, and Rebecca hugged all four of them, one after another. To ease the sadness of parting John invited the entire MacKenzie family for Christmas the following December and as a farewell gift gave each member of the family a voucher for free passage on one of his ships.

As the travelers climbed up into the carriage for their trip to Edinburgh, Katherine and Andrew approached John. Katherine hugged him for the longest time. "I will thank God every day for you and the gift of life you gave us. With your permission, we would like to name the boy after you, sir. He will be John Andrew MacKenzie."

"I am deeply touched and consider it a great honor. Thank you both," John said, smiling at them and kissing the baby on the forehead.

Brianda looked on with pride. He looked so handsome, was so sure of himself and did so much good.

The large carriage made its way slowly down the mountain and eventually out of sight of the MacKenzie home. Michael MacKenzie drove the horses, his frown holding back his tears. He would miss his son, but thanked God Angus now had a good Scottish woman at his side. Sighing heavily, he looked over at his youngest daughter. Alison MacKenzie accompanied her father in the carriage on the long trip to Edinburgh, and he was grateful to know he would have a companion for the trip home.

The *Maid of the Green* was waiting in port when the

carriage and horses arrived. Brianda stood up in the carriage to wave at Eric, Cappy and Bill, and was almost pitched over the side when the wagon's back wheel fell into a rut. Quick reflexes on John's part saved her from going over headfirst and probably breaking a bone or two.

Eric was the first to descend the plank and shake hands with John and Angus, giving them a giant grin. "Well, I see you two are still in one piece after a month with the fair Brianda! How many times has she been over your knee, Angus?" Eric asked, laughing.

Mary threw a questioning glance at Angus. Smiling, he assured her that he would explain later in the privacy of their cabin.

John and Angus were briefly diverted from their pleasantries, when they heard Brianda arguing with the sailor who was trying to lead the stallions up the plank. "I am getting old before my time with this woman!" John exclaimed, and all within earshot burst into laughter.

They saw that Brianda and the sailor had come to an agreement, so they returned to the carriage to see to the final unloading of their belongings.

28

Handwritten notes were delivered to the cabins of John and Angus, announcing that breakfast would be served at ten o'clock in the captain's quarters.

Brianda was fast asleep on John's chest, her arm thrown possessively over his waist. John heard the footfall and saw the note passed under the door. Supporting her head, he carefully lowered her to the mattress, slipped out of bed and retrieved the note. Naked, he stood in the center of the room reading the words.

Brianda woke and saw him standing there and marveled at the perfect proportions of his body. His extremely broad shoulders tapered to a slim waist and then down past well-muscled hips and buttocks to long, sinewy, muscled thighs and calves. With a sigh, she inquired, "Are you reading something? Or are you just standing in the middle of the room without a stitch to cover you . . . for another reason?"

Turning to smile at her, he said, "Do you find me attractive this way?"

"Certainly not!" Brianda had to force herself to look

away. "I think you shall catch cold if you don't dress, sir, it is still the dead of winter. I am only looking out for your best interests."

"Is that so? How nice of you. One would think you would be happy to push me overboard," he taunted, clearly unprovoked by the sneer she was directing at him.

"I don't think you would fit through the porthole, sir. I must wait for a better opportunity," she said matter-of-factly, her nose raised into the air.

Bursting into laughter, John walked to the closet and pulled on his clothes. "Get up, lazy one, we are invited to breakfast in the captain's cabin in fifteen minutes."

Brianda jumped from the warmth of the covers and hurried across the cold wood floor to her trunks. She dressed quickly in a red-and-green plaid dress that Rebecca had made for her. After pulling a brush through her long golden hair, she gathered it at the base of her neck and tied it with a ribbon.

Brianda and John were the last to enter the cabin, and found Mary seated at the table. Eric and Angus were looking at charts on the wall.

Eric looked up. "Good morning, sir, Brianda. I will ring for breakfast."

Everyone ate with relish. The food was delicious—eggs with cheeses, freshly baked bread and a spicy sausage. When the plates had been cleared away, the group of friends sat around the table and enjoyed coffee.

During a pleasant silence, Mary turned to Brianda. "What did Eric mean about you being over Angus's lap?"

Brianda froze and stared at the table. The three men said nothing. At the uncomfortable silence, Mary looked around at the tense faces and wondered what she had said wrong.

Finally Angus explained, "During our voyage to Scotland, Lord Fauxley was temporarily indisposed." He stopped and looked directly at Brianda, who studiously avoided his eyes. "The ship was caught in a storm, and Captain Bennett had his hands full trying to keep us all alive. Brianda is a headstrong, defiant young woman, and she chose to jeopardize not only her own well-being, but the well-being of the entire ship. With the verbal permission of her husband, who was unable to act at the moment, I put her across my lap, bared her bottom and spanked the holy hell out of her."

Brianda jumped up and stood with her arms braced on the table. Looking at Angus, she shouted, "You had better never try to touch me like that again, you big oaf!"

Angus, unperturbed, looked at her beautiful face and took a step toward her. Brianda stepped back.

"Brianda, I follow the orders that Lord Fauxley gives me. If, in the future, he requires my services in this regard, you can rest assured that I will do my duty to the best of my ability," he said, staring her down.

There was an electric tension in the room. Deciding that it was time to intervene, John walked to Brianda and escorted her back to her chair. He sat next to her and took her chin between his thumb and first finger, tilting her head so that she would have to look at him. "Angus and Mary are our friends. We will all live together in harmony. Additionally, you are well aware that Angus works for me. You need to recall that you have also been told that if I decide it necessary in the future, I will not hesitate to ask for Angus's assistance in dealing with you, little wildcat. The same goes for Eric, as well. We are three mature men, and have every intention of working together to keep our sanity, control and the well-being of our families."

Furious, Brianda shook her head from his grasp. Glaring at him, she responded, "That is totally unfair! We have no rights, then, as your wives?"

"Of course you have rights. You also have restrictions, restrictions that every marriage has. Behave yourselves, and we will all live happily."

"Restrictions, my backside!" she railed at him. "All you men are bullies, pushing your weight around, taking advantage of women because we are smaller and physically weaker than you are!"

"Thank God for that! Can you imagine, gentlemen," he said in mock horror, "if the ladies were equally as strong and as tall as we are? We would be in for some mighty battles!" Smiling at Brianda, taking in the hatred written all over her face, he stated, "You will just have to accept your plight and make the best of it."

"Go to hell," she said, not quite under her breath.

Mary waited in the hushed silence to see how John would react.

Then all three men burst into laughter. "She is impossible, my Lord," Eric exclaimed. "Won't you and Angus join me on the upper deck for a while."

Brianda was fuming. If it was the last thing she did, she would get away from that rotten bastard when they got back to England.

Mary put her arms around the smaller woman and hugged her close to her breast. At her kindness, Brianda felt an immediate wish to cry, and hugged Mary back.

"It will be a much easier life if we accept the dictates of our husbands," Mary, older than Brianda by almost ten years, advised. "Fighting back is counterproductive. Anyway, I do not find the things that Angus asks of me unreasonable. I will do whatever I can to make him happy. I love him."

Brianda pushed away from Mary and walked to the door. Before leaving, she said, "We are friends and I love you. But I will not compromise my principles nor will I accept willingly the dictatorship of any man." With that, she opened the door and walked toward her own cabin, head held high.

29

The door rattled on its hinges from being slammed so hard. With her hands balled into fists, Brianda stormed about the cabin. Everything she saw reminded her of him, and despair threatened to overcome her. Restless, she decided to go to the only place she really felt completely welcome.

Getting into the hold was easy. There was no one about, and she slipped through one of the small trapdoors and walked quickly to Dakota's stall.

Once inside, she threw her arms around him. He always welcomed her, no matter the circumstances. She felt hot, bitter tears slide from her eyes. They landed on his silky black coat and matted the downy hairs of his powerful neck. Dakota didn't mind, he nuzzled her and pushed her up against his body with his head.

Suddenly, Brianda felt very tired, tired of John Fauxley, tired of fighting for every bit of freedom, tired of it all. She slipped down into the hay next to Dakota and closed her eyes.

*   *   *

Once several hours had passed, the men decided that the female storm had most likely blown over, and returned to the cabin. Eric ordered lunch to be brought to his quarters. When the men opened the door, they saw Mary sitting near the bright light from the porthole, sewing.

"Where is Brianda?" John asked.

A startled Mary looked up. "I am not sure, sir. She left here just after you men did."

John, Eric and Angus exchanged glances. They had been topside all morning, and had not seen any sign of her. "I'll go to our cabin and see if she is sulking in there. We shall be back to eat in a short while," John said, taking his leave.

He opened the cabin door, ready to take on the task of smoothing Brianda's ruffled feathers, but the room was empty. Fear ran through him, and he decided to seek the aid of his friends. So as not to alarm Mary, he sent Cappy for Captain Bennett, Mr. Sanders and Mr. MacKenzie and instructed the first mate to be casual in his actions.

Together the four men discussed Brianda's possible whereabouts. Eric gave each man instructions where on board to search and to be quiet about it. He didn't want the whole ship in a turmoil, and he surely did not want Mary knowing that Brianda was missing. Not yet, at least.

Bill Sanders turned to his captain and said, "It is my wee lass making trouble again. But, do not worry, I will find her." When Eric nodded affirmatively, the old sailor smiled and added, "I have never known a woman with the spirit that this small lass has, sir. She's amazing, that one. Don't worry, sir," he said, bowing slightly in the earl's direction, "if she is on this ship, we will find her. She'll be back safe in your care soon enough."

"Not soon enough for me," John said under his breath. They departed then to their assigned directions to begin the search for the blond, long-haired beauty who was always stirring things up.

Not long afterward, Bill found John and Eric searching through the middle deck. "I've found the wee lass, sir. Please follow me."

"Is she all right, Bill?"

"Oh, yes, sir, she is just fine. She was in the first place that I thought to look for her."

Silently, they followed Bill down into the hold. When they reached the stall, Dakota stormed at them, not letting them come too near.

"When I first came down, Captain, I saw her in there, but the animal would not let me get close. I thought I'd better come for you, my Lord, as the animal knows you, and all."

"That was good thinking, Bill. I will take it from here. Thank you for your discretion. Please go and tell Mr. MacKenzie and Cappy that she is found, and that we will join them soon."

"Captain?"

"Yes, you may do as Lord Fauxley says. This was a job well done."

"Aye, sir. She is a special one, my wee lass. I hope you are not too angry with her, sir," he said, tipping his cap to John.

"No, I am not angry. I am just glad that she is found and well. Thank you."

John walked to the stall and called to Dakota. The stallion calmed at once. John opened the door and saw Brianda curled into a small ball in the right rear corner of the stall. She was sound asleep on a pile of hay. When he was close enough, he could see the remnants of the dried tears on her face. He felt a tug at his heart.

"Eric," John called softly, "I am going to take her to our cabin and let her sleep. Have some food brought there for us, will you? I wouldn't want her to have to face the rest of them now, after the difficult time we gave her this morning."

Eric left, and John lifted Brianda into his arms. She stiffened suddenly. "What are you doing?" she demanded.

"I found you here, sleeping, Brianda, and thought you would be more comfortable in your bed."

"Put me down, sir. I am capable of walking."

John set her gently on her feet. "To find you sleeping in the middle of the day is odd. Are you well?"

"I am just fine. I came down here to groom Dakota, and the heat down here made me sleepy," she explained, brushing the hay from her bodice and skirt.

"Well, then, if you are finished with Dakota, it is time for lunch."

"I am not hungry," she responded quickly, not wanting to face their so-called friends.

"I asked that the food be sent to our cabin. I have some work to do and need to be left undisturbed. Will you join me there?"

Warily, she looked at him to see if he were making fun of her again. Seeing nothing more than the sincere look on his face, she agreed. "All right. Maybe I could eat a little." With that, she walked off and climbed the stairs leading to the deck above. John followed.

The next ten days passed quietly. Brianda spent most of her time with Bill Sanders. He taught her how a lookout watches for weather changes, other ships and any sign of trouble. He explained that at times, when the winds were blowing hard, the men could not communicate by speaking, so they used signals. When a club was hit against the metal portion of the mast, it echoed loudly—

very loudly. The captain would hear the signals even in the worst of storms. Bill taught Brianda all the signals, encouraging her to learn more every day.

Brianda avoided Mary, and only took walks on the deck with her when John insisted. She was polite, but not overly friendly. With John, she was respectful and reserved, and when he tried to goad her into a verbal battle, she would back off and retreat to the safety of a book. In their bed, she did not fight John off. She simply did not participate. He wanted her daily—he could never get his fill of her—and she tolerated his physical attentions, but turned off her responses to him. Try as he might, he could not bring her to fulfillment.

John would have been glad if he thought she had finally accepted her role as his wife and had begun to live in peace, but he knew that was not the case. There was a falseness about her, but what could he do? He could hardly fault her for her seemingly perfect behavior.

While still one week from port, Brianda was walking alone on the main deck. It was a calm day, and as she walked, she glanced up and saw a vacant lookout post. It was the lowest of the three, and as it was only twenty feet from the deck, it was hardly used. However, it beckoned to her. Oh, how she would love to sit up there and watch the ocean, up away from everyone else. She could see Bill up on the highest lookout post.

Gathering her skirt in her hands, she ran to where Eric was talking to a crew member. Waiting patiently, she approached him when the sailor was sent off to work.

"Captain?" she asked quietly.

"Why, yes, Brianda. To what do I owe this unexpected visit?"

"I would like to ask a favor, and I would hope you won't say no, before giving me a chance to fully explain."

"I promise to hear you out," Eric answered, then waited patiently as she wrung her fingers and tried to think of an appropriate way to phrase her request.

"Captain, there is a lookout post on the port side of the ship that is usually unmanned. I would like your permission to climb up and sit for a while, so that I may observe the sea." Before he could refuse her, she hurried on, "It is a calm day, there is hardly a wind. I would be safe, and I am sure that Cappy would help me climb up and down safely. It would mean so much to me, Captain, Bill has taught me all about the duties of a lookout. Oh, please don't say no without some serious thought," she finished quietly. Only the gleam in her eyes gave away the excitement she was trying so hard to conceal.

"Have you asked John?" he asked.

"No, you are the captain. If you say no, then that is that."

"I will accompany you to the base of the lookout, and we will decide if it is possible," Eric consented. "I will consent only if I hear from John's own mouth that he, too, gives his permission for this adventure."

"Fair enough."

Eric called Cappy over to them and asked if he would escort Lady Fauxley up to the first lookout post. Surprised, but wise enough not to show it, Cappy said that he thought he would be able to do so without a problem. Eric sent Brianda off to get John's permission.

Brianda fairly ran through the ship in search of her husband. She found him bent over papers and charts, while Angus made notes. "May I speak to you a moment, sir?"

It was the first request she had made directly to him in many days. "Indeed you may, my darling."

"I have already obtained Captain Bennett's permission for something that I want to do. He will not allow me to do it until he hears your own voice tell him that you approve."

"And what is that?" he asked, his heart heavy. He could see the excitement in her eyes; if he refused his permission, he knew their relationship would worsen.

"As I am sure you have noticed, it is a gorgeous day. There is no lookout stationed on the lowest post over the port side of the main deck. I want to climb up there and watch the sea for a while."

His first reaction was to give her a flat refusal, but noting the desire on her face, he found himself quiet. "Show it to me, and I will talk to Eric before I give you my answer," he stated.

Brimming with excitement, she turned and led the way to Eric. Eric's and John's eyes met over the top of her head. It was obvious that they both felt exactly the same way.

Brianda was trying hard not to appear anxious, but was failing badly. Eric and John discussed the situation, and when she could hardly stand the waiting another moment, Eric announced, "You may go up with Cappy. He will tie a rope around your waist to secure you there. You are to hold on with both hands to the mast and wrap your legs around it also. If, for any reason, I feel that you are no longer safe up there, you will come down *immediately*. Do you agree?"

"Wholeheartedly! When may I go?" she asked with obvious delight.

"Right now, if you wish," Eric said.

Brianda ran as fast as she could and disappeared down the stairs that led to her cabin. She was back in a flash, dressed in her boys' clothes with a heavy wool overcoat. When neither Eric nor John said anything, she exclaimed, "Surely you didn't expect me to wear women's clothes! These clothes are much more decent than a skirt would be. Besides, it's cold up there." Turning to Cappy, she called, "I am ready now."

Cappy showed her how to climb the ropes and was surprised how quickly she learned and how strong she was. Eric and John stood just beneath her and watched as she progressed. When she reached the small round platform, Cappy tied a medium-sized rope around her waist and showed her how to best hold on to the mast. He explained that sometimes the ship would hit an unusually large swell, and that she would want to hold on securely, or suffer the sensation that she was about to fall forty feet into the icy water. When he was about to leave, he hit the mast with the club and pointed upward to the highest lookout. Bill looked down and, seeing his lass, waved down at her. Taking the club from Cappy, she surprised the first mate by sending Bill a series of signals. Bill answered back and all three laughed.

Winking, Cappy told her that she had better keep an eye out for pirate ships, and should she see the skull and crossbones, she had to signal the captain immediately! She agreed that she surely would do so, and surprised Cappy when she leaned up and kissed his cheek.

John was uneasy. Brianda was so far up there! He looked about at the calm sea and told himself that Eric would never have allowed her to go up to the post if he felt that there was the slightest danger. He went to get Angus, having decided that he would work on deck and keep an eye on her.

Scanning the horizon, Brianda had not felt this much at peace in such a long time. It was quiet, except for the wind. Bill signaled down to her for her report every so often, and with her hands, she would signal that all was well. He in turn would signal the captain or the first mate. It was great fun. Seated up high on the mast, she noticed the pitch and roll of the ship much more. She liked the sensation as the ship cut through the swells and soon let go of the mast with her hands.

After a couple of hours, Brianda was able to see patterns in the wave swells. Late afternoon was approaching, when suddenly she noticed a change on the horizon.

A dark band had appeared and they were heading straight toward it. She looked up, but Bill did not seem to be concerned. He was sitting as he had been earlier. Even so, she kept her eyes on the dark patch, and noticed it did not change for the next few minutes. But the wind did, picking up and turning very cold.

Once again she looked up for guidance from Bill. He was in exactly the same position he had been in the last time she looked. She tried her hand signals but he did not respond. Over the wind, she called up to him. He still did not move. Frightened, she beat the emergency code on the mast with her club.

Instantly Eric looked up at the top outlook. Bill was not signaling. His eyes went to Brianda. She was signaling the emergency code! Throwing down his chart, he called to John. John and Angus were on their feet in a second, running toward the mast that held Brianda.

The wind had now picked up considerably. Eric felt it and cursed Bill. He knew better than to let the girl decide if the weather was turning sour on them! When he reached the mast, he looked up at Brianda, and she signaled to him with her hands that bad weather was coming and that the man up top was in trouble.

Calmly Eric shouted orders to all assembled, and each man scrambled to his assigned tasks. Eric ordered Cappy and another sailor to go up for Bill and stated that he would go for Brianda. John wanted to go, too, but Eric stopped him. "I don't go into your surgery, Doctor. Now you let me do my job."

John agreed, but felt useless watching Brianda hold on to the mast while she swung about in the ever increasing winds. The pitch and roll of the ship increased.

Brianda watched as Cappy and the other sailor expertly climbed to the top rigging to help Bill. He still wasn't moving, and Brianda was frightened for her friend. In moments, Eric was beside her. He was just about to untie her rope when Cappy called to him that Bill was unconscious and that he and Will had to lower Bill down on a rope. Yelling to Brianda to stay put and to hold tight, Eric climbed higher to help Cappy and Will. After fifteen minutes, they lowered the unconscious man to the main deck.

The wind was howling, and Brianda clung tightly to the mast. She had stopped looking down at the deck, as the ship appeared to be moving so much beneath her that it made her nauseous.

Eric and Cappy climbed back down to Brianda's platform and ignored her demands to know about Bill as they quickly fashioned a tether and tied Brianda to Eric. Slowly, Cappy helped lower both of them over the edge of the platform. Holding onto the mast with one arm, Eric lowered them toward the deck. The closer they got, the fiercer the spray of the seawater as the ship rolled heavily in the tumultuous sea.

John reached up to grab Brianda's ankles while Angus grabbed her by the waist and cut the rope. Soon she was free, and John pulled her into his arms. She held on tight to his strong body.

Seeing Cappy and Eric lift Bill's body and start to carry him below, Brianda pulled herself from John's grip and tried to run to Bill. John grabbed her around the waist and hauled her back to him. "The sea is too rough for walking on deck," he shouted to her. "The sailors are experienced, but you aren't. You could easily slide into the ocean. Let's go down through this stairwell, and I will see to Bill."

John took her hand and guided her below deck to their cabin. Brianda was shivering with the cold, and John had to forcefully pull her wet clothes off, while she babbled to him about all that had happened up on the platform. Rubbing her quickly with a thick towel, he popped her into bed, stark naked. She was furious, stating that she had to go to Bill.

John called for Angus. "I am going to see to Bill. See that Brianda does not leave that bed," he ordered.

"She won't, sir."

Brianda called out to John. He turned to her. "I want to go with you to see Bill! Please, he may need me!"

"Brianda, Bill is quartered with many other sailors. They do not allow women on that deck. I will tell you everything as soon as I can."

Brianda fell back heavily onto her pillow. John was right—she would not be welcome in the crew's quarters. What was she going to do, anyway, leave the bed naked in search of her clothes with that big oaf standing right there? She frowned as the ship lurched against the onslaught of a huge wave. How she hated waiting!

The following morning, the captain, crew and passengers laid to rest the body of Bill Sanders. He was buried at sea, the victim of a stroke.

Brianda stood next to John and held on to his arm, crying as she heard Eric read the burial service. John put his arm around her and held her close to him. When it was over, she returned to their cabin, wanting to be alone.

At a knock on the cabin door, Brianda bade John and Eric enter.

"Brianda," Eric began, as he looked at the pained face of the young woman sitting so straight and solemn in the chair, "Bill was an old man. He died where he wanted to die, at sea. I want you to know that your love for him gave him many happy moments. You were a shining star in his life." Eric paused a moment, then continued, "Brianda, Bill left a note in his things. He wanted you to have his guitar." Eric lifted the guitar and handed it to Brianda. She took it without a word.

"I also want you to know that you saved the ship."

She turned her face to look at Eric. He looked tired and haggard. Slowly, she turned away.

"Bill had died, and in the face of grave danger, you calmly signaled me to warn me of the storm. All of us thank you for your heroic deed. If we ever sail again together, you can be my lookout," he said sincerely.

"Th-Thank you, Eric. I appreciate your words," she stammered, her eyes filled with tears. "It's just that I feel so sad. . . ." Looking away, eyes not focused on anything, she continued, "I haven't had many friends. I am sorry to lose Bill."

John motioned Eric outside, thinking to leave her alone for a while. There were no words of value at moments like this one. Only time would ease the pain of her loss.

30

The day that the Maid of the Green docked, it was rainy and raw, and moving the luggage from the ship was difficult in such conditions. Crew members slipped on the slick wooden decks as they made their way across the ship and down the loading planks. Thunder rolled and tumbled through the sky, as lightning shot jagged crackles of heat and light to the earth.

John found Brianda staring silently out the porthole at the city of London. "Darling, most of our things have been unloaded, and the coaches are waiting. Are you ready to leave?" he asked, looking about the cabin for any last remaining personal articles.

"I am ready to be on English soil again, sir," she stated simply.

"Then let's gather our things and get to the coach, all right?"

Eric laughed and slapped John on the back as he promised him that he would visit. Angus, taking Mary by the arm, walked her from the ship to the waiting coach. Brianda was just entering the coach, when she heard Dakota whinny in fear. She turned to see the massive stallion fighting the sailor who was trying to lead him down the wet plank. Dakota reared. His back hooves slipped, and he almost fell over the side into the murky waters of the harbor. Pushing away the restraining hands of Angus, Brianda bolted toward the ship.

Several men were now trying to calm the frightened animal. The rain was pouring from the gray sky overhead, and Brianda was soaked before she reached the plank. She yelled to the men to drop their holds on the horse.

Brianda finally got Dakota to calm down enough to grab his head. She pulled him to her and held him to her chest, all the while talking to him, settling him. There was a sudden roar of thunder, but the horse stayed with her, nervous, yet under her control, as they stood together on the ramp. At last, she began walking him down the slippery plank. He whinnied as he felt his hooves slide beneath him. Everyone watched nervously, afraid that the animal, in his fear, might turn and knock the brave little woman off the plank into the dirty, cold waters of the harbor.

With only a few more feet to go before they would be safely on the ground, Brianda kept talking to Dakota over the thunder and the patter of the rain, and never stopped stroking his nose, letting him know he was safe. When they touched ground, there was a cheer from all assembled, and John rushed to help her tie Dakota to the back of the coach, then led her inside.

Dakota had caused heads to turn all over the docks. Workers and the curious had come forward to see what was causing all the ruckus, and one of the onlookers was none other than Biff Blanders. When he saw the horse and the small young woman trying to calm him, he smiled. His rotten teeth showed through his sneer. He stayed out of sight, not wanting the earl to see him, not now. How happy Edward would be to hear that his precious little sister was back in England. Oh, he would drink well tonight, and when he was finished, he would enjoy his newest tart, a wayward fourteen-year-old girl from the country. She wouldn't last long.

Three footmen ran out to meet the coach. They held large covers up in the air, so that everyone could hurry into the house without getting drenched. Brianda refused to leave Dakota until she knew that he was safe, dry and warm in the stable. She insisted on taking him personally to his stall and ran out of the coach before John could grab her.

Brianda was just about to dry Dakota off with a large towel when John arrived. "You will let the stableman finish taking care of Dakota, and you will come into the house immediately! You are wet to the skin, and it is cold out here!" he yelled at her.

She had heard that tone of voice before and knew she had better do as he said. However, her ornery streak kept her standing with the horse, pretending as if she had not heard a word he said.

Calling to the stableman, John approached her, bent low, threw her over his shoulder and stormed toward the house.

Hanging over him like a drowned rat, she found it hard to breathe. She hit him on his back as hard as she could and tried to kick his thighs with the sharp edges of her leather shoes.

Enduring all that he would, he brought his hand up and smacked her on the bottom. "Stop that, you brat!" he raged at her.

The sting of his hand on the wet fabric sent shock waves through her, and she stopped fighting.

John burst through the kitchen door with the dripping girl slung over his shoulder. Cook and her helper stood with their mouths open wide, unable to say a word. This was not how they expected to welcome his Lordship home! Stevens came running when he heard the back door blow open and slam into the wall. Looking at the sight before him, he said drolly, "Well, sir, it appears that Lady Brianda has returned home. Shall I draw a bath for her?"

"That would be very good, Stevens," John said as if there were nothing wrong. "And see to it that all the guests have hot baths prepared as well and food within the hour. Have tea sent to each room."

"Yes, sir, immediately, sir," Stevens answered.

John leaned over and set Brianda on her feet. With a look that told her to keep her mouth shut, he removed her cloak and dropped it in a heap on the floor. Quickly, he grabbed her and carried her upstairs to their room. The tub was brought, steamy and hot. Without a word to her, he stripped her clothes off and slid her into the inviting water.

She glared at him, not knowing that he was assessing the blue pallor of her lips and the gooseflesh pimpling her skin. The water felt so wonderful that she forgot how much she hated him for a moment. She took the soap and lathered her hair and body. It had been a long time since she had had the luxury of an English bath with sweet soaps.

John stripped his clothes off and got into his own tub of water. Washing quickly, he rose and toweled himself dry. Brianda had her eyes closed, and he stood naked watching her. Even though she remained so slim, her body was perfection. He felt himself grow hard just looking at her. How different her face looked with her hair wet; her fine features appeared more defined and lovely without the mass of golden hair, wild and flowing.

He walked up behind her in the tub and slid his hands over her shoulders, down onto her breasts. She began to protest. "Take your hands off of me," she ordered.

"But, darling, you are my wife. I can touch you any time I want to."

"Don't call me *darling,* you ruffian. Does it not matter that I don't want you to touch me?"

Rubbing his hands over her breasts and feeling them tighten in response, he smiled. He held her securely with his left arm as his right hand continued down and stopped in the dark-blond triangle of hair.

She struggled but it was to no avail, he had all the leverage.

Moving his fingers down, he began to stroke the small bud that brought her so much pleasure. He shifted his left hand so that he could caress her breasts at the same time that his fingers worked, tormenting her sweetly. "Darling," he repeated with exaggerated slowness, "you can tell me that you don't want me to touch you, but I am an experienced man, and I can feel your responses to my touch. See how erect with pleasure your nipples are? Look how your hips move involuntarily as I massage you."

Stunned by the intimacy of his words, Brianda closed her eyes and tried to ignore what he was doing to her. She couldn't stand the fact that he was watching her like a specimen under the microscope.

He continued to touch her, changing tempo and pressure. She began to undulate under his touch, unable to stop herself. He kissed the sides of her neck, sucking softly on the special, soft spaces he loved so well.

She moaned deep in her throat. Her hips reached up to meet his fingers. She would have to hate him later.

As her hips moved forcefully upward, he slipped his long fingers into her, deep and sure. "Lift your arms and put them around my neck, Brianda."

She did as she was told, too hot inside to deny him.

Now with both hands free to use as he wished, he moved his fingers in and out of her and made tiny circles between the folds, making her gasp for breath. Just as he felt her tension building and saw her toes point, he withdrew his hands.

She moaned her protest, anxious for release.

Standing, he pulled her from the tub and lifted her into his arms. Turning her to face him, he carried her thus and sat in a large sidechair. Spreading her legs outside of his, he lowered her slowly.

He never took his eyes from hers.

Her body was still wet from the bath water, and she was wet inside with anticipation. She felt herself being lowered down across his abdomen, his few rough hairs rubbing along the inside of her thighs. Then she felt him, waiting, hard and unavoidable. His velvet tip gently spread the protective, soft folds. Without stopping, she felt him enter her. She put her hands on his shoulders to try to slow the advance, but his hands were on her hips, forcing her down onto him, inch by inch. The deeper he went the wider he spread her.

She had never been taken thus, and the sensation was new and almost frightening. It felt as if he had grown longer and larger, that he was invading her more deeply than ever before, and she wondered if he would split her. It hurt, but he wasn't stopping. Finally, when she thought she could take no more, he was fully embedded within her body.

She was breathing deeply, holding onto his shoulders with a viselike grip. She didn't want him to see her like this, so vulnerable, so much his.

Her face was inches from his. She could taste his breath, could see the satisfaction in his eyes, the gleam of the conqueror.

"Don't look at me," she whispered into his mouth.

"Why not? I love you like this, impaled on me, wet with desire, your fast, deep breaths sweet in my mouth. You are fully mine, and you always will be. No other man will ever know the pleasures of being within you. Brianda, you are mine. All mine."

"Stop saying those things!" she entreated.

"Why? Are you embarrassed?"

"Yes."

"You should not be. I've seen all there is to see, love. There is more to learn, though, and I want to spend the rest of my life finding out all about you, so that I can give you the pleasures you deserve." While whispering these words to her, he was sliding her up and down, alternating rhythms, driving her mad with desire.

"Please! No more! Don't look at me now!" she implored. He continued moving her up and down on him, causing the inevitable blessed torture to build. Soon she would be powerless to stop its path, and she did not want him to watch her like this, so close, so intimately.

He knew, too, that she was ready. He was on the brink himself and was just waiting for her to tip over the edge.

It was here. Her eyes closed halfway, and the sounds of release were born deep in her throat. She gave in to the glory, and he thrust upward at that very moment and felt himself disappear into the chasm of wondrous consummation.

Brianda's head fell backward, every muscle taut with pleasure. She heard herself call his name. He surged into her several times and then held her fast.

She fell forward, her head resting on his shoulder, small rivulets of perspiration flowing between their bodies. She was breathing in small gasps, and gave in to the inexplicable need to cry.

He said nothing. He understood and held her until she stopped.

* * *

Angus and Mary were waiting in the main hall for their one o'clock luncheon. When John and Brianda appeared, they looked uncharacteristically serene. John rang the bell for the food to be served and announced that Stevens would be accompanying the ladies while they shopped for necessities. In addition, the French seamstress, Madame Vibert, would arrive at three o'clock to take the measurements for new dresses for Mary.

Mary, who always agreed with everyone, was shocked. "For me, my Lord? I did bring clothing with me, sir." Angus grabbed her hand under the table and smiled at her.

"I am aware of that, Mrs. MacKenzie, but your husband and I decided that you are in need of some new dresses and other personal items. We hope to attend some balls before the season ends, and I doubt that you have brought such clothes. It will give me great pleasure to offer this gift from Brianda and me to you as a part of your wedding present."

"And what of you, my Lady?" John addressed Brianda. "Do you need some new dresses?"

"Absolutely not. I have new dresses that are only a few months old, some never worn. No further expense need be made on me," she answered, unable to look at him. The rush of the intimacy was still with her, and looking at him would only show the world her feelings.

"Madam, you need not worry about expense. I am a very wealthy man. I have no worries on that account."

"Thank you anyway, sir, but I have adequate clothing. I will enjoy accompanying Mary on her shopping trip." Finally turning to look at him, she asked, "Do we have to take Stevens, sir? He is such a prig!"

Stevens, standing just inside the door, straightened his back and squared his shoulders to live up to his reputation.

"If Stevens doesn't go, you ladies don't go, my darling."

"There are two of us, for heaven's sake. We can care for ourselves!"

"It is not heaven that concerns me, Brianda. Only God knows what mischief you could get into alone in London. No, you will go with Stevens or not at all."

"All right, my Lord. We will go with Stevens, I just want you to note that I am offering my formal objection."

"So noted, Madam."

At a loud knock, Stevens hurried to answer the summons. Elizabeth Martin was there, as pretty as a flower. She rushed past Stevens while he was offering his greeting and ran into the dining room. Squealing with delight, she rushed to embrace Brianda.

They hugged and laughed and hugged again. Breaking away, Brianda asked, "How on earth did you know we were home? We just arrived this morning!"

"We learned of your return from the newspaper. I sent a note to Paul at the office. I am sure he will come to welcome you as soon as he can."

Brianda did not see the look of concern that passed between John and Angus. Now John had less time than he thought to make his plans.

Brianda took Elizabeth by the arm and introduced her to her new friend. Elizabeth was thrilled to hear the Scottish lilt. They sat and chatted for a few minutes, and in no time, they knew they would all be friends. Brianda immediately invited Elizabeth to join them on their shopping trip.

She looked to John to see if one more woman would mean that they could go without Stevens. He shook his head no, and she didn't bother arguing with him further. The three women rose to gather their handbags. They only had three hours before the seamstress arrived! Soon they were ready, and they left, happy and excited.

John called Angus to him. Speaking softly, he gave his orders.

Edward and Biff watched as the three women got into the coach. Business had been fair in the smuggling trade, so Edward was wearing more expensive clothing. Biff, on the other hand, wore the same old clothes, the clothes he would likely wear until the day he died. Material possessions meant nothing to him.

They followed the women, taking great care that they were not seen. The butler seemed to be quite watchful of his charges.

Edward was waiting. He had plenty of time, and when he struck, he would be sure that he would get every drop of blood from that bastard Fauxley that he deserved. Planning was essential to his vengeance, and he had had adequate time to plan while his sister and her husband were out of the country. Now they were home and it was time to strike.

31

Madame Vibert and her assistants arrived to find the three young women gleefully poring over their purchases. She had to clap her hands together sharply several times before she gained their attention. When the three were seated, she brought out her array of fabrics, ribbons and buttons displaying the fabulous wares for all to see.

While Madame Vibert and her assistants led the Scottish woman to the corner and began taking measurements. Brianda and Elizabeth sat, heads close together, catching up on all the news. Elizabeth had not seen her since the day she had become Mrs. Paul Martin.

Looking carefully into her young friend's eyes, Elizabeth wanted to know what it was like being married to John Fauxley. Brianda thought for a moment and began to relate her tale from the beginning, and when she finished, she had told Elizabeth the whole incredible tale. There were several times when Elizabeth's mouth fell open and formed a perfect "O," so surprised was she.

Even knowing Brianda as well as she did, it was still difficult to believe the stories.

"Tell me, Brianda, do you enjoy, you know . . . being with him? As your husband?" Elizabeth asked with sincere concern.

"That is hard to answer, Elizabeth," Brianda said, as she rose and walked to the window. Her friend followed her there and put her arm around her.

"It is none of my business, Brianda, but I am willing to listen if you want to tell me about it."

"It is not that I don't want to tell you, Elizabeth, it is just that I don't know how to answer your question." Brianda felt as cold as the steel gray clouds that dotted the winter sky. "At times, I truly hate him. He is so bossy and unyielding," Brianda complained, reaching out for the solace in Elizabeth's warm fingers. "Then there are times when I feel respect and admiration for him. He is a wonderful doctor, Elizabeth. I have seen him with his patients. To them, he is kind, and understanding."

Brianda looked at Elizabeth, knowing that she had been skirting the true issue. "In our intimate life," she whispered to her friend, "I feel mostly . . . used. He takes me wherever he wishes, with no regard for my feelings. When I feel that I am only a receptacle, I try to do anything that will keep me from giving in to the desire. Sometimes I can accomplish that, and at other times, he carries me away to the most incredible places and feelings that I have ever experienced." Looking into the sympathetic eyes of her friend, she added, "I have never been with any other man, so I have nothing to compare it to. All I know is that he makes me know that I am a woman, a complete woman. That should give me pleasure and satisfaction. But feeling as I do, it doesn't."

Hugging Brianda close to her, Elizabeth sighed. "Brianda, Paul makes me feel like that, too, and I love it. What is wrong with enjoying the pleasure? It is the ultimate joining of man and woman," Elizabeth said, as she held Brianda at arm's length and looked into her violet eyes. "Why do you fight him? Why do you not accept what exists between you?"

"Because he does not love me. Never once has he said those words to me. I am sure he feels some closeness to me at the height of passion, but in the cold light of day, he is different."

"Have you told him that you love him?"

"Of course not! I am not sure that I do. I'm not sure that I know what love is."

"For me, it is the culmination of everything you share together. Your lives and the lovemaking. One day, a child will come of your union, then it will be complete," Elizabeth said, a small blush rising over her cheeks.

Brianda grabbed Elizabeth's hands and pulled them to her heart. "Are you pregnant, Elizabeth?" she asked excitedly.

"I was going to wait to tell you. I am just past the second missed cycle, so I think I am," Elizabeth said, her face glowing. "I have never been happier. I love Paul more than I can ever tell you."

Brianda felt the tears of joy in her eyes. "I am so happy for you! I would love to help you care for the baby. Will you let me?"

"Of course, silly! But soon you will have a baby of your own."

"No, I don't think so. I don't want a baby, not now. Not the way things are between us. I don't think it will happen to me."

"These things are not planned, Brianda, they happen."

"Not to me." Walking arm in arm with her friend, Brianda said, "I will enjoy your child, Elizabeth." She looked solemnly at Elizabeth then. "Please don't tell Paul what I told you about John and me. I have very special feelings for Paul, Elizabeth. He helped save my life. But

I just cannot discuss these things with anyone but you. Agreed?"

"Yes, of course. I feel proud that you shared these feelings with me. I love you, Brianda."

"I know. Thank you."

Paul Martin arrived at the same moment as the postman. He carried the letters into the study and tossed them onto the desk. Then he embraced John, and the two men spent an hour talking about the ocean voyages and the month John and Brianda had spent in Scotland.

Paul was astounded at what he heard. "Better you than I, old chum. Brianda would be too much for me to handle."

"She is too much for me, too! She just doesn't know it!" John retorted, and they laughed.

John sent Stevens to find Brianda and Elizabeth. While they talked about the medical practice, John sifted through his mail and found an invitation to a grand ball to be held in four days' time. After discussing the matter, the men decided that it would be a perfect first ball for Mary.

Brianda and Elizabeth entered the study, arms about each other's waists. When Brianda saw Paul, she ran and hugged him. Elizabeth walked to John and whispered into his ear.

"So, Dr. Martin, you are to be a father! That is great news!" John said, hugging Elizabeth and extending his hand to Paul.

Paul's smile was broad as he shook his friend's hand. He looked lovingly at Elizabeth. "We are very happy, as you both can see. The baby is due in seven months or so. We would like you to attend, John, and we would like to ask that you two act as the godparents for our child."

The four of them hugged and laughed as they collectively lost their balance. "Brianda and I would be honored to act in the name of the child, and I will attend the birth with great joy," John announced.

Just then, Brianda saw the open invitation on top of John's correspondence. Darting over to the desk, she grabbed the opened envelope and read the invitation fully. "Are we going to go to this ball, sir? Oh, please say yes!"

"Yes."

"That is wonderful! Wait until Mary hears! May I go and tell her right now?" she asked, fairly jumping up and down.

"I have not yet spoken with Angus. He will be here for dinner tonight. If he approves, you may make the announcement this evening. Can you wait until then to deliver the news?" John asked, smiling at his wife. It was good to see her spirited again.

"Must I wait?"

"I am afraid so."

"Well, I have no choice but to wait. Angus wouldn't be so mean as to say no. Mary will be so thrilled!"

John signaled to Stevens to serve the tea. Brianda and Elizabeth sat and caught up on news while John and Paul resumed the discussion of their medical practice.

Dinner was served at eight o'clock. Brianda sat on John's right and all through dinner kept looking at him for the signal that meant she could make her announcement. He hadn't yet told her whether Angus had agreed to attend the ball. She was bursting with anticipation. John had to remind her to eat.

When dessert had been served, John leaned over and told Brianda that she could make her announcement. Brianda smiled at Elizabeth and then stood up. "Mary, I have something to tell you! This afternoon, an invitation was delivered to this house. Since John and Paul conferred with your husband and obtained his approval, I am happy to announce that we are all going to a ball on Saturday night!" she declared, arms straight up in the air.

"Really?" Mary cried.

"Really! John sent a messenger to Madame Vibert, notifying her that the ball gown needs to be ready in four days' time. Isn't it wonderful?" she exclaimed to the entire table.

Everyone talked at once until Elizabeth caught their attention with her explanation that this ball was special, since all the guests had to wear a mask until midnight!

"Masks? How divine!" exclaimed Brianda, sitting back in her chair and listening intently to Elizabeth's descriptions of the ornate masks that the men and women would be wearing, and how at the stroke of midnight each man would walk to the woman closest to him on the dance floor and untie the ribbons of the mask to reveal her identity!

John was sitting in his study, when Angus entered and closed the door. John, seeing the look on Angus's face, motioned him closer.

"I saw them today, sir, Edward Breedon and the same man that was with him in the bar. I thought I may have seen them on two other occasions this week, but I was not sure. Today I know what I saw. They followed us the entire day as the ladies went about shopping for the ball. They do not know that I saw them, but they know now that I am somehow connected with the women, as I accompanied them all day. I don't think that they have definitely connected me with you, though, sir." Angus walked to the desk and punched his right fist into his left hand, angrily remembering what occurred next. "While we were in the last store, Mary was standing alone, admiring some scarves, when Edward approached her. He asked her very politely where she was going with all her packages, as if he were just passing the time of day. Before I could get to her, Mary answered that she and her friends were going to the gala ball the day after tomorrow and how excited they all were. Edward smiled, wished Mary a pleasant good evening, gallantly told her how much he hoped she would enjoy the gala, and then left."

"Damn it to hell!" John said, as he brought his fist down hard on the top of his desk, scattering his papers to the floor.

"Protecting you and Brianda might be difficult at the ball, sir. There will be so many people there, and it is required that the men and the women wear masks until midnight. It will be impossible to determine behind which mask Breedon will be hiding, and whether he will be trying to get close to Brianda or to you, sir."

"I know you are right, Angus. I cannot protect her there. I will have to think about how I want to handle this situation. Not a word to Brianda or Mary."

"Certainly not, sir."

Biff and Edward spent several hours planning Brianda's abduction. Biff's eyes glowed with desire. He had waited a long time for this prize and soon it would be his.

Edward, having stolen an invitation to the ball from the post, spent a large amount of money for clothes. The drug smuggling business had been quite slow of late, as the authorities had recently posted men to watch the harbor. Edward was running low on money. He had to get Cliffshead Manor back again, so he could use the ocean route to smuggle his illegal cargos. *Soon,*

soon, he told himself, an evil smile breaking across his dirty teeth.

Madame Vibert arrived Friday morning with the dresses for the final fittings. Brianda watched as Mary tried on her dress. It was pale yellow with emerald trim, and it looked truly beautiful with her chestnut hair.

John sat in the study alone, his chin resting in his left hand. Never before had he been so indecisive. He knew how much this ball meant to Brianda, but the danger would simply be too great.

The next day dawned with frost covering the ground and shrouding the evergreens. The morning sun soon melted the night's white crystal blanket and warmed the day.

John was still sleeping soundly when Brianda woke, and she lifted the arm that held her to him and slipped out from under it. She pulled on her chemise and ran to the window. Smiling in satisfaction, she hurried to dress in her riding clothes. Careful not to wake John, she ran down to the kitchen for a quick sip of tea and one of Cook's freshly made cinnamon muffins. She was just about to exit by the kitchen door, when a big hand grabbed her arm. Turning swiftly, she looked up at a very stern Angus.

"What are you doing? Let go of my arm, Angus!" she said, trying to pull her arm from his grasp.

"Just where do you think you are going, Brianda?" he asked in a tight voice.

"Take your hand off of me! You have no right to question my actions!" she said through clenched teeth.

He stood holding her arm. "Answer me!" he said sharply.

"How dare you treat me like this? Take your hand off me. Now!" she retorted, yanking her arm to loosen his hold on her.

"Brianda, calm down," he demanded. "You know very well that I have his Lordship's consent to question you about your plans, especially when I see you leaving the house just after dawn!"

"I am going riding. I have John's permission to ride whenever I choose, as long as a groomsman accompanies me. Now let go of me, Angus," she stated in a quiet, furious voice.

"You will not ride today," he said, offering no explanation.

"You have no right to make that decision," she said, turning quickly and kicking Angus in the shin as hard as she could. He doubled over to grab his bruised ankle, and she yanked her arm from his grasp.

Bolting for the door, she escaped before Angus could stop her and ran for the stable as fast as she could. Brianda ran through the open barn door past the astonished groomsman. She rushed to the middle of the barn, looking for anything she could use to protect herself.

Angus was just entering the barn, cursing under his breath, when he stopped short and halted. Brianda was standing in the middle of the passageway, feet spread wide, threatening him with a pitchfork!

"I am going riding now. If you try to stop me, I will shove this pitchfork right through you!" she warned him, her hands shaking with fury.

"I don't think his Lordship is going to like hearing about this incident, Brianda. I suggest that you put that pitchfork down and come into the house with me," Angus said calmly, not moving.

"Tell John what you will. I have done nothing wrong—I only intend to ride Dakota."

"You are not going anywhere!" came an all too familiar voice. Brianda looked around Angus to see John striding toward her, his face a mask of fury. When he saw the pitchfork aimed at Angus, he put his hands on his hips and glared at Brianda.

Defeated, Brianda let the pitchfork slip from her hands and fall to the floor. The situation was looking grim, and the set of John's face was enough to give her pause.

"Am I going to be allowed to explain what happened here, sir, or are you going to listen only to Angus's story?" she asked, squaring her shoulders and trying to look as tall and as brave as possible.

"You will go into the house now and march yourself directly to my study," John said with deadly calm.

"I am not moving from this spot until I tell you my side of the story, sir," she said staunchly.

John took a step toward her. "I am warning you, Brianda. You had best get moving, and fast."

Quickly assessing her options, she walked slowly toward them. They stepped aside and let her pass between them, and she hurried to the house and went into the study. They were right behind her.

John closed the door hard against the frame. He was trying to calm himself, and took a deep breath. "This had better be good, Brianda. If not, there is going to be hell to pay for what I witnessed."

Brianda winced. Gathering her thoughts, she began. "Sir, I rose and tried to leave the house for an early morning ride. Angus," she said with a sneer and a side-long glace at the Scotsman, "grabbed me and demanded that I tell him where I was going. He said I couldn't go out of the house and refused to give me an explanation. He has no right to tell me what I can and what I cannot do!" Brianda looked directly at John's countenance, but it did not soften at all. "As you well know, sir, I have often gone for rides with the groomsman in the mornings, and you were aware of my outings each time. Up until today, my riding was just fine with you. Now this morning, for no reason, I am a prisoner in my own home!" she stated with force.

John and Angus looked at one another. Both of them realized they had overreacted. Brianda's reasoning was correct, but she could not be told the real reason that Angus had been ordered to detain her.

Walking to where she was seated, John put his hands on the arms of the chair and said sternly, "Brianda, you have been told on several occasions that Angus works under my direct orders. Therefore, if he tells you something, take it as if it comes from me. Is that clear?"

"That is all you are going to say? You, too, are refusing to give me an explanation for this unjust situation?" she questioned indignantly.

"I am sorry, Brianda. You are not to disobey Angus again, understood?"

She refused to answer, and stared defiantly into his deep blue eyes.

"Decisions are made on your behalf that you might not agree with, Brianda, but you will follow the dictates of those decisions, like it or not. This rebellious nature of yours causes you a great deal of trouble."

"No, sir, it is your unfair decisions and orders that cause the trouble! Since when do I need an overgrown oaf telling me that I cannot go for a morning ride?"

"Brianda, the subject is closed. I will not hear another word about it!"

Stubbornly, she continued, "Why can you not tell me directly, when you decide that a change is in order? I am your wife, not a child or a servant. Do I not deserve more respect? Do you think the treatment I received this morning was fair or just?" she demanded.

"I have a lot on my mind these days, Brianda. There are matters that are more important than your morning rides. Angus has been directed to carry out my orders, and he will continue to do so. That is final," he said firmly. He turned and walked to the desk. "Now I would like to hear what prompted you to take up a pitchfork and threaten Angus with it. You had better consider your words carefully, young lady, and control your temper as well."

She felt an unpleasant churn in her stomach at his implication. "I grabbed the pitchfork to defend myself. Angus is much bigger and stronger than I am, and without an implement to aid me, I would have surely lost the fight," she answered honestly.

John and Angus turned their heads to the side at the same moment, stifling smiles. Gaining control, John looked at her again. "The pitchfork could do grave bodily danger to a person, Brianda, and it looked as though you would have used it if I hadn't come in."

"I was thinking of using it."

"Hurting someone just so you could go for a ride? Would you really do such a thing?" he asked, his voice lower, calmer.

"No. But I was very angry, sir, and felt that I was being unfairly treated. I wanted Angus to know that I wasn't some ant he could squash under his boot!" she said boldly. "I deserve more consideration, sir, and I deserve an explanation. If Angus had told me why I could not go riding then perhaps I would have understood, but he did not. He made me angry, and I tried to fight back," she finished lamely.

"I see. . . ." John thought to himself for a minute, then looked directly at his wife. "Brianda, you will receive direction from me, and when necessary, from Angus. You will obey. Do you understand?"

She looked at her lap, nodded, and waited for what was to come next.

"Apologize to Angus, and then go to your room and think about what your temper almost caused."

Brianda could not believe her luck! Would there be no punishment?

Standing, she walked to Angus and stood before him. Craning her neck back all the way, she looked up at his handsome face. "I apologize for trying to stab you with the pitchfork. I do not apologize for anything else." She turned and ran from the room and was up the stairs before John could respond.

John asked Angus to explain the details of this latest upheaval caused by Lady Fauxley. Angus told him how he had just happened to see the face of Biff Blanders lurking by the stable fence just prior to the time Brianda opened the kitchen door. "That was why I stopped her from leaving, sir. Brianda would have been heading right in Blanders's direction! She kicked me in the shin, and I lost my hold on her as she ran out the door. I looked for Blanders as I ran after her, but I didn't see him again."

John sat back heavily in his chair. "If Breedon and his henchman have the nerve to come onto my property, they must feel secure in their actions, Angus. I cannot take any chances with Brianda's welfare. We will implement our second plan of action. Leave immediately and do what we discussed. Unfortunately, knowing my wife as I do, there is going to be hell to pay."

32

By midafternoon, the main house was brimming with activity. The ball was only a few short hours away, and both Brianda and Mary were shut in their rooms preparing carefully for the grand event to come.

John climbed the stairs with a heavy heart. Angus had just returned and had brought very disturbing news. Edward Breedon would be attending the gala ball, as he had an invitation. It would be impossible for John to stop Breedon's entrance to the ball now. There simply was not enough time to accomplish all that was necessary to keep the man out.

Brianda had completed her bath and was in her chemise when John came into the room and shut the door behind him. She cast a glance his way. At his angry countenance she wrung her fingers together and waited for him to speak.

John could see that Brianda looked worried. He felt bad, but had no recourse for what he was about to do. "Brianda, an emergency has arisen, and you and I are leaving for the country immediately. I will send a servant to assist you in your packing." He turned to leave.

"Wait!" she wailed. "Do you mean that we are not going to the ball?"

"Precisely. Get ready to leave at once!" he ordered.

"This has nothing to do with an emergency, does it? This is my punishment!" she cried out, her words bouncing off the broad expanse of his back. "I apologized to Angus, just as you told me to, and I promise you I will never do anything like that again! Oh, please let me go to the ball!" she pleaded, grabbing his upper arm in her two small hands. She pulled him around so that she could see his face and beseeched him with her eyes.

"This decision has nothing to do with the incident of this morning, Brianda. Believe me, it is an affair out of my control. We are going to the country now, and there is nothing more to say." He turned toward the door, so that he would not have to see the pain and disappointment in her eyes.

She pulled on his arm with all her might, so that he faced her again. "This is not fair, sir! Why do you torment me so? Am I so wicked that I deserve such an unjust decision?" she demanded.

Their raised voices soon brought Angus to the master chamber on the run.

Looking into the violet eyes he loved so much, John's voice softened. "You would not understand, Brianda. You have to believe that I am doing what I think is right."

Glancing quickly at the man who had just entered her room, she said hopefully, "All right. You go to the country and allow me to stay in London and attend the ball accompanied by Angus and Mary. Angus will care for me and not let anything happen to me . . ."

"Brianda."

Hurrying, she continued, "You do not have to be at my side, sir! I promise to behave! I promise! Please!" she pleaded again, her fingers spread wide on the lapels of his jacket.

Pulling her to his chest, he looked over the top of her golden head at his friend. Angus had been informed earlier of John's decision to leave for the country and understood his reasoning behind the decision. There was nothing for him to do but remain silent.

Afraid she was losing ground, Brianda looked into his eyes and said, "I would rather you beat me than forbid me to go to the ball," she said, as tears she had been fighting off dropped over her lower lashes and ran over her anguished face.

John sighed and held her to him for a moment. "I am sorry, Brianda, but my mind is made up. Neither your words nor your tears will change it. Now, ready yourself, as we leave within the hour." John turned and left the room, Angus following him into the corridor.

They found Mary standing in the hallway. The loud voices from the master chamber had brought her from the guest room. The stern face on her husband and the deep frown on the earl's handsome face did not ease her concern for Brianda, who could still be heard crying inside her bedroom.

"Mary, please go to your room and remain there until you are joined by your husband. He will explain what has happened. You are not to speak to Brianda, under any circumstances, is that clear?" John stated in a tone that brooked no argument.

"Yes, sir." Fearful, Mary turned and retreated to her room.

John and Angus went to the study and carefully discussed their plans. Angus was to take Mary to the gala ball as planned, and once there, locate Paul immediately. John doubted that Blanders would be inside the hall. He was too coarse and crude to be allowed entrance, but he could well be lurking outside. Angus was given specific instructions on how to handle inquiries about the absence of the Earl of Manseth and his bride.

Angus was to stay in London for three days and gather what information he could about Breedon and his pal, Blanders. Most importantly, John wanted Angus to find out where Breedon and Blanders lived. After three days, Angus was to bring Mary to the country for an extended period of time and report any pertinent information to John.

Forty-five minutes later, John went to collect Brianda. She was sitting on their bed, head hung on her chest, her arms at her sides. Stevens had already seen that her luggage was loaded onto the carriage. Walking to her and taking her arm, he said, "Let us go now."

Brianda pulled her arm from his hand and walked slowly to the door. She turned and looked at her beautiful gown hanging on the outside of the chest. Biting her lip to keep from crying anew, she turned and left the room.

Standing like a sentinel, Angus watched them descend the stairs. Brianda looked at him and stated, "Please forward my wish to your wife that she may thoroughly enjoy her first gala ball in London. Please tell her, also, that I would have loved to accompany her this evening." Her voice was like steel, cold and unforgiving. She turned without another word and walked to the carriage.

Mary did not know that Brianda and John would not be joining them until it was time to leave for the ball. She was greatly saddened, and when she asked her husband why, she was told that an emergency had arisen. As the carriage carried them through the London streets, Angus delivered Brianda's message to Mary, but did not inform her that Brianda and John had left for the country. The fewer who knew that fact, the better for Brianda.

The ball was gala indeed. Music wafted through the air, and the fragrance of fresh flowers perfumed each room. Mary was transfixed when she stepped into the entrance hall. Men and women were strolling and dancing, each one in a magnificent mask that complemented their costumes for the evening. Laughter and the sparkle of jewelry decorated each salon. Mary had never imagined a night like this.

Excusing himself, Angus went in search of Paul and Elizabeth, who were waiting for him in the northeast corner of the main salon. When Angus found them, he quickly took Paul aside and informed him about John's decision to leave immediately for the country. He explained that he had been asked to quietly search for Breedon.

Paul escorted Elizabeth to the covered outdoor terrace. Carefully choosing his words, he told Elizabeth that an emergency had arisen, and that John and Brianda would not be coming to the gala ball. Elizabeth demanded to know if Brianda had become ill or had suffered an accident. Paul explained to her that John and Brianda were both well, but that he could not reveal the nature of the emergency.

"How is it possible that you expect me not to ask you questions, Paul? Brianda is my best friend, and I have never seen her more enthusiastic about anything than this ball!"

"I am sorry, my sweet, but I cannot tell you more at this moment."

"Well, then I am going to get a carriage and drive over to the house and ask Brianda myself why she is not here! It is probably another of John's unjust decisions!"

"Elizabeth, you are staying here."

"Are you saying that I may not go to speak to Brianda?"

"Yes."

"Paul, you are frightening me! You have never treated me in this manner before."

"You must trust me, Elizabeth. I promise to tell you the details when it is advisable."

"When will that be?"

"I will talk with Angus, and then I will decide when the proper time is to tell you. Now, Mrs. Martin, it is your choice, do we join the party or do we leave for home?"

"You are acting like John, and I don't like it!" Elizabeth said, her voice rising.

"Elizabeth, I am a quiet man and I love you, but I am telling you now that if you do not calm down, I will take you home and put you to bed. Emotional outbursts like this can be harmful to the child that you are carrying. Have I made myself clear?"

The look of hurt on Elizabeth's face made Paul feel terrible. "When you choose to tell me what has happened to my best friend I will be grateful to you." With that, Elizabeth turned and walked inside the salon in search of Mary. Maybe she would be able to get some information from her, since she had been in the same house with Brianda today.

John and his friends had not counted on Edward Breedon being smart enough to have John's house watched day and night. No one noticed the figure lurking near the carriage house. John's private driver enjoyed a casual conversation with the huge, gravel-voiced gentleman who explained he was visiting with the gentry next door. The man smiled in sympathy as the driver complained good-naturedly about the condition of the roads he would have to travel to get the earl and his wife to the country this evening.

Brianda sat huddled in the corner of the carriage seat opposite from John and refused to speak to him. When her mind wandered to thoughts of the ball and the wonderful time Mary must be having, her eyes grew hot with tears, which fell like burning raindrops on her hands. As hard as she tried, she couldn't prevent the irregular, rough gasps of breath that hurt her throat. It was possible that John heard her sighs, but he could not see the few tears that escaped from her swollen lids.

After several hours of silence, broken by occasional gulps of air on Brianda's part, John pulled a flask out of his pocket and offered Brianda some tea.

"I want nothing from you, sir."

"I want you to take a few sips of the tea, Brianda. Your mouth must be very dry by now. You have been shedding tears since we left London."

"My Lord, your sudden interest in my welfare does not impress me."

"Have some tea, Brianda, it will soothe you."

"I would rather die from dehydration. Then both of us will be out of our misery."

"We are not in misery, love. This was just a very unfortunate circumstance. There will be other balls, and we will attend them."

Brianda sat upright. "Why don't you admit the truth? You are sorry that you married me. You think I will disgrace you in front of your lofty friends, don't you?" Brianda was losing whatever control she had over her shattered nerves. "I wasn't worth all the land you gained by marrying me, was I? I have been nothing but trouble for you, and you wish you were well rid of me!" she cried out at him, covering her face with her hands.

"That is not true, Brianda. I will tell you again that when we married, I had no interest in possessing your father's lands, other than helping the people who lived there. I was already one of the wealthiest men in England. I married you for other reasons," he finished lamely.

"Oh really? Pray tell me what they were?" she demanded, her voice rising.

"I cannot tell you now. At an appropriate time, I will tell you everything," he said, maintaining his calm.

"You are insufferable. I want a divorce!"

"No."

Turning toward him with her arms half extended, she balled her hands into fists. "Is there no way for me to divorce you, if you are opposed?"

"There is no way. Married we are, and married we will stay, Brianda. Now sit back in the seat and calm yourself," he said strongly.

Something in her snapped. She lunged at him, trying to disfigure his handsome face with her fingernails. He caught her, and they struggled. She fought him with all her might. She wanted to smash his face, that perfect mouth that could not tell her that he loved her. Her anger and fury gave her added strength, and she wanted to hurt him.

John was surprised by her strength and her desire to inflict harm. He didn't want to hurt her, and just when he thought he had her in a hold, she would break loose and attack with another tactic. She kicked him wherever her foot would land, heedless of the pain inflicted on herself when she missed her mark.

The cramped quarters of the carriage worked against him, as he was such a big man. He could not maneuver easily and had to take care so as not to damage the vixen. He only wanted to calm her down.

Brianda made the fatal mistake of turning her back toward him for a second. Instantly his arms came around her, pinning her flailing limbs to her sides. He wrapped his long legs over hers and locked his ankles together.

She couldn't move. Struggling against him now was useless, as his strength was so much greater than hers. Frustration, greater than she had ever felt before, raged within her.

Suddenly, she relaxed against him, and tears of fury and pain fell. Great sobs wracked her. She hated him. In that moment she would give anything to die.

He unlocked his feet and pulled her into his arms to hold her while she cried against his chest. Had he broken her spirit? He hoped not. She was so difficult, so bright, so rebellious . . .

When, at last, the sobs lessened, he held the flask to her lips and tipped the container up. She was too tired to fight, and she swallowed the tea. Soon the sedative that he had put into the tea took its effect, and she slept heavily. He readjusted her position on his lap and let his chin rest on the top of her head.

"I love you, my Brianda, but tonight was not the time to tell you, for you would never have believed me. I will wait for the right time. Until then, you are worth all the battles, all the trouble. Someday you will know how much."

Edward was dressed early. He had manipulated an invitation to tea before the ball at the house of Lady Susana Smythe. He had met Susana in the park while she was riding, and had struck up a conversation with her. She had seemed intrigued with him, and when the time seemed right, he mentioned that he knew the Earl of Manseth quite well. It raised just the response he wanted.

Having heard all the rumors concerning John's mar-

riage, Lady Smythe had been dying for real information.
And thus, the invitation to tea.

Biff Blanders crossed town as fast as he could travel,
intent on reaching Edward before he left for the ball.
The streets were crowded in the late afternoon, and he
swore as he had to wait at the busy corners. No one
dared say anything to the giant for his offensive behavior.
No one wanted to irritate the ugly, mean man who
pushed his way along the street, mumbling obscenities
under his breath as he went.

Biff burst through the door of the run-down rooming
house to discover that Edward had departed five minutes previously. Swearing and throwing the chair
against the wall, Biff knew he would have to wait until
the ball began to tell Edward that Fauxley and Brianda
had left London. Furious, he decided to go up to his
room to try out a few new tricks on his latest chit.

The butler admitted Edward Breedon into the elegant
town house and showed him to the drawing room.
Susana kept him waiting for fifteen minutes. He didn't
care. All he needed was to convince Susana to allow
him to accompany her to the ball. Her presence would
assure him entrance, just in case it was discovered that
his invitation had been stolen and subsequently forged
to show his name.

When Susana entered the room, she flew toward him
and sat down opposite the tea service from him. "Pray
tell me how you happen to know Lord Fauxley so well,
Mr. Breedon," she asked, not even pausing to greet him.

"Lord Fauxley is my brother-in-law, Lady Smythe,"
he answered, smiling at her and accepting a cup of tea
from her gloved hand.

"Then it is true! He has really married, and a country nobody at that!" she spat. Almost at once, she realized what she had said and smiled at Edward. "I did not mean any offense, Mr. Breedon. I am sure you understand that. It is just that the Fauxley name is ranked so high in our social circle that it surprises one that his Lordship would choose to marry outside of it," she finished.

"I agree with you entirely, Lady Smythe. I am quite certain that the marriage will not last long. I ache to have my sister back with me where she belongs. She is a sensitive young thing, and she needs the love of her family."

"Quite right, Mr. Breedon, and please, call me Susana. Is there anything that I might do to be of help in returning your sister to you?"

"Thank you for offering, Susana. As a matter of fact, if I may be so bold in mentioning this, I have been told that you had a romantic interest in Lord Fauxley in the past. Is that interest still there?"

"Yes, very much so," she said, leaning forward with anticipation.

"Good. I know for a fact that my sister and his Lordship are unhappy together. Why, their divorce is almost certain. I would like to go to the ball with you this evening, and then while we are there, I would like you to distract John for a few minutes, so that I could speak to my sister without interference. You see, John doesn't much like me, as I was so opposed to the marriage. He will not allow me to speak to my own sister. Can you imagine that?" he asked, looking quite forlorn.

"That is terrible, Edward! I will do exactly as you ask this evening. I would love a chance to talk to John alone myself."

"Splendid. Shall we get our cloaks and leave for the ball?"

"I will be ready in an instant," she called back to him as she hurried off to gather her evening apparel.

Edward was helping Susana down from the carriage when he saw Biff signaling to him from the side of the main entrance. Giving Biff a prearranged signal, he walked Susana to the door, then feigned anger at himself as he claimed to have left his gloves in the carriage. He invited her to go in alone and told her that he would join her shortly. Smiling and waving at friends, Susana walked gaily into the ball.

At Biff's news, Edward stood straight, his eyes narrowed. So, the brilliant doctor had not been able to fool him this time. Whispering about their plans, the two men slipped off into the darkness. They had business to settle before leaving for the country. If all went well, they would be at Manseth Manor by dark the following evening.

33

Brianda awoke at dawn on her second day back in the country. The sun was just rising as she made her way to the chamber window. This was the perfect time to leave. If she waited much longer, the stable hands would be up and working.

She dressed warmly, putting on a blouse, a warm jacket and her boys' pants. Then she made sure to lock the door leading to the master suite. Afterward, she slipped very quietly from the bedchamber, and was careful to lock that door as well. She then hid the key behind one of the portraits in the upper hallway. Surely John and the staff would think she had decided to sleep late again.

She stopped in the kitchen and threw some food and a flask of water into a canvas bag. Hastily, she stuffed some bread into her mouth and washed it down with some coffee that had been left on the stove from the night before. It was bitter, but it helped her wake up.

At her approach Dakota thumped his welcome with his hooves. She had the bridle and saddle on him in moments, and tied her canvas bag to the saddle. Leading Dakota by his bridle, she snuck out of the barn and jumped onto the stallion's back and headed for the woods.

Mrs. Brady held the tray of tea and fresh muffins in her ample arms and tried to decide if she should take them in to the sleeping girl. She hesitated to knock on the door, as his Lordship had been so firm about not disturbing Brianda. But Mrs. Brady was worried, as Brianda had hardly eaten any food yesterday and would surely be hungry. After a few moments of thought she decided not to incur the wrath of the earl, as he had made himself quite clear with his orders. So she carried the tray back down to the kitchen and sat down to enjoy some hot tea.

John slept later than usual and woke up disgruntled, having grown used to his wife in bed with him. He walked to the door connecting the two bedchambers and tried the handle. Brianda had locked it from her side, making it plain that she wanted nothing to do with him. He was late in leaving for his business appointment, which necessitated riding to the neighboring county, and he knew that he would have to postpone talking to his wife until he returned.

As he breakfasted hastily, he sent word to have Sebastian brought to the front entrance. His stallion waited impatiently for his master and greeted John with a healthy whinny when he emerged from the manor. Patting the huge beast on his nose, John pulled himself into the saddle and called out to Stevens.

"Yes, sir."

"Lady Fauxley is not to leave the house, Stevens, not even to go to the stable. Make sure that every member of the staff is made aware of these orders. I will tolerate no errors. Angus is not here to help me with her today, so I am counting on you to handle anything that arises."

"You can rely on me, sir," Stevens said officiously.

"I plan to be gone half the day, and I will try to return as soon as possible." With that, he rode off at a gallop.

John never saw the stableboy waving his hands frantically after him. The black stallion was missing from his stall, and his riding tack was gone as well.

Brianda and Dakota rode through the forest, racing through the trees, jumping fallen tree trunks and dodging the low-hanging branches. The wind whipped her golden hair behind her like a veil. She stopped for a bite to eat at midmorning, sharing her apple with Dakota. They rested on the cool ground as Brianda decided where they would venture next. Then they were off again, cantering through the fields as they left the forest and headed for the ocean. Here on the flat plain, she let him run full out, and it felt as if they were flying. His powerful muscles contracted as he gathered his legs together and then hurled forward in long, graceful strides.

The wind blew much colder when Dakota and Brianda reached the ocean. Fresh off the water, its chill penetrated her jacket. Heedless of the weather, horse and rider raced through the waves breaking on the shore. The water was cold on Dakota's feet, and it felt like icicles to Brianda, as the droplets splashed onto her legs. But they kept galloping along the sand, the sheer exhilaration of total freedom making it too splendid to stop.

Finally, they climbed the path that led from the beach to Cliffshead Manor. She had gotten off Dakota's back, and they walked side-by-side up the steep hill.

She stopped to catch her breath at the crest of the hill. Cliffshead Manor rose in front of her like a decaying monument. Brianda stared at the house and felt nothing. No stirring in her soul for all the years she had lived there, for the parents she had lost. The manor looked more bleak than ever, boarded up and forgotten. She turned to walk Dakota around the house and stopped dead in her tracks.

Edward Breedon and Biff Blanders stood not twenty feet away from her. "Welcome home, little sister," Edward sneered. Dakota stamped his feet and tossed his head around. "Shoot the damn horse, Biff! He had been too much trouble as it is!" Edward shouted.

"No!" screamed Brianda. "What do you want, Edward? Money? My husband has a great deal of money. He will pay you what you want, but don't shoot my horse!" she pleaded.

Edward took a menacing step toward her. "I have missed hearing you beg, bitch." Turning to Biff, he laughed, "This has been easier than we planned. Why the little tramp walked right into our hands!" He started toward her, but the stallion lunged, teeth bared, his ears flat back against his head.

Biff raised his pistol and aimed it at the stallion. Screaming, Brianda ran and pulled on Dakota's bridle, dragging his massive head down. Dakota stopped his rush on Edward, but his hooves never ceased their prancing, his eyes locked on his foe. Brianda stepped in front of the horse, a small but adequate shield. "You will have to shoot me before you shoot my horse, you slime!"

Edward raised his hand, and Biff lowered the gun. "All right, Brianda. I will make a deal with you," Edward said, putting his hands in his pockets, assuming a less threatening posture. "You can put the animal in the old stable, and I promise you that we will leave him alone. In return, you will need to accompany me into the house. There are certain family matters that I need to discuss with you," he said amiably.

Brianda stood her ground, her face set and wary.

"What's the matter, Lady Fauxley? You don't trust me? Have you been listening to the cultured words of your rich husband?" he mocked. "He only says things that serve his own purpose." Seeing her wince, Edward continued, "How many times has he told you that he loves you? Are you so naive that you think the rapid union between a rich English earl and a chit raised in the kitchen was forged by love? Father would never believe that even you could be so blind." Noting that his words hit their mark, he softened his attitude toward her. "Brianda, I am your brother. Yes, I know that I got drunk and angry in the past and hit you a few times, but I am neither drunk nor angry now. All I want to do is talk to you."

Brianda was confused. She pushed her fingers through her long hair.

Biff, standing behind Edward, gulped. Just watching her run her fingers through her hair made him hard.

"I cannot imagine what you would have to say to me, now, brother. I am no longer your responsibility, as you well know. I am now under the rule of my husband. I cannot promise you money directly. You will have to deal with John." Standing with her back against the chest of the strong horse made her feel slightly less vulnerable.

Taking another small step toward Brianda, he inquired, "Have you no influence with him?"

"None."

"Good. This matter has nothing to do with money or your esteemed husband. It has to do with us, the only remaining Breedons. Are you not curious what it is that I have to tell you? I have a gift for you. I have had the gift for a long time now. Go on, put the horse in the barn and come with me, please," he entreated softly.

Looking at Blanders standing behind Edward, she said, "What of him? Will he go into the house, too?"

"Biff is harmless. He does just as I tell him and nothing

more." Opening his arms, he motioned to her. "Come on, Brianda, it has been such a long time since we have been together. I want to hear about your new life." The wind was picking up, blowing winter leaves up and about. "It grows colder. We will be more comfortable behind the walls of the house."

Brianda stepped back, and Dakota moved back with her. She felt the need to have more space between her brother and herself. She wanted to see if Edward would make a move toward her. He didn't. "You have done me grave harm in the past, Edward. I do not feel safe with you. Perhaps it is better that you speak to me in my husband's house. I will see to it that we are left alone so that we may speak in private."

Shaking his head sadly, Edward looked at her. "Brianda, your husband told me that I could never set foot on his property again, much less in his house. He would never permit it." Watching for her reaction, he sighed. "He threatened my life, Brianda. He said I would die, should I ever come close to you again." He forced a false tear from his eye. "I know I have done some bad things in the past, but to permanently separate me from my only living relative . . . is that just?" He took great pains in wiping the tear away with his sleeve. It was a gesture she had seen many times during her childhood, and she felt her heart soften toward him.

"If I tie Dakota in the barn, do you swear that after we have talked, you will let me leave with Dakota and return to my home?"

"Yes, I swear it." He looked so sincere.

Brianda turned and led the stallion to the old barn. She took off his saddle and tied Dakota to a post with the reins. Uneasy, he snorted his displeasure. She hugged him and kissed his nose. "I don't know if this is a mistake, Dakota, but I have to know if there is one person on this earth who truly loves me. I have to give

Edward one more chance." She turned and walked from the barn toward her brother.

Old Megan turned over in her small cot and slowly opened her eyes. She had been up late the night before with a very difficult birth. At her first stretch, her aged muscles protested painfully. Then, forcing herself up and out of bed, she reached out and put a hand on the bed frame for a moment. She was dizzy again. She had experienced dizziness for several months now, but the attacks were coming with more frequency lately. When the dizziness passed, she walked to the stove to make tea.

Feeling better after breakfast, Old Megan decided to visit Brianda. She had heard they had returned to the country, but had been unable to pay a visit immediately, as she had been committed to the pregnant woman. How she longed to visit and hold her darling girl. Suddenly the pain struck. It was heavy and oppressive, just below her breastbone, and she had to take a few deep breaths before it eased off. She sat down at the small wooden table and decided to forgo a visit to Brianda today, knowing she had to rest. However, she had to see the new mother and baby, so she waited a while longer until her breathing returned to normal, and then set off on foot to the village.

Aside from the nagging sensation in her chest, another troubling thought pulled at her. Something was wrong, and it had to do with Brianda. She felt it deep in her soul. The feeling was so powerful that she knew she would have to go to Manseth Manor after all.

Brianda emerged from the barn and saw only Edward waiting for her. She wondered where the thug had gone as, apprehensive, she drew closer to her brother.

Edward only had to wait for her to get a few feet closer to him. He forced the lazy smile on his face to stay put. The moment he had so long been waiting for was nearly upon him! He had even surprised himself with his loving, big-brother act. Maybe he should have taken up a career on the stage. The thought made him laugh.

Seeing Edward so relaxed, and laughing, lessened Brianda's fears. The wind whipped her hair with a sharp gust, and she glanced over at the ocean, noting that the water looked murky and tumultuous.

"Here, sister, take my hand and we will walk into our former house together," Edward said sweetly.

Brianda reached out and took his hand. He led her up along the stone path that was now almost completely covered with weeds. Her mother's gardens were gone, taken over by the stronger weeds that survived man's neglect.

Edward saw Brianda gazing at the forlorn gardens and felt a momentary pang of regret. He pictured his beautiful mother in his mind, planting and caring for her precious flowers. It had all been such a long time ago. His mother had left him, too, just like all women did sooner or later. And it was all Brianda's fault.

He smiled as he urged her along the path, as he was about to revel in the joy of his vengeance.

Following a tip regarding the present residence of Breedon and Blanders, Angus stood in the dingy vestibule, trying to convince the manager of the ramshackle boarding house that he was a trusted friend of Edward Breedon. The manager could tell by the way the gentleman was dressed that he did not belong in this part of London. Finally, when Angus offered a few coins, the nasty old woman allowed him to go upstairs to see if he could raise a response from Edward's room.

After several minutes of knocking on the door, Angus was sure that no one was inside. As there was no one in the hall, Angus tried the door. It opened with ease.

The filth and smell in the room made Angus's stomach turn. Old, empty bottles of cheap liquor littered the floor. Filthy clothes were strewn everywhere. Pieces of moldy food were on the table and between the grimy, dirt-encrusted sheets. Angus found a scrap of newspaper with pencil markings, underlining notations about the Gala Ball and the appearance of Lord Fauxley and his new bride. There was nothing to give him a clue as to the whereabouts of Edward and his half-witted sidekick.

"If you think this room is a mess, sir, you should see the room upstairs where the other one lives," said a voice from the doorway. Turning, Angus saw an elderly woman dressed in old clothing and clutching a wooden cane in her gnarled right hand. She was filthy, her hair hanging in lice-infested strands, her fingernails permanently stained brown from cheap tobacco.

"What information can you offer me, mother?" Angus asked, keeping his distance. She smelled worse than the garbage dump.

"If I tell you what I know about this man and his friend, have you got a coin or two for me?"

"I have several coins, mother, if your information is good enough."

"You'll not be telling anyone about this, will you? I have to live here in this house. Can't have myself getting a reputation for talking too much," she whispered through a mouth with only three teeth remaining.

"I swear that I will not tell another living soul. Now tell me what you know. I will make it well worth your while," Angus urged.

"You wait here. I will be back in a jiffy," she said as she hurried off, her ragged dress dragging through the dirt on the floor.

Ten minutes later, Angus was sure that the old woman was daft. He was about to leave, when she reappeared in the doorway. "Follow me, but quiet like. There's folk asleep nearby, and I don't want none of them knowing nothing."

Angus followed her up a flight of stairs on the back side of the house. The alley behind the house was littered with rubble and stank from the waste of human beings. He had to breathe through his mouth to keep from gagging.

His guide stopped at the top of the stairs. "I am not going any farther than right here." She pointed to the third door on the right. "That is his door, the evil one." She reached out a bony hand and grabbed Angus's sleeve. "Listen, sir, I have heard coming from within that room screams that weren't human sounding. There's been rumors that the girls that go in there don't come out alive," she said, squinting her rheumy eyes up at him. She started to leave.

Angus held up his purse and the coins jingled inside. She stopped and stared at it, the greed evident in her eyes. "Tell me, mother, what is it that you know about these two gentlemen? The one whose room I was in and the one who lives there," he said, motioning toward the door.

Stepping closer, she whispered, "Are you going to give me a fair share of those coins, if I tell you what I know?" She was salivating, and the spittle was dripping out of the corners of her mouth.

"If the information is good enough, I will give you the entire purse."

Her eyes bugged out for a moment. "All right. Come closer. I have to be careful that no one hears."

Holding his breath, Angus bent over and got closer to her.

"It is said that the gent downstairs used to be an

English lord, but he lost his title and all he owned. He is a nasty man, rude and coarse. They say he killed a bloke a while back over some drug-smuggling deal. He is the brains for the two of them. He can dress real nice when he wants to, like he did yesterday."

"Do you know where he was going yesterday, all dressed up fine?" Angus asked carefully.

"I heard tell that he was going to a ball. Can you believe that! The likes of one of us going to a ball!" she chortled.

"What else?" he prodded.

"The other one, he is an ugly, evil man. All of us around here is afraid of him. He is so big and has a look of a madman. Like I said, he takes girls into that room and only Heaven knows what becomes of them. Why one time, the manager went up to complain about the screaming, and the thug threw her down the stairs, cursing at her the whole way. That was the last time anyone tried to interfere with him," she finished barely audibly, her eyes darting about.

"Mother, where are the two men now?"

"Well, last night, the swell left early, all dressed up. Biff, that's the name of the nasty bloke, he came back and was furious when he couldn't find his friend. He stormed around here, and when it was dark, he left. About an hour and a half later they both came back. There was all sorts of commotion in their rooms, and then they left together with their traveling bags. But that ain't nothin'. They go out a lot together. They say the two of them's in the drug smuggling business. That is all I know, sir. Now do I get the money?"

Angus opened the purse and poured the money into her hands. She squealed with glee. "Mother, there is one more thing. Do not tell a soul about our conversation or the coins I just gave you. It is very important that these men do not know that I was here, trying to get information about them. Agreed?"

"Agreed, sir. I swear that no one will hear a word from my lips. I am going now. Take care if you are going into that room." With that warning, she slipped away into the squalid hallway.

Angus took a deep breath and walked to the door. The handle turned, and he entered. He gagged at the odor. Covering his mouth with a handkerchief, he looked around.

Tied spread-eagled on the filthy bed was a young girl. She was nude, and barely alive. Maggots crawled on some of the open wounds on her body. There were stains of blood everywhere, some older than others. Her pubic hair had been burned off. There were tooth marks all around her nipples. Dried blood covered her teeth and lips. At the end of the bed were handmade instruments covered with slime and mold. Angus didn't want to think what they had been used for. Not able to control himself, he ran to the window and vomited several times.

Shaking with horror, Angus went downstairs and filled a bucket with fairly clean water. He carried it upstairs, and with pieces of his shirt, he bathed the young girl. She didn't look older than twelve or thirteen years. When he was finished, he wrapped her in his long cloak and carried her down and out of the hellhole.

Yelling to John's driver to make haste, Angus gave directions to Paul's office. The girl didn't move in his arms as she stared at the top of the carriage, not making a sound.

Paul was finishing suturing a minor wound when he heard Angus call out for him. He motioned for the nurse to bandage the wound and ran out to the waiting room.

Angus was standing there, a small body wrapped in his cloak. There was a look of horror on the Scotsman's face.

For a moment, Paul's heart stilled. What if it were one of his friends, or his wife, in that cloak? Gathering his professional mantle, Paul motioned for Angus to follow him into one of the examining rooms.

Angus laid the girl gently down on the examining table. "I found this young woman tied to the bed in Biff Blanders's room, Paul."

At the sound of Blanders' name, the girl moaned deep in her throat, her eyes widened with fear.

Paul called for his nurse, and together they unwrapped the cloak. The nurse clapped her hand to her mouth and turned away. Paul found himself swallowing several times to keep his stomach contents in place. He had seen countless traumatic injuries and horrible burns, but this sight was unbelievable. He began cleaning the wounds, extracting the maggots with tweezers. There were several times when Angus had to hold the girl down so that Paul and his nurse could properly tend to her. Blessedly, she lost consciousness before they were finished.

When Paul finished the last bandages, Angus carried the limp body of the girl to the carriage. When he arrived at John's home, Mary put her to bed in one of the guest rooms and vowed to take care of her.

After serious consideration, Angus decided that he should leave immediately for the country. If what the old hag had told him was true, it was possible that Blanders and Breedon had left for the country the night before.

34

Edward took Brianda to the only door they could use to enter the manor, a small kitchen door that Biff had pried open when he and Edward returned to the manor after Fauxley had ordered the house boarded up.

Brianda let go of Edward's hand and wandered through the kitchen, feeling a sense of loss. Paying scant attention to her brother, she walked through the whole lower level of the house. The old draperies hung shapeless and forlorn. Most of the furniture had been removed, but there remained a few old pieces. It hadn't been long since Edward had quit the house, but it looked as if it had been deserted for years. She had seen enough, and turned to find Edward.

He stood just behind her, watching her with interest. "It looks very much different, doesn't it, sister?"

"So much has happened to me since I last saw this house, Edward. It seems like another lifetime ago," she said wistfully.

"It has been that, and more, for me. You can have no

idea how everything changed when the famous Earl of Manseth came into my life."

Brianda looked intently at him, his tone of voice suddenly stony, threatening. His face had lost its soft contours. They had been replaced by cruel lines and a self-satisfied smirk. She looked at him, confused.

"You were always so trusting as a child, Brianda. You are the same now, still stupid, still easy to manipulate." He started toward her.

She ran, her boys' pants making it easier for her to sprint, but she was no match for Edward's long legs, and he caught her before she left the salon. Grabbing a handful of her hair, he threw her to the ground. The look in his eye was maniacal.

"What is it that you want? All of your lies served to get me into the house, and I was fool enough to believe in you. So, it is money after all," she spat at him.

He pulled her hair and she cried out. "You are a stupid girl! You understand nothing! It isn't Lord Fauxley's money that I want, Brianda. It is you that I want. By making sure your death is a gruesome one, I will get my revenge on the earl. That is what I want, Brianda, and I intend to have it."

Recoiling from his hatred, she tried to pull away, her eyes wide with fear and the realization that her brother was mad. Completely mad.

"Don't fight me! There is no one for miles to hear your screams." The light of evil shone in his eyes. "Come with me upstairs, Brianda, to our special room."

"Why do you hate me so?" she asked him. "What did I do to you that you should hate me so?" she implored, trying to pry his fingers off of her arm.

Ignoring her efforts to free herself, he pulled her along the floor. Her feet made long continuous marks in the dust. Suddenly, he turned and hit her on the side of her head, knocking her senseless.

Brianda wobbled, her vision blurred from the blow.

Holding her upright by her shoulders, he screamed into her face. "Hate you? I hated you before you were even born! I hoped you would be born dead, or at least be another boy, but no, a girl was born. *You!* Then Mother died and it was all your fault! Even Father said so. He hated you, *hated you!*"

Brianda sobbed, hearing these terrible things. It was true. No one loved her, not really. She stopped fighting and let Edward pull her up the stairs. He was surprisingly strong, and he dragged her up three flights with little effort.

Biff was waiting at the entrance to the door. He noticed Brianda was limp, and for a second he thought that Edward had killed her. He stood silent, waiting.

Edward shook Brianda and forced her to look around the room. "Do you remember all the lovely things we did together in this room, sister?" he asked gleefully.

"You are mad, Edward," she stated matter-of-factly.

Edward slammed his fist into her stomach. The impact of the blow forced all the air from her lungs, and she doubled over, falling forward. Struggling for breath, she lay helpless on the floor.

Biff stood just inside the door, giggling.

"What justice there is, if one waits long enough!" Edward shouted to the world at large. "You ignorant bitch! You found a man who loves you and you threw it away!" He laughed and slapped his thighs.

Pushing herself into a sitting position, Brianda looked at Edward. "What do you mean, a man who loves me?"

"You don't know? The famous and powerful earl loves you! You are more important to him than anything in this world. I had a secret meeting with him in London before you married him. He told me that he would go to any lengths to keep you safe, and he forbade me to ever see you again. He loves you! Ha! A lot of good all that love will do him now. I have you, and you will be dead before he sees you again."

He picked her up then and pulled her face to within inches of his. Inhaling his foul breath, she thought how her life had been one torment after another. Maybe death would be preferable.

"Before I take great pleasure in killing you, I forgot that I have a present for you. How careless of me."

"What cruel joke are you playing now?" she asked feebly.

"This is no joke. I promised you as a very special gift to my friend, in payment for all the hard work he has done for me these past months. The present I am offering you is a splendid interlude with Biff, before I slit your throat and watch you bleed to death."

"God, no, Edward! If you must kill me, then do so. Please don't degrade yourself further by permitting such a thing!" she cried frantically, pulling at his shirt.

"Lower myself? I am going to watch him do what he does best! And I am going to *love* it!" He threw her across the room into Biff's massive arms.

Brianda screamed as she had never screamed before. Feeling herself fall against the horrid man, she kept on screaming.

Biff loved screaming. It made everything he did so much more enjoyable.

John knew immediately that something was very wrong as he rode up the lane toward his home. Stevens and Mrs. Brady were standing on the stoop waiting for him. He urged Sebastian into a gallop and jumped off before the animal had come to a complete stop.

"What has happened? Is Brianda all right?"

Neither one said anything; they just looked at him.
"Answer me!" he yelled.

"We are not sure, my Lord," Stevens replied. "It seems that Lady Fauxley left the house before you awoke this morning. She took some food and her stallion. The horse was discovered missing, just as you were riding off early today. We tried to call after you, but you did not hear us. Brianda has not returned, sir."

"It is now late in the afternoon, and she has been gone since dawn?" he asked in a deadly calm voice.

"I took the liberty of sending out men to search for her, sir. She has not been in the village. One of the men ran into Old Megan as she was walking here from the village, and she has not seen her. I put Old Megan in the library, sir. She does not look well."

"The men have looked all over the grounds?"

"Yes, sir, they have been all over the grounds and through the forest. I sent one man to search along the ocean and the others are riding about the county looking for her now, sir."

John felt a terrible sense of foreboding. Icy chills ran up and down his arms and he felt his gut churn. He ran into the house in search of Old Megan. She was the one person who knew where Brianda liked to ride.

In the library Old Megan sat holding her head, the pressure in her chest causing her to feel light-headed. She was terribly worried about her darling girl. When she heard John enter the room, she pushed herself up and walked unsteadily toward him.

John led her back to the chair. "Are you ill, Megan?"

"No, sir, I am just worried about my wee little girl."

Looking at her, he knew she was lying about how she felt, but he would have to see to her health after he found his wife. "Think, Megan. Where are her favorite places to ride? Tell me, I have to find her!"

"Sir, I will tell you every place I know, but she is not in any of those places."

"Do you know where she is?" he implored.

"No, sir, I wish I did. I do know Brianda, though, and she went out riding this morning to spite you. She may be willful, but she is not foolish. She knew you would be gone until at least midday. If all were well, she would have returned home before you did, and would be spending the day hoping that you would not find out about her ride. Sir, I am very much afraid that something has happened to her," she finished, short of breath. She wiped a few tears from her face with her cuff.

"Tell me where to begin looking, Megan. I cannot just sit here and wait for her to return. I have to find her!" he said, sitting heavily into one of the chairs. Something told John that this time Brianda wasn't going to show up with a defiant grin and a dare to throw her over his knee.

Just then Stevens came crashing into the room, knocking over a small table and a vase of flowers. In all of his life, the butler had never before lost control. Straightening himself, he announced to John, "Sir! Dakota has just returned! Alone!"

John was on his feet and out the door in seconds to find Dakota breathing hard and prancing around the courtyard. He had a wild look in his eye. John tried to get close to him but the stallion charged him and he backed off.

Thomas, the head groomsman, yelled to all assembled, "Everyone stand very still. Do not move. The animal is panicked. It will only make him worse if we try to get close to him."

Everyone froze, and there was a heavy silence. The only sounds heard were Dakota's hooves scraping about on the gravel. Thomas walked very slowly over to

John. "Sir, notice that he has no tack on. When Brianda left this morning, she took his bridle and saddle. He has no marks on his sides, but look at his head. It looks as though he may have ripped his bridle off. There is blood in the corners of his mouth where the bit cut into him."

Suddenly Dakota reared and ran a few yards down the drive and stopped. He turned and looked at John. "He wants me to follow him!" John shouted. "Thomas, get me another mount. Sebastian is too tired from our long ride today. I want the fastest horse in the stable!"

"Right away, sir. Do you want me to go with you?" Thomas called out as he ran toward the barn.

"No, stay here and wait for Angus. When he arrives, direct him to Cliffshead Manor in the carriage." Turning to Stevens, he ordered, "Get my medical bag and have it ready for me here."

In minutes John was mounted and following the stallion. He galloped down the long road that serviced the manor, and turned toward Cliffshead Manor.

Biff ripped Brianda's blouse down the middle and off her body with one pull. She beat at him with her fists while Edward sat in the corner and laughed.

Brianda landed a blow to the bridge of Biff's nose, causing him to stagger back a step. Furious, he pushed Brianda up against the wall; her flesh scraped against the old, dried wood. He stood in front of her and stared at her naked chest.

"I wanted to be the first man," he grunted, his eyes bulging. "Your brother promised me that I could take you and make you a woman. But the earl got to you first, didn't he, Miss High-and-Mighty? Well, I have some things in mind for you that I am willing to wager the earl has not done to you."

His words made Brianda nauseous. She would rather die than have this pig touch her, and wracked her brain to think of what she might be able to use against him.

Biff took his shirt off and threw it down to the floor. He opened his pants and pulled them down to his knees. Standing with a massive erection, he leered at her. "This is for you. I am going to put it places you never even thought of," Biff stated proudly, stroking himself slowly.

Brianda could do nothing but stare at him in horror. Edward's laugh was coarse and hard. "Biff, I am going down to get some liquor from my bag. I want to get a little drunk so that I can really enjoy the show. Don't have too much fun without me, little sister." She could hear him laughing all the way down the stairs.

At his departure Biff lunged at Brianda. She jumped to the side and ran to the fireplace. Just as he grabbed her from behind, her fingers closed around a small packet on the mantel.

Biff threw Brianda to the floor and pulled off her long boys' pants. He pinned her down and held her with one hand. His body odor caused her to gag, and she looked away. He laughed at her distress, then moved his hands to her rib cage and pressed her down hard against the floor. She was powerless to move from under him, but her hands were free.

Biff leaned over her and spread her legs with his knees. She could feel him probing her. She tried to squirm away, but his legs held her firmly. The trousers that he had thrown to the floor were within her reach. She grasped the fabric and slowly pulled the pants toward her.

Biff reached down and licked her nipple with his tongue.

Brianda gagged again, but forced herself to slip a match from the packet. She moaned loudly to cover the sound of the match scratching the rough surface of the floor.

It did not light.

Frantically, she pulled another one from the pack, just as he was about to enter her. She pulled the head of the match along the floor, moaning deep in her throat as the match caught and lit. Quickly, she put the match to the fabric of the pants, and it slowly started to burn. Brianda waited a moment, until the pants were burning well. With a toss of her wrist, she threw the flaming material onto Biff's back.

Biff screamed when flames from the burning material landed on him, searing his bare skin and igniting his grimy hair. He jumped up and hopped around, screaming and frantically trying to get the flames off him.

Brianda was up on her feet as soon as Biff was off of her. She grabbed her pants and torn shirt and started down the stairs.

In Biff's haste to rid himself of the burning pants, he did not notice that he had thrown them onto the draperies. They instantly erupted into flames, and in moments, the dry wood caught fire and the room was engulfed. Biff roared threats of death against Brianda as he ran toward one of the bedroom windows.

Brianda was looking behind her as she ran down the stairs and straight into Edward's arms. Without a moment's hesitation, she slammed her fist into his jaw. He recoiled, and grabbed for her. She would have gotten away, but he caught her long hair as it swung in an arc behind her. He held her fast and started down the stairs with his prize.

Flames spread rapidly to the second floor, and from there down toward the main floor. Biff was trapped in the third-story room, screaming for Edward to help him.

The fire was spreading fast, causing a tremendous heat and billowing black smoke.

Brianda tripped Edward as he pulled her behind him through the main salon. They wrestled and struggled as the smoke entered their lungs. Coughing, they fought each other in a deadly duel.

John saw the smoke long before he reached Cliffshead Manor. Already villagers were running toward the old manor house.

Dakota was first to arrive. Smoke was pouring from broken windows and billowing up into the sky. The stallion pranced about, panicked by the raging fire.

When John arrived at the front of the manor, it appeared that the entire house was engulfed in flames. Fear spread through John faster than the flames did along the old wood. Where was Brianda?

At a man's scream, he looked up and saw Biff Blanders ablaze in a third-story window. Horrified, he watched as Biff climbed up into the window and jumped. He fell, screaming, totally afire. His corpse lay burning, only a few feet from where John stood transfixed by the grisly spectacle.

At that very moment, John knew that Brianda was in the house with Edward. Without a thought, he jumped off his horse and ran toward the burning structure. To his horror, he found all the doors boarded up. He rushed around the house, frantically searching for a way to enter, and finally found the small kitchen door that had been pushed inward.

Brianda was dying from lack of air as Edward continued to wrestle with her. She reached her arm back in a wide arc, and her hand made contact with an old piece of shattered wood. Picking it up without hesitation, she swung it as hard as she could into the side of Edward's head, causing him to instantly loosen his grip on her. He fell to the floor, limp.

Brianda could hardly breathe. Gasping, she got on her hands and knees and put her face close to the floor, finding there a bit of air, and started crawling toward the kitchen.

She wasn't going to make it.

Thinking that there must be only one more breath of air, she reached the kitchen. It hadn't been engulfed yet, and she stumbled up to her feet and began running toward the open door.

Just then she was grabbed by strong hands. Panicked, she lashed out with all her might, kicking and flailing her arms in her struggle to get away.

"Brianda! Brianda!" John yelled at her over the roar of the conflagration.

She heard nothing, knew only that someone was trying to kill her. She fought like a wild animal, kicking, clawing, biting, emitting sounds that were not at all human.

Pulling her bodily through the door, John shook her so hard that her teeth rattled. "Brianda! It is John. Stop it!"

Still she fought like a crazed person.

"I am sorry, Brianda," were the first words to get through to her before she felt the sharp crack of a hand slapping her face. Once, twice, hard against her cheeks.

Reeling from the blows, she looked up and saw John! She was never so glad to see anyone in her life and threw herself, coughing, into his arms, clutching him as if she would never let go.

The villagers had been gathering water, but did not throw even one bucket. The entire house was an inferno. Seeing that there was nothing they could do, they left as they had come, quietly.

John held Brianda close as the coughing subsided. As soon as she could breathe more regularly, she began to cry. Her tears were for fear, for broken dreams and for what might have been, had John not saved her yet again.

In his arms she felt safe and protected. Eventually the crying stopped and she sat for a long stretch of time, her cheek pressed close to his chest. Surrounded by his enormous winter cloak, she began telling him everything—how she had enjoyed the early morning ride, visiting all of her favorite places. She sat as if she were a small child, elbows together, hands as if in prayer, resting on his chest. Her knees were bent with her elbows resting on them, while her bare feet rested on his thighs. She nestled the top of her head under his chin and reveled in the security of his strong arms.

Her voice dropped, and she tried to snuggle even closer to him, when she told him about meeting Edward and Biff.

John listened intently, not saying a word.

Haltingly, she described how Edward enticed her into the house with his false promises and lies. Fresh tears fell when she described how much Edward hated her and wanted her dead. Trembling all over, she repeated Edward's promises of torture and painful death.

"Don't tell me more if it causes you too much pain, my love," John said, his voice deep with emotion.

"I want to tell you all of it now, and then try never to think of it again, my Lord." Her voice was hoarse from the smoke and the tears as she continued slowly, describing the bestiality of Edward's offer of her body to Biff Blanders. Her small hands, cold and stiff, once again sought refuge in the warmth and security of his chest.

John had never before felt such rage at another human being. He had taken an oath to preserve life, to aid and assist the ill and dying. But he knew that if Edward Breedon were not dead inside the burning house, he would kill him with his bare hands and enjoy it.

Fighting renewed fear, Brianda burst into heart-wrenching sobs as she told him how she had hit Edward with the board, and how, after he fell, she had crawled toward the kitchen to escape. She turned her pale, pinched face to him, imploring him to understand. "I killed my own brother!" she wailed, grabbing his shoulders, and shaking him slightly.

"Darling, listen to me," he implored. "The man was evil, mentally deranged. You did what you had to do to survive. Do not torture yourself over this."

"But he was my only blood relative! Now I have no one in my family. I am alone," she sobbed.

"You have me. I love you. You have Old Megan, Mrs. Brady, Stevens, Angus and Mary, and Paul and Elizabeth. All of us love you, Brianda. Is that not enough?" he chided gently.

"You love me? Truly?" She searched the depths of his arresting blue eyes for a hint of insincerity.

"Yes, I love you. I have loved you from the first—you just didn't realize it, Brianda. You are very young, and you have been hurt so much that you strove to protect yourself from accepting love. Accept it now, and know that you are mine."

Slowly she wrapped her arms around his shoulders and rested her head on his cheek. Was it possible? Was this truth, or just another cruel jest? She wanted to believe it true; more than anything, she wanted it to be true.

*   *   *

Dakota had wandered over near the cliffs. The fire frightened him, and he was restless and uneasy. He called out to Brianda.

John carried Brianda to the deserted barn, and there she found an old pair of shoes. They were too big for her, but would do until she reached home. Sharing John's cloak, they walked, arms about each other's waists, toward the cliff and Dakota.

35

The butt of the revolver hit with a fierce impact on the back of John's head. He fell to the ground like a stone.

Shocked, Brianda heard the moan and felt her husband fall at her side. Looking up, she froze. Edward stood two feet from her, arms limp at his sides, feet planted apart, his eyes filled with madness. He let the revolver fall to the ground.

Brianda heard herself scream. She dropped to her knees and shook John. He did not respond. Terrified, she called his name, shaking him harder.

"He is beyond helping you now. Did you think you could get away from me so easily, bitch?" Edward smiled a lazy smile. His face was covered with soot, making his uneven teeth look whiter and more evil.

Shaking, she asked, "Is he dead? Have you killed him?"

"Oh, I am sure he is dead, Brianda. Look, he doesn't move."

Edward stepped up and kicked John in the leg. There was no response.

"No! Please God, no!" she pleaded, eyes turned toward the sky.

"Cry for help all you want. I enjoy hearing your pleas. But nothing and no one is going to help you now. You will die by my hand. It has been preordained." He moved to her and pulled her off John's inert body. Brianda tried to hold on to John, but Edward found it easy to overpower her and drag her behind him as he headed for the cliffs.

As she was being pulled by only one arm, Brianda tried to slow Edward's progress by dragging her feet and scraping at the ground with her free hand and fingernails.

Edward reached the edge of the cliff and stopped. The wind was blowing hard, carrying icy moisture from the sea. He turned to pull Brianda to her feet and held her directly in front of him. Then he threw his head back and laughed.

Brianda felt his fingers dig into her upper arms. The pressure continued, and she thought he would break her bones if he didn't ease his grip. She lashed out with her boot, trying to shatter his shin. Sensing the oncoming blow, Edward moved her intended target, and she missed him completely.

Savagely, he drew his hand back and struck her neck. She collapsed under the blow. He pulled her back up and spat in her face. "I am going to strangle you slowly. The life will ebb from your eyes, and your body will go limp. Then, just before you suffocate, I am going to hurl you out over the edge of the cliffs and let you fall to the rocks below. I will watch gleefully as the waves come in and take your body out to sea. Too bad you won't be able to feel the teeth of the ocean creatures that will be feasting on your flesh."

She was lost. Helpless.

Edward's hands closed around her throat, and instinctively Brianda's hands flew to his wrists to try to ease the pressure. He delighted in the fight—it made the kill that much more fun. With great satisfaction he began increasing the squeeze on her throat. He could feel the frantic beating of her carotid arteries as they tried to supply her brain with oxygen against the rising pressure. His thumbs on her trachea pushed inward, and he could feel the hollow tube bending inward, about to collapse.

Dying, Brianda thought only of John and Dakota. Bringing up a knee with her last ounce of strength, she caught him in the groin. In the pain, Edward momentarily loosened his grip.

From the depths of her soul Brianda called out, "John! Dakota!" It was an anguished farewell to those she loved most.

Edward, furious now, increased the pressure and watched as Brianda's pupils expanded, and he felt her begin to go limp.

At the sound of his mistress's call, Dakota raced forward, ears flat, teeth bared.

Edward never saw the animal approach. He was too involved in the kill to notice anything else.

Suddenly Dakota was upon him, hundreds of pounds of muscle descending on him with a fury. The horse's eyes sparkled with a deathly determination that not even Edward could match. Terrified, he let go of Brianda and brought his hands up to protect his face from the huge teeth that were closing in on him.

Brianda fell to the ground, inches from the cliff's edge, gasping for breath. Her throat was swollen and she could barely breathe.

Dakota bit off a section of Edward's face. Edward shrieked in pain and terror as the horse reared and knocked him to the ground, then reared again, crashing down on the man's chest. An agonized wail spurted from Edward's mouth.

Pushing herself up to a sitting position, Brianda witnessed Dakota attacking Edward. It was horrible. The hooves rose and fell, breaking bones and crushing flesh.

When Edward lay inert, the stallion put his nose under the body and shoved. Edward rolled over and over, and slowly, almost gracefully, fell over the side of the cliff and crashed on the rocks below.

In shock, Brianda could not move. Dakota rushed to her and pushed her with his nose. When she didn't respond, he pawed the ground and whinnied loudly.

Angus, who had just arrived at Cliffshead Manor, ran forward to John's deathly still body. He put his head down on his master's chest and listened for a heartbeat. Gratefully, he raised his head. John's heartbeat was strong and steady.

Rallying, Brianda pulled herself up and held onto Dakota's neck for support. Together they walked toward her fallen husband. She noticed Angus, and idly wondered when he had arrived, little that it mattered now.

When Angus lifted John's head, his hand came back covered with blood, and he laid him down again and turned him over. The hair on the back of his head was covered with blood. Inspecting more closely, he found the scalp wound, which was bleeding profusely. Angus applied pressure to the wound with a handkerchief. It was lucky for John that it was so cold, the low temperature kept him from bleeding faster.

As Brianda drew close to John, he opened his eyes and, appearing suddenly alert, tried to push himself up. Angus held him down. "Angus? Where is Brianda? She is in danger!"

"She is all right. She is walking toward us right now. Stay down. I have to get you into the carriage and return you to Manseth Manor. Paul should be there by now."

Brianda saw Angus's hand come out from under John's head. At the sight of blood, she gasped. But then she saw John move, and hope filled her heart as she tried to reach him. Suddenly the exertion was too much for her, and she didn't make it, fainting in a heap onto the frozen ground.

Stevens was the first to see the carriage and called out for help. Paul, Elizabeth, and Mary had arrived from London, and now they all gathered at the front steps to watch the carriage approach. Thomas saw Dakota trailing along behind, untethered, and, calling to his son, moved in behind the carriage as it stopped and put a halter on the horse. Dakota allowed the men to lead him to his stall without a fight.

Paul jumped up into the carriage. *My God, my friends,* he thought as he quickly assessed the damage. John waved him off and motioned toward Brianda.

Paul made a cursory examination, noting the angry marks all over her neck. Her breathing pattern was regular and her heart's rhythm was faster than normal, but steady. He moved his hands over her, checking for any obviously broken bones, but found none. "Angus, carry Brianda into the house and put her into bed. Have Elizabeth and Mary warm her with heated blankets and notify me as soon as she regains consciousness," Paul ordered, then turned to examine his best friend.

"It is as good as done, Paul," called Angus. He lifted Brianda and carried her to her room.

Mary and Elizabeth removed Brianda's sooty undergarments and tenderly bathed her. The fire was well-tended, and the room was kept quite warm to ward off any chill. Were it not for the slight rise and fall of Brianda's chest, she looked like she might be dead.

In the library, Paul washed the back of John's head. "I will need to suture this wound. It is long and deep." He asked John some questions, to see if John was able to answer coherently. Putting a candle close to John's eyes, he watched to see if John's pupils would constrict correctly. They did. "You may have a slight concussion, John. You will need to take it easy for a few days," he stated.

John gave him a look and tried to rise, but Angus held him down with his strong hands. "You are not going to get up out of this chair, my Lord, until Dr. Martin has finished his work."

"Angus! To hell with my head wound! I need to get upstairs and see to my wife! Now let go of me!" John said angrily.

"I am sorry, sir, but Dr. Martin is shaking his head. You will not get up until he says you are able." Angus was immovable.

"Paul, tell Angus to let me up!"

"Sorry, John, I need to put those sutures in now. Now sit still, or will I have to ask Angus to sit on you," the young surgeon commanded, smiling at his friend.

"Both of you can go to hell," John raged, but he let Paul sew his wound together. It hurt like holy hell; only thoughts of Brianda got him through it.

The next morning Brianda opened her eyes to find John sitting on the side of her bed. Tears sprang to her eyes. "Are you well, my Lord?" she whispered in a hoarse voice.

"I am much better now that you have opened your eyes. I was worried when you stayed unconscious for so long, my lady," he said, touching the tip of her nose with his finger.

Suddenly her love was so strong that she could no

longer hold back the tears. In a last effort to keep from crying, she swallowed hard. Pain exploded in her throat. Worried, she looked at John and pointed to her injury.

"It is all right, love. Don't worry." Gently, he ran his fingers down her cheek and onto her damaged throat. "You remember that Edward tried to strangle you?"

At the mention of his name, she cringed. John grabbed her hands and brought them to his mouth. "He is dead now, Brianda. He will never threaten you again. You can live in peace."

"His body . . . Dakota trampled him, and then he fell over the cliff . . ."

"His body was recovered this morning, and it has been buried alongside your parents. I hope that he rests in peace, wherever he is now."

She pulled herself up and rested her head on his chest. "John, I can hardly swallow." Worry was evident on her battered, beautiful face.

"Your throat is swollen from the trauma of Edward's brutal assault. With all the smoke you inhaled, it is a wonder that you can speak at all! It will take several days, possibly a week, before the tissues return to normal. Soon enough, though, you will be back to driving us all crazy," he said, rubbing her back as he held her close. He had come so close to losing her, he promised himself to always hold her near.

"Is Dakota well? He was truly an animal possessed yesterday."

"Dakota saved your life twice! First he came here to lead me to you, and then he attacked Edward. I owe him more than I will ever be able to repay."

Feeling tired, Brianda lay back against the pillows. "When will I get to see Dakota?"

"As soon as you are out of this bed. Please advise me before you plan to go to the stable, and I will accompany you."

"When may I leave the bed?" she croaked.

"Whenever you feel up to it."

"I am ready now! Let's go!" she said, pulling the covers back and swinging her feet over the edge.

"I should have known better," he said, as he helped her put on her warm clothes and shoes. She stood and had to wait a moment for the dizziness to pass. Undaunted, she took a few steps. Though every muscle ached, she kept going.

John simply shook his head in amazement all the way to stables.

The next few days were slow-paced and wonderful. Brianda's neck bruises were beginning to fade, when Paul and Elizabeth left for London, with promises to visit soon. John vowed that he and Brianda would come to London for the birth of Elizabeth and Paul's baby.

John allowed Brianda to ride Dakota on his properties without an escort. With each passing week she became stronger, physically and spiritually, and was soon able to ride for hours. The freedom and sheer exhilaration of the country air helped her forget the last trauma. John constantly reminded her how much he loved her, and with that knowledge, she blossomed.

John decided to tear Cliffshead Manor down. He planned to build a church there with large glass windows, so that the beauty of the ocean could be appreciated by those worshiping there. Brianda intended never to worship at that church. It would be many years before she would feel comfortable above the cliffs.

One beautiful morning three weeks after Edward's death, Brianda rode over to see Old Megan. She hadn't seen much of her in the past few days, and worried constantly about the old woman's dizzy spells and pale complexion.

There was no one about the small cottage, and the door was open slightly. That was strange. Old Megan was meticulous about latching the door when she left. Too many herbs for some stray animal to get into, Old Megan always told Brianda.

With a sense of foreboding, Brianda pushed the door open. Old Megan was lying on her bed gasping for breath. Brianda ran to her side and demanded to know what was wrong.

Old Megan looked into the worried eyes of the person she loved most on earth. How beautiful she was, her violet eyes huge with concern, her glorious hair hanging freely down her back. "My girl, I think I am not long for this life. Do not grieve . . ."

"You just wait, I am going for John. I will be right back," she said over her shoulder as she rushed from the house, tripping over a potted plant as she went.

Dakota and Brianda raced through the woods at top speed and galloped up the road to the house. She was off him and running as Dakota slid to a stop. "John! John!" she shouted at the top of her lungs.

Every staff member came running to see what was wrong. Angus and John emerged at the same time from the library. "What is it?" John demanded. Brianda looked frightened.

"Grab your bag and come quickly! It is Old Megan!" She turned and ran from the house and called to Thomas to saddle the master's horse immediately.

Sebastian was ready and waiting when John ran from the house with his medical bag. Without a word they rode off at full speed.

Old Megan couldn't expand her chest against the pain. She lay without moving, looking around her small house, taking in all the treasures that had been part of her home for so many years. She felt a sense of pride as she looked at all the bottles of herbs and medicinal powders. They had been her life's work.

Bursting through the door, Brianda led John to Old Megan, then paced while he talked quietly with her and examined her. All the while, he held her hand.

"Why aren't you doing something, John?" Brianda demanded. "Give her some medicine, do something! Don't just sit there!" she cried.

"There is nothing I can do, love. Old Megan knows that, too. I can sit here with her and let her know that she is not alone now. You can do the same. What she needs from us now is our love."

Brianda walked over to the bed and looked at the woman who had taught her so much about life. "Please don't leave me, Old Megan! I cannot bear another loss," Brianda begged, as she sat on the floor near Old Megan's pillow. She reached out and caressed Old Megan. "I love you. I need you."

Looking first at John and then to Brianda, Old Megan smiled at the girl. "I love you, too, Brianda. You filled a spot in my heart that ached with loneliness. I promise I will watch you from wherever it is that I am to go. His Lordship will take good care of you, my girl. Love him. Be happy." Old Megan closed her eyes, and her chest rose no more.

Brianda, panicking, grabbed Megan by her shoulders and shook her. When there was no response she called out to her, "Megan, oh no, Megan . . ."

John gently removed Brianda's hands from Old Megan's body. "She is gone, darling, we must let her rest in peace now."

Tears streamed down her face. "What happened to her? Why did she have to die now?"

"Her heart was tired. It was time to rest. Old Megan knew that it was time to leave. She was very happy that she got to see you before departing." Taking her to the comfort of his chest, he said, "Don't cry so, darling, she would want you to be happy. Let's go and we will make the arrangements together."

Old Megan was buried three days later next to her mother and grandmother. The entire village came to the funeral.

After the funeral, Brianda had the cottage cleaned and closed. No one would ever again live in the Medicine Woman's cottage.

36

Brianda woke up and looked around the bedroom. It was empty, and, from the looks of things, John had already dressed and gone down to breakfast. One month had passed since Old Megan's death, and they were still in the country. John refused to take Brianda back to London, as he wanted her living a quiet life, but promised they would go to London in time for the birth of Paul and Elizabeth's child, but not before.

Brianda dressed in a pale blue cotton blouse and skirt and hurried to join John at the breakfast table. She kissed him and sat down on his right. When the servant put the food in front of her, she couldn't bear looking at it. Suddenly, she pushed away from the table and ran from the room.

John watched her leave and then rose slowly from the table and followed her down the hall. Brianda was vomiting in the small bucket in the kitchen while Cook held a cold towel to her forehead. "When are you going to tell his Lordship that you have been sick every day, Brianda?" she scolded.

Leaning his tall body against the door frame, John said, "What is this I am hearing?"

Guiltily, Brianda looked up at him.

"How long has this been going on without my knowing?" he asked sternly.

"Not long, I promise. I thought if you knew, you wouldn't take me to London!"

"How long, Brianda?"

Looking at the floor, she tried to decide if she should lie to him. He would never know the difference, anyway.

"Brianda, I asked you a question."

"On and off for . . ." She looked at Cook who was standing with her arms folded across her ample chest and a very stern look on her face. "A couple of weeks or so."

"More like a month, my Lord," stated Cook. "I know it is not my business to interfere in the lives of the masters, but this has been going on long enough now."

"Thank you, Cook. I appreciate your telling me." Looking grim, he said, "Brianda, you will come with me."

Brianda stomped her foot and glared at Cook. "There you go, Cook, opening your big mouth, and now I am in trouble again!"

"I only spoke up for your own good, my Lady," Cook stated flatly.

Noting that Brianda was not following him, John retraced his steps, took Brianda by the hand and led her down the long hallway to the northwest corner of the manor, where he had installed examining rooms. Since the death of Old Megan, the villagers had no one to depend on, so John offered to care for the sick and injured. He had also hired a young physician to assist, and anticipated his arrival in a few weeks' time.

John pulled a reluctant Brianda into one of the examining rooms and closed the door behind them. "Up you go, sweetheart," John said, as he lifted her up onto the examining table. He took off her blouse and listened to her chest. Then he looked into her throat and felt the glands under her chin. Her body temperature was normal. He looked at her feet as they hung over the edge of the table. They looked fine. Finally he swung her legs up and laid her down.

Brianda felt uncomfortable. She didn't like any part of this procedure and barely tolerated his pulling off her skirt. Lifting her chemise over her head, gently he began palpating her stomach and abdomen.

"Are your breasts sore, darling?" he asked, not looking at her face. He continued to palpate the center of her abdomen.

"No," she lied.

He walked over to the instrument table, and she could hear him moving things about. When he returned, he raised her knees and spread them apart.

Brianda tried to close them, feeling ill at ease.

"Leave your legs as I put them, love. How can I examine you if you resist me?"

She let her legs fall apart. This, too, she barely tolerated.

Gently he slipped two fingers into her. With his left hand he palpated her abdomen from the outside while his right hand did the same on the inside.

He removed his hand and let her legs fall to the table softly. "I would estimate that you are approximately three months pregnant, Lady Fauxley."

Brianda sat up, hopped off the table and hastily pulled her clothes on, avoiding looking at her abdomen. She wandered about the room for a moment an then blurted out, "Me, a mother? Why, I know nothing of such things. I am too young to have a baby."

"Too young or not, you will be a mother soon. You and I will have to have a serious talk about how you must comport yourself from now on."

Those words brought Brianda to her battle stance. She faced him squarely, legs apart, hands on her hips. "Do you mean that I cannot go on living my life as I choose to?" she asked, challenging him.

"You will need to make some adjustments," he said, holding her eyes. "We will work out your activities together. You will not sneak out and do things that are not allowed."

She just looked at him, her chin held at an elevated angle.

"This is no game," John stated in his most professional voice. "By not doing as you are advised, you could lose the child and put yourself in danger, Brianda. If you refuse to cooperate, I will take measures to see that you do. I have done so in the past and I will do so again. Am I making myself clear?"

"What? Will I have Angus the Oaf watching my every move?" she taunted.

"If necessary," he said just as firmly.

Realizing that she had better change tactics, she turned to him and smiled. "Can I still ride every day?" she asked hopefully.

"You can ride for a while, but Dakota should only walk. No trotting, cantering, or galloping like you two like to do. Then later on, you can take him for walks when I won't want you riding anymore."

"You are serious, are you not, my Lord?" she asked, hoping that he was having a bit of fun with her.

"Dead serious, Brianda. Will you cooperate or do I call in the troops?"

"I will behave. But I want you to know that I am opposed to unfair restrictions."

"I am glad you are showing some maturity," he said, happy that it wasn't going to be the battle he had anticipated.

Brianda merely turned and stormed out of the room.

*   *   *

All went well until Brianda's fifth month of pregnancy. The morning sickness faded away in her third month. She ate better after that and was gaining a little weight.

She did not tell John about the headaches.

In her solitary moments, Brianda was becoming more used to the idea of motherhood. It seemed so alien, having a tiny person dependent on her. Why, she had trouble running her own life!

Then one day she felt the baby move. She was supine on the thick virgin grass, moving her foot slowly through the murky water of the pond, remembering how she had received her first kiss at this very spot, when she was surprised by a definite thump inside her abdomen. It was a miracle. She lay still and waited to see if it would move again. Sure enough, she felt another ping. Bursting with joy, she grabbed Dakota's halter and side by side they walked home, sure that the earl would want to feel the activities of the next Earl of Manseth.

John looked up from his reading when Brianda burst into the office. Seeing her face alive with excitement made him smile.

"Sir! Come here! You aren't going to believe this!" Running to John, because he wasn't moving fast enough for her, she took his hand and placed it on her abdomen. "Just wait!" In a few seconds, the baby kicked her. Eyes wide with astonishment, she looked up at him.

There were times when he thought he might burst with the love he felt for her. She was still so young and innocent. He left his hand there and waited for another kick. "He is letting us know that he will be one to be reckoned with." Staggering back and putting his hand to his forehead with mock dismay, John said, "I don't think I can handle two of you! Obstinate, rebellious, opinionated and stubborn. What am I going to do?"

Laughing, she reached up and kissed him squarely on the mouth. "You have a patient, Doctor, and I have to see to my horse." She left then, waving to a farm hand who had punctured his hand on a hoe and was waiting patiently for the doctor.

That night in bed, John made love to Brianda more tenderly than he ever had before. He caressed her with long strokes, letting his hand make circles over her slightly bulging abdomen, and then dipping down into the honeyed sweetness that was reserved just for him. She writhed and moaned ancient sounds of sexual response, and finally, when she thought she would explode, Brianda sat up and swung around, taking the length of him into her mouth. She taunted and pulled, swirled her tongue, and ran her teeth over him. He, too, was lost in another plane. When she knew he was ready, she straddled him, lowering herself onto his slick shaft. Up and down she slid herself, with eyes closed, concentrating on the sensations that only he could bring to her. With a smooth motion, he rolled her onto her back and continued the stroking. Just before Brianda tipped over the edge, he whispered into her ear, "I love you, darling. Did you know that I'm rocking the baby to sleep?"

She smiled at his statement, and then her smile expanded into the face of a woman in the throes of ecstasy.

When Brianda was in her eighth month, word came by morning post that Paul wanted John in London as soon as possible. Elizabeth was showing signs of early labor.

Brianda's headaches were worse, at times affecting her vision, and her feet were always swollen. At times, the swelling reached as high as her midcalf. To deceive John, she would sit with them elevated until they returned to normal. She had stopped taking walks with Dakota. When John inquired as to her state of health, she would lie easily, telling him that she was fine, just feeling tired. She was afraid that if she told him the truth, he would not let her go to London. And she wanted more than anything to go to the city.

John and Angus readied the carriage, fashioning a special sling for Brianda so that she would ride comfortably on the long journey. John was sorry he had waited so long to get Brianda to London where better care was available. Mrs. Brady waved farewell to the travelers and watched as Stevens passed her in the second carriage, loaded with valises and trunks.

The tired travelers arrived home at midday. The house buzzed with activity as bags were unloaded and the new arrivals made their way to their rooms to unpack and freshen up.

A note was delivered an hour after their arrival, asking that John hurry over to the Martin residence at his earliest convenience. He gathered his medical bag and Brianda, and left at once.

Elizabeth lay in her bed, catching her breath between contractions, when the door burst open and Brianda entered. Brianda rushed to her and held her in her arms just as the next pain started. Elizabeth stifled a moan, her face beet red. Frightened, Brianda ran to find Paul and John. They were together, discussing the progress of the labor, when Brianda hurried in to tell them to come immediately.

With Paul and Brianda standing away from the bed, John examined Elizabeth. He inserted his hand and found that her cervix was well thinned out, dilated halfway open. The baby's head was presenting, and its heartbeat was strong. "You are doing fine, Elizabeth, it won't be too much longer now." He and Paul both knew it would be longer yet, and much harder, before it was over, but they wanted Elizabeth to feel secure and as calm as possible.

John wondered if he had done the right thing in letting Brianda come to help with the birth. Watching the contortions of Elizabeth's face and hearing her cry out with every contraction was difficult for even the most seasoned caretaker. But Brianda remained calm, staying with Elizabeth and talking to her, wiping the sweat from her forehead and frequently reminding her of how well she was doing.

When the cervix was fully dilated, John asked Elizabeth to push with the contractions. She pushed without being asked, as pushing was now beyond her control. Grabbing the wooden handles that Paul had affixed to the sides of the bed, she pulled with all her might, pushing and urging her child down. Her face was bright red and contorted with the strain. Finally, the tiny head appeared. John carefully made a small cut under the baby so that he could ease the child out without tearing the mother's pelvic tissues.

"One more push, and your child will be born, Elizabeth. After the head is delivered, I don't want you to push again until I tell you to do so," John said kindly.

Exhausted, but anxious to get it all over with, Elizabeth nodded that she understood. The next contraction started and she screamed. Pushing with all that was left in her, the baby's head was delivered. John cleaned off the little face and made sure its mouth was clear of mucus. Pulling down slightly, he delivered the first shoulder and then, lifting the child in the opposite direction, he delivered the second shoulder. The rest of the baby slid out easily after that. "You have a baby girl, Elizabeth and Paul," John announced as he held the tiny infant upside down and smacked her tiny bottom. The baby screeched in response.

After drying the baby off and cleaning the blood from her face and head, John wrapped the infant in a blanket and put her into her mother's arms.

Elizabeth and Paul cried as they looked at her, overjoyed with the blessing of their child. Brianda cried too, relieved it was over and happy that all was well.

While Elizabeth put the baby to her breast, John delivered the placenta and sewed up the small cut. All had gone as expected, and he was sure Elizabeth would do very well. Soon, mother and child slept, the child cradled, warm and welcome, in her mother's arms.

Paul hugged his best friend, his gesture saying all that was in his heart. He knew that he would soon be delivering John's child, and fervently hoped that everything would go as smoothly.

Over the next week, Brianda's condition worsened considerably. She couldn't hide the headaches or her swollen limbs from John any longer, complaining of strange sensations in her head. Whenever John checked her pulse, it bound against his fingertips. She began retaining water in all parts of her body.

John consulted with Paul in his study. "I am frightened, Paul. I have seen this before. If she doesn't deliver soon, she could convulse, and then I will lose her and the child." John put his head in his hands and wept.

Placing his hand on John's back, Paul let his friend cry. Indeed, the consequences of Brianda's obstetrical condition raised concern that she would meet the same fate as her mother. . . .

Paul took John by the shoulders. "John, listen to me. Do you remember Old Megan telling us about Brianda's mother's untimely death?"

Raising his head and looking directly into the eyes of his friend, John responded, "Good God! Yes, I remember now." Standing, John turned and thought for a moment. "We have to get Brianda into the hospital right away, Paul. We will monitor her there for as long as possible, and when we decide that we can wait no longer, we will take the baby by Cesarean section."

"That is very difficult surgery, John."

"Yes, but you and I are going to do it."

"You cannot do surgery on your own wife!"

"I shall indeed! There is no one in London with better hands than mine, and you know it. Come, let's make the arrangements. Then I will talk to Brianda."

Brianda listened while John explained that he was going to take her to the hospital for the delivery of their child. The thought of complications terrified her, and she cried in John's arms and tried to convince him to let her stay at home for the delivery, but he was unyielding.

Brianda lay in the hospital bed for three weeks. She was constantly monitored by the nurses. All of her friends visited, which helped to pass the lonely, frightening days. Elizabeth even visited at the end of the third week and brought baby Morgana. She and Paul had named the baby after Elizabeth's grandmother.

Very early one morning, John came into Brianda's room dressed in surgical garb. The sight of him dressed like that frightened Brianda.

"What is wrong, John? Why are you dressed like that?" she asked, not really wanting to know the answer.

"Darling, I want you to listen to me carefully . . ."

Tears brimmed in Brianda's eyes and her hands shook. She knew the news was bad.

"Don't be frightened, darling. I have conferred with the best doctors in London, and we all agree that we must take the baby surgically."

"Oh no! Please, John! That is so dangerous. Please

give me a chance to deliver my baby normally!" she begged, holding his hand in hers.

"Brianda, I have known for some time that this was the only way. I didn't tell you because I didn't want you to worry."

"Well, I am worried."

"I know, sweetheart, but you are in peril now. I will not take any further chances with you or our child," he said gently, trying to keep the trepidation out of his voice. "We must do the surgery this morning."

The operation was performed quickly, and Brianda did not hear the first lusty cries of her son, for she slept, a captive of a drug-induced world.

Handing the baby to Paul, John made quick work of removing the placenta and suturing the womb.

Brianda was up walking in four days, scandalizing the whole ward by defying the charge nurse. She paid no attention to any of the rules and stayed in bed only after John threatened to tie her to the bed frame. Two weeks after Peter Fauxley was born, mother and son went home on the arm of the Earl of Manseth.

Epilogue

It was Christmas in the English countryside. The snow was deep this year. It blanketed the trees and shrubs in cloaks of brilliant white.

Peter Fauxley was two and a half months old. He was smiling and cooing. He had his father's black hair and his mother's violet eyes. Peter was the joy of John and Brianda's life.

The MacKenzie clan had arrived a few days before, to celebrate Christmas, as they had all promised one year before. Michael and Rebecca were thrilled to be reunited with their son and pregnant daughter-in-law. Mary had never been more beautiful. Her child was an unexpected gift, one she and Angus would treasure beyond all others.

When Rebecca found a few moments to be alone with Mary, she gave her a gift for her unborn child from Mary's mother. It was a hand-carved rosary. Mary cried for a few minutes and then let Rebecca hold her close in her arms. Mary had written to her mother regularly and fervently hoped that the day would come when she would see her mother and sisters again.

At noon on Christmas day, Brianda sat with John, watching their friends enjoy each other. Peter's nanny, Elizabeth and Mary were caring for the babies. John and Brianda were planning to sneak out and go for a ride, seeking a chance to be alone. Looking into his eyes, she felt the flame of love grow.

John pulled her to him and put his chin on the top of her head. She was so precious to him. "We have guests, Lady Fauxley, and we wanted to get a quick ride in. Shall we go?"

"All right. But, after everyone has returned home, I want you all to myself. Promise?"

"I promise, my love."

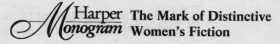

COMING NEXT MONTH

DREAM KEEPER by Parris Afton Bonds
The spellbinding Australian saga begun with *Dream Time* continues with the lives and loves of estranged twins and their children, who were destined to one day fulfill the Dream Time legacy. An unforgettable love story.

DIAMOND IN THE ROUGH by Millie Criswell
Brock Peters was a drifter—a man with no ties and no possessions other than his horse and gun. He didn't like entanglements, didn't like getting involved, until he met the meanest spinster in Colorado, Prudence Daniels. "Poignant, humorous, and heartwarming."—*Romantic Times*

LADY ADVENTURESS by Helen Archery
A delightful Regency by the author of *The Season of Loving*. In need of money, Stara Carltons resorted to pretending to be the notorious highwayman, One-Jewel Jack, and held up the coach containing Lady Gwendolen and Marcus Justus. Her ruse was successful for a time until Marcus learned who Stara really was and decided to turn the tables on her.

PRELUDE TO HEAVEN by Laura Lee Guhrke
A passionate and tender historical romance of true love between a fragile English beauty and a handsome, reclusive French painter. "Brilliant debut novel! Laura Lee Guhrke has written a classic love story that will touch your heart."—Robin Lee Hatcher

PRAIRIE LIGHT by Margaret Carroll
Growing up as the adopted daughter of a prominent Boston family, Kat Norton always knew she must eventually come face-to-face with her destiny. When she travels to the wilds of Montana, she discovers her Native American roots and the love of one man who has always denied his own roots.

A TIME TO LOVE by Kathleen Bryant
A heartwarming story of a man and woman driven apart by grief who reunite years later to learn that love can survive anything. Eighteen years before, a family tragedy ended a budding romance between Christian Foster and his best friend's younger sister, Willa. Now a grown woman, Willa returns to the family island resort in Minnesota to say good-bye to the past once and for all, only to discover that Christian doesn't intend to let her go.

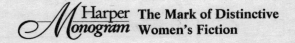

Harper Monogram **The Mark of Distinctive Women's Fiction**

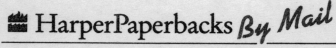